In HIS CAGE

RUSSIAN ALPHAS BOOK 1

ELLA JACOBS

IN HIS CAGE

http://www.ellajacobs.com

ISBN 978-87-974182-5-3

First Edition: September 2023

SHA-256 hash: eff8c6be56491aeb046e5218c
22a6ffdf56fe74f7432cefd2d3c399022fea41b

To all the girls who find the world
can be an overwhelming place,
and to my Dom for making my world less so.

AUTHOR'S NOTE

I had someone who knows Russian translate the Russian phrases in this story. You'll find a glossary at the back of the book.

Prologue

CRACK!

The whip tears through the air with a horrible, obtrusive sound.

Then it strikes. Searing pain flares in my back, and I buckle in the chains as my knees give in beneath me. Black dots form in my vision as my world narrows to a dark tunnel of agony and despair. My scream fills the space, tearing through my throat and causing more pain.

But the pain isn't the worst thing. The pain I can somehow handle. What nearly breaks me is the sting in my eyes, tears prickling to burst free in endless streams that I won't be able to stop once started.

My captor may have my screams and my despair, but not my tears. I refuse to give in to him—refuse to give him my vulnerability.

A large arm comes around my waist, catching my weight as it presses me back into a hard body. The protective grip feels safe against all rational judgment. I want to sink into it, soak up the feeling as I let go of my strength.

I want to cry and take the sweet reward of his comfort.

But I can't. Resistance is the only thing left that's mine. So I stubbornly gather my strength, force back the despair, and straighten my legs.

"I hate you," I grit through clenched teeth, pouring all my fury into the words. I desperately try to mean them. He was supposed to be the man who fulfilled my dreams, but he took me from my life instead, crushed my dreams, and cast me into this nightmare that becomes harder to fight with each passing day. I should genuinely mean those words, but they don't ring true any longer, and he knows it.

"*Ladno, prosto povtarayem i ty sdashsya.*" Knuckles brush my cheek as a deep voice croons next to my ear. "We'll just go again until you give in."

Chapter 1

"PRISHOL! PRISHOL!" NATASHA squeaks as she rushes up to me and grabs me by the shoulders. "He's here!"

My heart flutters with the hope that she means who I think she does. For almost two years, I've been waiting for him, and time is running out. I only have three months left. *It has to be him.*

Natasha's tall heels click against the floor as she scurries to the stage door. She moves like she was born in stilettos. Peeking into the concert hall, she waves her hand for me to join her.

I bunch up my black gown and wobble to her. I might have learned to play the piano in thin heels, but I still can't manage Natasha's natural grace.

"There." She continues in English as she tries to point discreetly. "I think that's him. In the fifth row."

I peek my head out and scour the rows of antique wooden chairs beyond the stage. Chandeliers and sconces fill the hall with warm light, keeping out the darkness lurking outside the tall windows. But even so, I can only make out shapes and outlines from up here.

"On the far right by the corridor," Natasha clarifies. "Black suit and red tie. Short, blond hair. Broad shoulders."

"Are you sure it's him?" Since I came to study at the St. Petersburg music conservatory, this man has been my biggest hope, but I wouldn't recognize him even if I came face to face with him. Being one of Russia's top businessmen, Aleksandr Pletnev is surprisingly good at staying clear of the media. And since I steer clear of Facebook and news channels, I've gone this far without seeing a picture of him. It's become quite the little superstition of mine, thinking I'll somehow jinx my chances if I see his picture.

"It's him, alright," Natasha blurts, her excitement throwing her back into her mother tongue. She glances back at me with big, sparkling eyes. "Anna saw him when he came."

"It is him," a warmer voice confirms in accented English as a slender hand comes to rest on my shoulder. Anna leans against my back to join my inquisitive perusal of the man in the fifth row. "Aleksandr Pletnev. We're finally getting our shot, Astrid." Her fingertips dig into my shoulder, reflecting the anxious nervousness she hides so well on the outside.

I turn my head to look into her almond-shaped eyes. "Are you sure?"

"Positive." She sweeps her long brown hair to the side as her delicate lips stretch into a thin line. "I've met him."

I thought she would be excited, but there's this somber gravity to her, laced with a sliver of hope. And... fear?

"Where? You've never told me."

Her nose scrunches up like it does when she struggles to keep up her brave façade. "Somewhere else. It doesn't matter. He's not very nice."

I pull back into our hideout behind the stage and drag her with me. "You say that about all rich men, Anna."

The shudder in her shoulders doesn't escape me. "This one is in a class of his own." She tries to cover her unease with a smile. "But who cares? He might get us to the Mariinsky."

"Who cares?" I echo, grabbing her hands to give them a reassuring squeeze. This man is the biggest patron of The White Nights Festival, and for several years, he's been attending recitals here at the conservatory to scour for new talent. If he singles me out, I'm as good as guaranteed a spot on the festival program, playing at the famous Mariinsky concert stage. So it doesn't matter if he's nice or not—he holds the power to fulfill my biggest dream.

Natasha blabbers on in Russian, too fast for me to understand.

"*Spokoyno*," I tell her to make her slow down.

I started learning Russian several years ago when I decided this was where I wanted to get my postgraduate degree, but it still doesn't come naturally to me. People have to speak slowly, or I'll only understand half of it.

Natasha goes on at a slower pace—something about her dress choice. But it's still too fast, so when another girl joins us, I leave Natasha's girly chatter to her and step up to Anna. She's peeking out at Aleksandr Pletnev again.

I can hardly believe he's finally here. I'd almost stopped hoping since I'll graduate in three months.

He's only going to pick one—if any at all—and though he tends to favor pianists, he could just as easily pick a violinist or an oboist. The competition is harsh. Tonight's concert is meant to showcase the conservatory's finest students rather than a specific instrument group or genre, so most of the postgraduate students are playing. He'll have plenty to pick from, and I'll have plenty of competitors. But I'm not losing hope. I've already defied the odds by getting into the conservatory back home in Norway and getting my master's degree there. The odds were even more stacked against me when I pursued the piano performance program here in St. Petersburg. But here I am, earning my postgraduate degree at the conservatory I've always dreamed about attending. So maybe—just maybe—I'll get lucky this time too.

Most students here end up with decent careers, playing their instrument for a living, but as with everything else, only a few reach the peak of the mountain. I've been aiming for that peak all my life, and Aleksandr Pletnev is the most certain ticket.

He's not hard to find in the crowd. His authoritative posture and unnerving calmness make him stand out like a sore thumb. He's far outside his natural habitat. This man belongs in private booths in grand concert halls, watching the world's foremost musicians—not measly students clawing like beasts to reach the top.

Anna leans back to let me step in front of her. We might have the same slender hourglass figure, waist-long hair, and the same age of twenty-five, but the similarities end there. Anna is tall like a model; I'm short like a pixie. Her chestnut hair and amber eyes lend her a mysterious look, whereas my blond locks and round gray eyes give off a sweet and innocent vibe.

"How old is he?" I whisper. I had thought him to be fifty, at least. A balding, fat man like so many other rich Russians. But this man is the opposite.

"Thirty-five, thirty-seven."

"Is he tall?" He appears tall as he sits there among the commoners with his broad shoulders and proud posture. Though, maybe it's just his way of carrying himself that makes him appear so.

"A head taller than me." Her voice takes on a playful lilt as she brushes her hand over my head. "You'd strain your neck if you spent more than five minutes talking to him."

I reach behind me and pinch her side, making her squeal. "I'll just stand on a chair then."

"Ooh, that would get you in trouble. That man couldn't stand a woman looking down at him. He's a major misogynist."

"We're looking down at him right now, aren't we?"

Anna pulls me back into safety and makes a yikes-face. I cover my mouth and snicker. If anyone can make me laugh, it's Anna and her crazy faces. She doesn't make them often, but when she does, it's priceless. I'm one of the few lucky people who gets to see beyond her protective façade—the result of two years of living together.

A pang of sadness claws at my chest. In three months, we'll each go our own way. I'll return to Norway, and she'll stay here. Or maybe she'll land a string of concerts taking her across Europe. Maybe Asia. Who knows? She has the potential.

My face must reflect my troubled thoughts because Anna gives me a sympathetic smile. "Maybe he'll pick us both," she offers, misinterpreting my worry.

He *has* to pick us both. I need that spot on the Mariinsky stage—the grandest stage in Russia. It's all I've ever worked for. Without it, I have to return to my parents' "We told you so; now find a real job and a husband." I can't go back to that *steady* existence. It has always sucked the life out of me.

I give her a tight smile. How ironic that I'm the gloomy one and Anna is the optimist, when she's the one who's spent her whole life in this unforgiving country. But despite the harshness of it all—our worn-down apartment, the icy winters, and all the poverty—there's more spirit and vigor here than I've ever found anywhere else.

Maybe I should stay—try my luck in these uncertain waters instead of going back home.

"Come." Taking my hand, Anna leads me to a couple of chairs as our department head goes on stage to announce the first student.

"Do you think he'll like my Rachmaninoff prelude?" I whisper. "Maybe I should have chosen something flashier like you? One of his etudes?" I've played plenty of flashy concert etudes and could easily whip one out, but the thought alone has my lips tightening.

Anna is the one who's all virtuosic rapid-fire of impossible notes, whereas I'm more expressive depth and melodic beauty. Or rather, dark and brooding, restless and searching as of late.

"Are you kidding me?" She laces her fingers with mine. "He'd be an idiot not to appreciate the depth of your music. No etude could showcase it like the G minor prelude."

"He'll love your piece too," I say when I feel the strain in her grip.

Nerves are an inevitable part of performing, but with all the concerts we've played throughout our lives, we've learned to use them to our advantage. Tonight, though, these well-practiced strategies fail us. My hand quivers in Anna's long pianist's fingers, and her palm is more clammy than usual, our reassuring smiles more strained.

We sit like this for the next half hour, tense and silent, listening to the other performers.

"Our next student is Astrid Berger from Norway," our department head announces.

Anna brings me into a tight hug. "You'll do great. You always do."

Squeezing both her hands, I give her my bravest smile,

straighten my spine, and walk onto the stage.

Blood rushes through my veins, making my heart pound quicker than the music I'm about to play. I try to keep my breathing level, my steps firm so I won't slip on the glossy floor in my too-high heels.

My eyes dart to the fifth row, and I catch a glimpse of the powerful man watching me—the man who can pull me from the swamp of normalcy and into greatness. I've always yearned for more. Something beyond the confining routines of life—something to ease the restless yearning pumping in my veins. This man can give it to me if only I prove myself worthy.

I gracefully sink onto the piano bench and turn the knobs at the sides until it's high enough for my small figure. Then I settle in the seat with my feet flat on the ground and rub my clammy hands on my gown. A familiar rush surges through me as I feel the weight of a hundred people watching me. Only me. But the eyes feel more insistent today. More oppressive.

I block it out and place my right foot on the sustain pedal, balancing it on the thin heel as my toe hovers above the golden metal. It's taken a long year of frustration to get comfortable playing in heels. You can't play in flats on the concert stage of the Mariinsky. You just can't.

Closing my eyes, I take a deep breath and remind myself there's nothing to be nervous about. I've been doing this since I was seven. Playing the piano is second nature to me. Like breathing.

When I open my eyes again, the first notes of Rachmaninoff's prelude rush through my mind as I visualize the pattern on the keys.

I know exactly what to do.

I lift my hands, wrists loose, fingers spread to accommodate the large chords, and then I burst into the nervous notes. The music seeps from my fingers and through the instrument, encompassing my entire world.

People say this piece is about being buried alive, and I understand the interpretation. The darkness and frustration are palpable. But to me, it represents my own mind.

The burden of the deep notes is my own. The rapid-fire of octaves is the longing crawling in my veins. And when the anxiety explodes in the mid-section, it's my own frustration that crashes through the hall.

I breathe it all in, feeling every note in the depth of my soul. The music swamps me, and I merge with it until neither I nor it holds any meaning beyond the other.

Four minutes of pure ecstasy.

I fire off the last notes and lift my hands from the keys. Clapping becomes a thunderous noise around me. I've always hated the clapping. I'm grateful for the intent, but the sound is stifling. I have to subdue the urge to cower.

With a steadying breath, I step out to the middle of the stage. The clapping is part of it, and like the audience shows their respect, I show mine with an elegant bow.

Summoning all my confidence, I gaze out over the sea of people. It's as claustrophobic as the noise, but I have one last statement to make before I go.

I scan the fifth row until I find *him.* He's still watching me, and suddenly, I feel dizzy as I fall into the trap of his gaze. I can't see his eyes clearly, but I can feel them. Their intensity is as palpable as a roaring fire. Dangerous and oppressive. But I don't let them intimidate me. I hold my chin up, spine straight, and will him to see me. Will him to pick *me.*

He stares back with a force that has my resolve wavering.

Something tells me this is not a man to be trifled with, but I keep watching him. I don't think I could break away even if I wanted to. Clutching my hands in front of me, I fight the need to lower my shoulders—lower my chin. I don't know if I succeed, and I don't know that I care anymore.

I don't see or feel anything except those eyes burning into my skin, trying to take something. Something more than my music. Part of my soul? It scares me to the bone yet thrills me to the core.

The applause keeps beating, but I only hear my pounding heart, only see the man holding my eyes—holding my future in the palm of his hand.

Pick me!

My heart is bursting with the need to shout it out loud. But I feel helpless under his gaze, unable to move, unable to speak. So I force the message into my eyes, praying he'll see it.

He makes a slight tilt of his head, almost like he's trying to decipher my message. Then he stands, the motion strong and resolute. Closing the top button of his suit jacket, he gives me a firm nod.

Then he turns and walks down the corridor between the seats.

I can almost hear the clicking of his leather shoes as I watch his steady gait. Anna was right. He is tall. But even more so, he carries himself with the authority of an unconquered king.

I might be the one up on the stage, but I feel tiny as I watch his tall frame disappear out the side door.

It takes me a full minute to realize the clapping has died down and I'm supposed to leave. My feet move on autopilot as they take me across the stage.

"How did it go? Did you see his reaction?" Natasha's eager

questions are an assault on my dumbfounded mind.

I stare at her, unable to comprehend her words despite hearing them clearly.

"Are you okay?" Anna's soft voice breaks through the blur, and I turn to meet her concerned eyes.

"I think so."

"What happened?" Anna asks.

"He gave me a nod. Then left."

"What? When?" Natasha's eager voice is a shrill sound, but I only notice Anna's reaction.

Her curved brows furrow, and her beautiful eyes fill with sadness as she shakes her head. She wants this as badly as I do, and she didn't even get a chance to show her talent.

Natasha doesn't see it. She keeps spurting questions, and Anna has her well-practiced façade back in place before I can tell her how sorry I am.

"That nod means everything," Anna says, holding her spine deceptively straight. "He left because he didn't need to see more. It's the biggest compliment of all."

Our department head calls Anna's name, and Anna gives me a supportive squeeze and leaves. It's truly difficult being each other's greatest supporters and biggest competitors.

I'm left with an eerie feeling that I've missed something. And as Natasha bounces at my side, saying he's picked me, I can only think of the fear in Anna's eyes when she said Aleksandr Pletnev was here. I felt that same fear when he locked his eyes on me.

Chapter 2

ANNA IS ABOUT to go insane from my incessant pacing over the weekend. I retreat to the bedroom to give her some peace, but then I'm the one going insane, needing more space for my restless energy.

We usually have no problem sharing an apartment meant for one, but today we feel the consequences. Technically, the place has two rooms—a bedroom and a living room slash kitchen—but it's not much bigger than a traditional studio in the Western world. And the walls are far from thick enough to contain the sounds of my stress.

"Will you stop pacing already?" Anna calls.

"I'm sorry." I open the door and throw my hands into the air. "I can't help it."

"If you keep this up much longer, I'll have to find my own place."

"Please don't," I say, though I know she doesn't mean it. If not because she can't afford it, then because we've grown inseparable.

Anna rolls her eyes. "Alright then. I'll stay until someone kicks me out." Anna is not supposed to stay here. The conservatory offered me the place at a cheap rate because I'm an international student, and the rules clearly state one person per apartment.

"Don't even say that." I start pacing again. I know it's not likely—many others do the same, and the conservatory won't kick anyone out. They'd just lose talented students who can't afford to move. But right now, even the slightest worry gets my heart rate going.

"Sorry." Anna gives me an apologetic smile and waves the remote. "TV time?"

I glance between Anna and the couch. I don't feel like sitting still.

"It just might help settle your nerves," she adds.

With a sigh, I drop onto the couch beside her. "Alright. But none of those Russian sitcoms."

Anna puts on an American sitcom instead, and it only takes twenty minutes before I lose focus and start thrumming my fingers.

Anna grabs my hands to stop me, but then I tap my feet instead.

"God, you're impossible. Do I need to tie you up, or will you just start rolling around?"

I push out a long breath. "Maybe I should go for a walk." I get up and grab my jacket. "Walk off some of the stress."

"Yeah, you do that. And stop worrying, will you? That nod was as good an answer as you'll ever get."

"You really think so?" I stop buttoning my jacket, giving her a hopeful look.

Her expression becomes solemn. "He couldn't even acknowledge my presence with a nod when I met him, so yeah. A nod sure means something coming from that man." Her mouth twists as she stares at the coffee table. "He's too caught up in himself to care about anyone else."

"He sounds like an asshole," I say, offering my support. "How did you meet him anyway?"

"It doesn't matter. Just make sure not to be alone with him when he comes with a proposal."

"Aye, aye, captain." I salute her in an effort to brighten the mood.

"I'm serious, Astrid. He might get you to the Mariinsky, but you should be careful with him."

"Okay," I agree, gulping at the serious warning in her eyes.

"Now go." Anna throws a pillow at me. "Get out of here, you restless girl. And bring me a tub of ice cream."

"Aye, aye, sir." I repeat the salute and tap my heels together. This time, I get a wide, teeth-revealing grin that has me smiling too.

I spend an hour pacing the streets. It's better than the tiny apartment, but my restlessness won't fade. If anything, I become more anxious. Paranoid even. I feel like someone's watching me, and I keep glancing over my shoulder. But there's nothing suspicious; the Russians are minding their own business as usual.

The foreboding feeling grows when I enter a grocery store, but the most suspicious thing I see is a babushka nearly knocking down a lanky man in a blue windbreaker. They curse at one another, and the man leers at me as the babushka trudges on with her cart. But not even that is noteworthy.

I grab a large tub of ice cream and a few other groceries I hope to sneak in without Anna noticing. She always insists on splitting the bill even though she can barely afford tuition and rent. She's too proud to accept my help. But I won't have her take more of those shady jobs she used to resort to whenever she was low on money. She never told me what they were, but once when she was drunk, she let the word Bratva slip. Since then, I've been hellbent on making sure she doesn't repeat it.

So I sneak a bag of groceries into the apartment, hiding it in the bedroom until she takes a bathroom break and I can fill the cupboards without her noticing.

When she comes back out, she grabs the ice cream, drags me to the couch, and shoves the remote and a spoon into my hand. "Pick something."

I put on *Twilight*—my ultimate guilty pleasure. Plus, to get back at Anna for all her Russian sitcoms.

She can't stop complaining, and that's part of the fun. "Oh Bella," she mocks. "You're my own personal brand of heroin." Later, she levels me with a priceless glare. "Seriously, Astrid, vampires don't twinkle like fucking stars."

I laugh out loud. "Sorry, miss imagination-less. Would you rather he burst into flames or die from sniffing garlic?"

"Yes, please," she deadpans.

My phone vibrates on the coffee table, and my laughter dies when I see it's my mom.

"You have to pick up eventually," Anna says as my fingers twitch with indecision over the phone.

She has a point. I've already ignored her calls three times this week. So I give Anna a wry smile and swipe the green icon.

"Hi, mom." I try to sound happy, but my voice is flat.

"How are you?"

I barely get an answer in before she launches into a stream of questions about my studies, my living situation, and money.

I keep my answers brief, but she continues prodding until I

reluctantly tell her we are low on money this month too.

"It's about time you come home," she says with that condescending *I know better* tone she's mastered to perfection. "You already have an education, and you could get a good teaching job instead of chasing that foolish dream of yours."

I want to tell her that one of the patrons of the White Nights Festival has singled me out, but I still don't dare believe that nod was a yes. So I keep my mouth shut, hearing my dad in the background, "Don't waste your energy. She'll be back in a few months, and then she'll come to her senses."

Long, slender fingers tug at my fisted hand, and I unclench it to allow Anna's fingers to interlace with mine. With a small squeeze, she silently lends me her support.

She knows it hurts more when my parents call than when they don't. When I don't hear from them, it's easier to forget that they haven't been here to visit me once and only call to persuade me to go along with their standard idea of what life is supposed to be like—a steady job, marriage, and children. I detest the idea. Always have.

At the conservatory on Monday, everyone is looking at me. I get a mix of snobby glares of envy and genuine smiles of congratulations. People I've never talked to come up to me, wanting to hear all the details about Aleksandr Pletnev's nod and demonstrative departure.

Rumor travels fast, apparently.

Anna comes up beside me as I walk down the hall during my lunch break, lacing her arm into the crook of my elbow. "Everyone's talking. They're all sure he chose you." She's the more talkative one of us—not that it says much—but if she goes snooping for information, she usually gets it.

"Do you really think he's going to pick me?"

"I do." Conflicting emotions war in her eyes, revealing how she tries to be happy for me even though she's sad she lost her chance. I've been too preoccupied with my own confusion to truly notice.

The need to repay her support flushes out the cocktail of nervous emotions. "I'm sorry."

Her eyes fall to the ground, and I'm about to bring her into a hug when the quick clicking of heels announces Natasha. Her face is alight with unrestrained excitement when she jumps up at my side. "Congratulations."

"He hasn't picked me yet," I say, my tone more irritable than intended.

"He's going to," she declares with the gung-ho excitement of a four-year-old holding a giant ice cream cone.

"You don't know that." I go for a calmer tone and squeeze Anna's arm as I feel her heavy silence beside me. She's done her best to hide her disappointment during the weekend, and it's clear that by acknowledging it, I've given her a much-needed permission to feel sad.

"No one's heard of him walking out before. Much less giving a nod like that. He's a cold-ass rich guy who never says more than needed. So I do know."

Turning to Anna, I get an apologetic shrug saying *I told you so.*

So I let myself believe it. I let myself feel excited at the prospect of the department head taking me aside one day or the rich man coming here to tell me the good news himself.

A week goes by, then two, and everyone keeps saying he's

just taking his time.

But when a month passes without a word, people start to whisper in the corners, giving me pitying looks—and a few gloating ones.

This is why I didn't want people to draw premature conclusions. I feel like a joke and avoid the halls, keeping to myself—except for Anna.

When we have a long weekend off for Victory Day in early May, she asks me to come home with her to celebrate with her parents. She argues her case ardently, saying I need to get out of the city and clear my head.

It doesn't take much persuasion, though. I spent Victory Day with her family last year and have visited them on several other occasions. Her parents always welcome me with open arms. They even invited me for Christmas last winter. So I tell her I'd love to go, though I can't stay for the celebrations on Sunday since I have a piano gig at a private party.

We take the train to see Anna's parents. It's a four-hour ride, and when I tell Anna it's a long time to spend on a train, she grins. "You're so spoiled coming from such a small country. When I was little, we would spend nine hours on a train to go see my grandparents. And even that's a short train ride to some people here."

"I guess you're right." I lean my head on her shoulder to take a nap. Being around her is easy. It feels like I've known her forever and not just for two years. How it happened, I don't know. I've always had a hard time getting close to people. Maybe it's the single-minded determination we have in common. Who knows?

I wake up an hour later when Anna stirs me.

Her eyes are wide and worried, the corners of her delicate

lips pulled down. She looks scared. And that scares me.

"What's wrong?" I ask.

"That man... the gangly one in the blue windbreaker." She stares into the back of the seat in front of her, her voice trembling. "He keeps watching us."

I lean over to glance down the hall and instantly see who she means. A lanky man in his late twenties with a blue wind jacket, unwashed hair, and thin cheeks is leering at us. She's right. There's something off about him.

Swallowing the lump in my throat, I sit back and muster a reassuring expression. "He's just looking at a beautiful woman."

She shakes her head. "I know how it looks when men watch me like that. This is not it. I think he might be following us."

"Anna—" I'm about to tell her it's nothing, but she cuts me off.

"I saw him two times before we boarded the train, watching us the same way."

I lean over her again to find the man's protruding eyes glued to us like a sticky cobweb.

"It's just a coincidence that he's on the same train," I say, despite the anxiety knotting up my insides. I want to think she's just being paranoid. She's had the same suspicion a few times before, and it's always proved to be nothing. But I also know she's dealt with some shady people and seen some of the dangers lurking in the dark corners of this country. I, on the other hand, feel too safe, coming from a place where corruption, human trafficking, and the mafia are foreign concepts of another world.

I try to brush it off—talk about something else to calm both of us.

But when we get off the train in the small town where Anna grew up and the gangly man also gets off, my fear spikes. I'm no longer able to hold on to my rationality. So I hold on to Anna as we walk down the street.

Anna leads us in the wrong direction, taking several aimless turns to see if the man truly is following us. Whenever we turn our heads and think we have lost him, he shows up behind us seconds later. We are both shaking when we circle back to the station.

"Come," Anna urges in a low voice and picks up her steps, steering us straight for the public bathroom. The smell of urine and sweat hits us as she slams the door shut, but neither of us cares. Anna fumbles in her bag and takes out her phone to call her dad.

Her voice trembles as she fires off rapid Russian phrases, and I hear the soothing rumble of a male voice on the other end.

I imagine how my dad would react if I called because I was afraid someone was following me. He'd say something like "Astrid, don't be preposterous" or "The world revolves around other things than you."

Luckily, Anna's dad is nothing like mine. It only takes a minute before she puts away her phone and says, "He's coming."

I breathe a sigh of relief—a small one, though, since the lanky man might be lurking right outside.

We barely wait five minutes before there's a knock on the door accompanied by Anna's dad's voice. "Anna, Astrid, it's safe to come out."

Her dad brings us both in for a long hug, and Anna's mother does the same when we step into their homey apartment fifteen minutes later.

At first, her parents' worry does nothing to soothe my anxiety. On the contrary. Because if they take us seriously, it means we had good reason to be afraid.

It takes a few hours of reassuring conversation, a hearty home-cooked meal, and the warm atmosphere of the traditional Russian home and the people living in it before we both calm down and are able to enjoy the rest of the evening.

We spend Saturday helping Anna's mom prepare food for the celebration. I'm a bit sad I won't be here tomorrow to join the feast and see the military parade and fireworks. In many ways, it's much different than our holidays back home, and even though I'm not part of the cultural heritage, I still felt like I was part of something bigger when I joined the festivities last year.

Unfortunately, well-paid piano jobs don't come around often, so both Anna and I are quick to strike when the opportunity arises. We need the money. Plus, more jobs mean more referrals, which might lead to something steady when we graduate in early July—in two months. God, time moves fast.

I still haven't decided whether to stay in St. Petersburg.

My parents have been calling a lot recently, adamant to make me drop this magical fantasy-land idea of becoming a concert pianist. It makes me want to stay just to defy them, but they know exactly which buttons to push to scare me.

There's no safety net here. If I go unemployed and my meager savings run out, I'm forced to go home and rely on my parents until I get back on my feet. That would be a kick in the stomach on so many levels. A failure of epic proportions. But I've come this far and am not ready to give up.

Anna, on the other hand, has her plan laid out. She already has several potential jobs lined up. She's going to play at restaurants and fancy hotels until she can save enough to get a manager to help her land important concerts.

Maybe I could do the same.

Or maybe it's too big a risk.

All these uncertain thoughts scurry around my head like squirrels scrambling to gather the final acorns for winter.

When I say goodbye to Anna and her family Sunday morning, this melancholic feeling is stuck in my throat. A feeling of finality.

"I'll see you again soon," Anna's mother says in slow Russian, lifting a hand to catch a stray tear running down my cheek. "We'll be in St. Petersburg to see both of you play at your final exams."

She's more of a mother to me than my own mother these days, and I'll truly miss her if I decide to go home.

Anna pulls me in for a tight hug. "I'll see you tomorrow," she whispers reassuringly. "I promise to bring a piece of mama's Sharlotka."

"Thanks." I make a final wave as I walk into the stairwell with Anna's dad. He insisted on driving me to the train station, and I'm more than grateful for it.

Once I'm settled in one of the comfortable seats on the train, I push my earbuds in and start my playlist of soothing Debussy piano. Then I spend the next hour blinking up toward the ceiling or down at the carpeted floor, trying to hold back the tears prickling behind my eyes.

When my phone vibrates in my hand, I look down to see a text from Anna.

Everything good so far? No creepy men?

A smile pulls at my lips as I punch in my reply.

No creepy men :) Enjoy Victory Day and send a smile to a pretty soldier for me.

Neither Anna nor I have much interest in dating. The few dates we've been on during the past two years have been disappointing, to say the least. I think we've both decided it's better to avoid the distraction for now—save our time and energy for the piano. But we did enjoy waving at the stately soldiers at last year's Victory Day parade.

Will do. I'll even blow them a kiss or two for you ;)

My smile widens at her response, and right then, I make an important decision.

I can't leave her. There's nothing at home worth leaving Anna and my life here for. Her parents are more parents to me than my own, and Anna is the only person I've ever felt this close to. Hell, I even feel more at home in this country despite the uncertainty and the occasionally creepy men.

Why leave all this? For the security of money? Anna and I have made it this far without a single penny from our parents, and we're both great at what we do. We'll figure something out.

I'm going to stay in St. Petersburg. Indefinitely.

I'll tell Anna tomorrow when she comes home. She'll be stoked. She often talks about how we can get a shared apartment if I decide to stay. "Maybe even a cat," she'll always add with an excited smile.

I think she likes the prospect of being alone as little as I do, but she's too polite to let on, not wanting to pressure me.

I breathe a satisfied sigh. This feels right.

Looking up from my phone, I glance around the cart with a small smile.

Everyone is celebrating today, so there are not many people

on the train. An elderly couple, a mother and her child, and a businessman.

My eyes fall back to the latter. He sits on the opposite side of the aisle, facing my direction. He's engrossed in something on his laptop, so I allow myself to study him for a minute.

There's something familiar about him, but I can't put my finger on it or imagine where I would have seen him. Maybe at the fancy dinner party I played last week. Everyone there was upper-middle class, clad in suits and pretty gowns. This man would have fit in with his black slacks, polished shoes, and crisp, white shirt pressed to perfection. But then again, something about him makes me think he'd stick out. It's the air around him, I think. The innate authority emanating from his every move and the self-assured way he carries himself, like he knows he's important.

Everyone at the dinner party had to make an effort to fit in at the five-star hotel lobby. They had enough money to appear rich for a night, but the fancy garments weren't their normal clothes, their proud postures not their natural ones. However, this man seems at ease in the tailored suit and the big Rolex around his wrist. He oozes money and wealth in a way only men born into riches can.

His inch-long blond hair falls perfectly straight to one side without a single strand astray, and his clean-shaven skin sports the same perfection, leaving an unobstructed view of his square jaw and the straight line of his lips. Judging by his smooth skin, which only bears slight lines across his forehead, it seems he's in his mid-thirties. However, his commanding presence suggests a level of maturity only a few men of his age can muster.

And those eyes... They are the most striking blue I've ever seen. Like the sky on a cloudless summer day—or rather, the blue shades of an icy winter landscape. I would have remembered those eyes if I'd seen them before. The same goes for the calm authority rolling off him even as he reclines in a train seat, tapping away on his computer. So I suppose he just resembles someone I know.

Realizing I've stared too long, I look away. But my eyes dart back of their own accord, unwilling to adhere to my usual propriety.

Aleksandr Pletnev had short blond hair and broad shoulders, I suddenly remember.

I study the man for a minute more, trying to gauge if it really is him. I didn't get a good enough look at the man in the fifth row to discern whether the features are similar, but the confident posture looks the same.

With a shake of my head, I turn my gaze away. *It can't be.* It would be too much of a coincidence, and a man like Aleksandr Pletnev wouldn't take the train.

Even so, I can't stop looking. Something about him draws me in.

He never catches me, but he must surely sense me watching. Most people would. Especially a man like him who emanates control enough to govern several countries.

Maybe he knows but doesn't care.

A stab of disappointment shoots through me.

Why does that thought bother me?

I force my attention to the window. But I can't shake the hope that he's watching me—seeing my long waves of blond hair and the fullness of my rosy lips. I may not have Anna's delicate features or almond-shaped eyes, but I know my round cheeks can be sensual when tinged with a warm shade of pink, and I've been told my gray eyes can hold startling amounts of passion when I find something to evoke it.

I rarely do, though. The piano seems to be the only thing that will stir any kind of excitement in me, and these days, even that is rare.

Suddenly, this pounding yearning for passion grips me. Passion directed at something besides black and white keys.

I peer back at the man, and a strange longing clenches my chest as I take in his masculine beauty. His strength. I wonder what it would feel like to have his arms wrapped around me while he whispered seductive words into my ear, his fingers slipping beneath the edge of my pants, skimming the skin on my mound.

My thighs twitch. It's been so long that the mere thought of a man's touch will make me all hot and bothered.

I swallow past the lump in my throat as tears suddenly prickle behind my eyes.

What's wrong with me today? Usually, I steer clear of all these heavy emotions. I'm always focused—restless, but unwaveringly determined. And now, it all bubbles to the surface.

I take out the book that has remained untouched in my bag all weekend. It's one of those crime novels that are popular back home in Norway. I don't see the appeal, though. One month, and I've only reached page one hundred. It never captures my attention, and today is no exception.

I keep sneaking furtive glances at the man on the other side of the aisle, trying to be discreet by letting my eyes scan the surroundings, settling for the small glimpses I get in passing.

The landscape outside begins to change; trees and fields become buildings and streets.

I pack up my book and fold my jacket over my arm since the May sun offers plenty of heat today. Then I spend the next fifteen minutes resting my head against the seat, gazing out at the emerging city.

One last time, I let my eyes drift to the businessman. He has packed up his laptop and has his attention on his phone. He's impassive and unreadable, like he's been the whole time. But then, by some small miracle, a smile tugs at his lips, crinkling the corners of his eyes as he watches something on the screen. And that smile... It's utterly charming. Like the sun on a cold February day in St. Petersburg.

I wish he would look up and direct the smile at me. Let me bask in its warmth for just a second—feel the intensity of those blue eyes on me.

But he doesn't, of course.

The train pulls into the Ladozhsky station, the large, modern glass front coming into view. I heave a silent sigh, get up, and walk toward the exit.

A smile would have been nice—especially now that I didn't get to smile at the soldiers. But I didn't even get that.

Loneliness creeps up on me, and my fingers drum on the handrail as I wait for the train to come to a stop.

Shoes click on the floor behind me. I'm about to look back to see who's joining me, but then I feel his presence, the man with the laptop and formal attire. It's a palpable energy that fills the space—sucks out the air and heats my skin. I force my eyes to remain on the window as my heart rate spikes.

The train comes to a stop, and I press the button for the door. My feet are heavy as I step onto the first step, and my focus wavers as I feel the man towering behind me.

I move my other foot but somehow miss the second step and fall into the air, face-first.

I gasp as I prepare for impact with the platform. But I don't hit it. Not with anything but my stumbling feet. I somehow remain upright, unhurt. Besides my rough landing, the only discomfort is a tug on my arm.

That's when I realize the man has caught me. And his fingers are still locked around my arm, my muscles aching from the force of his grip.

"Watch your step," a low voice says with a hint of irritation.

"I'm so sorry." I turn to face the stranger, embarrassment flushing my cheeks. The air lodges in my chest as I look up, up, up to meet his gaze, and I stumble away from him.

I've been watching this man for four hours, and his eyes have been calm and controlled the whole time. But now they hold the intensity of a thousand storms, piercing me like icicles.

He gives me a curt nod, as cold as his glare, then moves on.

My feet remain glued to the platform as I stare after him, my heart pounding, my hands quivering. It's only when he disappears from view that I can finally get my legs to move toward the escalator.

I halt again when I reach the grand hall, barely remembering which way leads to the bus.

Usually, the space buzzes with life, people milling in and out, waiting on benches, and buying food in the shops. But today the place is dead. Metal roll-up doors cover the storefronts, the rows of seats and benches are empty, and the single person in here quickly disappears down to a platform.

I feel lightheaded and disoriented. Maybe I should get something to eat. I had a hearty breakfast at Anna's parents' place, but that was several hours ago. Furthermore, I'm not ready to go back to the empty apartment yet, so I decide to scour the place for an open bistro or something. But first, I need to use the restroom.

I make my way to the end of the lobby and head down a long, lonely corridor.

It's eerie how quiet it is, and I quicken my steps until I reach the door with the female icon. I quickly slip into a booth and lock myself up with a feeling of unease creeping down my spine.

I shoot Anna a quick text, needing the illusion of safety from being in contact with another person.

Arrived safely at Ladozhsky. No signs of the creepy man.

It must be the episode with the man following Anna and me that has me on edge. Luckily, there's been no sign of the gangly man since we fled into the dingy bathroom two days ago. It's just irrational anxiety, I tell myself as I step out of the booth to wash my hands by the long row of sinks.

My phone vibrates in my jacket, and I take it out to read Anna's reply.

Good to hear. We're at the parade, waving at the soldiers and blowing kisses as promised. Text me when you get home.

Leaning back against the counter, I breathe a heavy sigh that eases the weight in my chest. It feels safe to have someone know my whereabouts—especially when it's someone who cares about them. I quickly type my reply as I push through the door and walk down the hall.

Will do. I'll grab some food here first, though, so it might be a while.

When I get back into the open hall with tall, arched ceilings and large glass fronts, I notice an open coffee shop at the other end. I head straight for it, my stomach growling at the prospect of food.

I make it four steps and startle when someone grabs my arm. I'm about to sputter my offense and rip my arm free when I feel a cold prickle on my back—something sharp piercing my blouse.

Cold steel, right on my skin, I realize to my horror.

My feet falter, but a hard body presses against my back and the firm grip on my arm steers me on. "Keep walking," a deep voice commands, all too calmly.

I want to turn my head—see who's got the nerve to grab me and press a knife to my back in broad daylight. But I can't. Fear has me paralyzed, unable to think or act. My legs are the only thing working, and only because they have to.

All I can see from the corner of my eye is his left side—white and black clothes, tall and broad frame. He's so tall his face is hidden way above my head where I don't dare cast my eyes up. His fingers are large enough to encompass my upper arm in an unbreakable grip. It's not forceful, but the potential strength is palpable. He could easily snap my bones.

Icy shivers skate down my skin, and my legs quiver, threatening to give in. But fear is not the only thing churning in my stomach. There's this feeling of powerlessness that tugs at something deep inside me—some magnetic pull, against all rationality, that flutters and sends heat coursing through my veins.

It's his presence. It looms over me like a great building casting its shadow over several blocks, calm and powerful. Commanding in a most masculine way that speaks to my feminine soul and keeps my heart from speeding too fast. It's like the unwavering stability steadies me through the fear that wreaks havoc on my insides.

Fuck. I must be sick. There's nothing alluring about a stranger who presses a knife to my back, possibly kidnapping me.

The blood drains from my face and bile rises in my throat.

Is that what's happening? He's kidnapping me?

I'm going to be sick at any moment. The telltale stomach

cramps have already set in.

"That's it," the man says, voice slow and deep—praising? "Keep going. Straight ahead." It's almost like he senses the oncoming nausea. Like he's trying to reduce the immediate threat with soothing words.

It's ridiculous. I know there's nothing safe about those words. They're a twisted illusion.

Yet my stomach settles.

He guides me through the exit and onto the raised parking lot on a large platform. I hear a train pull in below us, screeching on the tracks as it comes to a halt. A woman walks past us with hastened steps—maybe to catch said train—and she doesn't even spare us a glance.

I want to reach out and tug at her, scream for help. But I don't dare. And as the man behind me moves us across the platform, toward the stairs at the corner, help slips out of reach.

I know what's down there beneath the long set of stairs.

Nothing.

The stairs lead to the secluded side of the station, where people only come when the parking space up here is full. And it sure isn't today.

The shaking spreads through my body, and I start staggering.

I abruptly halt at the edge of the stairs and stare down the immense amount of steps. "I can't," I croak. Somehow, it seems worse falling down all those steps than being dragged away by this stranger. "I'll fall."

"*Dershu tebya.* I won't let you fall." As if to prove his point, he tightens his grip on my arm.

It's like déjà vu—the steadying hand and deep voice.

That's when it hits me. The man on the train. White and black. His suit.

I turn my head and stare straight up into chilly blue eyes. Cold as a block of ice, yet warm with the promise he just made. It doesn't make sense—not the dichotomy in his eyes, not the kidnapping.

I'm so stunned my fear fades for a moment, making my feet move on autopilot as he nudges me.

Fresh notes of citrus and something masculine waft past my nose as I move my feet onto the first step, and I inadvertently inhale a deep whiff of the intoxicating scent. *His scent.*

"One step at a time. I'll catch you if you fall."

He must be mocking me for my unsteady feet—or maybe my fall on the platform earlier. But I find no ridicule in his words. They are smooth and warm. Tender even. Maybe he actually means it?

It can't be. How can someone be tender while holding a knife to my back?

My brain fogs over with all the questions and contradictions. Yet somehow, I manage to zero in on the task of placing one foot on each step—a task that seems more like climbing a mountain than a simple everyday action.

I barely notice that the sharp tip at my back disappears and a flat palm presses against my waist instead. Supporting me?

It takes forever to descend those stairs, and when I finally have both feet back on solid ground, it takes me a moment to gather my thoughts. Before I can think of running, the knife is back against my skin. The man leads me to the dusty parking lot in front of the rails, where a single large SUV is parked in the shadow of the platform.

My skin stings beneath the tip of the knife, but the pain is nothing compared to the one bearing down on my chest. I can barely breathe through it, and my inhales become more and more ragged as we approach the car.

The faint noise of traffic hums in the distance, but it's so low I barely notice it. My wheezing breath and the crunch of shoes on gravel seem to be the only sounds around us.

Stopping by the SUV, the man opens the back door, and I see the silhouette of another man in the driver's seat. The driver is large and bulky, like one of those men you see pulling a truck on TV.

Heavy blocks of ice settle in my stomach. I can't get into that car. When I'm in, there's no out. I know it like I know sunsets leave darkness, heavy clouds bring rain. And like the weather, I see no stopping this. Yet my mind scrambles to work something out.

Should I fight? Scream? Is it worth risking a knife in my back?

Indecision pounds in my head, dragging on in a single second that seems to last forever.

Then the last question becomes void as the knife hits the ground with a metallic sound. The sharp tip is gone, and I know what I have to do.

There's no way I'm getting into that car.

With a forceful yank of my arm, I open my mouth to scream. But I'm too slow. Before the shrill sound can ring out into the open space, a large hand clamps over my mouth.

"Don't even think about it." The words are a low snarl, and for a moment, I think it's someone else—maybe the man in the car who has come out. It can't be the same voice as the one crooning in my ear moments ago. "The knife was just a means to keep you calm. But down here, I'm not beyond using force."

It's the same man. The citrusy scent from before wafts past my nose again, and the other man is still in the driver's seat.

There's no one else here. The man snarling in my ear is the same one who pressed a supportive hand against my waist and promised he wouldn't let me fall.

Maintaining the punishing grip on my bicep, he removes his palm from my mouth, and what little courage I had gathered fades fast.

There's a rustle of clothes—a hand digging into a pocket. The seconds stretch on, and I don't understand why he doesn't shove me into the vehicle.

Something new drops to the ground. Plastic? I glance down, and yes, there on the gravel lies a small, oblong plastic cap, and somehow, that lid is more terrifying than the knife beside it.

The man pulls down my arm, stretching my shoulder. And then I feel it. The most terrifying thing of all. A small prick, then an aching pressure as liquid seeps into my muscle.

I whimper—a small, weak sound. My body slackens as my strength seeps out with frightening speed. My limbs go numb, and my knees give in. I collapse.

As the man promised, he catches me. Strong arms easily support my weight, holding me against a hard chest.

Using my last sliver of strength, I crane my neck and gaze up into a set of blue eyes boring into my very soul. I don't recognize the features around them, but I recognize the intensity of those eyes.

It *is* him. Aleksandr Pletnev.

"It's you..." My voice fades before I can say more.

"You're mine now." His lips tip up into a wide, charming smile—the smile I so badly wanted on the train. Now, he finally aims it at me, and it's the most terrifying thing I've ever seen.

The last thing I see before my world goes black.

Chapter 3

THE RUMBLE OF an engine vibrates gently, and the sound of soft jazz seeps through speakers. It's peaceful. The steady roll of wheels lulls me, keeping me on the edge of sleep.

I stay there for some time, but inevitably, I have to wake up. Even though I try to fight it, somehow knowing it will bring me no good, I slowly regain consciousness.

Pressure builds in my head, working its way up to a painful throbbing. My hands and feet start to tingle, and when I open my eyes, my sight is blurry. All I see is brown leather, windows, and daylight. A car?

I don't remember getting into a car.

"Where am I?" I moan.

"You're safe," a deep voice reassures, but something tells me I'm not.

Blinking against the light, I catch a glimpse of the broad-shouldered figure in the driver's seat—a large hand resting on a leather-bound steering wheel.

My head spins as I try to focus my gaze, and nausea suddenly churns my stomach. "I don't feel so good," I croak through heaving breaths as I fight the urge to throw up.

Wheels screech as the car veers to the side, coming to an

abrupt stop. I press a hand to my mouth, nearly vomiting at the sudden movement. The jarring sound of the driver's door slamming shut makes another surge of bile rise in my throat. I vaguely notice someone rushing around the car, and then I'm hauled out just in time. My knees barely hit the ground before I'm retching. It all happens in a flurry of limbs, flashes of green grass and red metal. Now also yellow spew.

My stomach goes into cramps as I expel its contents. I hover above the pool of vomit and have no idea how I don't fall into it. My limbs are dull and lifeless, my hands not even touching the ground. Someone must be holding me.

When I'm finally empty, I realize I'm lying over a sturdy thigh. It presses into my stomach, provoking my nausea, and I keep dry heaving.

Someone is stroking my back. It's the same person whose thigh I'm hanging over—whose arm keeps me above the pool of vomit. The long strokes are calming. I close my eyes and try to redirect my focus to them, but the acrid smell stings in my nose, and I groan as my stomach keeps contracting painfully, moisture trickling down my cheeks.

"Calm breaths," someone says. "*Dershu tebya.*" The hand keeps going, up and down along my spine, underlining the spoken promise that he's got me.

I take in a long, shuddering breath and push the air back out.

"That's it. One more."

I take another deep breath and focus on the soothing hand. It's warm. Warm and big. The heat easily seeps through my blouse, easing the nervous prickling in my skin. It coaxes me to let go, so I do. I go slack in the foreign arms and sink back into that dull, hovering place between consciousness and sleep.

"Everything's okay," the voice reassures.

Deep down, I know it's not. But I can't refuse the comfort, so I soak up the gentle words.

My hands start to tingle like they did in the car, and I try to ignore it. But it slowly gets worse, a thousand needles pricking my arms as if I've slept on them. That's when I realize my hands are caught between my hips and the man's leg.

I try to wrest them free, but they're stuck. Or maybe I'm too tired to make an effort.

The man seems to sense my discomfort and shifts me to sit in his lap. It's a clumsy hassle getting me settled. My arms are useless weights, and my feet are dragging along, not wanting to move of their own volition. When I'm finally leaning against him, my head flops down on the offered shoulder.

He takes one of my twitching hands and gently presses his thumb into my palm, massaging with just the right pressure to alleviate the discomfort. That's when I feel something around my wrist—something that makes my other arm rise too as he lifts my hand.

Opening my eyes, I'm startled to find brown rope twined around my wrists and ankles too.

My heart starts thrumming in my chest. *Why are my hands tied?*

It's not right.

I twist my wrists against the rope, but there's no give. They remain trapped, and panic builds as I pull and yank, gaining nothing but pain as the rope digs into my skin.

Two strong hands close around my wrists. "Don't," he says, and I think it's meant as a comfort rather than a rebuke. Yet a command hovers somewhere in the soft rumble, and it's that hidden note that makes my arms go slack.

"Good girl," the same voice croons.

At the warm appraisal, I lift my gaze for the first time to face the man who holds me. Suddenly, it all comes crashing. The train ride, my stumbling feet, his sharp gaze. But more so, the knife against my back, the angry snarl when I tried to scream, and the smile when he robbed me of my consciousness.

Aleksandr Pletnev. The man I thought would fulfill my dreams.

I don't waste any time on feeling betrayed. It doesn't matter what this is or why he took me. I just know I need to get away.

Tumbling from his arms, I barely miss the pile of vomit. To my great relief—and stunned surprise—he doesn't try to stop me as I start crawling. Instead, he rises to his feet.

"Try to avoid the vomit. I don't want you dragging it into my car," he says tersely, walking to the sleek, red sports car—not a large black SUV like the one at the train station.

My head pounds with confusion, and it only gets worse when I stagger to my feet. My legs won't carry me, and I fall back on my knees, hitting the ground with a jarring thud.

Desperate to get away, I scramble forward on my elbows and knees. But with my feet bound and my entire body sluggish, I crash flat on my belly.

Refusing to give up, I try to worm my way through the grass instead. It takes all my strength, but I keep going even though a turtle could outrun me.

Steps approach behind me, and I claw at the grass to go faster. But it's no use. A heavy foot slams onto my back, shoving the air from my lungs.

I fist the itchy grass, heaving through the pain.

I expect more cruelty when he comes down to his knees, but his touch is surprisingly gentle as he plucks strands of grass from my hair and brushes dirt off my blouse. "You look like a mess."

He grabs me under the armpits and hoists me up on my knees. I don't protest when he presses me back against his legs. I'd fall if he didn't, and I feel oddly grateful for the small gesture.

"Drink." A water bottle appears in front of me, and I realize my mouth is dry as cotton. I bring the bottle to my lips and chug down half its contents.

"Easy now." Aleksandr pushes the bottle away. "We don't want to upset your stomach again."

I don't want him to be right, but he is. So I drink the rest in small sips.

Once the bottle is empty, he hoists me up on my feet, and I struggle to make my weak legs carry my weight. But they don't have to. Without effort, Aleksandr lifts me into his arms and carries me to the car. I don't know much about cars, but I recognize the silver cat on the hood, which tells me it's a Jaguar. A very expensive one.

I feel utterly helpless when Aleksandr returns me to the back seat and rounds the vehicle. The door is unlocked, and there's no immediate threat—no knife to my back, no hands holding me down. It would be so easy to flee the car, run through the tall grass, and disappear into the line of trees. Freedom is right there within my reach. But nothing is easy in my bound, drugged state. I can't do anything but lie here and watch how he takes me away—farther into the depths of this desolate country.

If we're even in Russia, that is.

The sun mocks me with its bright beams, tinting the green trees in an idyllic light. The engine does the same, humming joyously as Aleksandr starts the car. I keep still on the smooth leather, watching the trees disappear out of sight, leaving only blue sky and power lines in my view.

Aleksandr turns the music back on, humming along and

tapping the rhythm on the wheel, making the day seem as bright as the sun.

We pass through a couple of small towns, where road signs in Cyrillic confirm we are indeed still in Russia. Purple, green, and red houses come into view, some well-kept, some old and tattered. A bus-sign. A road sign. A bus with passengers.

The fog slowly lifts from my mind, and my throat feels less raw after having downed a bottle of water.

I want to ask him something. *Who are you? Where are we going? Why have you taken me?* But all these clichés seem like a wasted effort. I already know who he is, and it makes no difference which hellhole or deserted nook of this godforsaken country he takes me to. I probably wouldn't even recognize the name of the place if he were to tell me. And the reason for taking me... I'm not sure I want to know—if there even is one.

So I end up choosing an entirely different question. "Aren't you afraid I'll jump up and bang on the windows?" I ask as another bus passes us.

"Who would care? Besides, the windows back there are tinted."

My stomach churns. But lucky for me—or maybe his car—I have nothing left to expel. Ignoring the nausea, I keep talking. "How long have I been out?"

"An hour or so. More than plenty to get you out of the city without a fuss."

"Where are we going?" I say, feeling stupid for asking such a ridiculous question after having decided not to.

He answers this question too, surprisingly talkative for a kidnapper. "My estate up north, by Ladoga."

Ladoga is a large lake north of St. Petersburg. It's supposed to be beautiful there. That much I know. But what difference does it make? He might lock me up in a basement where I won't see the light of day. Take me to some human trafficking auction to be shipped off to God knows where. Kill me for the pleasure of it and throw me into the lake, never to be found.

My hands are shaky and sweaty, clinging to each other when I continue. "What are you going to do to me?" I have to know.

His voice takes on a stern tone, his entire demeanor shifting to match it. "Whatever I please."

I don't dare say more, regretting I asked in the first place. My head is already stirring up vivid horror scenarios worse than the ones before he answered.

We are both quiet for a while. I'm shaking with fear, and he's enjoying the music like it's a regular sunny day. But it's not for me. Far from it.

His innocent humming takes on an ominous note as it becomes the soundtrack to the horror scenarios playing out in my head.

"Hey."

I look up at the sound of his voice and meet his gaze in the rearview mirror.

"Try to get some sleep. We've still got an hour to go." Aleksandr grabs his suit jacket from the passenger seat and tosses it back to me. "I didn't bring a blanket, so this will have to do."

The jacket falls over my hips, and I stare at it, not wanting to cover myself with anything of his.

"Stop being a brat and put on the jacket." His voice carries the same threat as when he stopped my scream in the parking lot, and it has the same effect this time too. My courage disappears as hopelessly as the line of trees did. So I take the jacket, and after a minute of fumbling with my bound hands, I manage to cover myself. It feels wrong, and I tense up. I'm not going to fall asleep here. Not even if I try.

The music changes, and Debussy comes on. "Clair de Lune." It's an overused piece, but unlike so many other banged-up pieces of classical music that have been ruined by ridiculous commercials and bad movies, this one never fails to move me. I still remember the first time I managed to play the beginning. I didn't have the required technique, but I was ecstatic, making those notes with my own hands.

What if I never get to play it again?

Tears spring to my eyes at the thought, a sharp ache wrenching my chest.

I feel Aleksandr watching me again, and when I peer up at the mirror, his eyes are soft and gentle. Full of sympathy.

Jerking my hands up, I dry at the moisture spilling over my cheeks. I hate that he sees this vulnerable side of me. He may see me scream, puke, and thrash for all I care. But the tears are mine. I don't ever want to give them to a man like him.

With a couple of clumsy movements, I manage to turn around and escape his gaze without losing the jacket—I don't dare to lose it.

I close my eyes and try to keep my breath steady so the tears won't turn into sobs. Deep inhales through my nose, long exhales through my mouth.

A citrusy scent drifts into my nostrils as I drag in a breath. It's his. The scent is already branded into my mind as his. It should evoke fear—and it does that too—but it also makes me feel something entirely different. A sliver of something warm, a sense of calm. Protection.

I try to shove it away, but my throbbing head and exhausted body want to dwell on it—let it drag me under. And finally, it does. I fall asleep with the scent of citrus and danger in my nostrils, the soothing notes of Debussy and the quiet humming of my kidnapper drifting into my ears.

Chapter 4

I WAKE UP WHEN someone lifts me out of the car. I whimper and shove feebly at the arms taking me. I don't want to go. It was peaceful here. Painless.

Now, sharp spears of pain shoot through my head as I bounce against a hard chest.

I don't want to open my eyes and face reality. I know nothing good awaits me on the other side of the drowsy veil shrouding my memories. I'm perfectly happy in this oblivion.

So I shove at the person who carries me again. "Go away."

"You can go back to sleep in a minute. I'm taking you somewhere more comfortable." The resonant voice is a rumble in the chest beside my ear—an acceptable replacement for the humming engine.

I blink and see gray clouds marring a blanket of blue sky. The clouds look like they want to rain as they hang there, heavy and dull, dragging their weight along as they impose on the sun.

My eyes feel as heavy as those clouds as I slowly scan my surroundings.

Neatly trimmed trees, colorful flower beds, large lampposts in Victorian style. And... turrets? Looking farther to the left, I see a gigantic mansion. Turrets, pillars, and balconies. It has it all. But it's big enough to carry the ornamentation without being vulgar. It's beautiful, really, with its sand-colored stone, wrought iron, and ornamented window frames. Yet it's ominous, and a nagging voice at the back of my mind tells me nothing good comes from a place like this.

What is it Anna says about rich men?

I can't remember. I can barely remember how I got here. Only a few flickers of memories peek through the haze. The train station. A red car. Green grass scratching my palms. I don't want them. I want to stay in this blissful ignorance a while longer before my world crashes. So I let my eyes fall shut and rest my head against the firm chest. It's warm. Safe. Strong enough to protect me.

Danger, a voice in my head says.

I ignore it and whimper at the bumping movement as I'm carried up a set of stairs.

A door moves smoothly on its hinges—a heavy one—and then there's the echo of hard soles in a large space. *Click, click, click.* More stairs, more pain.

I inhale sharply and catch the citrusy notes of an aftershave.

Citrus.

My eyes snap open, and I stare straight up at the man carrying me. Every muscle, nerve, and fiber of my being curls into rigid coils of fear.

It can't be.

I squeeze my eyes shut, willing it all to go away. It's just a bad dream. When I open my eyes, I will be in my bedroom. Maybe on the train. Someplace safe that doesn't smell like lemon and fresh air.

I peek my eyes open, and my breath sticks in my throat, my heart pulsing with alarm. The man carrying me is very real, and so are the marble columns, intricately carved banisters, and heavy chandelier.

Money is power, power is danger. Stay away from rich men.

The words come back to me with an icy surge of fear. Anna usually says them with a haunted look in her eyes. She's had her taste of danger in the shifty waters of Russian dating life. I never really grasped those words, but now they seem to ring truer than any other words.

Stay away from rich men. Didn't I do that? I don't remember seeking out anyone with loads of money. I don't remember approaching anyone at all. I'm a recluse. Me, my piano, and Anna. No dating, no men.

A memory hits me like a hammer to my aching head. He took me from the train station—forced me at knifepoint.

Why would he take me? Because I willed him with my eyes, begged him to choose me?

Fuck. My head is running too fast, the unfamiliar surroundings spinning around me like I'm on a crazy carousel.

I try to focus on the white ceiling as he carries me down a hallway, through a sitting room, and into another room. It's only when he sets me on a sofa and the carousel stops that I can focus my eyes on the space around me.

We're in a large room with high ceilings, gilded moldings, and another chandelier—though less monstrous this time. Dark wood, gold, and warm shades of rosy pink dominate the space, and arched windows let in plenty of light while offering an outlook over an expansive garden and a lake in the distance.

For a second, I'm lost in the mesmerizing beauty. But when my eyes land on the broad iron structure in the farthest corner, icy shivers shoot down my spine. A thick, queen-sized mattress on the floor is surrounded by golden bars on all sides.

A cage.

If it wasn't for the solid steel and the fact that it's surely built to keep someone locked up, it's sort of beautiful with the gold and rosy beddings. It looks like something meant for a cherished possession—or a beloved pet. But not a person. A person shouldn't be locked up. And that's what this is for.

I gulp hard as I stare at the thing. No, there's really nothing beautiful about it. The gold is meant to deceive, and somehow, I just know that cage is for me. I'm about to become a captive behind golden bars.

"Don't forget to breathe," a deep voice says close to my ear.

"Wh—what?" I stutter, taking my gaze off the terrifying thing to stare at the man crouching in front of me—equally terrifying. "You're not..." I point one of my tied-up hands at the disturbing thing, unable to finish the sentence.

"Shh." A hand comes up to brush loose strands of hair from my face. "Just breathe."

I shake my head, my eyes back on the golden bars. *I can't.*

Large hands cup my cheeks and turn my head to face the cold blue of a warm gaze. Like ice in the sun. It doesn't make sense. None of this does.

"Who are you?" I say, asking the last question on my list of stupid kidnap-clichés. But this one I don't mean in the traditional sense. I already know his name, his job, his status.

And he knows I do. "I'm the man who owns you." He says it like it's the simplest thing in the world.

I shake my head in the frame of his hands. *Owns me.* A person. It's nonsense.

"You'll learn the meaning soon enough." He releases my head and lets his hands hang over his thighs. "For now, you just need to know that you're safe. You don't have to fear any of the other men coming in here. They'll just bring food and take you to the bathroom. They won't touch you. Not unless I tell them to."

I part my lips. *But you will touch me?* The words hang on the tip of my tongue but won't move further. I stare at him in horror. There's no emotion, no sympathy in his features. This man is danger incarnate. Pure and unadulterated danger. Other men might not harm me, but what difference does it make when this man is on the other side of that equation?

Aleksandr starts loosening the knots on the ropes, massaging my joints as he goes. I barely notice the fingers rubbing my wrists. I'm paralyzed with cold fear, staring off into the room, unable to do or say anything, and my hands hang limply in my lap when he's done.

He gets up and crosses the room with long, steady strides—the gait of a predator—and my eyes follow him like magnets. When he opens the long lid on top of the cage, my pulse becomes a painful pounding in my neck.

Steady footfalls bring him back, and the sound of fancy men's shoes echoing in the large space is a bad omen that has my hands trembling. I know what he's going to do, and I'm terrified, but I can't move. My brain screams at me to leap from the couch and run out the door, but my body refuses to listen. I can't do anything but sit here, staring at him as my chances of escape wane with each click of his soles.

It's only when he hoists me into his arms that my brain connects with my body. The stagnant message shoots to my limbs, and I go frantic, kicking and scratching.

"Let me go!" I yell.

I might as well be fighting a lion. Aleksandr easily loops an arm around my knees and holds me immobile with frightening strength, and as we approach the cage, my frantic protests turn into pathetic pleas.

"No, no, no, no," I whimper. "Please don't."

I grab onto his shirt when he lowers me into the cage, but he pries me off without effort.

"Don't do this to me." My voice is shrill and desperate, and I hate the sound of it, but I keep going. My pleas turn into senseless clichés when he presses me down and closes the lid. "I'll behave," I squeak. "Just let me go, and I won't tell anyone. I promise."

He puts a padlock through the latch. *Click.* The sound is like the clank of a metal bar to my weary mind, and I start rattling the golden steel above me.

Crossing his arms over his wide chest, Aleksandr studies me for a moment. "Don't waste your energy." He shakes his head like I'm a foolish child, then turns on his heel and leaves.

As soon as the door shuts, I slip my hands through the bars and yank at the padlock. But it doesn't budge. So I ignore the pounding in my head and use my weight to push at the top bars, then move to my back and kick at them with all the strength I can muster. But the bars are solid. Not even a metal bat would make a dent, I'm sure.

Panting, I drop my legs to the mattress and slap my hands over my eyes. If I watch those bars a second longer, I'll break into tears.

Why is he doing this? The question rattles my mind with the same uselessness I rattled the bars. The only sensible explanation I can come up with is some sick fetish, and that thought only drives my anxiety higher. So I try to stop thinking altogether. An equally impossible task.

It's only when my bladder starts screeching with the urge to pee that I can drag my thoughts away from the mind-numbing terror.

I haven't peed since... the station. And I gulped down that entire bottle of water. The thought alone makes me writhe to keep control over my bladder.

God, I need to use the bathroom. I toss and turn, squeeze my legs together, and toss and turn again. Why didn't I feel it sooner? It's like I've chugged three pots of tea, and I don't think I can hold it much longer.

Minutes feel like hours, and when Aleksandr returns, I feel like I'm going insane.

"I need to pee." I cringe at my pathetic tone.

He sets a plate on the desk near the door and crosses the room in a casual gait that makes me want to scream. But I know it may just prolong things, so I bite back my curses. He stops in front of the cage and takes his time to observe me, lording his power as if to make me feel how utterly helpless I am.

He strokes his knuckles against his chin like he considers what to do with me, then cocks his head. "Do you promise to behave if I let you out?"

"Yes," I say in a tiny whimper and shift on the mattress.

He watches me for another minute, then takes the key from his pocket and opens the lid. Half the top and half the side come up, leaving plenty of free space to climb out—or for him to lean down and grab me.

His features are impassive as he holds his hand out to me, and I can't tell whether it's a friendly gesture or some kind of hoax. Desperate as I am, I take it and cling to his whole arm as I scramble to get over the bars. The bars are now low enough for me to climb over easily, but with my legs still being useless and my pressing bladder sending me into uncoordinated stress, I can't seem to manage.

Strong hands clamp onto my hips and hoist me over, and I scamper forward as soon as my feet hit the hardwood. But the drug is still in my system, and I stumble, my legs buckling under the sudden strain. I whimper as I prepare for the collision with hard ground, but it doesn't come. A large hand wraps around my arm and holds my weight until I regain my balance.

"Watch it," Aleksandr reprimands, and when my gaze collides with his piercing blue eyes, I'm back at the train station, rescued from my fall by a dangerous stranger.

I scramble to pull away, but this time, his grip remains. He drags me to the en suite bathroom, orders me to drop my pants, and only lets go of my arm when my bare thighs hit the toilet seat.

I'm so relieved I release my bladder before he's gone, and when I realize he's watching me, it's too late to stop.

"Please, privacy," I beg as the humiliating sound of trickling urine permeates the space.

Aleksandr doesn't relent. He just stands there, arms crossed, eyes fixed on me until my bladder stops dripping.

Shame burns hot within me when I dry myself and reach for my pants. I still don't trust my legs enough to get up before I have them over my thighs.

"Don't bother."

Hunched over and clutching my pants, I look up at Aleksandr. "What?"

He doesn't repeat himself but hauls me up by the arm and sets his foot down on the fabric between my ankles. "Step out."

With all my courage from before gone, I pull my feet free. Defeat settles on me like a pile of bricks as I gaze down at my bare legs beside Aleksandr's slacks.

"Are you going to rape me?" I sound weak and dejected, a

mere shadow of myself, and I know I won't fight if he tries to. There's simply no energy left.

"Shh," Aleksandr unclenches his fist around my arm, and when he tightens again and steers me back to the room, it seems almost gentle. "I'm going to get some food in you, and then you need to rest."

It's not a promise not to rape me at another point, but for now, it's good enough. When he lifts me back over the bars and my feet touch the soft sheets, I'm so grateful for the soothing sensation that I sink to my knees of my own accord.

The lid gives a heavy clank, the click of the lock telling me I'm trapped, but I don't have it in me to react. I just watch with heavy eyes as Aleksandr retrieves the plate on the desk along with a bottle of water and returns to crouch in front of me on the other side of the bars.

"I must say, I didn't expect you to react so strongly to the sedative. I don't want to upset your stomach further and risk you vomiting all over your new cage. So crackers will have to do for now." He breaks one of the crackers on the plate into four, then stretches a hand through the bars to offer me a piece in his open palm.

I reach out to take it but get a firm reprimand as he snaps his hand shut.

"Uh, uh. Eat from my hand."

He folds his fingers back out, and I stare at the white piece of biscuit.

"Eat," he demands, all gentleness from a minute ago gone.

Angry tears gather at the corners of my eyes, and I quickly wipe them away, refusing to break down in front of him.

"Eat," he repeats, his voice dangerously low. "Show me what a good little bitch you are."

Fury surges through me like a raging storm. I don't know where the sudden burst of energy comes from, but I snap my head to him and hiss, "I'm not a dog, you fucking asshole."

His other hand darts between the bars with frightening speed, fisting my hair and slamming my face into the cold steel.

His voice is right by my ear, his breath hot and words furious. "Don't. Ever. Talk to me like that." He yanks at my hair, eliciting a pained moan from my throat. "You get a pass today, but it's the only one you'll get. Next time, I'll whip your ass blue and wash your filthy mouth with soap."

I pant and whimper as I clutch at the bars digging into my skin.

"*Yasno?*" He tightens his grip on my hair and repeats in English, "Are we clear?"

"Yes," I croak.

"Now, eat the goddamn cracker." He slams his palm over my mouth, and the cracker crumbles against my lips. I try to pull away—reach up to catch the pieces with my fingers—but the hand in my hair keeps me in place, forcing my face into the crumbs.

"Eat!"

I dart out my tongue, licking and gnawing at his hand to get all the pieces, feeling every bit the dirty animal he's reduced me to.

Once I've eaten every last crumb, he shoves my head into the mattress. "Clean up the mess."

I lick at the sheets. There's nothing else I can do. *Survival,* I tell myself as I angle my head to drag in air before burying my head back into the mattress. But the explanation does nothing to alleviate the humiliation as I lick the sheets clean.

I keep licking until he releases my hair, and not even then do I dare stop, too scared to find out what he'll do if I misinterpret his intent.

Only when he orders, "Sit up," do I straighten into a kneeling position.

He takes another piece of cracker and holds it out for me the same way he did before.

Fear has wiped out my dignity, so I bow my head and take the piece. Without my dignity, the humiliation is a deep cut to my soul. It sears through my insides, slouching my shoulders and making my head fall forward as I chew.

"Good girl." His voice is back to the steady calm of before, yet I flinch when he moves his hand to my stinging scalp. He only pets me, though, gently stroking my hair. "You're already learning."

His words are meant to praise, but bitter hatred churns in my gut, and it's only because I'm so drained that I bow to eat the next piece of cracker from his palm. It's only because my head is pounding, my limbs dull and lifeless that I don't bite down on his hand and scratch at the one petting my hair.

"Try to get some rest." Aleksandr rises to his feet after having fed me five crackers. In my peripheral vision, I see him point to the side of the cage. "There's a bell in the corner. Use it if you need to pee or feel sick."

His shoes click over the floor as he leaves, and I hear the door close. Like he said, there's a bell. Golden like the bars. But I'm too numb to truly see it. My head nods with the effort of staying upright, my eyes are blurry and unfocused, and before long, I collapse on the mattress and sink into a heavy sleep.

Pale moonlight seeps through the windows when I wake up,

penetrating the darkness of the room. At least some of it. The moon may be bright, the windows wide, but the room is big, and the light only reaches halfway across the floor, every corner laid in eerie black. Mine too.

I must have slept for hours, but I still feel exhausted, my limbs sluggish and my head the same. Maybe the drug he gave me has taken its toll on my body. Or maybe it's the emotional stress of being kidnapped.

Kidnapped. I gulp down the thick emotions piling up in my throat as the realization hits me. I'm trapped in a cage by a man who seems to hold no moral scruples. A rich man in a corrupt country.

The door opens, and the chandelier comes on, bathing the room in bright light. I steel myself, using what little energy I have left to hold up a façade of bravery. But I'm not brave. I'm scared shitless, and when two large dogs come running, barking and sticking their snouts through the bars, I cry out and curl into a ball, hugging my head to my chest.

"Brunja, Luna, out." Aleksandr delivers the command with cutting precision, not even raising his voice.

I peek up to see the two dogs dart back from where they came, wagging their tails and bouncing joyously.

"Don't worry. They won't bite. I've trained them well." He sinks down beside me and places a hand on my shoulder. I jerk away, wiggling across the mattress as I try to get out of his reach.

"Don't." It's a firm command, reinforced by a hand clasping my nape.

I go still, panting through my nose, feeling every bit the cornered animal I am. The hand on my neck isn't out to hurt, but it's firm enough to render me helpless, and I bite my lips to repress the devastating feeling of defeat.

He holds on for a minute, ensuring I've gotten the message. And I have. I don't move a muscle when he releases me and slides his fingers down my neck, shoulder, and onto my arm. With a featherlight touch, he trails his fingers up and down between my elbow and shoulder, dragging up goose bumps on their way.

"I'll train you too," he says, voice gentle like it's supposed to be a good thing, and some instinctive part of me wants to believe it. "I'll get rid of that nasty bark of yours." His fingers move back to my neck, onto the vulnerable spot above my windpipe, brushing up and down.

A shudder runs through me—cold yet warm. It gathers between my legs, where it becomes a slow hum. The intimacy is too stark. Too terrifying. My hips want to arch even as my hands want to fight. But I don't move.

It's only when he rises to his feet that I suck in a hard breath and release my reply on an exhale. "I'm not a dog."

Aleksandr rounds the cage and spears his eyes into me with a force that has me shrinking. "You most certainly aren't. I wouldn't put a dog in a gilded cage. A dog would have been grateful for the crackers. Easier to train." His nose twitches with something feral, and I think more rage is coming.

But the hint of violence passes over his face, and his eyes become impassive as he studies me like he's considering how to go about this training.

My stomach churns with bitter hate, and I want to repeat my words but hold them in.

Aleksandr pulls a chair up beside the cage and sits with his hands interlaced across his belly. His eyes almost become curious as he keeps studying me.

A minute passes like this. Two more. The silence grows tense on my end. My eyes dart back and forth between him and the wall, and I curl up under the comforter, becoming small as if it could protect me.

"Why have you taken me?" I finally ask, needing to break the tension.

Aleksandr scoffs. "Do you really need to ask?"

I give a confused lift of my shoulders.

"You looked so lost up on that stage, begging me with those big eyes." Aleksandr moves to crouch in front of me, his movements slow and measured, revealing a strength matching the intimidation in his eyes. He reaches between the bars and grabs a fistful of my hair to keep my gaze on his. It's not punishing like earlier, but I feel just as small.

"You may not be a dog, but you *are* a stray I've taken in. Just like Brunja and Luna were. And like them, I think you'll thrive with a master." He seems to muse on his words for a moment, then adds, "Once you learn your place."

Bitter tears gather in my eyes, and I blink to force them down. I won't give him the satisfaction of seeing me break apart. So I clench my jaw and gather all the rage I can muster in my eyes.

"Such spite." Aleksandr gives a shake of his head. "Luna would growl and sneer too in the beginning. But she was all bark and no bite. Once she accepted me as her master, she became even more cuddly than Brunja. I wonder if you'll be like that too." His hand loosens around my hair to stroke me instead.

"I'll never accept you as my—" I can't even say the word.

"We'll see about that." There's a knock on the door and Aleksandr gets up. "We'll see."

I don't bother turning to see who's there, but I know it's Aleksandr who returns once the door closes again. Something in his step gives him away. A firmness. Determination. Something in the air. Powerful yet stable.

"Sit up." I hear his voice before I see him, and I slowly move to sit on the mattress, dragging the comforter with me to keep my half-naked body covered.

Aleksandr hands me a wrapped-up sandwich and a bottle of water and sits on the chair, watching me with unnerving intent. "Eat."

I fumble to unwrap the paper with my unsteady fingers. It's clean white, and I wonder if Aleksandr has his own personal chef who has prepared it. I don't think there are any takeaway places nearby.

The scent of pancetta and semi-dried tomatoes fills my nose as I peel back the wrapping, and I realize how hungry I am when my stomach rumbles in anticipation. I bite down on the golden bread and almost moan at the delicious taste. Flavorful basil pesto, creamy mozzarella, and a delicious crust. It's nothing like the cheap sandwiches Anna and I would buy at the small deli around the corner from our apartment. Actually, it's not like anything I've had in a very long time. Maybe ever. I scarf down two more bites and am shocked to find I have completely forgotten about Aleksandr when he speaks.

"Slowly. There's no need to upset your stomach."

I pause mid-bite and peer up. To my relief, he doesn't seem angry or irritated, but I slow down and take a small bite instead of the large one I had prepared for, suddenly feeling very self-conscious.

"Much better." His pleased tone dulls the anxious jitter in my stomach. It's not the type of jitter caused by fear, though. This particular feeling has always been there, turning and twisting, urging me to go on, rendering me unable to sit still.

I try not to think about how this man, who has drugged and

kidnapped me, eases the constant restlessness that I've never been able to soothe with anything but the piano.

Gazing up at him, I swallow. He's pure male power as he sits there on his throne, towering over me like a king. There's no taunt or derision as he looks down at me, caged and reduced to base instincts. He's calm and collected, like he doesn't need to lord over others to know he's in charge.

I keep glancing up at him as I eat, unable to keep my eyes away despite fearing it might provoke him. Something about him draws me—like it did on the train. Against all good judgment, I somehow feel calmer when watching him.

Calm enough to repeat my question from earlier once I've finished the sandwich. "Are you going to rape me?" I ask straight out, and my breathing becomes ragged as I await an answer, hoping it's not the same vague one he gave me before—hoping it's not a *yes.*

"I didn't bring you here as a fuck doll. I have no use for that." Aleksandr rubs his knuckles on his chin. "But I'll probably want to use you at some point." He gets up, and I crane my neck to meet his icy blue eyes as a smirk spreads across his face. "I'm sure you'll beg for it when the time comes."

With that, he walks away and turns off the light, leaving me in darkness and with a whole lot more questions spinning in my head.

Chapter 5

THE NEXT MORNING, another man comes in, and thudding footfalls reveal it's not Aleksandr. I keep my back to the door and tuck the comforter closer as he approaches the cage. Maybe it will all go away if I block it out hard enough.

The sound of clanking metal rips into my hopefulness. "Bathroom break," a coarse, heavily accented voice says as the lid goes up.

I remain unmoving, praying he will leave if I stay still. I don't want to face another person in this dehumanizing state.

"I can leave, and you pee bed." The coarse accent makes the words ring even cruder than they already are. Yet there seems to be no mockery. The flat tone purely states facts.

And I do need to usc thc bathroom, so I turn around and keep my eyes lowered as I push up to sit. Since my limbs are weak, I take a moment to rub my eyes and gather my strength before I rise to my feet. I'm wearing nothing below my waist, and I must stop myself from thanking the man when he hands me a long silk robe. I shrug it on and tie the belt, and with a bit of my dignity restored, I feel some of my strength returning as I climb out of the cage.

I don't look directly at the man, but I see enough to make my skin chill. He's bulky like a bodybuilder. Or rather, like a troll—like the man in the driver's seat when Aleksandr took me. He could easily throw me to the ground and have his way with me, but he doesn't even touch me. He just walks beside me, leading the way to the bathroom, and thank God, he gives me the courtesy of privacy as he closes the door behind him. Maybe Aleksandr's promise about no one touching me wasn't empty words after all. I don't dare to be convinced quite yet, but this small gesture gives me hope.

There's no lock on the door, but the sound of receding steps is reassurance enough, so I hurry to the toilet to relieve myself before the bulky man returns. The privacy is a small luxury, much like the spacious room I have to myself. When I'm done washing my hands, I seize the opportunity to activate my legs by walking back and forth over the warm tile for a few minutes.

One day, I berate myself. One day of imprisonment is all it takes for me to appreciate the small things my captor gives me—the robe, the privacy, men not touching me. Am I really that weak?

I stop at the mirror to take in my reflection. I look no less pathetic than I feel. Straws of grass poke out from my tangled hair, and grime and makeup streak my milky skin.

I must have looked the same when Aleksandr brought me in here yesterday, but I was probably too shaken to truly notice.

Now, a sort of panic grips me as I tear my fingers through my tangled hair. I wince when I tug at the sore roots at the back of my head, but I keep going.

Then I notice the brush on the shelf beneath the mirror and halt. God, I need to calm down. But the settling breath I inhale does little to settle me, and I hiss as I drag the comb through the rat's nest that is my hair.

I still haven't worked through all the tangles when I notice the unopened toothbrush and the toothpaste. I glance over my shoulder at the door. The man might come back at any moment, and I at least want the feeling of a clean mouth when he puts me back in the cage. So I drop the brush, rip open the packaging, squeeze a dollop of paste on the toothbrush, and jab it into my mouth.

There's still no sign of the man when I spit in the sink and turn the golden faucet to rinse. I go to the door and press my ear against the wood. There's a light rustling sound like sheets being changed, but no "hurry up" or angry steps approaching the door.

So I pick the brush back up and finish combing out my long, blond hair. It's one of my best attributes, waist-long, smooth, and thick. This time, I treat it with more care, starting at the tips and working my way up. It takes several minutes before I'm able to drag the brush all the way from the top and down.

Still no sign of the brute.

Maybe he'll let me come out on my own time.

Or maybe not.

There's only one way to find out, and I decide I might as well get cleaned up—take my time and postpone going back as long as I can.

Turning in a full circle, I take in the room. The floors and walls are in the same beige marble as the countertop. The cabinet knobs, lamps, and hangers are all gold like the faucet. Even the towel hanger beside the walled-in shower is flashy with its shimmery gold. I walk to it and wrap my fingers around the white terry cloth hanging there. It feels as expensive as the linen in the cage.

My stomach churns. I know I'm going back there when I step out of this room. I'd much rather be trapped in here than behind bars like some animal. Plus, I need a shower. I don't care if the brute drags me out of here naked and dripping if it means I've gotten to rinse off all this grime, fear, and sweat.

Hurriedly, I strip out of my clothes, run the water until it's hot, and step under the spray. The warm water wraps me in a familiar sense of comfort as it cascades down my body. It's such a relief that moisture gathers in my eyes.

Suddenly, the weight of it all overcomes me, and it's a struggle to rein in the tears. I'm sniffling and drying my eyes when the door opens.

Freezing in place, I steel myself for the onslaught of angry words and punishing arms hauling me from the shower, but the bulky man just pokes his head in, finds me with his eyes, then leaves.

Relief assaults me, sending a wave of tremors rolling through my body. I fall back against the wall and sink to the floor, where I hug my knees to my chest as I succumb to a shaking fit. There I sit, chattering my teeth under the hot water, until the air is so dense with steam it's hard to breathe.

Reluctantly, I push back up on my feet and make quick work of washing myself before shutting off the water and wrapping myself in the fluffy towel.

Then I scour the cabinets by the sink, where I find deodorants, tampons, and assorted creams. I only use the former since I feel too base for the luxury of fragrant lotions. Finally, I put my clothes back on—including my bra and blouse. They might be dirty, but I won't go naked under the robe if I can help it.

Tightening the knot on the robe, I step up to the door and squeeze my eyes shut as I grip the handle. Anxiety prickles like needles beneath my skin as I prepare to return to the nightmare that is my new reality.

If I weren't so frazzled, I would marvel at the beauty that meets me when I step out of the bathroom. The large room is bathed in warm sunlight, making everything shine and twinkle as the light reflects upon all the gold.

"Sit," the bulky man says, his Russian accent eschewing the vowel to a long *seet.*

I cast a glance at the sofa where he reclines with a book, pointing to the large, wooden desk where breakfast for one is set out.

"Maybe cold." He gestures to the food and then to the bathroom. "Too long shower."

English clearly isn't his strength, and as I peruse his gruff, weathered features and the bulk of his muscles, I think he might not have many strengths besides those that are purely physical.

But then my eyes fall to the book in his hand. *Dostoevsky* the cover says in Cyrillic letters.

Don't judge a book by its cover, I guess.

If that's the case, then I probably shouldn't rely on him to keep up his patient demeanor. He might well flip if provoked, and this is not a man I want to instigate. So I go to sit in the pink swivel chair by the desk. After all, being offered a seat at a table and a meal is far better than the cage.

At the thought, my eyes flicker to the large enclosure in the back of the room. It might be in a corner, but said corner is so big the cage by no means seems put to shame. Rather, it might as well be on a pedestal with the way it's angled from the wall, taking up much more space than needed. Even the brute could walk around the monstrous thing without a problem. And all that gold... If the room was any smaller, it would look tacky. But really, as I hate to admit, it's beautiful in its own warped, special way with its clean lines and shiny gold around the rosy bedding.

Beautiful or not, I hate it.

I grab the fork and clutch it until my knuckles turn white. If they ever leave me alone in here—and not locked up in that thing—I will do whatever I can to destroy it. Or at least destroy its offensive beauty. I'd shove it all the way into the corner like a shameful thing no one should see.

A shudder turns my stomach.

Then I would become part of that shame when they put me back into the cage.

"Eat," the man says, breaking me out of my distressing thoughts.

My stomach growls as I turn my attention to the plate in front of me. Despite the large sandwich I ate last night, I feel like I've been starved for days. It must be all the strain of the last twenty-four hours that has taken its toll on my body. So for the next fifteen minutes, I forget about the cage and the dangerous-looking man as I fill myself with eggs, pancakes, and sweet cherries.

"Finish." The Dostoyevsky-reading brute gets up from the couch and approaches me.

Not sure what he means, I peer up at him.

"You finish?" He points to my empty plate, and I want to shrink at the feeling of his large bulk looming over me.

I give him a meek "Yes."

"Up," he says with a nod toward the cage.

My feet are like blocks of lead as I cross the room. The only thing driving me forward is the threat of the man following right behind.

I want to plead with him and fight if he doesn't relent. But for some reason, I can't do it, and when I'm close enough to touch the metal, I freeze—just like I did in the parking lot when Aleksandr took me and again when he brought me up here. I feel weak. Useless. And I hate myself for it.

"Get in." It's more a suggestion than an order. He doesn't need harsh words. I'm small and he's humongous. When I don't move, he simply grabs me under the arms and lifts me into the cage. Then he presses me down by the shoulders, and before I manage to break free from my paralysis, I hear the clank of metal and the click of a lock.

The cage is tall enough for me to remain sitting even as it's closed, but the bars above me are like heavy weights pressing down on me, so devastating I can't keep upright. With an acute need to become as small as I feel, I curl up in a fetal position.

I notice the sheets have a new pattern as I slink under them. They're as silky as before, but there's no comfort in this luxury. Aleksandr could have wrapped me in brown sacks of jute, and I wouldn't have felt the difference.

The sound of heavy steps crossing the room is followed by the sound of a door. Then I'm alone again with nothing but silence to keep me company.

I lie here for hours. At least I think so. There's no way to tell time. No clock, no activity, no sound. There's just the sun, which is all I can see beyond the windows from down here. But not even the sky will reveal the pace of time as dreary clouds slip over it, covering the golden globe in a static gray.

At some point, the brutish man with the calm disposition returns to ask if I need to use the bathroom. I shake my head. This frozen stillness, staring into the sky, keeps me in a drowsy state akin to calmness, and I don't want to ruin it.

It doesn't take me long to realize my mistake, though. The tea and juice I drank this morning is working its way to my bladder, and pressure keeps building until I'm desperate for release.

I consider using the bell, but I can't make myself do it. It would be another step toward accepting this fucked-up situation. Instead, I stubbornly shift on the mattress, squeezing my thighs together and clamping down my inner muscles.

My stomach is cramping with the effort when a new man finally comes in. This one is more normally built but without the calm disposition to ease the harshness rolling off of him. He looks like a rough biker with his thick beard, tousled hair, and tattoos running up the side of his neck.

I'm ready to beg and plead when he opens the cage and gestures toward the bathroom. I scramble over the bars and rush over there, slam the door behind me, and sink onto the toilet seat. It feels like heaven to ease the pressure. I'm so relieved when I go back out that I step back into the cage without hesitance.

The top slams shut, and the lock tells me I'm trapped with a startling click. How can such a small sound be so terrifying?

I cower behind the bars as I peer up at the man, expecting some kind of mockery. But his face remains expressionless as he hands me a sandwich and a bottle of water, then leaves.

Several more hours pass, and I feel like I'm going insane just lying here, hugging the pillow, hugging the comforter, counting the rows of flowers on the linen. All the while, my head throws frightening questions at me, to which I have no answers.

The light fades outside, finally letting me know the day is nearing its end. By the time the door opens again, the sky is a black sheet with yellow dots, and the room is cast in shadows.

I'm grateful for the light that floods the space when someone flicks a switch, less grateful for the man who appears.

With long, confident strides, hands tucked into the pockets of his dress pants, Aleksandr crosses the room and stops in front of the cage.

"I'm sorry I couldn't be here earlier. Busy day. Lots of phone calls. Online meetings." He lifts a hand to rub at the faint stubble on his jaw before crouching beside me and picking up the untouched water bottle.

I devoured the whole sandwich, but I didn't dare touch the water, afraid to repeat the bladder-bursting incident.

"You need to drink." He unscrews the cap and hands me the bottle through the bars.

Pushing up to sit on the mattress, I gingerly accept it and take a few sips while eying him suspiciously.

"Drink it all." His eyes darken. "And use the bell next time you need to pee. I might not feel inclined to give you a new mattress if you soil this one."

Breaking away from his intense stare, I fixate on the floor as blood flushes my cheeks.

"Besides that childish folly of yours, I was happy to learn that you've behaved yourself. I was afraid you'd kick and scream like a rabid beast again today."

I don't respond, just keep my eyes trained on the floor as I chug down the rest of the water.

Aleksandr reaches in to take the empty bottle. "Maybe it won't be so hard to train you after all, huh?"

Anger spikes inside me, hot and livid. I can't control it, and I snap my eyes back to his as my nostrils flare. "You can't keep me locked up in here."

"I can do whatever I want. You're mine." He says it like he's stating a fact, and it pisses me the hell off.

"It's sick…" I don't know how to argue with his fucked-up notion that I belong to him, so the words blurt out of me, fueled by my rising fury. "It's fucking sick is what it is. You can't just take a person and lock them up in a fucking cage."

Spearing me with an icy glare, he rises to his feet calmly. Too calmly.

I know something is coming, but I keep throwing curses at him. It's like a wheel that can't be stopped once it's spinning. "I'm not yours. I never will be, you sick fucker. You can't do this to me!"

He pushes a key into the padlock, then lifts the lid. "Get up."

I don't do it. Of course I don't. And when he reaches down for me, I jerk back and throw my hands at his. But it's uncoordinated and no use either way. He simply grabs one of my wrists and hauls me off the mattress, up in the air. It happens so fast I don't perceive it before I land on his shoulder with a thud that knocks the air out of me. It takes me a moment to recover, and then I kick and scream and claw at his back like the rabid beast he accused me of being.

Aleksandr throws me onto the couch, stomach-down, and pins me with a hand on my back. A gust of air chills my skin as he flips the silky robe from my butt, and I flail and kick and snap my teeth, but it doesn't change a thing.

Smack!

A large palm slams onto my left butt cheek. I wheeze through clenched teeth and squeeze my eyes shut as I try to process the pain.

Smack!

The sound rings through the large room, and my right cheek bursts into flames.

Smack! Smack! Smack!

I try to say something—anything to make him stop. But the words stick in my throat, and all I can do is whimper and groan as he keeps raining down his hand on my ass. Moisture gathers in my eyes, and I clutch the edges of the couch and clamp my eyes shut as I force back the pressing emotions. It's all I can do not to combust into tears and let him have the one thing I vowed to keep to myself.

But even as I somehow manage not to cry, my vulnerability must be evident in my every whimper and choked breath—the way my body desperately tries to sink into the couch and avoid the cruel punishment. He's reduced me to sheer instinct. A helpless creature caught in agony.

I can't think; I can't move.

I can't feel anything but searing pain swamping my mind and body.

When I finally do manage to lift my upper body, I fall right back down, that single hand on my lower back rendering me utterly helpless. Devastation seeps into my veins, pressing on my chest like a mass of lead squeezing out what little fight I had left. I collapse on the couch as all fight drains from my body and devastation takes its place.

Five more smacks land—each one a blow to my ears, flesh, and mind.

Then it stops. The room sinks into a startling silence.

I want to cry. The need has never been so urgent. Yet I can't feel anything.

Aleksandr eases the pressure on my back and trails his fingers under my blouse. I squirm as I expect more pain. But it doesn't come. The large palm simply settles on my lower back, spreading waves of heat into my nervous skin. Then it starts moving, back and forth in circular movements.

My mind struggles to cope with the drastic change. Such gentleness shouldn't be possible after such brutality. Especially not from the same man. I can't take it. The burden of the shift is no better than the pain. I begin to heave, unable to drag in air past the constriction in my chest, unable to see through the fog in my mind.

A second hand curves over my head. "Breathe," a tender voice croons by my ear. "It's over now. Just breathe."

I try. And with a couple of sharp inhales, I somehow manage to get air through my constricted throat. But my muscles remain coiled tight, and I can't release my death grip on the couch. I feel shattered.

Empty.

Aleksandr keeps rubbing, up and down in long strokes, broad circles that encompass my entire back, comforting me.

It shouldn't be possible and I shouldn't accept his comfort, but I'm so hollowed-out I can't reject it. So I soak it up, needing it to mend my frazzled mind and chase away the hurt and pain—eradicate the shame.

"I told you not to swear," Aleksandr says with the gentle *I told you not to* tone a father would use with his hurt child. He keeps rubbing, and the languid motions are like a gateway to my mind. I'm too shattered to close it off, and his words sink into me and settle deep within the essence of my soul.

I shouldn't swear.

Part of me wants to gather a final ounce of strength and expel his decree before it's too late. But the desperate part—the one craving his comfort—overrides everything and lets the correction stay lodged inside me.

Aleksandr pulls me up to sit, then gets down on his haunches and drags the pad of his thumb over my cheek to catch a single tear that has spilled free.

"Go take a shower. You reek." There's no mockery in his tone. He's just stating facts. It's warped and fucked, and some part of my brain knows it but won't recognize it.

Like a mindless beast, I obey, my shoulders slumping with exhaustion as I pad across the floor.

"Keep your clothes off," he calls after me, and I make a small nod without looking back as I slip into the bathroom and close the door.

I take a quick shower, too tired to prolong my time in here. I just want to go to bed, and I don't care if it's in the cage. Any place to rest my head will do. I'm so depleted my lack of clothes doesn't even bother me as I wrap a towel around myself and step back into the room.

I'm about to walk toward the cage of my own accord when Aleksandr puts a hand on my elbow and guides me to sit on the sofa.

"Please, can I sleep?" I gaze longingly at the soft mattress and silky covers.

"We need to get you fed. Then bed." Aleksandr puts a bowl of steaming hot beef stew into my hands, then leans back against the heavy desk to watch me like a hawk—or a prison guard—as I eat.

Once the bowl is empty and I've downed a glass of water, he lets me use the bathroom. With some nourishment in my body and a reprieve from Aleksandr, I feel more collected and slowly find my way back to myself. I take my time brushing my teeth and combing out my hair before opening the door with a deep breath.

Aleksandr motions to the cage. "Now to bed."

Anger flickers in me again. I want to snarl at him and say it's not a bed. It's a fucking prison. A cage. A place where you shouldn't keep a person.

The cage has now lost all its attraction despite the mattress looking very comfy, so when Aleksandr takes my arm, I pull away, and when he tightens his grip, I start struggling. There's not much fight left in me, though, so I use whatever little willpower I have to stop myself from leaning into him when he picks me up.

He lowers me into the cage and pulls the covers over me. It's a strange thing to have someone who has just beaten you tuck you in. Everything about my predicament and this man is so very strange, but I don't have it in me to try to solve the riddle.

The iron clanks and the lock clicks, and I curl up into myself as I try to shut out the sounds of my imprisonment, which keep ringing in my ears.

I startle as a hand moves over my hair, and I try to move away.

"Shh," Aleksandr soothes and strokes me again. Somehow, that small comfort breaks my last ounce of defiance. I can't resist him. I'm utterly depleted, physically and mentally. After the brutality he unleashed upon me earlier, I need the comfort. So I let it happen. And somewhere along the way, I fall asleep.

Chapter 6

THE FOLLOWING WEEK goes by in a similar fashion. I spend most of the time locked up behind the golden bars, except for bathroom breaks and meals.

In the mornings, it's always the same giant of a man who comes to let me out and feed me. He lets me take my time in the bathroom, and I try to make the most of the small reprieve—long showers, brushing my teeth twice, and combing out my hair for several minutes.

Then I eat breakfast at the desk while the brute sits on the sofa reading Dostoyevsky. The food is always delicious, and I consume it with the same gusto every day, like it's my last meal. And maybe it is. In some sense. I don't really fear for my life—I'm not sure why. I'm more afraid they'll stop feeding me and stop giving me bathroom breaks. Simply let me rot in the cage.

I try not to think about why Aleksandr has taken me. If not for his own sexual pleasure, I can't imagine why. To sell me off? Then why the beautiful room and golden cage? And why speak like he intends to keep me? He doesn't strike me as the type who likes to fuck with people. He's more of a straight-shooter, saying the truth no matter how harsh.

Pondering his intentions spirals my mind into chaos. I fear it could easily render me insane when I lie in the cage with nothing but solid iron and worrisome thoughts to keep me company.

So most of the time, I just stare into space—or the sky or the wall—and try not to think at all.

It's nearly peaceful when I manage to blot everything out. No thinking, no worrying, no pressure. Just lying there doing nothing.

I've never been good at doing nothing. Restlessness always kicks me into gear, forcing me to be productive, study, and work toward my goals.

It's wholly wrong that I need to be trapped to clear my head, and whenever I linger on the thought, bile rises in my throat.

So that's another thing I try not to think about.

One thing I do allow myself to ponder is why I fight Aleksandr, but not his men.

With the brute, I just stand there and let him pick me up and put me in the cage. With the others, I go along meekly, feeling like the humiliation of losing a fight would be worse than stepping into the cage.

But when it's Aleksandr, I sputter with fury from the moment he enters the room. Some days, I don't even need an arrogant comment; his mere presence is enough to instigate me.

I rattle the bars, demand that he let me out, and scream and yell. I even throw the remainder of a sandwich through the room one day. The only thing I don't do is swear.

Some days, he's eerily calm and gives me a wide smirk as he tells me he'll let me out when I stop acting like a petulant child. Then he watches me until I can't stand the weight of his stare anymore or wear myself out.

On other days, his eyes go ablaze as he rips the cage open and shoves me into the mattress with a large hand around the nape of my neck, pinning me down until I stop flailing.

He could easily subdue me in a more effective way—use his weight or hold my limbs. Instead, he chooses this primal symbol of superiority, like a lion holding its prey, an alpha asserting its dominance. I think it's deliberate. He wants me to feel the impossible helplessness deep in my bones.

And I do.

Knowing a single hand is all it takes for him to overpower me is devastating. But what's even worse is my reaction. I can't help it. When he grabs my neck, I'm flooded by the urge to give in—accept his control and the futility of it all. But my mind won't allow it. I tell myself it's just a base reaction and fight the urge until it turns into smoldering fury.

Going against those basic instincts takes all I have, and one day, I'm too exhausted after having barely slept and spent the day buried in worrisome thoughts.

"Get up," Aleksandr orders after opening the cage.

I remain sitting on the mattress and pull my knees up in front of me like it could protect me. My chest shudders with the need to cry, and I have to trap my bottom lip between my teeth to keep it from trembling.

"Get up." His voice becomes frighteningly low, and the rough edge reveals that today won't be one of the days he goes easy on me.

When I still don't move, he reaches into the cage and grabs my arm.

"Let me go." I try to imbue my words with anger as I push at him, but they come out as a weak plea.

He grabs the back of my neck instead, his strong fingers curving around my nape in a devastating grip. Ever so slowly, he presses me down, making me feel every little nuance of my defeat. When my forehead hits the mattress, everything swooshes out of me—the anger, the pain, the hurt. Even the exhaustion. I feel nothing but powerlessness, so stark it numbs my brain and slackens my limbs.

The only thing left is a tiny voice in my head that tells me I've hit rock bottom. A few tears leak from my eyes as I vaguely realize what a low point this is.

"Good girl," Aleksandr praises. "You're finally starting to feel it."

Feel what? I want to ask, but no words come out.

His thumb moves back and forth along my hairline, comforting and tender. It's everything I've been yearning for as the loneliness has gnawed its way into me throughout the day.

I can't resist it. My shoulders lift with my long breaths and fall back down as I push air out on ragged blows. I feel like I can actually breathe after having spent an entire week burdened by fear and self-loathing.

"That's it, keep breathing," he croons, and I keep my airflow working in long inhales, slow exhales. "*Takaya horoshaya devushka.*"

Aleksandr strokes my hairline continuously even as his fingers dig into the side of my neck. "Can you be a good girl for me and come out without a hassle?"

I manage a small nod, and during the rest of the night, I'm pliant and silent like on the second day after he beat me—except this time, I don't even fight when he puts me back in the cage. And when he leaves the room, I masturbate myself to sleep with the feeling of his large hand lingering at the back of my neck.

The next day, the brute doesn't return me to the cage like usual after breakfast. Instead, he unlocks the door and makes a hand motion for me to step out.

I stare at the opening like it's a magic portal to another world. I haven't left this room for over a week. I have barely even seen the other side of the door since Aleksandr put me in here.

Hugging the soft robe around me—which is the only clothing I get—I take a tentative step forward, glancing at the man like it's some kind of ruse. But he only nods for me to go ahead, and I take one more step, and one more, until I'm standing in a large sitting room.

"Come." The brute leads the way down a wide hallway, and I glance around with equal parts fascination and trepidation.

I've never seen riches like this. I'm from a good old-fashioned middle-class family, and whatever few wealthy homes I've set foot in can't compare—not even the five-star hotels I've played at. It's even more mesmerizing now that my head isn't clouded by the drugs Aleksandr injected into me, and today I also notice the majestic paintings and Persian rugs that lend the place an air of elegant grandeur.

We descend a wide marble staircase to the first floor and continue down another hallway. Enormous sitting rooms and vast dining areas open up on each side until we reach a more enclosed hallway with closed doors on either side. It splits into two, and then we walk through yet another lobby with a wide staircase.

I've lost my bearings when the brute finally opens a door for me.

He nudges me into a large open fitness room full of all the types of gear you'd find in a fitness center. Tall windows light up the space, offering a serene view over the garden. I've always found fitness centers cold and uninspiring, but this place almost makes me want to jump onto one of the machines.

"Work-out or pool." The man points to the fitness gear and then to the open door across the room.

Taking a step closer, I realize the open door leads into a huge, oblong room with a pool stretching out across the space.

I take a few more tentative steps, and when my guard shows no sign of stopping me, I go up to the opening and stare at the mesmerizing turquoise water. My stomach does a little flip as the water exerts its magnetic power over me.

It's not just the pool. The entire room pulls at me. Tall windows line the walls in a long L-shape, letting the bright daylight filter in and glitter on the blue water. Delicate imagery of trees and bushes adorn the walls in watercolor style, and the calm colors blend with the sandy tile to create a harmonious whole.

I step over the threshold, feel the cool tile beneath my feet, and inhale the nostalgic scent of chlorine.

When was the last time I went swimming? Fifteen years ago?

I used to love it as a child—free and careless when I was in the water. Then life assaulted me with expectations and aspirations, and I lost the joy of water lapping against my body. I haven't felt the urge to go swimming in more than brief flashes for ages.

Now it comes rushing back, and my entire body itches to sink into the water.

When I glance down over myself, the enthusiasm fades. I can't bear to lose the black silk protecting me from invading eyes. Not even to be in the water.

I turn to the lounge chairs on my right. "Can I just sit here?"

"Swim. Need exercise," the large man says in his usual gruff voice. I'm about to protest when he points through the fitness room to another door. "Bathing clothes. Go change."

Really? I hurry through the fitness room, eager to find out if it's real.

No ruse, no scam. Like the brute promised, there's a bikini along with a small pile of gym clothes and shoes my size. Aleksandr could make me walk around naked, but instead, he offers me the bare minimum of coverage. I wonder if it's for the sake of my modesty or to keep other men from ogling his property.

Probably the latter. Though I don't see the point. Why care about other men looking when he barely ever does it himself?

A surge of disappointment prickles at the corners of my mind. Part of me wants him to desire me—regard me as the woman I am. But all I get are unreadable looks and harsh stares, no signs of lust.

A bit disturbed to realize I'm craving his attention like this, I force myself away from the unwelcome thoughts and turn around to take in the dressing room. It's big and luxurious, like everything else in this house. It has a closed-off toilet and fancy shower stalls, upholstered recliners, and a wall with a long counter, sinks, and mirrors.

I notice the white shirt on a hanger and trail my fingers over the soft fabric. I wonder if it's Aleksandr's—if he comes here to work out often.

Without thinking, I lift the sleeve to my nose and inhale. His fresh, citrusy scent swamps my senses, and a fluttery sensation sparks in the pit of my belly. It's yet another feeling I don't want to confront, so I quickly step away and try to expel the scent lingering in my nostrils by focusing on getting changed.

After a week of being confined to a cage, only getting out to use the bathroom or eat by the desk, my limbs are weak. I'm spent after only five laps and end up hanging at the edge of the pool. The brute remains in one of the lounge chairs, keeping an eye on me while reading. He never shows any sign of impatience, so I stay in the water until my fingertips are wrinkled and I'm so tired holding on to the edge takes effort.

After a quick shower in the dressing room, I follow the brute back to the cage where I fall asleep as soon as he closes the door behind him. I don't wake until another man enters with my lunch.

This is how I spend my mornings for the next few days. Bathroom time, breakfast, and swimming.

Slowly, I build up my strength, going from five to ten laps a day. It feels good to move around and use my body, knowing it won't deteriorate in the confines of my golden prison. My mind also benefits from the small change of scenery—the small freedom.

Watching the verdant garden while kicking my feet in the turquoise water brings me into a meditative state. The water washes away my worrisome thoughts, and the beautiful scenery holds my attention so they won't drift back. The cage room offers the same view, but I can only see the sky from down in the cage, and when eating by the desk, I'm too preoccupied with the food or too nervous to truly enjoy it. Here, it's different. Even when the sky is gloomy, shedding streams of rain over the flowers and bushes, I feel nothing but peace and quiet.

On the sixth day, the peace breaks. I'm taking a break on the far end of the pool when Aleksandr comes in, stark naked, and dives into the water. He sets off in a swift crawl toward my end, and panic grips at my chest when I see the bulky man leave. I don't want to be alone with Aleksandr. Not here, in a skimpy bikini with him fully naked.

I feel somewhat safe around the brute, trusting Aleksandr's promise that none of his men will touch me. But I also remember Aleksandr's response when I asked if he'd rape me. The threat of him wanting to use me at some point looms over me like a boulder hanging from a thin line.

Wasting no time contemplating, I push off the edge in a breaststroke toward the ladder on the other end. Only halfway there, I hear the splash of Aleksandr turning directions, and I pick up speed, panting as I push through the water. The steady splashing of his arm-strokes closes in. Just as I grab the metal bar, a large arm wraps around my waist and pulls me from the edge.

I struggle against him, splashing my legs aimlessly, afraid he'll drag us both down since neither of us has our arms free. But he has me locked against his wide chest, and to my surprise, there's no water in my nose or eyes except the splashes I create myself.

Aleksandr keeps us perfectly steady above the water as he sneers into my ear. "You're not going anywhere until I say so."

Then he's gone. The steady splashing starts anew, and I struggle to make my shaky limbs bring me back to safety.

I flop my arms onto the edge, panting as I stare into the space before me. Shock and exertion pound in my body, and the awareness of Aleksandr's strong frame lingers, dangerous and oppressive, in my skin. But it's not just that. There's also something else—a surge of heat tingling in my bones, pooling between my legs. The heat doesn't clash with the fear like it should. Not at all. The two seem to go perfectly well together.

"Swim." Aleksandr's voice breaks into my disturbing thoughts. "Five laps aren't enough."

How does he know how many laps I've swum? Did the bulky man keep count and tell him?

Glancing to my left, I see Aleksandr push off the edge, this time for a lap of butterfly. He moves swiftly and effortlessly. A shark in the water. Deadly and dangerous.

But also beautiful.

I push off the edge, needing to swim the unwelcome fascination off. But it won't quite go away. Whenever I pause at the edge of the pool and see Aleksandr swimming, I'm struck by the effortlessness of his strokes and the strength of his body.

When he finally stops swimming, my muscles are achy and dull. I've swum more than usual, not daring to stop for too long, afraid to become caught up in my disturbing thoughts about my captor.

Aleksandr jumps out of the water, his strong arms flexing as he lifts himself up. Patting his face with a towel, he turns to me, and I struggle not to let my eyes flit to his cock. It's not that I want to look at it, but for God's sake, it's hanging right there, begging for attention, large and thick.

"That was quite the effort you put in today." He walks up to the ladder and holds his hand out to me.

I tentatively take it as I step onto the first metal step. A searing hot sensation rushes through me even as icy cold crackles down my spine at the feeling of his large hand closing around mine. The strength in his arm is palpable as he pulls me up without effort.

"I'm impressed," he says, leading me toward the dressing room with a hand on my back.

My skin flushes, and I'm not sure if it's the compliment or walking beside a naked Aleksandr. Maybe both.

I feel tiny next to him. He's tall, even for a man, and I'm short and petite. He could snap me like a twig if he wanted. Somehow, the thought doesn't scare me like it should. Rather, it sends more heat rushing between my legs.

What's wrong with me today?

I shouldn't get turned on by my kidnapper—my degrader and jailer.

"Wash up and put on a new robe," Aleksandr orders and disappears into a shower stall.

I hurry into one myself, hoping I can finish before him, so I won't have to come out naked while he's watching.

No such luck. I'm still washing my hair when I hear the door of his stall open. So instead, I try to prolong the shower, hoping he'll leave once he tires of waiting.

This strategy proves just as useless. Five minutes later, Aleksandr opens my stall, dressed and ready to leave. "What's taking you so long?"

His eyes roam over my naked body, taking it all in. His features are impassive, showing no signs of lust, and I can't decide if I'm disappointed or relieved.

I instinctively cover my breasts and gather my legs. "I'm done in a minute," I say, hoping it will make him leave.

But he doesn't. "Remove your hands and spread your legs."

Staring at him with wide eyes, I give the smallest shake of my head.

"You might as well get it over with. We're not going anywhere until you obey." His tone is as impassive as his features.

I watch him for a long moment before I finally lower my

hands and move my feet apart. Just a smidgen.

"More," he orders.

Blood rushes to my face as I spread my legs a bit further. But it's not enough. He urges me on with a nod and another until my feet are as wide as my shoulders.

The water beats against my back as I stand there, trapped by his intense stare. It's so stark I can almost feel the trail of his eyes as they travel down my body, sharp and hot on my skin. I want to bury my face in my hands, but I can't. His sheer will has me frozen in place.

Something dark flickers in his eyes, and I take a step back, blinking against the water as it cascades over my face. When I see movement, I take another fearful step back, expecting him to follow.

But he doesn't. The door glides shut, and I'm alone, my heart pounding as loud as the water over my ears.

Aleksandr reclines in one of the chairs when I come out, tapping away at his phone. He doesn't spare me a glance, and I make quick work of drying myself and grabbing a fresh robe from the closet, which is always full of them.

Pressing a hand to the small of my back, Aleksandr leads me back through the house.

"Take a nap," he says when we're back in the cage room. "Anton will bring you lunch in an hour, and then he'll take you out for a walk."

"A walk?" I stare at him in bewilderment.

"Yes. On the grounds."

"Outside?"

"Yes."

My heart skips a beat. I haven't been outside for weeks, and I'm pining for fresh air.

The words slip out before I can stop myself. “Thank you.”

Aleksandr’s lips curve into one of those charming yet frightening smiles. I lower my head as my eyes flicker between him and the floor.

I shouldn’t thank someone for letting me outside. Fresh air is a human right. Even prisoners in oppressive countries get to go outside. Yet I can’t stop the gratitude from blooming in my chest as I watch the man who holds my life and freedom in his hands.

Chapter 7

I START TO LOSE count of the days. Thirty, maybe forty, have passed since Aleksandr took me. A month doesn't sound like much, but it feels like a small eternity when locked up with nothing to hold my attention—only a silent brute and a rich maniac to keep me company.

The swimming and the walks in the vast garden help pass the time, but I'm starved for normal conversation. So one morning, I try to strike up one with the brute.

"What's your name?" I ask, beginning with introductions like I would in the normal world.

"Boris." He turns a page in the worn book he's been reading for the last two days—*Anna Karenina* by Leo Tolstoy. It's a tome, and he's already halfway through.

I must admit I'm a little curious about this man. He looks harsh and weathered but gobbles up Russian classics like a bright, sensitive soul.

"Is it good?"

He lifts his gaze from the pages. "Good book," he confirms, holding it up. "You read." His falling intonation makes it sound like a suggestion, but I recognize it as a question, knowing Russians don't rise in pitch at the end of enquiring sentences.

"No." I've never had the patience to read books, especially not heavy classics.

"Shame," he says, and silence stretches between us anew.

I'm not ready to end the conversation, so I shift to Russian, hoping it will make him a bit more talkative. "Do you like... Russian classics?" My Russian wasn't exceptional before, and after several weeks without practice, I have to rack my brain to find the words.

"*Ty russki znayesh*?" His voice suddenly holds a new kind of zest as he shifts to his mother tongue.

"Yes. Some," I continue in Russian, feeling as inept as he must have felt in English. "I had to learn, to... study here."

My face falls as I remember where I'm at now and how I got here. But Boris pulls me out of the onsetting melancholy before it can fester.

"Would you like to borrow a book?" he asks, continuing in Russian. "I only have Russians, but I can get you something shorter." He turns the tome in his hand, and I give him a small smile.

"Sure." Anything to occupy my mind while I'm in the cage.

I'm surprised at how talkative Boris is after having changed to Russian. I had pegged him for the silent type, but I guess that's what language barriers will do.

Boris gets up and puts his book away. "Let's go for a walk."

"What about swimming?"

"Not today. Aleksandr wants you to take a day to rest. He says you pushed yourself hard yesterday."

"Oh." I guess that makes sense. My muscles are quite sore now that I think about it, and I did swim forty-two laps. That's a record.

My stomach flutters at the pride swelling inside me. It's

always like this when Aleksandr notices my effort in the pool. Maybe that's why I push myself. Every time he gives me a "good job" or an "I'm impressed," I go all warm and fuzzy inside.

I can't help it.

"Get dressed." Boris tosses me a pile of clothes that I catch in the air. "It's a bit chilly today."

There are jeans, a cute blouse, and a sweater—the usual attire for a chilly day. When the sun is out, I only get the silk robe. It was strange at first, walking around outside half-naked, but I'm getting used to it. I get a few glances from some of Aleksandr's guards now and then, but they are discreet about it, and the robes offer enough protection to cover all the important parts. Plus, I'm not afraid they'll touch me. There have been at least five different men up here, and none of them have tried anything despite my vulnerable—and underdressed—position.

I go to change in the bathroom, and when I come back out, Boris is gone. Not knowing what to do with myself, I simply stand in the middle of the room. When I'm alone in here, I'm always in the cage.

Could Boris be waiting in the adjacent sitting room? Am I supposed to go to him? Or wait here?

Uncertainty churns in my stomach, and after several minutes of uneasy contemplation, I try the handle on the door. It's locked. So I sit on the couch, my hands working like crazy in my lap. I look down at them and see my thumbs rolling around each other and my fingers nipping my skin.

When was the last time I fumbled like this? I used to do it all the time, so much so the habit comes quite automatically. But I can't remember having done it for a long time.

I clutch my hands to put an end to the nervous restlessness. I've always hated the habit but never managed to kick it. And now I'm here, locked up and at the mercy of my kidnapper, and finally, it's almost gone?

I startle as the door opens. Boris enters with a smile carved into his rough features.

"Dostoevsky." He holds a book up, then hands it to me.

I turn it and read the title in Cyrillic. *Crime and Punishment.* I've heard the name but have no idea what it's about.

"One of his best and not too long," Boris says in Russian and gives me an encouraging nod.

"*Spasibo*," I say, flipping onto the first page. A tightly packed page of Cyrillic letters assaults my eyes. A month ago, I would have shut the book immediately. But I'm not where I was two months ago.

I try to make out the first line, and it takes me a full minute to comprehend the meaning. Not only is it Russian, but it's also a long and complex sentence with several words I have to guess at.

I read a few more sentences and feel a small sense of achievement when I have decoded the first paragraph.

"You like it?" Boris asks.

It's too early to tell, but I like the stimulation for my brain, so I smile up at him and nod. "What does this mean?" I point to one of the words I don't know.

Boris sits beside me and pulls the book closer. "*Kamorki.* Small room." He points to the ceiling. "Below roof."

Maybe a garret? No wonder I barely understand half the words.

I point to another word, and Boris eagerly explains.

He points to another one. "You know this one?"

We end up reading the whole page like this before Boris finally gets up. "Time to get out."

I hand him the book a bit reluctantly, sad to already part with the first entertainment I get in a month.

Boris holds up a hand, pushing the book back to me. "No. You keep it. I'll get you another when you've finished this one."

"Oh. Thank you." I glance around the room. I'm not sure Aleksandr wouldn't take it away, so I need to hide it. But I also want to have it when I'm in the cage. Otherwise, there's no point. So I end up crossing the room and sliding it under my pillow before following Boris.

He leads me through the house and out front like he always does. Then it's up to me to decide the way.

I pick left and go around the huge mansion to follow the path I found the other day, leading through trees and to the lake. It's a long walk—at least half an hour—but I like strolling through the beautiful garden, and I want to see the water up close again. It's peaceful.

Boris follows at a distance, close enough to keep an eye on me, but far enough to give me a sense of privacy. It was strange in the beginning, walking freely yet being followed, but I'm beginning to get used to it.

The grounds around the house are huge. I don't think I've reached the limits yet. And I haven't tried.

Maybe I should, though. Since Aleksandr started letting me out two weeks ago, I've been thinking I should contemplate ways to escape. Start planning. Isn't that the normal thing to do when kidnapped?

The thought crosses my mind whenever one of his men comes to take me out. I tell myself I should spy for the bounds of the grounds, places to hide, and ways to escape. But I always end up getting caught up in the beauty of the place, watching the lively colors of the flowers or the small droplets of water on the leaves after it's rained. So I tell myself I'll do it the next day.

Tomorrow, I can think about how worried my parents must be. But I don't want to spoil a peaceful day with thoughts of them. I miss Anna, though. So much my heart aches when I lie in the cage at night and think of the loss and worry that I'll never see her again.

But when I'm back in the garden the next day, telling myself I'll search for ways out this time, I remember all the other things I'd be going back to. The constant pressure to succeed, the stifling amounts of people, my parents' constant nagging, and all the horrors of the world. So I let my eyes drift back to the peaceful water as I approach the lake and get lost in the sound of a bird singing in the treetops above me.

Why leave this peaceful beauty to go back to the chaotic streets of St. Petersburg?

On a rational level, I know this place is more dangerous than the world out there, but I can't quite feel the danger. Not anymore. Not in the same way I feel it when I walk down the dark city streets or even the crowded halls of the conservatory. Anxiety has always been my companion. I've learned to cope, but it's never gone away. Not until I came here.

I'm quick to shoot the thought out whenever it rises. It's wholly wrong, I know. And so is this irrational feeling of safety, but I can't quite help it.

There's the threat of Aleksandr wanting to use me, sure, but with each passing day, it slips farther into the distance. He's seen me naked countless times in the dressing room after swimming. He often watches me when I'm in the shower like that first day, and sometimes, I even think I see a flicker of hunger in his eyes, but he never acts upon it. And I'm half convinced that his way of insinuating he might let his men use me at some point was just a way to emphasize the power he holds over me.

He rarely even touches me himself. Only when getting me out of or into the cage, when leading me from one place to the other, or the occasional caress. Besides that, he hasn't laid a hand on me. There's been no further sign of the cruelty of the spanking, and his degrading words have become fewer. He even seems somewhat protective at times even though I still sense the dormant brutality simmering behind his blue eyes.

I think it's because I've grown more compliant, and I intend to keep it that way.

So the threat is there, but I don't really feel it anymore. After all, I'm well-fed, get to swim and walk the beautiful gardens, and have a comfortable place to sleep—except for the bars. And now I even have a book to read.

I must be brainwashed to feel so excited about a book—something I've never cared for. The thought wants to stir up self-deprivation and doubt, but I don't let it. I shove it right back down and spend several hours reading after Boris locks me back up in the cage. My mind feels like it's waking up after a long hibernation, and I gobble up the words even though it's a battle to string together the meaning.

I end up feeling exhausted after all the mental exertion, and after the bearded man—who I've found out is Anton—has brought me lunch, I fall asleep.

I'm quick to hide the book when I hear footsteps outside the door late in the evening. It's Aleksandr coming with dinner, like he usually does.

"I hope you're not too hungry. I got held up in a meeting in St. Petersburg." Aleksandr is not very talkative, but sometimes, I get these voluntary tidbits of information. So far, I've found out he prefers to work from home but often goes to St. Petersburg for meetings that he can't hold online or when there's something he needs to oversee.

"Anton brought me some fruit a while ago." I push up to sit, feeling less vulnerable facing Aleksandr this way.

I'm not sure why Anton didn't bring me dinner while he was at it. Maybe Aleksandr has some weird rule about doing it himself. Only twice has someone else brought me dinner, and that was because Aleksandr was away for the night.

Why he would be adamant about doing it himself, though, I can't figure.

The fragrant scent of spicy meat and mushrooms drifts through the air as Aleksandr places a tray on the desk and comes to let me out of the cage.

I take his proffered hand and let him help me to my feet.

"How are you feeling today?" he asks, wrapping a supportive arm around my waist as I lift my legs over the bars. A surge of heat rushes through me at the feeling of his touch, causing me to lose my balance and fall into him. I stagger on the floor like I did on the platform the day he took me, and like then, he catches me.

I land flush against his chest. For a second, I can't think as his scent swamps me and his strong arms engulf me. I want to lean into him, press my palms against his warm abdomen and let go of my control—let him be the one to hold me up. But before I can lose my senses like that, Aleksandr takes my arms and steadies me on my own two feet.

"I'm okay," I say, finally answering his question. I actually feel quite good today. Better than I have in a long time. But I don't want to admit it to either him or myself.

"Are you sore?" His hands travel up to massage my

shoulders.

I blink up at him, feeling so very small as I crane my neck to meet his gaze. “A little.”

He holds my eyes as he deftly works his fingers against my muscles. I let out an involuntary moan when he hits a sore spot, and I tense up at the sound.

“Relax.” Aleksandr presses down on my shoulders as the sharp blue of his gaze spears me with a command I can’t refuse. Slowly, I let my shoulders sink back in place, and his fingers start moving again, working out the kinks in my muscles.

My breathing deepens as I give in to his steady touch and lose myself in the depth of his gaze.

I fall so deep under his spell that I don’t even protest when he opens the belt on my robe. With a small nudge, he pushes the silk off my shoulders, and it slides off me like water and pools at my feet.

I half expect him to move his ministrations to my breasts, maybe down between my legs, but he keeps working on my shoulders and down my arms until I’m so loose I feel like jelly. Pressing his palm to my chest, he drags it down between my breasts and over my belly in one long motion. Just as slowly, he sinks onto his haunches and gathers my robe in his hands like he’s about to bring it back up. He hovers right before my pelvis, and his hot breath tickles my sensitive folds.

His hands travel up my legs, dragging the silk along, and small tickling shivers shoot into my skin as his hands come to rest on my hips. Ever so slowly, he leans forward and presses a long, soft kiss to my mound.

My nether region flares to life, humming with expectation and need.

But then he gets up, and I watch him, startled, as he wraps

the robe around me, closes the belt, and brings me to the sofa where he places the tray with dinner in my lap.

I gulp as I watch the delicious-looking pasta dish. Disappointment, maybe even hurt, nags at me. I don't think I've ever felt this confused and rejected.

Doesn't he want me?

He must. Why else would he touch me so intimately?

"Eat," Aleksandr orders.

I pick up the fork and scoop pasta into my mouth. It's a robotic motion, and I don't taste the flavors. My gaze remains blank as mind-boggling thoughts take up my focus. I have no idea what just happened or why he hasn't done anything sexual to me. He said he'd want to at some point, but I'm starting to think he didn't mean it.

Only one explanation makes sense.

"Are you gay?" I blurt halfway through the meal.

He huffs and shakes his head like I've lost it. "Of course not."

I swallow the food in my mouth. "Then why..." I can't finish the sentence. I don't want him to think I want him to use me.

"Then why don't I fuck you?" He lifts his brow with a hint of mockery and continues before I get a chance to answer. "Unlike so many other men, I don't let my dick control me."

Heat flushes my cheeks as I ponder his words.

So that's what this is? A matter of control? I know control and power can drive people to do insane things, but I've never seen it with my own eyes, so the possibility didn't enter my mind.

It does make sense, though. He seems like a control freak—locking me in a cage instead of a room, having men guard my every move, and counting how many laps I swim. It could explain why he's taken me too. Power is what gets him off. The power to control someone so completely they can't eat, pee, or even walk without his permission.

I'm not sure if this is better than him taking me for my body, and I don't dare to consider what it means. Not now, at least.

So I focus on my food until the plate is empty.

"Back in the cage." Aleksandr jerks his head toward the barred-in mattress and takes the tray.

I pad across the floor, feeling Aleksandr follow me a moment later. His long steps catch up with me, and when I lift a leg over the bars, his fingers curl around my arm. I wonder if this is also a control thing or a genuine desire to help me.

I sink onto the mattress of my own accord and keep my eyes down, unable to face my helplessness by watching Aleksandr as he locks me up. The clatter of the bars and the click of the lock is more than enough to remind me how powerless I am.

Expecting Aleksandr to leave, I'm about to lie down under the covers, but then he lowers himself to his haunches and reaches through the bars under my pillow. I watch with wide eyes as he retrieves the book.

"You don't have to hide this," he says, holding up the contraband.

Confusion mingles with shock and renders me speechless.

"Boris knows better than to give you something without my permission," Aleksandr clarifies.

"Do you have cameras in here?" I manage, wondering if that's how he knew where to look.

He gives a light chuckle. "Why would I have cameras?"

I shrug. It seems like something a wealthy kidnapper would do.

"You're locked behind solid iron." He gives one of the bars a firm yank to prove his point. "And why would I watch you on a screen when I can go two doors down the hall and see the real thing?"

He speaks of me like an animal in a zoo. And that's exactly what I am. Except, I'm the only attraction here. At least, so I think.

An uneasy feeling snakes its way through my stomach. I shouldn't care, but I can't stop the words from blurting out of my mouth. "How many women do you keep here?"

His lips tip up in a wicked grin, only to shift into something dark a moment later. Stretching his hand out, he grabs my throat and pulls me up to the golden wall between us, forcing me into an awkward position.

"This is the only cage I have—the only one I've ever had. I bought it especially for you." His lips make an evil twitch. "Does that answer your question?"

I start panting, both from fear and the strain of my position. Why would he buy a cage for me? It was here when I came. Was this some kind of sick, premeditated plan?

"Why?" I croak, swallowing past the lump in my throat.

He shifts his hand to my chin in one quick move and rubs his thumb over my jaw. The gentle touch of his thumb clashes with the bruising grip of his hand, and my head spins, unable to cope with the contrasts. "I don't think you're ready to hear the answer quite yet. You're struggling enough with yourself as is."

He releases my jaw and I fall back on my ass, watching him with dumbfounded confusion. What does struggling with myself have to do with anything? I remember him saying something about me begging him with my eyes when I asked why he took me, like that was the reason. I wonder if he actually thinks my silent begging from the stage was about something else than playing the Mariinsky.

The idea of me bringing this on myself has bile rising in my throat.

He's warped and depraved, and I must be too. I should hate him and sputter curses all the time, demand he let me out, but instead, I find myself trapped by his stark, blue eyes, not wanting to break free.

"Are you ever going to let me go?" I ask.

Aleksandr rests his arms over his thighs and gives a shake of his head. "It would be cruel to give a stray a home just to let it back onto the streets five weeks later, don't you think?"

My stomach twists with bitter longing. But it's not from the prospect of staying here. It's something else that I've been avoiding thinking about for a long time. Something that has my heart aching so unbearably I'd rather shut it down and let it fester. But now it hits me like a slab of concrete.

I might never play the piano again.

A strangled whimper rises from my throat, and my chest heaves under the weight of the realization.

"You are mine now." Aleksandr reaches through the bars again, but this time to pet my cheek. It's a startling solace—one that lets me hope he might hold some kind of care for me, even if it's no more than the care he has for his dogs. It sparks a small sliver of hope. Maybe he's not so cold and callous to keep me away from the thing I love the most, after all.

So I ask him, my heart burning with the hope he'll say yes. "Can I play the piano again?"

His answer comes without hesitance. "You're not ready." He keeps stroking my cheek, comforting me as tears start to spill from my eyes.

"Why?"

"You need to accept that you belong to me first."

I shake my head with utter powerlessness. I can't do that.

Not ever. Not even to play the piano.

"Lie down." Aleksandr gives me a final stroke and gets up. I see him take out his phone and go to the other end of the room. He bustles with something, and a moment later, the peaceful notes of Debussy seep through speakers embedded in the ceiling.

The sound of the piano sends a deep ache through my heart that makes me collapse on the mattress. I curl up on myself as I weep, unable to control the burst of grief. I don't know if he's trying to comfort or taunt me. It works both ways. I've been pining for the pure piano sound, and this is the next best thing to be playing myself. But it's also a stark reminder of how much I miss touching the keys and making the music myself.

I feel heartbreakingly empty. There's a deep, gaping hole in the middle of my soul. A place I've only ever been able to fill with the roll of fingers and the pure sounds emanating from the piano. Now I have nothing left to fill that void.

The lights go off, and the room plunges into darkness, leaving only the pale shimmer of the moon to cast a dreamlike glow over the space. I think Aleksandr is going to leave to let me sleep, so I'm surprised—and maybe even relieved—when he returns to sit on the floor with his back against the wall.

"I've always loved Debussy," he says in a low voice that blends into the stillness of the night. "As a child, I had difficulty sleeping. My mother would put on classical music when she put me to bed, hoping it might help. First, it was Mozart for a long time. Everyone thinks he has such a great effect on the mind, but it did nothing. Then Beethoven, Bach, Schubert, Schumann. All the greats. It wasn't until she came around to Debussy that it helped. I would go still within minutes and drift into a calm, deep sleep."

As I listen to Aleksandr's warm voice and the soothing notes of Debussy, something sparks in that empty pit inside me. A flicker of warmth—or life. Maybe even hope.

It's far from enough to ease my deep sorrow, but it's something. I grab onto it with all my might and let it be my beacon of light in this dark, narrow tunnel.

Aleksandr stays the whole night, talking to me and caressing me as I keep crying. My grief seems to have no end. The tears keep flowing, the sobs straining my throat.

After what seems like hours, I'm so exhausted I can't do anything but lie here and stare into space as the early morning light seeps across the floor toward the cage. I don't know how or when I moved closer to the bars, but I'm lying right in front of them so Aleksandr can easily touch me.

I feel utterly broken. The only things holding me together are his touch and voice. I'm so broken that panic rises in my chest when Aleksandr gets up.

"Please don't leave."

Aleksandr sinks back down and traces the line of my hair. "Don't worry. I'm just closing the curtains."

I turn around and stare after him, afraid he'll disappear if I stop holding on to him with my eyes. When he returns, I turn back and slip my hand through the bars in search of his touch.

Aleksandr grants me it as he folds his large fingers around my tiny hand and strokes the backside with his thumb. "*Krasivaya devushka.* Go to sleep. I'll be here when you wake up."

With that, I finally drift away.

Chapter 8

WHEN I WAKE UP, the sun is high in the sky, casting its rays through the windows and glittering on the golden bars. I rub my eyes and blink against the light. It's too bright. Too happy. I don't feel like bathing in sunshine today. I just want to curl up under the covers and forget about everything. So that's what I do. Pulling the comforter up to my chin, I turn my back to the sun.

It's only then I hear the rapid tapping of a keyboard. Startled, I jerk my head up to see Aleksandr at the large desk, his attention zeroed in on the laptop in front of him.

That's when I remember what I asked him before I fell asleep. I begged him to stay, and he promised to be here when I woke up.

And here he is.

He looks like he hasn't left the room. His light blue shirt is the same as yesterday, only now with the top buttons hanging open and the collar slightly crooked, and stubble covers his jaw. The small flaws do nothing to compromise his powerful air of control, though. Rather, it gives him a rugged look that I would find extremely sexy if he weren't my kidnapper.

I don't think I've ever seen a crooked hair on his head before, and I can't help but watch with fascination. He doesn't seem to notice, and it reminds me of the first time I saw him—the first time I saw him up close. He was caught up in whatever was on his computer that day too, and I watched him for four hours without him ever catching me.

"Are you hungry?" he asks without lifting his eyes from the screen.

I drop my head to the pillow as shyness washes over me. If he knows I'm awake, he has surely felt me watching too.

The tapping of keys stops, leaving the room eerily quiet. I lift my head again and meet Aleksandr's intent gaze. The air swooshes from my lungs, and I sit up, wrapping the comforter around me like it could shield me from those eyes.

"Erm... a little."

Aleksandr lifts his phone to his ear and fires off a couple of Russian sentences as he holds my gaze with a startling intensity. And then he's back to his computer.

A few minutes later, Anton comes in with Brunja and Luna on his heels. The two dogs run directly to Aleksandr, wagging their tails and bouncing around him.

Aleksandr pushes away from the desk, and his stern features soften as he bends to scratch one dog, then the other, behind the ear. "*Kakaya khoroshaya sabatjka*," he says cheerfully, when one of the dogs jumps up with its front paws on his legs, and he rewards it with an extra-long scratch.

"*Sidet.*" He orders them to sit, and they both go still as he starts typing again. I can only see a tail sweeping the floor beside the desk and four ears poking into the air.

Anton lets me out to use the bathroom, and on my way across the room, I can't stop myself from glancing back over my shoulder with fascination. Aleksandr's attention is back on the screen, but once in a while, he reaches out to pet one of the dogs.

I remember how he petted my cheek yesterday, and an unwelcome feeling of envy surges through me as I cast one last glance at the dog receiving his attention.

When I come back out, the dogs and Anton are gone, and there's a tray full of food on the desk. Two plates, I notice.

"Pull up a chair." Aleksandr points toward a chair across the room, eyes still glued to the screen.

I remain still for a moment, uncertain about this new situation. Aleksandr hasn't been here when I woke up before, let alone been working here or eating with me. I rarely ever see him before I go swimming, and then only again when he brings me dinner.

I go get the chair and tentatively take a seat at the end of the desk.

"Eat," he orders.

I look down at the two plates. One has a healthy portion of scrambled eggs, sausage, and white cheese; the other has Belgian waffles with fresh strawberries, syrup, and cream.

My mouth waters at the sight of the waffles, but I don't dare presume they are for me.

When I don't react, Aleksandr closes the lid on his laptop and trains his eyes on me. "How are you feeling?"

I lower my head, letting my long hair spill over the sides of my face to hide my red, puffy eyes. "Fine."

Aleksandr leans in and pushes my hair to the side and nudges my chin up. I feel exposed as I stare into his perceptive eyes.

"You're not fine," he states like it's a well-known fact. He places the waffles in front of me and takes the protein-rich meal himself. "Eat something." Pushing a fork into my hand, he levels me with an uncompromising stare. "It's not a suggestion."

We eat in silence—Aleksandr working and me trying not to watch him. The sweet waffles are soothing to my frazzled soul. I haven't had anything sugary besides breakfast pancakes since Aleksandr took me, and it's like discovering chocolate for the first time. It only gets better when I get to the bottom two waffles and see there are chocolate chips in them, and I forget about Aleksandr while I gobble up the sweet treat.

"Did that help?"

I peer up to find Aleksandr leaning back in the chair, hands folded over his stomach and a warm expression shimmering in his eyes. I wonder if he's the one who ordered waffles for me.

Turning my gaze down, I give him a shy, "Yes." *It really did help.*

"I thought so." His smug tone doesn't even irritate me today. Rather, I feel warm at the thought of him caring enough to get me waffles—and staying because I asked him to.

"Let's go swim," he says, pushing up from the chair.

Swimming with Aleksandr has become a daily routine that I'm beginning to get comfortable with. There is no talking or intense stares when we're in the water. It's just swimming—him on one side of the pool, sweeping back and forth in four different styles; me at the other, dragging along in a slow breaststroke.

My energy always runs out before he's finished, so I hang at the edge of the pool, catching my breath and enjoying the water until he gets out.

Today is no different. Aleksandr is still going at it, full speed, when my lungs feel like they are about to combust. I sling my arms up on the edge and flop my head onto them. There I hang, feet kicking lightly at the water, until I realize the space has gone silent. There's no splashing, no sign of Aleksandr coming to help me out.

I turn to see what's going on and find him hanging on the opposite edge by his elbows.

"How many laps? Twenty? Twenty-five?" he asks.

"Twenty-three." I lower my gaze, embarrassed I didn't manage more.

"That's good," he says, surprising me. "I didn't expect more than fifteen laps after the night you had."

"Oh." I flutter my eyes between him and the water as a tinge of red creeps into my cheeks at his compliment.

The room goes quiet again except for the slight lapping of water. It's eerie, such a large space without sound. But also sort of peaceful. I watch my legs move languidly in the water. His are doing the same, and he seems calm and approachable like this. It gives me the courage to repeat my question from last night.

"Why are you doing this?"

"What? Letting you swim in my pool?" There's a flicker of something playful in his eyes that I didn't expect, and I think he knows that's not what I meant.

But I also want to know the answer to this, so I stay quiet.

Aleksandr rubs his chin with his wet hand. "You belong in that cage, but I don't want you to waste away in it."

I gulp, and it takes me a minute to work up the nerve to ask the real question. "Why do you lock me up?" It's only a small part of the flood of questions blasting through my mind, but it's the most pressing one.

Something dark settles over his features. With a sudden burst, he dives into the water, pushes off the edge, and glides toward me. He's at my end in a matter of seconds, closing the final distance with a few long strokes.

I shrink against the tile, hoping it will swallow me up and shield me from the dangerous man coming for me.

The water splashes as he breaks the surface right in front of me. Grabbing the edges, he cages me in, his face so close I can feel his breath.

"The answer is the same." His eyes flicker to my lips, my neck, and back to my eyes. "You belong in the cage."

I shake my head as I try to sink further into the tile, but I only end up sinking lower into the water and becoming even smaller.

He leans closer, dwarfing me with his immense size, spearing me with his intense stare. A finger comes up to play at the edge of my throat. "It's okay. You're not ready to admit it yet."

"You're wrong." I push at his chest and groan when it gets me nowhere. I push again, but he only moves closer, and that's when I feel it—his hard cock.

I swallow and stare at him with wide eyes.

His eyes narrow as he stares back, and there's only a flicker of movement to warn me before he throws his head forward and bites down on my neck. Hard.

Using all my strength, I shove at him through the water, and this time, he loses his grip on the tile. But he only bites down harder and wraps his arms around me, bringing me with him farther into the pool.

Pain shoots into my shoulder, and I flail and yelp. But it gets me nowhere. Aleksandr has my arms trapped at my sides, rendering everything but my legs immobile.

We start to sink, and I go absolutely frantic. I kick against the water, but it's no use. Aleksandr keeps straight and still, and the water slowly takes us.

I manage a deep gasp of air before we go under, and then I'm teetering on the edge of panic. I want to scream from the pain searing into my shoulder, but I know I'll choke on water if I open my mouth.

We bounce as Aleksandr's feet hit the floor of the pool. And then I'm stuck at the bottom—stuck in Aleksandr's arms, stuck in the vise of his teeth.

I stop struggling as I realize it only makes it harder to hold on to what little air I have. The moment I go still, everything changes. The pain becomes bearable, and my panic recedes as I realize I have enough air to last a little longer. The need to escape morphs into a need to be saved, and I cling to Aleksandr like he's my last lifeline. He *is* my last lifeline. He might be the one who has me trapped here, but he's also the only one who can get me out, and my mind seems to be stuck on the last part.

Leaning my head into his shoulder, I surrender to him, hoping he'll save me.

Aleksandr's response is almost as strange as my own. I'd expect him to loosen his grip since I've stopped struggling. Instead, his arms grip me harder, and they're filled with a strange urgency—almost like a promise to protect me. His teeth slacken around my muscle, and his mouth becomes something like a kiss on my shoulder.

I tighten my arms around his waist in return. For a moment, all the struggle, fight, and tension between us is gone as we're caught in this strange intimacy. But then my lungs start to convulse with the need to breathe, and panic creeps back in. My hands flex on his back, and I squirm against him, fighting to subdue the reflex that's about to set in.

With a burst of motion, Aleksandr pushes off the bottom, and we surge upward. Water sputters around us and runs down my face as we breach the surface, and my gasp brings me as much water as air.

I cough and gasp, cough and gasp, all the while clinging to Aleksandr. He's the only thing keeping us above water since I can't coordinate any useful movement. And I don't need to. Aleksandr is strong enough for both of us. His legs move in smooth circles under the water, effortlessly keeping us up despite his arms still holding me tight.

I drop my head to his shoulder, spent with the effort of breathing and coughing up water, shaken by the fear of being trapped underwater.

Tears drip into the water, which has settled around us, and soon weak sobs follow. I cry like a child on Aleksandr's shoulder, and he holds me as tenderly as if I were one.

"*Dershu tebya,*" he soothes, kissing the side of my head. "Just breathe. There's nothing else you have to do. Only breathe."

And I do. I take in all the air I can get, almost choking on it.

As my crying dies down and my breathing settles, I find there's a strange sense of comfort in losing control—being reduced to the bare minimum of breathing.

Aleksandr turns my back to his chest, hooks an arm around my waist, and swims us to the edge. There's no effort, not even a labored breath. He hoists me up on the edge and jumps out of the water and onto his feet in one smooth motion.

He's so strong and proficient, moving with grace and ease, and I can't deny the safety I feel in his presence. I wrap my arms around his neck and bury my face in his shoulder when he picks me up. *My savior, my protector.*

A small part of my brain scolds me for this irrational gravitation toward him, but the need for protection drowns it out.

He carries me to the shower in the dressing room, where he

takes off my skimpy bikini and soaps me up from head to toe under the hot spray.

It's not overtly sexual, but he doesn't hold back either. Wrapping an arm around my shoulders, he pulls me back against him and takes his time kneading my breasts with a soaped-up hand.

I feel his cock harden against my back, and I can't help my reaction. I arch my hips back, my body feeling like it's about to overheat with need.

I haven't been touched like this for years. The few men I've been with since I left Norway have been one-night stands—quick fucks to satisfy my most immediate needs. No one has taken the time to explore my body, and feeling Aleksandr's firm, capable touch makes tears spring to my eyes anew.

I half whimper, half moan when he moves his hand between my legs to clean me there. There's still no prodding or touching without the purpose of washing me, but his cock is growing harder against my back.

Suddenly, he slams his hand onto my sex with a primal grunt, and the sexual charge flares alive between us.

His breathing comes hard as he growls against my ear, "Beg me."

"What?" I pant as I try to grind my pussy against his hand, but it's impossible to gain any traction with the way he holds me. I just need a little more, and I'll fall over the edge.

"Beg me, and I'll make you come."

"Noo," I whimper. My mind may be fogged over with the desperate need for release, but it's not enough to let me forget who this man is—my kidnapper and captor. He's the man who locks me away in a cage every night, strips me of my dignity, and denies me the thing I love the most. I can't let him take this too. It doesn't matter that I'm already begging him with my body. If he drives me to orgasm like this, I can still live under the pretense that I had no choice, but if I say the words, the responsibility will lie on my shoulders. I can't live with that.

I keep squirming and grinding my hips, and when he doesn't budge, I cry again. Tears drip from my eyes, merging with the water falling from above, and my chest shakes with silent sobs.

Please, please, please. The word hovers right on my lips, and I think I'm about to say it, but it never comes. I just can't.

"I haven't had a good fuck in over a year," Aleksandr rasps into my ear. "I'm not dependent on pussy, so I can hold out quite a while longer." He tightens his hold on my sex to the point of pain. "Or, I can just get a whore if I want."

He releases me with an abrupt motion, and I fall forward. If not for Aleksandr catching my arm, I'd crash into the tile. But he never lets me crash. Not physically.

"Brace your hands on the wall," Aleksandr orders, and when I'm too slow to obey, he grabs my wrists and slams my palms onto the wet tile. Using the handheld shower, he washes the soap off me, and this time, his touch is cold and mechanical.

A minute ago, I was an attractive woman with curves and forms worth exploring; now I'm a dirty thing that needs to be cleaned in a quick and efficient manner.

"You, on the other hand," he continues. "I'm not sure how long you can handle not having your pussy filled. Don't think I don't know how you masturbate at night. Boris can smell your juices in the mornings. So I'd reconsider that answer if I were you. If you ask nicely, I might shove my fingers inside you or have one of my men take you."

"You wouldn't do that," I blurt, horrified at the prospect. Full of disbelief. He might have told me no one would touch me without his permission, insinuating he'd let someone else use me at some point, but I didn't think he meant it. I thought he was too possessive to let someone else touch me.

Like he reads my mind, he explains. "You're mine. That means I get to whore you out to whomever I like. I enjoy having that kind of control over you. But even more so, I enjoy denying you my cock until you deserve it."

"I don't want it."

"No? Then why did you grind against my hand when I touched your pussy? Are you such a little *slyuka* that you'd do that with anyone?"

I can't answer. I simply can't. Either option is too demeaning. This whole situation is more humiliating than any of the previous things he's done. First, making me want him—making me feel wanted—then throwing me away like I'm nothing.

Aleksandr makes quick work of washing himself. I remain where he placed me, muscles taut with the hurt of it all.

I don't even move when he turns off the water and leaves the stall. I just stand there, shaking and breathing shallow gasps until he returns, dry and dressed, and towels my body down.

He's gentle again, like he needed the time to cool off—like he was angry that I didn't beg him and he didn't get to fuck me. The shift hurts almost as much as his detached touch did. Still, I can't deny the comfort, and when he picks me up in his arms, I have to resist the urge to cling to his neck and weep into his shoulder.

He carries me naked through the house. We pass a couple of his men on the way, but Aleksandr acts like nothing is out of the ordinary, and I'm too lost to care.

Once we're in the cage room, he curls me up in his lap on the couch. I try to remain stiff and draw in on myself, but it becomes increasingly difficult as Aleksandr caresses me. His firm hands glide up and down my body like they did in the shower, and it's so easy to fall into the illusion of affection. I don't have the will to fight it after all that's happened during the last twenty-four hours, so I curl up against his chest and find solace with the same man who has ripped me apart.

"Good girl," he croons, kissing my hair. "I wish you'd stop fighting yourself so much. If you'd just admit that you belong here, everything would be so much easier."

He must be delusional. That's what I want to believe. But when he pulls me closer and starts rocking me like a child, I can't deny his words.

It would be so much easier if I could stop fighting and just flow along with the current.

Chapter 9

I MUST HAVE FALLEN asleep in Aleksandr's lap because when I wake up in the cage, I don't remember how I got here.

My arms are stretched above my head, achy from the awkward position. When I try to bring them down to my chest, something tightens around my wrists, halting the movement.

I crane my head to find my wrists encased in brown leather cuffs locked and chained to the bars. Like the bars, the metal rings and padlocks, even the chain, are golden.

Always gold, mocking me with the beauty where no beauty should be found.

A strained moan escapes my throat as I tug at my wrists, but the cuffs fit snugly against my skin, and there's no give when I grab and yank the chain. The delicate appearance is as deceptive as all the other pretty things in here.

Still, I keep pulling, squirming with the effort. But soon I realize it's not just my struggles that have me writhing on the mattress. It's also the almost painful throbbing between my legs, and to my horror, I find that the pulsing heat only intensifies with each fruitless yank on the cuffs.

No, no, no, no. It can't be. This insanity shouldn't turn me on.

My mind refuses to acknowledge the sick need, but it's smeared between my thighs, slick and wet, pulsing and pounding, growing more urgent by the second.

Soon, I can't focus on anything else—not the chains, not the ache in my arms.

The only thing that exists is this desperate urge for release that has my skin prickling and my inner muscles clenching painfully.

Grinding my thighs together, I try to gain enough friction to relieve the pressure, and when it only drives it higher, I flip around to rub my pelvis against the mattress. Still no use.

I feel like a beast in heat—a chained-up, desperate beast.

Is this what he wanted? To humiliate me yet again? Or is this my punishment for not begging him?

It's a terribly fitting consequence—and terribly torturous. I'd rather take a spanking than this insane need clawing at my insides to get out. I don't think I've ever been this desperate for an orgasm.

Anger, frustration, and painful arousal coalesce inside me. It spirals into a panicked desperation that clenches my chest until I can hardly breathe.

I hate Aleksandr fiercely, yet I crave him with my entire being. I want his fingers, his cock, between my legs. Anything to alleviate this terrible pressure. And if he won't grant me a release, then at least I want his hands on my head, stroking and soothing with tender caresses like he did last night. I want him to chase the hurt away even though he's the very root of it.

I consider calling for him, but it would be as bad as begging. So I shove down the urge and somehow manage to get a grip on myself, shut off the emotions, and ignore the twisting pulsing between my legs.

Straining my arms against the restraints, I manage to reach under my pillow, needing a distraction to stay calm. But the book is gone.

Fury builds anew inside me, and when the door opens, I'm ready to sputter and throw curses at Aleksandr. But it's not him. It's Boris.

I can't decide if I'm more disappointed or relieved. He comes up to the cage and crouches beside me, and humiliation runs ice-cold through my veins as I watch him break off a piece of bread and hold it to my mouth.

"Please unchain me," I beg.

"I'm sorry, I can't do that," he says, sounding genuinely regretful.

"Please. I promise not to tell him."

Boris and I have become the closest thing to friends possible, considering he's my jailor. He spends a lot of time here in the mornings, talking about books and teaching me Russian, and I've come to enjoy our time together. So maybe, just maybe, he'll do this thing for me.

Boris watches me with furrowed brows, and I think he's going to relent. But then determination hardens his features, and he moves the bread closer to my mouth.

"Will you at least cover me?" I glance down at my naked body. I've kicked the comforter off and haven't managed to cover more than my legs again.

Boris sets the bread aside and reaches into the cage to adjust the comforter.

I consider refusing when he holds the bread back to my mouth, but I can't make myself launch into an unwinnable fight. Not with him.

With Aleksandr, I can somehow bear the indignity of

behaving like a crazy person. He'll make it all worse by calling me a belligerent child or making me lick up crumbs. He'll revel in the devastating power difference and make me feel it to the bone. But he's also strong enough to keep me steady through the madness. I don't feel so lost with him. When he's close, the crazed insanity feels more like a storm passing through than a strike of lightning that will crack the earth beyond repair.

In the steady presence of his command, I can bear to lose the fight and lose myself.

With Aleksandr, I don't need my dignity; with Boris, I do.

I hate myself for thinking like this, but I'm unable to stop it. And when I accept the bread from Boris's hand, I no longer wish he would unshackle me or let me eat on my own. I only wish Aleksandr was here to feed me himself.

When my eyes flicker up to Boris, I find his gruff features softened with pity. I hate it. I absolutely hate it. A stab of indignity shoots through me as I take the next piece of bread. Squeezing my eyes shut, I imagine how Aleksandr would watch me. His eyes would be full of unrelenting power and maybe even a hint of mockery. But not pity.

I keep this image firmly glued to the forefront of my mind until Boris finally stops feeding me and unchains me. Only when he opens the cage to let me out to use the bathroom do I open my eyes, but I don't meet his. I obediently leave the cage, use the bathroom, then lie back down on the mattress and stretch my arms above my head for him to reattach the cuffs and chain.

"Do you want me to read to you?" His soft voice reflects his startling concern for me.

Tears gather in my eyes, and I tuck my face closer to the comforter to hide the moisture as I shake my head. *I don't want him to see me like this.*

Boris lingers for a moment, then I hear the receding thuds of footsteps and the click of a shutting door.

Then I'm alone again.

Time drags on at a painfully slow pace. I force myself into a numb state, ignoring the ache in my arms, the heat between my legs, and most of all, the internal battle raging in my head.

When the sun hangs low in the sky and the door opens, I expect it to be Aleksandr bringing me dinner. This time, there are no foul words hanging at the tip of my tongue, no rage buzzing in my limbs. The only thing I feel is relief that he's finally come.

Lying here, feeling so utterly helpless, has made me desperate for comfort. My entire body still pulses with painful need, and I'm desperate to be touched. I don't care how or where—I just want to feel Aleksandr's hand on my skin.

Maybe if I behave, he'll stay and comfort me. Maybe he'll even release my arms. And maybe—just maybe—I'll shut off my brain and finally beg him.

All these hopes die a quick death at the sound of a sleazy voice. "*Nakonets-to, vot plennaya slyuka Aleksandra.*" The door falls shut, and heavy, booted footsteps cross the floor. They're not steady, even thuds like Boris's gait. These thuds are squeaky and haphazard, sending icy shivers down my spine.

I scramble to turn and see who it is, and fear becomes a vise around my chest when I see a gangly man with hollow cheeks and eyes like a hungry hyena.

I know him. It's the man from the train.

Immediately, I start tugging at the cuffs. Somehow, I know this man is not like the others who come in here. None of them ever touch me unless necessary—like Boris lifting me into the cage. They all seem to accept Aleksandr's rules without difficulty. But this man is of a different breed. Unrestrained hunger and sleazy defiance hang thick and pungent in the air around him.

I consider screaming, but it seems ridiculous. Who would come to my aid? My kidnapper? My jailor?

A choked sound escapes me, and I'm not sure if it's a whimper or a laugh. How could I ever have felt even a flicker of safety here?

The gangly man has no food or water to indicate someone has sent him. Hope flickers as he just watches me hungrily through the bars. If he's not here to feed me, he might not have a key. Maybe the bars will keep me safe?

The irony doesn't escape me, but I'm too scared to linger on it.

"What a shame no one uses such a pretty little thing," he drawls in Russian as he leans down to touch a bony hand to my face. A stale smell of smoke and sweat hits my nostrils, and I scoot further down on the mattress until the leather cuffs prevent further retreat. He can just step to the other side and reach me there, but I can keep scooting, and even if I'm not quick enough, he can't do more than touch me.

But just as I allow myself to find a little security down here, he retrieves a set of keys from his pocket. My eyes widen at the sight of the small golden one resembling the one that goes in the padlock.

The man's lips tip up in a nasty smile as he jangles the key above me and says in Russian, "Aleksandr thinks he has everything figured out. You know, he fired me after you and that little bitch friend of yours made me on the train. But Pavel easily lent me the keys at the sight of a little weed."

My mind scrambles to translate and process the words. *Pavel, Pavel, Pavel.* I might have heard Boris mention a Pavel. He must be one of Aleksandr's men, but it could be anyone of the nameless men coming up here—or any of the guards I've seen on the grounds.

It doesn't matter either way. As the gangly man unlocks the cage, my mind scrambles to find a way out of this hellish situation. Frantically, I yank at the chain and the cuffs, but there's no give. I don't even have the chance to hop out of the cage and run. I'm trapped like a defenseless animal, and this man can do whatever he wants to me.

Icy fear shudders down my spine when he leans into the now open cage and trails dirty fingers down my neck. It takes everything I have not to flinch. Something tells me a display of disgust would only instigate him—my fight turn him on. But when he pushes the comforter aside and drags his clammy hand down my stomach, I can't hold it in. I squirm and whimper, kicking my feet.

The man laughs at my pathetic resistance, showing off his yellowish teeth in a sleazy smile. "The little whore can't get away?"

It doesn't matter how much dignity Aleksandr takes from me, I've never felt as small and worthless as I do at this very moment. So utterly helpless. Even when Aleksandr pins me with as little as a hand, I feel some kind of worth in being under his control. But this is humiliation in its cruelest, most devastating form.

Fat tears roll down my cheeks as the crude hand reaches my pubic bone, and I whip my head from side to side as I try to squeeze my thighs together. But it's no use. The man rips my legs apart, and when he shoves two fingers inside me, I let out a wail so painful it shakes me to the core.

A bony hand slams onto my mouth, choking the next scream. The vile smell of tobacco and sweat stings my nostrils and forces itself into my breath.

Blinding panic seizes me as the man pumps his fingers in and out. I thrash against the restraints and scream into the hand, gasping for air through my nose. But I'm not getting enough, and dizziness blurs everything to the point where I'm about to pass out.

A door flies open and feet pound against the floor. Then the gangly man flies off me.

I heave for fresh air, but the putrid smell still infests my airway. I keep hyperventilating, unable to fill my lungs.

With my vision still blurry, I can't see anything but a huge, imposing figure looming above me. For a moment, it drives my panic even higher until I realize it's Boris.

He actually came when I screamed.

The realization brings a trickle of relief. But it quickly dies in the blinding panic that pounds red-hot and livid in my head.

Another set of feet rushes across the room, a terrifying voice barking orders. There's the dull sound of a fist striking flesh and the crash of a man hitting the floor. Then someone is in the cage with me, working to free the cuffs.

I still can't stop thrashing, and when my hands finally fall free from the leather, I hit blindly at anything I can reach.

"Sh, sh, shh," someone soothes, lifting me up against a chest, cradling me like I'm something precious. "Just breathe. *Dershu tebya.*"

The air fills with the fresh scent of lemons, and I heave for it, desperate to cleanse the vile smell sticking in my nostrils. I cry into Aleksandr's shoulder with agonizing desperation, and my muscles throb from the strain of holding so hard onto him.

I know I shouldn't cling to this man. He's the very reason this happened.

Bitter hatred rises inside me, and I pound at his chest. "I hate you," I croak, raising my voice to a hoarse cry. "I fucking hate you."

I keep pounding, but the soothing touch never lets up. He just holds me as he tells me to let it all out. The anger, the hurt, the pain. He doesn't even react to my swearing.

When I finally exhaust myself, I slump against him and drift off to some numb state full of... nothing.

The rest of the day is a blur.

I'm detached from everything and everyone around me. Even myself. It's like I'm floating adrift somewhere outside it all, watching through a bleary lens.

I'm carried to the bathroom where firm, familiar hands wash me under the hot spray. Then I'm wrapped in a warm blanket and strong arms. A familiar voice encourages me to eat while another person prods a spoon at my lips.

I don't open my mouth, not when the spoon keeps prodding and not at the encouraging words drifting into my ear. Finally, they give up and allow me to curl up in that safe space that smells like lemons and fresh air.

Dusk settles over the room, and I still sit here, wrapped up in warmth, yet feeling cold and shaky.

"*Prosti menya*," a regretful voice whispers, and soft kisses pebble over my hair. "I promised no one would touch you without my permission, and I didn't keep that promise."

Aleksandr leans his head against my shoulder and presses soft lips against my skin. If I wasn't so shaken, the vulnerability in the act would shock me.

I curl closer to him, wanting to feel the rare intimacy, soak it up and let it soothe my frazzled nerves. I snake my arms around him. *Aleksandr.* The man who took me from my life and put me into this depraved one, made me a captive and took away my free will. Degraded and dehumanized me.

None of that matters right now. I just need him close.

Shifting my legs, I move to sit astride him on the couch, wanting to feel his heartbeat against mine as I lean into him. I rest my lethargic head on his shoulder, seeking comfort where none should be found. But here I find it. Aleksandr holds me tenderly and rests his cheek on top of my head. It's easy to think he's my lover and not my captor, and for a while, I give in to the illusion.

Minutes drift by in silence—ten, maybe twenty—before Aleksandr speaks in a regretful voice. "I knew Yury was flaky. But he was the only one I could spare at the time, and I needed someone to keep an eye on you to make sure you were safe until I took you. But I should have known you weren't safe with him. I was livid when I found out how he had scared you. I should have gotten rid of him right then and there." He presses his lips against my skin, then heaves a sigh as if regaining his composure. "I won't make that mistake again. From now on, Anton and Boris will be the only ones to come in here. I know my word doesn't mean much right now, but you'll come to trust it again. I'll make sure of it. *Ty imeish moyo slovo.*"

I shouldn't ever trust a man like this. He's the one who committed the biggest crime of all when he stole my freedom.

But somewhere along the way, on some warped level, I think

I did trust him.

He thinks he's broken that trust now, but I don't see it that way. I do experience a break of confidence, but it's not directed at him. It's all directed at myself for ever trusting this man and the twisted existence he's made for me. I'm the one I don't trust.

I realize a despairing sound has fallen from my lips when his arms tighten around me.

"Shh. I'll take care of you. I'll keep you safe."

I want to believe him so badly. I *need* to believe him. So I do. For now.

Chapter 10

I WAKE UP IN the middle of the night. In the cage.

The moon casts a careful glow through the closed curtains, leaving most of the room tucked into darkness. But it's enough light to make out the bars. I always see the bars.

I shudder through the onslaught of icy chills. But my body is burning hot, and I wipe a hand over my clammy head and toss the covers aside. Then I pull them back as the chills spread down my skin.

For almost two months, I've slept like a child behind these bars. Ever since the searing fear of the first week faded, I've felt safe here, enclosed alone in the darkness. Now the safety is breached. The smell of smoke and sweat lingers even though Boris has changed the sheets and Aleksandr has washed me.

In some sense, I'm happy I no longer feel safe here. Knowing I ever did makes me resent myself. But as this sticky fear creeps up on me, it's difficult to feel relieved about anything.

Shadows crawl around the cage, and I toss and turn with slithering paranoia. Invisible ropes snake around my torso, constricting my chest and making me gasp for air. I grab the iron bars above me and push.

They don't cave.

So I shake them. The padlock rattles wildly, and the iron clanks as the lid rattles with half an inch of leeway. It's an ominous soundtrack in the chill of night that enhances the dreariness of the blue moonlight breaking through the curtains.

My fear keeps building, higher and higher. Panic lends frantic energy to my fight until I'm wheezing and dizzy.

The door opens and light spills into the room in a long triangle across the floor. I cry out, scrambling back in the cage when I see the tall shadow blocking the doorway.

The ceiling light flashes on, stabbing my sensitive eyes. And there he is. The man who is my nightmare. The man who has taken everything I had. The man who made me easy prey for another to prod and abuse.

"Let me out," I yelp, still rattling the bars. "Let me out," I cry with more force.

With hurried steps, Aleksandr crosses the room and unlocks the cage. The moment the lid goes up, I leap over the bars and dash toward the door. I don't know where I'm going. Anywhere that's not the cage. Anywhere but here.

I only make it three steps before firm arms snatch me. I crash back into a hard chest, and the collision knocks the air from my lungs.

Suspended above the ground, I kick my feet into the air and shove at the arm around my waist. "Let me go!" I yell.

"Calm down," Aleksandr says with surprising patience and carries me across the room to settle on the couch with me in his lap.

I keep writhing and yanking at his arms. "Let me go! I fucking hate you!"

Suddenly, he's off the couch, slamming me down on it, flat on my stomach. "What have I told you about swearing?" he sneers into my ear as he wraps hard fingers around my nape.

"Fuck you! I don't fucking care!"

Three hard smacks on each of my butt cheeks send fire bursting through my system. Anger mixes with pain in a keening sound that rings through the dead of night. Six more strikes echo in the room and draw an equally harrowing sound from my throat.

Boris's concerned voice breaks into the nocturnal hell. "*Vso horosho s neĭ?*"

"Poshol!" Aleksandr barks, and then his harsh breath is back at my ear. "You get off easy today because you're still in shock, but if I hear a single curse out of your mouth tomorrow..." He doesn't finish the sentence, but the threat is palpable in his low tone. "Do not test me."

"Let me go," is all I can say.

"Yasno?" He shakes me and repeats in English. "Do you understand?"

"I don't care," I whimper, tears dripping rapidly from my eyes. "Just let me go."

He starts rubbing my back. It usually soothes me, but not tonight. Nothing will make me want his touch tonight.

"Please let me go. I can't stand to be near you." There's no malice in my voice. My plea is a pure, agonizing need to get away from him.

My sniffles and soft whimpers are the only things breaking through the heavy silence that wraps around us as I wait for an answer.

Aleksandr's hands flex against my back, and when he speaks, there's an uncertainty to his words I haven't heard before. "This time only."

His hands lift from my back, and I waste no time, scrambling off the couch and darting to the other end of the room. I press myself into a corner and stare at him with fearful eyes. What I find on his face almost breaks me. His brows are furrowed in a worried expression, his eyes wide with something akin to hurt.

The air lodges in my throat, and I blink hard.

When I look again, his face is hard as stone. "Get back in the cage."

Not daring to protest when he's like this, I move to the front of the cage, trepidation slowing my steps as I keep my eyes on him. I climb in and curl up under the covers, hating myself for being such a coward.

He locks the cage, barely sparing me a glance, then walks to the door.

"Please leave the lights on." My feeble voice barely carries through the large room.

He pauses at the door, his back to me, and some forbidden part of me hopes he'll turn around. That he'll say something. Anything.

But he doesn't. He just steps out and closes the door, leaving me alone with the blaring light and my blaring thoughts.

Chapter 11

AFTER THE HORRIBLE incident with the lanky man, I draw in on myself and become distant and angry. I don't talk to Boris when he brings me breakfast. I barely answer when he asks me how I like the new book he's given me. I've stopped reading anyway.

Whenever Aleksandr comes in, I glare at him with bitter anger, hating him with all my heart—or, as much of it as I can muster.

He tries to soothe the hurt away, caressing me through the bars or taking me out to sit with me in his lap, but I always pull away from him. No matter how much it hurts to refuse his touch, I pull away.

I think it angers him. I can see it in the way his jaw clenches, the way his grip hardens when he drags me back to the cage. But he doesn't say anything. He just leaves me alone, heeding my unspoken plea.

He stops coming to the pool in the mornings, and I barely swim. I just hang on the edge, staring out at the whipping rain or the radiating sun. It doesn't make any difference if the sky is blue or gray. It all looks the same.

I should be grateful. For once, Aleksandr grants me my wish.

Yet it's like a stab to the chest every time he walks out the door or lets someone else bring me dinner.

As he promised, only Anton and Boris come into the cage room, and after a week, they are the only two people I ever see.

For four long days, I don't see Aleksandr. On the fifth day, I'm so wrought with nerves I break the deafening silence between Boris and me at lunch.

"Is Aleksandr away for one of his business meetings?"

Boris lifts his eyes from his book and shakes his head. "He's here." Something akin to hurt flickers in his eyes when he watches me expectantly and I don't say more.

I hate shutting him out like this. Some warped part of me thinks he's innocent. But he's not. He locks me up in the cage every day, witnessing this dehumanization without doing anything. He wouldn't even release my arms so I could eat for myself that day.

So I turn away from him and stare into the food that has tasted bland and gray for the past two weeks.

As with everything else, I shut out the regret of hurting Boris. I've been repressing everything since the gangly man forced himself upon me. Terrible feelings of hurt, sadness, and worthlessness want to swamp me in terrifying pain, but I refuse to acknowledge them, and every time I do, I grow a little more numb.

It should be a relief to shut off all emotions when in a predicament like this. But it isn't. It's hard and lonely. My muscles are constantly tense, my very core frozen.

I hate it. I hate what I've become. I hate the bars, the man. Even the goddamn air I breathe.

When I push the plate away, only halfway through the meal, Boris gets up and motions for me to follow. He presses his thumb to the biometric door lock, which was installed the day after the attack, and the lock opens with a click.

Thinking we are going for a walk, I glance out at the pouring rain. "Don't I get any clothes?"

Without response, Boris strides through the sitting room and down the wide hall. I trail behind him, worry accumulating in my belly.

"Where are we going?" I ask, unable to hide the tremor in my voice.

Boris opens the door at the end of the hallway with yet another newly installed biometric scanner and leads the way without granting me an answer.

We descend the stairs and walk through the same halls as when we're going to the pool. But I've already been there today, so what the hell are we doing down here? I've never been here—or any other part of the house—if not to swim.

Is Aleksandr going to drown me?

What starts as a sarcastic remark to myself quickly piles more dread onto the worry in my belly and sprouts a whole new line of fearful thoughts.

Maybe Aleksandr has grown sick of me, decided I'm no use to him? That I'm untrainable? Maybe drowning would be the cleanest way to get rid of me?

No, Aleksandr is not a psychopath. He can't be. Not with the caring way he sometimes holds me. Right?

And why sully his pool with a dead body when he can bring me to the lake—or simply snap my neck?

Fuck, my mind is spinning out of control, and when Boris finally opens a door for me, my hands are shaky and clammy.

I dry my palms on the silky fabric of my robe as I scan the large empty room, which looks like a dojo. Minimalist Japanese-style art adorns the wooden walls, spotlights lend a warm light to the space, and gray foam mats cover the floor.

What the hell are we doing in a dojo?

Aleksandr and Anton are in the middle of a sparring session, both clad in nothing but white karate pants. I think they've been going at it for a while. Anton repeatedly tries to make a move on Aleksandr, but Aleksandr gracefully dodges, and when he sees Boris and me enter, he finishes by throwing Anton to the ground in one swift move.

Anton quickly takes his leave, shutting the door behind him.

I watch as Aleksandr removes two floor mats a few feet apart. My eyes go wide when he attaches leather cuffs to O-rings embedded in the floor, using chains.

I reflexively take a step back, but Boris blocks my retreat with a hand on my back. So I just stand there, frozen in place as Aleksandr proceeds to attach two new leather cuffs to the ceiling.

"Restrain her," he orders, stepping to the side and wiping a sheen of sweat from his brow with a towel.

I try to jerk away when Boris grabs me, but his massive hand encompasses my arm, rendering escape impossible. So I drag along behind him, unsuccessfully digging my heels into the floor. I have no idea what's coming, and I don't want to find out.

I start squirming when Boris places me between the cuffs. It's the first time I've struggled against him, and it's as useless as every other fight I've had in this house.

"Please don't," I whimper as he wraps a leather cuff around one of my wrists. My pulse pounds frantically at the restrictive feeling.

As soon as Boris releases my arm to dangle in the cuff, I throw my free hand up to open the clasp. There's no lock. I can just rip it open. But before I even touch the buckle, Boris has my other hand wrapped in leather and is closing the clasp on this one.

I frantically try to reach my hands toward each other, but they're too far apart, and soon all four limbs are caught in a spread eagle.

"Please." My eyes dart back and forth between Boris and Aleksandr, seeking some small mercy, which I never get. Boris doesn't meet my eyes, and Aleksandr's gaze is cold and detached as he watches from the sideline.

"Give me your knife." Aleksandr steps up to us and holds his hand out, and I watch in horror as Boris places a spring knife in his open palm. A glistening blade pops free with a click before me, and I pull back, yanking at the chains as they block my retreat.

Aleksandr bunches the short sleeve of my robe up at my shoulder, and I squeeze my eyes shut and lock up every trembling muscle as the knife tears through the fabric. Two swift cuts and the silk disappears, leaving me naked and exposed, goose bumps raising on my skin.

"Poshol!" Aleksandr demands.

Boris's heavy steps resound behind me, and the thud of the closing door leaves an ominous silence. Peeking my eyes open, I watch Aleksandr go to a side table and pick something up. I stare at his hand as he approaches me, trying to make out the object. It's round and black. Leather coiled into a circle.

A whip.

Cold sweat drips down my back.

"What are you doing?" I stutter through labored breaths.

Aleksandr walks behind me, inducing more fear into my veins as he disappears from my view.

I jerk at the touch of fingers on the side of my neck. They

just stroke, ever so gently. His tone, though, is firm power and unrelenting control. "This is not a punishment. It's for your own good."

"That doesn't make sense," I croak, giving a yank at the chains. *Has he lost it?*

Aleksandr might have kidnapped me and locked me in a cage, but I never truly thought him a madman. I just thought him to be an unscrupulous business magnate who took whatever he wanted. But now, I'm starting to reconsider.

The signs have been there all along. These small hints of craziness. Like his fucked-up logic, insinuating I asked him to take me, and the premeditated plan to steal me. And now, I'm going to feel the full brunt of it.

I should have planned my escape when I had the chance. I should have fought more, tried harder to get closer to Boris and appeal for help.

Now it's too late.

Tears prick behind my eyes, but like every other time during the last two weeks, I refuse to give in to them. I refuse to let him have this part of me.

I shut down and go rigid everywhere—my body, my brain. He can't have this. Not any of it. He may use and abuse me physically, but the vulnerability is mine.

Aleksandr presses a warm palm to the top of my back. It takes everything I have not to arch into his hand as he slides it down my skin, all the way to the juncture above my butt. It takes everything to keep the pressing tears at bay.

"It will only hurt more if you tense up, Astrid."

Why does he care? He's going to hurt me anyway. I bite my lips together to hold back the bitter words.

His hand turns, his knuckles trailing back up along my spine.

“I’ve done a lot of thinking, and I’ve realized you went pliant too fast—well, before Yury broke into your cage.” Aleksandr grunts in displeasure.

“It’s your fault,” I accuse with venom.

I expect him to lash out with anger, but as his hand ends its trail by my nape, he turns it back onto the palm and travels back down gently. “It is. But it won’t happen again. Boris has taken care of both Yury and Pavel. No one but me, Boris, and Anton can enter your room. The new locks make sure of it.”

I shudder at his words. Even though I want to, I don’t dare to ask what *taken care of* means, and I’m both terrified and relieved that I’m now even more cut off from the world and everyone in it.

Aleksandr’s hand changes direction upward again. “What I was saying is that you accepted your new life too quickly. It’s not natural. You needed more time to adjust. More training. I should have seen it before.”

I seethe at his rationale. “Nothing about this is natural. Not you, not the cage...” my voice trembles so hard I’m afraid the anger will morph into tears if I keep going.

“Shh. I’m going to help you let go of all this pent-up rage. You’ll feel better afterward.”

“Please don’t,” I whimper as terror creeps up my spine.

“This will help, Astrid. I promise.”

I shake my head, wanting to cry or curse. But I hold it all in.

Aleksandr takes a step back. And one more. I tug and yank at the cuffs, but it’s no use. And when I hear the swish of leather ripping through the air, I steel for the onslaught of pain with a fierce grip around the chains.

At the first lick of the whip, I almost cry out. But then I realize there’s no pain. Only a slight sting. The thin tip simply flickers back and forth on my back in a gentle rhythm, traveling up and down like Aleksandr's hand did. It's almost as soothing, like small caresses extending directly from his arm.

I want to release the painful tension straining my limbs and give in to the soothing rhythm. But I can't. Instead, I shut everything out. Both good and bad.

Suddenly, the whip cracks through the air, loud and harrowing. The tip bites into my skin with an agonizing swish that tears straight through my walls. I thought I had solidified them; I felt strong and resilient. But at the crack of the whip, my defenses are dust and dirt.

A scream rips through my throat, filling the space with resounding misery. I yank at the restraints, trying to contain the fire burning in my skin.

"That's it," Aleksandr croons, like I've done good. "Let it out."

The warm appraisal lights up my simmering rage. When the whip strikes again, I burst into another frantic scream that renews itself with a fury unlike anything I've ever experienced.

"I fuc—" Aleksandr slaps a large palm over my mouth to block the vile string of curses I'm about to fling out.

"Don't you dare," he snarls into my ear. "Scream and cry all you want—claim that you hate me. But if I hear one filthy word from your mouth, you'll feel just how hard this whip can strike."

He holds me there for a long minute, the rapid rush of air through my nostrils the only sound around us.

Slowly, he releases my mouth, and I let out the only three words of anger I'm allowed. "I hate you," I say with all the vehemence I can muster.

"Do you know why I allow those words?" he asks, skimming his knuckles down my arm.

"Because you're—" I bite back the curse and sputter the next word, "sick."

Aleksandr ignores my accusation. "Because you don't mean them." Pressing a soft kiss to my neck, he adds, "Not truly."

I cry out, pure fury ripping through every fiber, and when the whip cracks a moment later, I choke on a harrowing scream.

Two more cracks and I'm shaking like a leaf. Two more and I feel the threatening onslaught of tears.

"Stop, please stop," I cry, knowing one more strike will tear through the floodgates. And then I'll have nothing.

"Stop fighting, Astrid." The whip hisses through the air and sears into my flesh like burning acid. I slump under the pain, falling limp in the chains as a sob spills from my lips.

With an arm around my waist, Aleksandr catches my weight and presses me into his hard chest. Reaching his other hand up, he trails his fingers through the moisture slipping down my cheeks.

"Good girl," he soothes.

"I hate you," I whimper through tears. "I hate you so, so much." I struggle against his arm, but it's a halfhearted attempt.

"I knew this would help." He rocks me gently, and I want to sink into his embrace—accept his comfort—but those words trigger a new wave of fury.

Fucking arrogant prick. He knows nothing about me.

I don't know how I manage, but somehow, I shut off the tears and lock myself back into numb tension.

"It's okay." Aleksandr trails his hand down my spine as he steps back. "We'll just go again."

The whip cracks through the air, and I bite back a wail. But with five more strikes, Aleksandr rips through my walls and reduces me to tears and screams.

Again, he holds me with startling gentleness, and I tell him with burning fury how much I hate him, struggling against his arm even as I sink into him.

Once I manage to shut down the hurt and regain some composure, Aleksandr steps back and keeps going. Whipping, then comforting. Whipping, then comforting.

It goes on forever, and with every round, it becomes harder to stay in control. I just can't allow myself to give in to him, but eventually, I have no choice. A severe round of screaming and straining through agonizing pain leaves me hanging limply in Aleksandr's arms. My legs are shaking beneath me, barely able to hold my weight when he steps back.

A single lick of the whip tears apart the flimsy remains of my strength. I crash into deep despair with an ugly sob that gives way to a torrent of tears and despairing sounds.

My legs buckle beneath me, leaving my weight hanging in the wrist cuffs. Aleksandr steps around me and gathers me to him, holding my weight and my worries as I sob into his chest, letting everything go.

"Good girl," he praises, having achieved what he set out to do.

I'm so broken I can't hate him. All the anger and resentment, the self-blame and guilt, is washed away by the pain, leaving only tears and desperate longing for comfort.

Supporting my weight with an arm around my waist, he frees me from the cuffs. Then he hoists me into his arms and carries me to the opposite end of the room. I cling to him with whatever little strength I can muster. I don't care what's going to happen or where we're going as long as he keeps me tucked into the safety of his arms.

Aleksandr grants me my unspoken wish as he brings me to a sitting room with three walls of floor-to-ceiling windows that lend a perfect view of the rain-soaked garden. It's not the outside garden that has me blinking to focus through the veil of tears, though. It's the inside garden of potted trees and plants which surround us in a cloak of flower-scented peace.

It takes a while for the peace to reach my shattered soul, though. Aleksandr brings me to an L-shaped couch where he half lies with me in front of him, spooning me with my back pressed to him. He grabs a box of tissues from a side table to dry my eyes, then hands me one whenever my sniffling gets out of control.

I have no idea how long it takes for my tears to cease. When they finally do, I'm blinking my heavy eyes against the beautiful splashes of verdant colors surrounding me. The rain still patters on the roof of the garden annex, and Aleksandr caresses my hair with languid strokes. It's peaceful and still. Everything the dojo wasn't.

"We'll do this again." Aleksandr trails his hand down my arm and hips before returning to my hair. "Until you shed your inhibitions and give in to me."

My heavy eyelids fall shut, and I mold myself a bit closer to him. I wince as my raw back moves against his naked chest, but it fades again as I settle into the new position. He's much bigger than me, longer and broader, yet my petite form fits perfectly into him. His legs wrap mine up in safety, and his torso curves perfectly against my back, enclosing me in a cocoon scented with notes of lemons and fresh air.

I should fear his words and fret for my near future, but all I can think as I drift off in his arms is that I want this again.

Chapter 12

THE NIGHT HAS restored some of my strength, and I'm back to being spiteful when Aleksandr comes in after breakfast. I sit in the cage, glaring at him. He stares back for several minutes, seeming to study me, maybe considering how to proceed.

"Are you ready to drop this little tantrum of yours and accept where you belong?"

I feel utterly broken after what he did to me yesterday. Part of me wants to collapse on the mattress and accept defeat—give in and take the sweet price of his tender caresses. But I can't. I just can't. Because then what do I have?

Nothing.

The choice to resist him is the only thing I have left. So I shake my head and glare at the mattress as tears threaten to spill. After I woke up in the garden room last night, I cried on and off for the rest of the day until I finally fell into a deep sleep in the cage—Aleksandr by my side, stroking my hair.

Now the same man crouches beside me and reaches through the bars to tip my chin up. "You're mine." He says it like it's a proven fact. "The sooner you get it into your head, the easier it will be for you."

"You can't own a person." I cough and swallow to ease the

raw feeling in my throat from having screamed my lungs out. "I have rights," I add, pulling away from him. The loss of his touch is painful. I'm not sure if it's that or his fucked-up ideas that have angry tears dripping onto my hands as I try to wipe my cheeks. "There are laws. It doesn't matter that you lock me up and whip me. It will always be a delusion. You can't register me like a fuc—" I bite back the curse. "Like a dog."

Aleksandr's lips curl up in a cruel smile. "You are aware that you're not in Scandinavia anymore, right? You're not protected by their humanitarian rights."

"You can't own a person," I repeat, lacing my voice with venom and truth. "The law won't allow it. Not even here in Russia."

"No?" He shoots me a challenging look. "You wanna bet?" He rises to his feet and adds mockingly, "Oh, I'm sorry, I forgot—you have nothing to put on the table."

With that, he walks away, leaving me with tears falling in endless streams. All the while, rage burns hot and livid inside me, and his words mess with everything I once thought I knew.

Aleksandr remains absent for the next three days. It's maddening and relieving. Before the whipping, I didn't see him for four days, so if that's any indication, his absence won't bring any good. Another whipping? Something worse?

I can't stand to contemplate it, but I don't have the energy to shut it down either, so I flit between bursts of fitful sobbing, harrowing fear, and painful loneliness.

Whatever little strength I do have goes into keeping myself in check whenever Anton or Boris comes in. Though, I don't know why I bother. My puffy, red eyes say it all, and Boris keeps giving me these worried looks. He tries to get me to read and talk, but I refuse both. If our relationship was tense before, it's cold and distant now. I simply can't forgive him for handing me to Aleksandr and his whip on a silver platter. He feels the strain of that action too. I can see the guilt flickering in his eyes. But it doesn't change anything.

When Aleksandr comes in early in the afternoon on the fourth day after the whipping, my shoulders fall from their tense position as a loud exhale passes through my lips. I don't know how or when his authoritative presence came to mean safety because it's the most dangerous thing I've ever encountered.

Getting a grip on myself, I avert my eyes—back to the cloudy sky outside the windows.

When another set of steps enters, I glance back to see a short, chubby man with rosy cheeks and a suit that hangs awkwardly from his plump body.

"This is my lawyer," Aleksandr says, not bothering to introduce me back. And why would he? I sit here in a cage like an animal, a thin robe the only material covering my body.

The chubby man sets his briefcase on the desk and takes out a laptop while Aleksandr comes to open the cage. I shrug free from his grip when he tries to help me out, and it hurts more than I dare to admit when he lets me pull away and step out on my own.

The next moment, Anton comes in with a bathroom scale and a tape measure. I stare from him to the chubby man, then at the scale he places before my feet.

"Up," Aleksandr orders, nudging me onto it.

My feet move on autopilot as worry turns my stomach. When Aleksandr rattles off the numbers to the lawyer, I feel like an animal up for auction.

"Up against the wall." Aleksandr points to the wall, his eyes matching the sharp command in his voice. I want to disobey, and

I'm not sure if it's to retain my self-respect or to make him drag me just so I get to feel him. It doesn't matter. The thought is only a flicker. I don't dare to test him when he's like this, so I force my feet into motion and press my back against the wall so Anton can measure my height.

Once again, the lawyer gets the numbers and taps them into his laptop before closing it. "I have everything now. We just need to get the documents printed."

"Lock her up," Aleksandr says to Anton as he leaves with the lawyer, not sparing me an extra glance.

"What's going on?" I ask once I'm alone with Anton. I usually don't talk to the bearded man—somehow, I find him less approachable than Boris despite his less giant-like build—but I need to know.

He urges me toward the cage with a hand on my back. "I can't tell you."

I give him a pleading look before I climb in. "Please." My voice is shaky, my legs the same as I step over the bars.

"You'll find out in a few minutes." Anton locks the cage and leaves the room, and I stare at the closed door as dread pounds through my system.

One minute becomes two. Two become three. Three become ten. There's no clock in here, but I can hear the time ticking loud and clear. I keep staring at the door, and I jump when the handle moves.

This time, a whole slew of people enters. Aleksandr, his lawyer, Boris, Anton, and two men who each carry a bag that appears to be full of different equipment as they both start unpacking. I haven't been around more than two people at a time for months, and the sudden commotion makes me anxious. It doesn't help that I'm locked up like an animal for all six sets of eyes to see.

I cower behind the bars, tucking the comforter around me like it could protect me. But it can't—not from the eyes, not from whatever Aleksandr has planned.

When Aleksandr stalks across the room, I try to hone my focus on him and forget about the other men. I tell myself it's because I should be wary of the most dangerous one, but really, it's because his authority settles my nerves.

I close my eyes and try to shove the thought out along with everything else. But then another dreadful thought shoots into my head.

Snapping my eyes open, I stare up at the man who has become my entire world. He's opening the cage, watching me with hard, emotionless eyes.

"Are you selling me?" I croak, my eyes wide with fear.

Surprise softens Aleksandr's expression. "No, *krasivaya devushka.*" Leaning down, he pets my cheek with startling affection. "Quite the opposite."

A small surge of relief washes away some of my anxiety, but there's still plenty to make my hands shake.

"Then what's going on?"

Aleksandr hands me a small pile of documents. "I had an English version drawn up for you."

A sliver of hope eases the tension in my shoulders as I take the documents. His tone makes it sound like this will be good. But as usual, what's good for Aleksandr is not good for me. Cold ice slithers through my veins when I read the header.

Pet registration.

My breathing becomes ragged, my heart pulsing hard as I read further. The top of the document states Aleksandr Pletnev as the owner, along with his personal information.

Then there's the information about the pet. Nausea roils in my stomach already at the first line, and I have to gulp it back repeatedly as I read on.

Name: Astrid Berger
Gender: Female
Date of birth: 20/03/1998
Species: Human
Breed: Norwegian
Color: White/blond
Desexed: No
Height: 5.3 feet
Weight: 128 pounds
Microchip number: 945000482928122
Ear tattoo: AZX215

I shake my head. This can't be. It has to be some cruel joke.

Flipping the page, I find all my medical records. The documents contain everything from my first vaccination to getting my contraceptive implant replaced.

How did he get all of this?

I turn my eyes to the man who thinks he owns me, praying this is a cruel hoax to make me more complacent.

"It's not legally binding." I gulp, not believing my words even though I know for a fact that I'm right. "You'll never be able to enforce it."

"Are you sure about that?" he asks without humor.

"This is the twenty-first century. Not even Russian laws will allow you to own a person." My hands shake around the paper as I remember his smug arrogance from a few days ago when he told me I was no longer protected by Scandinavian human rights.

"You'll never be able to enforce it," I repeat to convince myself.

"No?" he challenges. "I'll give you ten lawyers and ten politicians on any given day who'll enforce this contract." He removes his phone from his pocket and starts scrolling. "Where do you want to start? The prime minister? We go way back. Or maybe the minister of justice? He owes me big after I lent him one of my hackers to cover up some shit he'd done."

He gives me a hard look that shoves my incredulous words into my throat before he scrolls on.

His lips curl up in a cruel smile. "Or the president." His eyes burn with dark intent as he fixates on me. "He'd love it if I owed him a favor. In fact, I'll bet half my fortune on that. I'll even do you one better and throw your tight little ass into the pot." He points his phone at me, then shoves it back into his pocket.

I stare at him with blank fear. I don't know who's more crazy—him or his country?

He gives me a wide smile that would look utterly charming on any other man. But on him, it is terrifying. There's nothing nice about it. He revels in my fear, enjoys the power rush of seeing me writhe helplessly in the muck at his feet.

His lips twitch in a snarl as he leans down and grabs my hair. "Don't worry. I'm not reckless with my property. I won't throw you into a pot I'm not sure of winning." He raises his eyebrows in a dark promise. Then he's gone, leaving me shaken and disturbed, my mind reeling to grasp the magnitude of his sordid connections.

I stare at the document. *Ear tattoo.* It has to be a joke.

But when I turn my gaze up, I see a man with a tattoo gun.

This can't be real. No, no, no. It just can't. It's too fucked-up. I must be dreaming.

Squeezing my eyes shut, I will it all to go away. But when I look again, it's the same horrific scenario playing out before me, and the very root of it is walking straight back for me, holding two bundles of rope.

"Are we doing this the easy or hard way?" Aleksandr asks, towering over me. "I don't mind either way."

Shaking my head frantically, I scamper back on the mattress as panic builds with each passing second. I dig my nails into my skin, praying I'll wake from this nightmare. But I'm already wide awake.

"You don't have to do this," I say, for lack of better words.

Aleksandr leans down for me, and I claw at his hand, refusing to go willingly.

"Hard way it is." He hops into the cage and throws me onto my stomach, pinning me to the mattress with his weight.

I keep fighting, bucking and writhing beneath him. When it gets me nowhere, I grab the bars and try to drag myself out from under him. It doesn't matter that he's proven my struggles useless countless times. I have to try, or I won't be able to live with myself.

His hands close around my wrists, and I grip the steel so hard it hurts. But Aleksandr squeezes harder too, draining the strength from my hands. I let out a helpless mewl as they pop open and I lose them to Aleksandr.

Defeat wraps around my lungs, making me breathe hard as he gathers them on my back. He's so impossibly big and strong, and there's nothing I can do. Not even a yank fueled by all my strength nudges his grip in the slightest.

Aleksandr makes quick work of tying the rope. The coarse material goes around my wrists a couple of times, then between them, fastened with a tight knot.

I strain my hands against the ropes, and when my fingers

start to prickle, panic rises anew. My hands are my most precious thing. If he damages my nerves, I can't play.

Flexing my fingers frantically, I whimper, fearful urgency suddenly replacing my fury. "Noo, pleease, no."

"Sh, sh, shh, I'll fix it." He must understand because he immediately unties the knot and runs a finger under the ropes to loosen them before fastening anew. "They won't damage your hands," he assures with a warm palm on my back.

Part of me wants to be grateful, but when he lifts me out of the cage and I see the five men watching us, whatever gratefulness I felt dies a quick death.

"Don't do this." I strain in his arms, not caring he might drop me, or maybe stupidly trusting him not to. "It's... it's sick! I'm not a dog!" I use the only weapon I have left—my teeth—and bite into his pectorals, feeling a small sense of victory at his growl.

"You think I treat you like a beast, huh?" He drops me onto the couch, grabs my throat, and sneers into my face. "Maybe I should put a muzzle on you. That should teach you the difference."

His eyes bore into mine, and I tremble beneath their raging force.

"Or maybe I'll do you one better and stuff that foul mouth of yours. Then we'd get rid of that nasty language *and* your bite. Two birds with one stone. Isn't that how you westerners say it?"

I want to hold on to my anger, but it's quickly slipping under his ruthless control, and I barely fight when he shoves me onto my side.

Aleksandr curls his hand around my nape, fingers flexing with feral dominance as he tightens his grip. And that's it. The final sliver of resistance slips away. Helplessness takes its place, and silent tears drip from my eyes.

There's nothing I can do. This will happen whether I want it or not. The realization is a vise around my chest, yet there's freedom in the acceptance.

When Aleksandr feels the change, his hand loosens and his thumb takes up a soft stroking along my skin.

Someone speaks, and Aleksandr answers in a hushed voice, like he doesn't want to disturb the warped calmness that has finally settled over me.

A few more strokes and Aleksandr lifts me by the shoulders to sit under me with my head in his lap. I make no protest, don't move a defiant muscle.

Stroking my hair, Aleksandr lowers his voice as if speaking to a frightened animal. "A doctor will insert a small chip into your shoulder. He'll start by numbing the place, so you won't feel a thing. Just a small prick from the anesthetic."

Tears slip in a steady stream from my eyes. *Drip. Drip. Drip.* Down my cheeks, into my blond curls, and onto the smooth fabric of his slacks. I want to hate him so badly, but I can't. Not really.

Someone moves a chair up behind me, and I tense when a foreign hand grabs the skin on my shoulder.

"A small prick," Aleksandr says softly, holding one hand on my head and the other on my arm.

I clench my teeth at the sharp prick of the needle. The liquid inflames a tightening ache in my muscle, and I whimper, fisting my tied hands on my back.

"Good girl." Aleksandr's appraisal sparks a flicker of anger in me. I try to cling to it, but my desperate need for comfort snuffs it out, and I sink into him instead.

The doctor prods at my shoulder and asks in Russian how much I can feel. I understand perfectly, yet Aleksandr repeats the question in English.

"Can you feel anything?"

I don't think he does it to translate. He certainly knows I understand Russian—he'll often switch to Russian briefly when angry or particularly sincere. I think it's something else. He wants me to answer *him*, not the doctor. I don't know if it's another control thing or part of his warped brand of comfort. And I'm not sure it matters. Because it does calm me. It's just him and me in this fucked-up bubble. No one can reach me but through him.

I shake my head, and Aleksandr gives the doctor a go-ahead.

I make the mistake of turning my head, staring straight up at a thick syringe. Poisonous fear fills the bubble, and suddenly, I can't breathe. "No, no, no, no," I plead, squirming in the ropes, kicking my legs.

"*Derzhi za nog*," Aleksandr commands someone while he tightens his grip on my arm.

I see Anton grab my ankles from the corner of my eye, and I start weeping when my range of movement narrows to inches. Everything is so damn hopeless.

The doctor pinches my numb skin, and I feel the tiniest prick as he jabs the syringe into me, chipping me like an animal. I sense no form of regret from this man, no sliver of compassion. He's here to do a job, and I'm a means to make money. It's the same with all the other men here.

Loneliness hurts as much as the icy panic creeping up my neck.

The only man who shows any flicker of sympathy is the man who put me here.

"All done," Aleksandr soothes, stroking my hair—stroking the panic away. I badly want to resist his touch, but I can't help it.

I lean into him and soak up the comfort he offers. It doesn't matter that he's the one doing the grandest violation of them all. He's also the only one who will get me through it without me splintering into tiny fragments of myself.

Next, the guy I saw holding the tattoo gun rinses the skin behind my left ear.

"Please don't do this," I whimper through tiny sobs.

"Shh." Aleksandr runs his knuckles over my arm. "You'll be mine now. For good. You need this to understand it."

What kind of warped world does he live in? The whipping was also for my sake. How can anything so horrible be for my own good? I've been miserable ever since.

But isn't sadness better than numb loneliness? a small voice inside me asks. Despite all the crying, I've felt better during the last couple of days than any of the fourteen days leading up to the whipping.

But that's because of the catharsis. This... there's nothing cathartic about any of this. It's pure humiliation.

I tense up at the buzzing of a tattoo gun, hardly breathing when Aleksandr presses my head down to hold me still.

"Take a deep breath."

I try to shake my head under his hand.

Aleksandr lowers his voice to an impossibly dark command. "Take. A deep breath. Astrid."

My lips fall apart of their own accord, overriding my pathetic attempt at defiance, and I draw in a long shuddering breath. It levels me for a moment, but when a latex-clad hand pushes my ear forward and the prickle of a needle touches my skin, I cry out. It doesn't matter how many commands Aleksandr issues, I just can't do this. Black panic folds around my mind, and I start thrashing like a wild animal.

The needle disappears as quickly as it came, but it doesn't help. I flex my fingers and strain my hands against the rope, desperately needing something to hold on to—needing to move, needing to breathe.

Aleksandr tries to soothe me with his touch, and when it doesn't work, he says, "Can you keep your arms still if I untie them?"

I nod even though I'm not sure I can. I just need to get them free.

I vaguely notice Aleksandr issue a command to cut the ropes, and then I feel Boris's large figure looming behind me. It's not as frightening as it should be, and when he slips a knife under the ropes, I barely flinch. I just need to get them off.

At that moment, I realize something fucked-up. I may resent both Aleksandr and Boris, but part of me trusts them. It's a warped kind of trust because I don't trust them not to hurt me. But I trust Aleksandr not to let anyone else harm me, and I trust Boris to make sure no harm comes to me under his knife.

The moment my hands are free, I scramble to get them in front of me. I don't get to fumble for purchase long before Aleksandr grabs them both. His hands are as effective restraints as the ropes, but they don't feel restrictive. They're comforting.

I grab onto him like my life depends on it—and maybe my life doesn't, but my sanity sure does. It hurts—both his strength and mine—but it distracts me from the pain inside, so I bid it welcome.

"Breathe," Aleksandr says, and my entire world hones in on him. His deep voice, his unrelenting grip, his scent. His order that spurs my instinctive obedience.

Closing my eyes, I drag in staggered gulps of air, but my lungs seem to repel it. None of it will stick, and my heart thrums with the frantic rhythm of my panic.

"*Smatri na menya,*" Aleksandr demands with an authority that overrides my every self-protective instinct.

I obey and stare straight up into the sharp blue of his gaze. There's both the reflection of his command, unmerciful will, and something soft—sympathy or maybe sincere care for me. It doesn't make sense. But that's Aleksandr. Nothing about him makes sense. And this time, I don't try to comprehend him. I just fall captive to his eyes and let him suck me into the trance as he takes a deep breath that forces me to follow.

Finally, the air sticks, and Aleksandr keeps guiding my breaths until I can breathe on my own.

Even as the panic recedes, I keep watching him, because if I don't, I'll tumble straight back into it.

"Boris, *dershi golovu,*" Aleksandr orders, never releasing me from his gaze.

Two large, calloused hands become a vise around my head, and the buzzing starts again. My eyes go wide, but my only reaction is to renew the strength with which I clutch Aleksandr's hands. He gives a slow nod. To reassure me? To say I'll take this?

The needle hits my skin, and my eyes clamp shut, dragging me straight back toward a black pit of panic.

I don't think the pain is truly bad, but to my frazzled mind, the needle is like a knife cutting my skin, the buzzing like a jackhammer in my ear.

"Stay with me." Aleksandr's harsh command prompts my eyes back open. Tears stream down my cheeks and sobs shake my chest, but I keep watching Aleksandr, granting him entrance to the deepest parts of my soul—where I vowed I'd never let him in. It's all I can do to stay afloat.

At some point, Anton releases my legs, and Boris relaxes his hands around my head. There's no use restraining me anymore.

The fight has drained. Left is only reckless survival.

It takes forever before the gun stops buzzing. I only think it's half an hour, but it seems like several. Then the tattoo guy cleans the mark and wraps it in tattoo film as he instructs Aleksandr how to take care of it.

All my muscles are taut and achy, but I don't relax them before the room is finally empty behind me and I'm alone with Aleksandr.

"This will help you." He releases one of my hands to caress my hair. He sounds so sure, and I think he actually believes it. This is not merely some egotistical means to boost his control over me. He believes I will gain something from being marked as property—giving me papers that snuff out the last illusion of freedom.

Part of me wishes he was right. But not even my brain has any power left to ponder the notion, so it drifts away along with everything else, leaving a blank void.

Chapter 13

ALEKSANDR IS STILL here when I wake up—in the same place, stroking my hair. A blanket is draped over my body and the ceiling light is off. Only the dwindling light of day keeps us out of the shadows.

At some point, I must have turned around since I'm now facing the room. I blink my eyes against my surroundings. There are no signs of the crime committed here. No scraps from the tattoo artist, no documents on the desk, and not even a chair beside me. Everything is back in pristine order.

Except me.

I feel shattered, scrambling through the drifting pieces of my mind. Yet everything is quiet. Almost peacefully so.

Something comes down in front of my mouth. I look to find a piece of strawberry between two large fingers. I take the offered berry and close my eyes to the world as I chew. Juicy sweetness coats my tongue, in perfect harmony with the sweet touch on my hair.

Another piece of fruit prods at my lips. This time, melon. Then a straw that lets me gulp sweet apple juice.

I could almost be led to believe that the struggle is over and everything will fall into place now.

But when a deep voice speaks, my world once again shatters.

"I have one last thing for you," Aleksandr says, still stroking and feeding me with deceptive care.

"Please don't. I can't take any more."

"Shh, it won't hurt. No needles, no people."

The promise of no pain or people takes the brunt of my fear. It's disturbing how easily he placates me despite everything he's done. But I don't care. I don't have anything left to care with. So I say in a broken voice, "Do you promise?"

"I do." His hand stills on my head as if to underline his sincerity. "*Ty imeish moyo slovo.*"

Aleksandr slowly helps me up to sit, then gets up himself to retrieve a flat, square black box.

"Kneel." He points to the floor at his feet.

There are no thoughts left to stop me. I just do it. I sink to the floor in front of him, kneeling at his feet like it's the most natural thing. I don't look up as he opens the box. I sit there in silent acceptance, knowing I can't do anything to hinder whatever's coming.

"Bow your head and gather your hair on your head."

Leaning my head forward, I gather my thick locks like he said. A shiver runs down my right arm as fingers trace the side of my neck. I can't help angling my head to the side, welcoming his touch.

"*Takaya horoshaya devushka,*" he praises. "I hope your obedience will stick this time. I much prefer this beautiful submission to the belligerent childishness."

I catch a glimmer of gold as he holds something down. Cold steel wraps around my neck in a snug fit, closing with the click of a locking mechanism. The sound sends a strange surge through me. It's not the desperate fear the lock on the cage spurred in the beginning. It's a surge of peaceful helplessness.

Nudging my chin up, Aleksandr studies the thing around my neck, and a warm smile crinkles the corners of his eyes before his gaze returns to firm control.

"You may release your hair and touch the collar."

Carefully, I lift my fingers to the metal, tracing it around my neck. It's a band of steel, barely an inch wide. There's a small ring at the front, and then it's thin and smooth metal until I reach the back of my neck where it bulges out. I fiddle a bit with the thick part and find a small hole for... a key.

Aleksandr catches my line of thought. "It's locked. Only I have the key." He dangles a small, oddly shaped piece of metal that must be said key in front of me, then pockets it. "It's proof that you're mine, and if anyone doubts it, my name is engraved beside the lock. You can shower and sleep with it, and I expect you to wear it with pride and reverence."

At this moment, something vital breaks in me. The will to fight? The will to be free? I don't know. Emotions flood me like a tidal wave, threatening to drown me and wash away everything I once knew.

Aleksandr presses my head against his leg. "Can you feel it? That you're mine?"

I nod. Because I do. I feel it in the very depth of my soul, his ownership carved into me with irrefutable precision. I neither can nor want to deny it. So I let it fill me to the brim, and tears spill over again. But this time, it's not the hard and desperate kind. It's tears of gratitude.

Chapter 14

I WAKE IN THE middle of the night, drenched in cold sweat, panting through the onset of panic.

Frantically, I scan the place for something to reassure me, but all I see is darkness. And cold steel. Bars surround me on every side. I shove at them—the top, the sides, one bar at a time, several at a time.

Nothing gives.

Then I feel it. Steel around my neck too.

My hands shoot up to the collar, fingers sliding around the band, feeling the unforgiving metal, the tiny lock on the back, and the ring at the front.

I can't breathe. So I yank at this steel too.

Nothing gives.

I start heaving, my chest aching with desperate attempts to take in air. Slipping my fingers under the metal, I try to loosen it. I get a smidgen more room by my windpipe, but the metal digs further into the back of my neck, refusing to let me forget.

My chest shakes, and white-hot panic blinds what little sight the darkness allowed me—blinds every thought in my mind.

I flip to my side, trying to angle my fingers differently, then toss to the other side and pull at more angles. Shooting up to sit, I put in more energy, coughing as the steel digs into the front of my neck. Now my windpipe is truly blocked. But I don't care if I choke myself in the process. I just need to get this thing off. So I keep yanking, whimpering, and coughing, clawing at my skin.

Nothing gives.

Searing powerlessness sends my hands to my scalp, pulling at my hair.

Finally, something gives. I feel hairs loosen from their roots, and I welcome the stinging pain that makes me forget about the steel—just for a split-second.

I feel like a lunatic—a crazy person that should be locked up.

I already am.

A painful scream rips through my throat. Loud and desperate. Filling the darkness like a demon's wail.

The sound prolongs my insanity; my insanity prolongs the scream. I claw at the prickling skin behind my ear and rip away the plastic. If I can't remove the steel, I can remove the tattoo. Digging my nails into the already burning skin, I scream anew with manic frustration.

The door flies open and the light comes on, but I don't see anything but the blinding fury that keeps my hands clawing and scratching.

Metal clanks, and suddenly, my hands are trapped too. I writhe and thrash, snapping my teeth to hurt whoever has grabbed me.

"Stop it!" a hard voice commands, but it only drives my insanity higher. I keep fighting like a trapped beast as I'm lifted out of the cage.

I manage a few scratches on a naked chest, but then I'm trapped in someone's lap on the floor. Trapped against a hard chest. Trapped in the unbreakable shackles of two big hands.

Always trapped.

A familiar scent of citrus tugs at something inside me, but I can't see what it is through the panic. So I keep fighting. I whip my head back and forth, into a hard shoulder, hurting myself. Ugly sobs rip from my throat, alternating with horrid screams.

A hand locks onto my forehead, and with my arms still immobilized, the only thing left to do is bang my heels into hard wood. So I do that.

Someone else comes bursting into the room, footsteps thudding across the floor.

"Put something under her feet," a hard voice snaps beside my ear.

A massive figure moves above me, and then someone folds the comforter up under my feet. But I kick it away, needing the pain because it's the only thing that's mine.

The comforter returns, and two calloused hands press my legs into it, rendering me completely immobilized.

"Breathe," someone urges against my ear, and that same someone starts rocking me.

I try to fight it, but straining and bucking get me nowhere, and soon my energy runs dry. My sobs and screams fade into heartbroken weeping, and my muscles slacken in defeat.

"Go get tape and towels," a voice says, and the thudding steps from before recede. Then the same voice is at my ear. "Shh, *dershu tebya*," it soothes. "You're not alone."

Those words break me—break me out of the blinding panic and into a deep hurt that's always been lodged inside me. I don't want to be alone. I've never wanted to, but I've always been. Not even when I met Anna could I chase away the feeling and let her in. Not truly.

"I've got you," the voice repeats in English, and the scent of lemons fills my nose with each staggered breath.

"I don't want to be alone," I whimper as I struggle to turn and bury my head in the shoulder I'm trapped against.

"You're not alone. You're mine." Arms loosen around me, and I scramble around to press myself into the man who offers me something more—the man who chases away the loneliness with soothing caresses and tender words.

Footsteps return, a gruff voice speaking in Russian. "What do you want me to do with these?"

"Wrap her hands up." Aleksandr presses me closer and kisses the top of my head, almost like he's trying to calm me for what's next.

I don't register his words until someone pries one of my hands free. Glancing up, I see Boris wrap a towel around my fist, and panic builds anew.

"What are you doing?" My voice is shrill as I push against Aleksandr.

"I don't want you marring what's mine." There's no rebuke in Aleksandr's voice. It's a perfectly calm statement. He truly believes he owns me. It's not a game or a means to fuck with my mind. In his eyes, I'm property. He believes it's his right to do whatever he wants with me. And worst of all, I'm starting to believe it too.

There's nothing I can do as Boris wraps a small towel around my hand and secures it with plenty of duct tape, then does the same to the other. So I bury my head against Aleksandr, where I can't see the humiliation, and soak up his comfort as he strokes my hair.

When my hands are all wrapped up and useless, Aleksandr rises with me in his arms. I expect him to put me back in the cage, but instead, he carries me through the sitting room and to the first door in the wide hallway. Firing off a couple of quick orders to Boris, he brings me into a huge bedroom.

The sheets are tousled, the lights on, clothes hanging over an armchair. I peer up at the man carrying me. Does he sleep in here? Right next to my room?

The realization sends a warm feeling through my weary bones. It shouldn't be possible, but here in the dead of night, cradled in his gentle arms, I see Aleksandr as my protector.

He carefully places me on the bed, and his scent lingering on the soft sheets dredges up all kinds of emotions I've tried to deny for so long. I stare up into his eyes, taken aback by the gentleness I find there. I want to hate this man so badly, but I always seem to fail. Maybe I should stop trying.

Averting my gaze, I dispel the scary thought only to see my wrapped-up hands. I try to flex my fingers against the terrycloth, but I can't even open my fists. Humiliation stabs into my chest. I'm so ugly and useless.

"*Smatri na menya.*" Aleksandr nudges my head to catch my eyes. "I don't know what's going on in that head of yours, but snap out of it. You're mine. You're not out there any longer." He nods toward the window. "It doesn't matter what the rest of the world thinks of you. They can't see you. The only thing that matters is what I think. And I happen to like my mark of ownership on you."

He trails his fingers along the collar around my neck, then up to flip my left ear back. His mouth curls in a hint of a snarl as he sees the damage I've done.

"What I don't like is you trying to destroy my mark." He grabs my jaw and looks me straight in the eye. "So when you destroy my property, you're gonna wear goddamn towels on your hands."

I should be angry, but all I can muster is regret as I see the truth of his words in his willful gaze. *I don't belong to myself anymore. The only thing that matters is what he thinks.* So I stop thinking altogether.

"I'm sorry," I say in a low voice. And I mean it. I'm not sure exactly what I'm sorry for. Scratching up his mark? Or maybe for not seeing that I belong to him sooner? I'm not sure it matters.

Aleksandr's lips curve into a smile, and for the first time since I saw him on the train, I don't find it scary. It's warm and soothing. "You're finally getting there," he murmurs, absently stroking my jawline.

My lips part, almost releasing a devastating *yes*, but Boris saves me as he enters the room.

Aleksandr remains at my side, soothing me with tender words and soft caresses, as Boris cleans the mark and reapplies new tattoo film.

Once we're alone again, Aleksandr turns off the lights and crawls into bed behind me.

Trying to become as small as possible, I gather my arms against my chest. I'd almost forgotten the towels and the tape, and feeling how useless my hands are is so devastating I start weeping again. I try to keep the tears silent in the still of night, but Aleksandr can surely feel my grief in the shakes in my chest as he pulls me to him.

His hand splays on my stomach, fingers gently moving against my skin. "Do you want to forget? Just for a little while."

I have no idea what he means, but I'll do just about anything to chase away the hurt and humiliation tearing at my soul. So I nod.

His hand makes a slow journey down my stomach, speeding up my breath as I realize where it's going. When it reaches my mound, I tense up, but the arm tightening around my chest quickly chases away all thoughts of right and wrong. So I let up the mental fight and sink into him.

"That's it," he whispers, sliding a long finger between my folds.

I gasp at the sensation, my nerve endings flaring to life. No one has touched me there for months, maybe half a year, and when he slowly circles my clit, I mewl like a starved cat. Unable to hold back, I grind my hips against his naked groin, and I feel all too clearly how his cock comes alive. But I don't stop.

"Please," I say with a weak moan even as tears keep spilling from my eyes.

"Please what?"

"Please make me come." I don't care if he shoves his cock inside me or uses his fingers. I've masturbated in the cage plenty of times, but I badly want to feel the sweet pleasure of a man driving me to the peak.

The smug smile is palpable in his words. "You know, I was going to make you come anyway. But since you asked so nicely"—he shoves two fingers inside me—"I'll make it extra good."

He starts pumping, in and out, and I cry out from pleasure so intense it's painful. I strain against his arm, but for the first time, it's not to get away. It's pure, unrestrained need. Need for more. Need to be closer to the man I've tried so hard to get away from.

Aleksandr tightens his grip and rasps into my ear, "Show me what an obedient girl you are and come for me." He grinds his palm against my clit as he adds another digit, expertly fucking me with three fingers. But it's not the added touch that drives me over the edge. It's his words.

Painful pleasure mixes with all the hurt of the day as the

orgasm rips through me, and when I cry out, it's a half moan, half sob.

"*Horoshaya devushka.*" Aleksandr prolongs my orgasm with a few more thrusts before pulling out. His cock is still hard against my butt, but he does nothing to take his own pleasure. He just wraps me in his arms and rocks me gently as I cry a few soft tears before the strain of the day knocks me out.

Chapter 15

I WAKE UP IN Aleksandr's bed with vivid memories of yesterday flashing through my mind. The struggling, the crying, the devastating defeat. The documents, the chip, the tattoo. The collar.

When I notice my hands, I let out a broken whimper. The towels.

I sink deeper under the covers, refusing to acknowledge the humiliation. Somehow, those towels are more devastating than anything else. For a fleeting moment, I consider gnawing at the duct tape to get them off, but it would make me feel even more base, so I force my attention away.

The dull throbbing in my shoulder and the sting behind my ear draw my focus instead. Marks of property.

With the need to get as small as possible, I pull my legs up to my stomach and feel leather around my ankle, attached to... a chain?

The degradation has no end.

It freezes me in place and locks up my muscles. I lie there, stiff and still, until the door opens. Heavy steps announce Boris—one of the men who witnessed and abided my dehumanization. How will I ever be able to look him in the eye again?

He stops beside the bed, and I shut my eyes and draw my hands under the comforter.

A gentle stroke along my hairline surprises me. Boris never touches me. Not like this. It's only a fleeting touch, but the tenderness is palpable.

I flicker my eyes open and peek up at him. There's no pity or judgment. Only sympathy.

"He didn't do it to punish you, you know," Boris says, again surprising me.

I watch him for a minute before I swallow through my raw throat and ask in Russian, "Then why?"

"He wants you to accept your situation."

Bitter tears sting my eyes. "That's one fucked-up way to do it." I flinch at the sound of my curse, but Boris doesn't react to it.

"He really cares about you."

"He doesn't," is all I can say.

Boris is quiet for a moment, and I can feel the gravity in the air before he speaks. "Trust me. I've known him my whole life, and I've never seen him do so much for anyone before."

Two days ago, I'd have made a bitter remark, but the snark is gone. I stare at the wall and remain silent. At least for a while, because I do need the distraction of conversation.

"How do you know him?" I finally ask, my eyes still staring straight ahead.

Boris sinks onto the edge of the bed. "I grew up at their estate. My father worked for Aleksandr's father."

"Has he always been so cold?"

I can see Boris's shrug from the corner of my eye. "To most people. But he always treated Anton and me with respect even though he wasn't expected to."

I shake my head, not following. "He always barks at you."

Boris huffs. "That's not disrespect. It's just how he is. No, if you want to see disrespect, you should have seen his father."

"What about him?" I look up at Boris, almost forgetting about my useless hands under the comforter.

"When Aleksandr's mother died, Leo—his father—took to drinking. From then on, everything went south. He neglected the business and started treating everyone like shit, including Aleksandr."

"How old was Aleksandr?"

"Eight."

The distraction works as my curiosity grows. "What happened to the company? Isn't it his father's business he's running now?" This is one of the few things I knew about Aleksandr before seeing him the first time. He'd inherited a billion-dollar company from his father, who had bought large parts of the steel industry for pennies at the collapse of the Soviet Union.

"Leo's best friend stepped in and started grooming Aleksandr to take over the business, and Aleksandr even lived at his place for long periods."

"Because of his father?" This is the most anyone has divulged about Aleksandr since I came here, and I'm soaking up every drop of information I can get.

Boris's gruff features tighten like the memory is painful. "Him and the women he brought home—foul-mouthed creatures who only wanted Leo for his money and thought they could control Aleksandr."

"I can't imagine him being happy about that," I mutter half to myself.

Boris huffs. "You don't say. Aleksandr was barely a teenager the first time one of them fled the house with a red handprint on her cheek."

It's hard to imagine a thirteen-year-old boy slapping a grown woman, but when I imagine that boy being Aleksandr, it's quite plausible. "Is it because of those women that he hates swearing so much?"

"Probably."

I'm about to ask another question when Boris takes out one of my arms from beneath the covers. I'd almost forgotten about my towel-wrapped hands, and the sight knocks me straight back into tense silence.

Boris removes a spring knife from his pocket and cuts the tape.

The relief is minimal as I flex my free hands. Not even the removal of the chain will free me from the devastation pounding within me. There are so many other things weighing me down, and Boris leading me to a huge en suite bathroom and insisting on staying while I pee and shower is yet another one.

"I need to make sure you don't harm yourself," he says when I beg him to leave.

Thus, the humiliation continues. My shoulders slump in defeat when he finally leads me from the bedroom. Thinking he's taking me back to the cage, I veer right, but Boris grabs my arm and steers me left.

"Where are we going?" I ask. The only place I've been besides the cage room is the pool and the dojo, and we're surely not going to either place before breakfast.

"To Aleksandr's office." Boris grabs the handle on the next door.

"Here?" Why would he have his workspace so close to his bedroom when he has such an enormous house?

Boris pauses. "He moved his office up here when he got you."

With that, he opens the door, and I step inside with this new information fluttering in my head.

My eyes find the cause of my bewilderment immediately. Aleksandr is sitting by a huge, heavy desk at the other end of the room. Seeing us enter, he closes his laptop and leans back in his leather swivel chair, hands folded over his stomach. I cast my gaze down, feeling so utterly small under those eyes—feeling so small after being broken into tiny fragments of myself.

"Come here," he says.

Hesitantly, I make my way across the large space, unable to lift my gaze from the floor as I go. Beside the desk, I halt at the sight of the large dog lying beside Aleksandr. It glances up at me with lazy eyes as its tail sweeps back and forth on the floor.

"She's harmless." Aleksandr leans down to pet the dog. "Come, see for yourself."

When I don't move, he holds out his hand and urges me on with a nod.

I step around the dog, giving it a wide berth, and take Aleksandr's hand. He guides me onto my knees and sinks down behind me. I'd rather he'd sit between me and the dog, but feeling him close to me is still reassuring.

Slowly, he guides my hand toward the creature's nose. "Always let a dog smell you if you don't know it."

The sound of the door catches my attention, and I glance up to find that Boris has left. Unease creeps along my skin as I realize I'm alone with Aleksandr and his dog in this strange new setting.

The feeling of a wet snout makes me jerk my hand back with a gasp. But the dog only looks curious when I return my gaze to it. There's no apparent threat.

Aleksandr gives a warm laugh. "You're not used to dogs, are

you?"

I shake my head.

His hand comes up to brush my damp hair behind my shoulder, his fingers tracing my skin right above the collar. "Were you bitten, or have you just never been around them?"

"The first."

"Where did it bite you?"

"My ankle." Unconsciously, I cover the place with my hand. The sickening feeling of teeth sinking into my skin remains all too clear. I was only a little girl trying to pet a cute dog in front of a store. I've never repeated that mistake.

Aleksandr covers my hand with his protectively. "My dogs won't ever bite you. Only poorly trained dogs bite. I've trained mine well."

I expect a remark about how he's training me, but he just curves his other hand around my waist to stroke me. It's almost like he's making up for the comfort I didn't get back then. My mother was so angry I touched a random dog, and I think I cried as much from her berating me as the pain in my leg.

"Now, try touching her back. Her fur is incredibly soft. I think you'll like it."

Carefully, I reach for the dog and pause right above its fur as I turn my attention to its face. It watches us with lazy eyes like it doesn't have a care in the world. So I slip my fingers into the long, golden fur. A small smile tips up my lips as warm softness engulfs my fingers. Feeling brave, I move my hand a little, and soon I'm stroking the dog from its head down the length of its back.

"Where's the other dog?" I ask, suddenly curious about these fluffy creatures.

"Probably out running the grounds. Brunja is the active one;

Luna here,"—he ruffles the dog's head—"is the lazy one. She spends most mornings here with me."

"What breed is she?" I don't know much about dog breeds, but this one doesn't look like a regular one.

"I'm not sure. I found her in an alley in St. Petersburg when she was a pup. But I'm thinking a mix between Golden retriever and Collie."

I glance back at him. "Golden retriever because of the color?"

"Exactly," he says with a warm smile as if impressed. "Do you see the slightly elongated face?"

I turn my eyes back to the dog and nod.

"That's typical collie. Plus, the long fur. You know, like the movie *Lassie*?"

I smile, a bit surprised that this Russian business magnate knows an American dog movie. "Have you always liked dogs?"

"Always. My family spent a lot of time with my father's friend's family. They had six dogs that—"

"Six dogs?" I interject and immediately cover my mouth as my eyes shoot to Aleksandr. I've never interrupted him. I expect him to grab me or at least glare at me, but he simply smiles.

"Yeah, he used them for hunting. And Vasily, his son, loved to train them. He's five years older than me, and when you're a kid, that's a lot. He was my hero. I remember being awestruck by all the tricks he could get the dogs to do."

"Did you have a dog of your own?"

Aleksandr's eyes darken. "My mom got me a beagle for my seventh birthday, but my dad had it put down a year later. He didn't like its barking." He hides his anger well, but I can feel it in his hand tightening around my waist.

My heart breaks at the thought of the little boy losing his new best friend because his dad didn't like its bark. It's so pointless I almost can't bear it. He must have been eight. That's when he lost his mom. Did his dad kill his dog right after his mom died?

Suddenly, I'm sniffling, and I shoot my hand up to catch a tear on my cheek. "I'm sorry," I say, apologizing for both his loss and my tears. I try to rein them in, but the emotions keep flowing.

"Shh, sh, shh." He gently turns me around, cupping the back of my head as he presses me into him. "I have two beautiful dogs now." He strokes my hair the same way he'd pet his dog, with tender affection. "And you."

Two days ago, I would have hated being compared to his dogs, but now I see it for what it is. A dog is not a vile, base creature to him. It's a creature worthy of love. Maybe not the kind a normal person would crave, but I think it might well be the only type of love Aleksandr is capable of.

Boris's words come back to me. *He really cares about you.* Could it be? This morning, the idea seemed ridiculous, but in light of all the new information I've learned today, it seems plausible.

My tears come faster, and I press myself into him. Right at this moment, I don't care about any of the violations or degradations he's put me through; I only care about the firm arm holding me close and the soft kisses pebbling down on my head. It's fucked-up, wrong, and sick on so many levels, but I can no longer deny that my entire being gravitates toward this man, and more so, that I care about him too.

I spend most of the day in Aleksandr's office. He makes me kneel at his side and eat breakfast while he's on a conference call, then he takes me to the pool for a swim. When we come back, he spreads a large fur over the floor along with a pillow and a blanket and lets me take a nap at his feet.

My head is unusually calm. All thoughts of right and wrong, should and shouldn't, have quieted.

Have I finally come to accept Aleksandr's self-proclaimed ownership over me?

No, not accept, but maybe I've stopped denying it. The distinction is subtle but nonetheless important to me. Accepting his ownership would mean I'm a willing victim, but not fighting just means I've realized there's nothing I can do about it.

I wonder if he's finally broken me or if it's sensible rationalization that has drained the fight from me. I don't give it much thought. What I think doesn't matter anymore, and with each passing day after the tattoo, my self-image becomes less important as Aleksandr's opinion takes precedence.

The first few days post-tattoo, I'm an emotional mess. The tears come without warning, and I'm helpless to control them.

After a few days of weeping and feeling broken, I regain some self-control and start shutting off my emotions again. It's not a conscious choice, really, but more of a habit after having done it adamantly for weeks.

"Astrid," Aleksandr says one morning when I'm sitting on the floor in his office, sniffling as I force down the sudden urge to cry. This has become my new morning routine, eating breakfast at his side while he works and Luna snoozes on his other side. "Look at me."

I wipe a quick hand under my eyes before peering up, tightening my features to keep the sorrow out.

He takes a long look at me, then tuts. "Not this again?" He

shuts his laptop and rises to his feet. "Get up."

"What... where are we... I'm sorry." I don't know what I've done, what's going on, or where we're going, but I know it's not good.

"You can't keep shutting off your emotions. It's not good for you. So I'll keep whipping you until you learn to come to me on your own."

"No, no, no, no, no." I pull at my hand when he snatches my wrist. "Please don't. I promise I..." The words die on my tongue. I know I won't come to him on my own, and for some reason, I can't make myself lie to him.

I pant and jerk my arm to get free as he drags me from the room. Aleksandr remains adamant, his hand an unbreakable grip around my wrist, his authority permeating the air around us.

Somewhere on our way through the house, something in me flips. I don't want to fight him anymore. I want to give in—give up the burden of choice and fall into the steady current of his control.

So that's what I do. My arm slackens in the shackle of his grip, and my breathing steadies as I fall into an even pace beside him.

My surrender changes something in him too. The tension drains from his shoulders, and his arm becomes surprisingly protective as he tucks me into his side. It no longer feels like he's dragging me off to be punished, but rather shielding me from the pain of the world.

It doesn't make sense because he's the one to inflict the worst pain I've ever known as he once again restrains me in the dojo and assaults my back with the thin tip.

The licks of the whip send me careening through an onslaught of pain, and harrowing screams rip through my throat.

It breaks out all the terrifying emotions I don't dare to confront, and I feel raw and broken, inside-out, when he finally drops the whip to the floor.

But I'm not broken. When Aleksandr gathers me in his arms, he holds the tattered fragments together. He gives me a safe place to cry out the pain and confusion.

He takes me to the garden room and rocks me until the tears finally let up. Then he takes me to his bed and makes me come on his fingers as he holds me in a fierce grip against his body.

"Say *thank you, Master,*" he says as I shudder through the fading current of my orgasm.

I tense in his arms. "Please don't make me say that." Somehow, I know there'll be no way back once I say the word. I still feel like I'm hovering somewhere on the edge, holding on to the last piece of myself, and that word will plunge me straight into the pit of his control with no way back.

His hand comes up to my cheek, coaxing me with soft caresses. "Say it, Astrid." There's no harsh command forcing me into obedience. There's just the soft voice and sweet touch, and it makes it that much more devastating when my lips part and the words slip out.

"Thank you, Master," I say, just above a whisper. Something shifts inside me. But it's not the devastating brokenness I expected. It's something entirely different and much brighter.

Peace.

"*Takaya horoshaya devushka.*" Aleksandr trails his fingers behind my left ear, caressing the wrapped tattoo. "You're mine now."

You're mine now. The words repeat themselves over and over in my mind, and slowly, I realize the truth in them.

I'm his now.

Chapter 16

THE NEXT DAY, I wake up from someone stroking my hair. I'm in the cage. I don't have to open my eyes to know; the bars are a palpable weight around me. But they're not stifling. Rather, they're like a heavy blanket. I don't know when I allowed myself to be so comfortable here. It's become increasingly difficult to deny the peace I feel at being locked up with no choice. It's so simple.

Curling up under the warm comforter, I lean into the hand. Notes of citrus drift through the air, and there's the sound of a dog breathing with its tongue sticking out. Not even the latter bothers me anymore.

"I have something for you today," Aleksandr says.

I rub my sleepy eyes and crane my neck to meet his gaze. The last time he gave me something, it was a chip, a tattoo, and a collar to mark me as property. But his eyes are warm today, holding no warning of a new degradation to come.

"Something you've deserved," he adds, brushing my skin above the collar. "But first, a shower and breakfast."

Aleksandr lets me out of the cage, and I rub Luna behind the ear before I go about my morning routine—with the small difference that Aleksandr is here and not Boris. That in itself is a treat. Aleksandr comes into the bathroom once I'm out of the shower and takes the towel from my hands to dry me off. After all the whippings, showers after swimming, and orgasms on his fingers, I no longer feel self-conscious at the feeling of his hands on my naked body. Rather, I enjoy his touch, and I soak up the feeling of his firm hands roaming over my body with the terry cloth.

Next, he takes me to his office and orders me to kneel on his left side by the desk, Luna on his right. It's been like this most mornings for several weeks now. But the large plate of waffles he hands me is special. It's not unusual per se, but waffles are for special occasions—a consolation after a hard night or an award when I've been particularly good.

My mouth waters, and Luna strains her neck and sniffs the air.

"Can I give her a piece?" I ask.

Aleksandr shakes his head. "Those are especially for you."

"Thank you," I say, truly grateful. But also a little confused. Usually, I know why I get waffles, but today I have no idea.

It's only when Aleksandr speaks a moment later that realization strikes.

"Say the word, Astrid."

I've only said it once, yet I immediately know which word he means. Saying it last night shifted something within me, and I think it did for him too—so much that he rewards me with waffles. Folding my hands, I close my eyes and lower my head, shutting out every self-inflicted thought of belittlement that wants to ruin the moment.

"Thank you, Master."

A wave of warm gratitude washes over me when his hand curves around my nape, holding my head in the humble position.

"Good girl. Now eat your waffles."

After breakfast and our daily swim, Aleksandr brings me back to the hallway with his office, bedroom, and the cage room. But instead of leading me to any of those rooms, he stops at the fourth door, through which I've never been.

He studies me for a beat, a small smile pulling at his lips, and I realize this must be the surprise. I'd forgotten all about it, thinking it was the waffles, but he actually has something new for me.

Before opening the door, he levels me with a stern expression. "You'll do well to remember that I can take this away again."

I nod as I stare up at him, my breathing coming in small drags as the importance of the moment swells inside me.

Aleksandr pushes the door open, and everything stops. My breath, my heart, my words. Aleksandr has to nudge me forward because all my focus is frozen on the centerpiece in the room.

I can't believe what I'm seeing. Right in front of me is a large, shiny grand piano. The lid is propped open, the keys bared, inviting me to touch. The polished surface twinkles under the bright sun seeping through tall windows. There's nothing around it to draw away attention—only an old-fashioned couch, a side table by the piano, and a long line of bookcases filled with... sheet music.

Tears well in my wide eyes. It's too much. A dream come true. It's everything I've ever wanted.

Aleksandr was the one to take it away, but what should be a significant detail fades into irrelevance since he's now the one to give it back. I don't know what happens. He must have broken me for good because I turn and fall to my knees before him. Bowing my head, I grab his legs with fervent hands.

"Thank you," I say, my voice thick with reverence. "Thank you, Master." The words slip past my lips without effort. Suddenly, this title is the most natural thing, and I repeat the words over and over until they become a mantra. But it's not enough. The gratitude is about to rip me open. Tears drip in rapid streams, and I fall lower, all the way into the humble dirt at his feet, where I rest my head on his shoe.

Aleksandr sinks to his haunches and places a hand on my head like a prophet would a disciple.

"How beautiful." His voice is a gentle hum, like he's mesmerized by my humble display of submission. "I knew you were ready to receive this gift—that it's the right time."

His words break me open. I burst into full-on crying. Tears stream down my cheeks as I sniffle and whimper. I don't even try to hide it. I lay it all out there for him to see—my hopes, my dreams, my vulnerability and sorrow. I want him to have it all.

"That's it," he soothes. "Let it all out."

And so I do. I let go of all the festering fears as I lie there at his feet, feeling small and fragile yet somehow safe. Everything except Aleksandr—my master—fades. There are no hopes and dreams so intense they hurt, no burden of expectations coming from ten different directions. There's only his command and the one thing he wants from me.

Submission.

Once the tears fade and I'm breathing steadily, Aleksandr brings me up to sit in front of him. Stroking my long hair from my damp face, he says, "I want you to go find whatever sheet music you'd like and bring it to the piano."

It might well be the best order he's given me. Wasting no time, I push to my feet and go to scour the tall bookcases. They seem to contain all the music I could possibly dream of—all the big composers, some less known, and even a few I've never heard of.

The sheet music is sorted by period—baroque, classical period, romantic, modern. I run my fingers over the contents of the nearest shelf. Bach, Händel, and Scarlatti. This music has never pulled me in—too sturdy and stiff. Next are Mozart and Haydn, but I don't want the pretty elegance they offer. I want music that can fill my soul. And for once, there's no teacher telling me I need a varied repertoire. I can play whatever I want. This is the one choice that is mine to make, and it's the only one I want.

The first romantic music I see, I take out. Schubert's Impromptus. Next is Schumann, Liszt, and Chopin. I take several books by each composer. Then comes the Russians. Tchaikovsky, Mussorgsky, Glinka, and my favorite, Rachmaninoff. Music that can express the heavy grief lodged in my chest. Music that can fill the hole in my soul. And lastly, the delicate beauty of impressionistic Debussy.

Finally, I can't carry any more, and I turn to Aleksandr with an apologetic look as I realize how large the pile is. "I'm sorry. I've taken too much." I lower my eyes and take Debussy's *Suite Bergamasque* and put it back on the shelf, and a longing ache tightens my chest at the loss of the beautiful music. It no more deserves to be discarded than any of the others.

I take the next book from the pile—Rachmaninoff's beautiful preludes—and lift it to the shelf, but Aleksandr stops me with a hand on my arm.

Staring up at him with big, melancholic eyes, I watch as he

takes the Rachmaninoff sheet from my hand and returns it to my pile, then retrieves Debussy and adds it on top.

"This is for you." Pressing a hand to my back, he guides me to the piano, where he relieves me of the huge pile and places it on the side table. I tense at the loss of the music but force myself to relax since it's right there within arm's reach.

"Sit." Aleksandr points to the piano bench. It's one of those fancy ones with a thick upholstered leather seat.

I sink onto it and feel the rush of excitement as I watch the black and white keys begging to be caressed.

It's only when Aleksandr crouches at my side that I notice the chain and manacle attached to the piano's front leg. My heart makes a hard thud at the rattling sound, but the sharp breath rushing past my lips at the feeling of steel around my ankle is not defeat or devastation. It's a rush of deep-seated belonging.

Aleksandr brushes a hand over my hair and leaves my side to sit on the upholstered couch in front of the windows. He doesn't say a word as I flip through the large pile beside me. A light tremble creeps into my hands when I open Rachmaninoff's preludes to the one in C sharp minor and set it on the music stand before me. I haven't played for months. *Do I even know how anymore?*

The first three strokes of keys are simple. Three different notes, each played in unison. I place my hands above the keys and play the first. The tones ring innocently on their own, yet I can already hear the ominous music to come. Playing the next two, I relish the trembling depth of Rachmaninoff's low notes, and then my hands move on to the large chords of their own volition, remembering every note without help from the sheet music.

I play through the entirety—the ominous depths of the

beginning, the trembling middle, and the violent chords at the end.

When I lift my hands, my entire body is trembling. All the loss and longing I've felt over the last couple of months stir wildly inside me, clashing with the extreme relief of feeling the keys beneath my fingers.

I stare at the piano, unable to play another note, all energy having left me in one fell swoop.

I barely register Aleksandr crouching at my side and unlocking the manacle. It's only when he lifts me into his arms and carries me away from the piano that I react.

"No." I reach for the instrument. "I only got to play one piece."

"There'll be more tomorrow."

"Please," I whimper, barely hearing his words.

"Shh, you need rest." Aleksandr carries me back to the cage room and sits with me on the couch, holding me until the shaking finally dies down and I'm left hanging limply in his arms. Then he puts me in the cage, and sleep quickly claims me as the lid shuts, the click of the lock settling me into the peaceful knowledge that I'm trapped.

Aleksandr takes me to the piano room every day. Playing is almost like taking up swimming after a week of inactivity in the cage. The first few days, I'm exhausted after barely fifteen minutes. Unlike with swimming, though, it's emotional strain that wears me down.

I spend a lot of time crying. The emotions seem to keep bubbling to the surface. But for once, I don't try to shove them back down—not even when Aleksandr comes into the cage room and finds me weeping into the pillow. I willingly wrap my arms around his neck and let him carry me from the cage, and then I press myself into him as he rocks me through the onslaught of tears.

He stops taking me to the dojo. I don't ask him why. I don't have to. I clearly remember his words from a few days after I got my collar. *I'll keep whipping you until you learn to come to me on your own.* I guess I've learned that now. He's succeeded—torn my walls to shreds, broken me down to crave my captor's comfort.

Gradually, the soul-shattering emotions wane, and playing the piano becomes a peaceful activity. Aleksandr lets me spend hours shackled to the instrument whenever I have the energy, and I relish every minute of it.

Not once does he tell me what to play. He may decide how much and when I get to play, but the choice of music remains my own. He often sits in here, listening but never commenting. I can tell he finds a certain peace in my music. His expression is impassive as ever when he listens, but I notice how his shoulders seem more relaxed, the sharp air of control less acute.

It's like I'm playing the music especially for him. He gets every note, every nuance of emotion, and somehow, I feel the music stronger when he's here.

But I'm starting to miss something. The piano pieces that have always been able to fill the hole in my soul don't seem to cut it anymore. I crave something more, but I'm not sure what.

One day, a piece of melody pops into my head. It's from Borodin's "Polovtsian Dances"—an orchestral piece I've always loved and wanted to play. But I could never find a piano transcription that truly captured the beauty of the piece.

Now, my fingers seem to be adamant to get the music out,

and I find myself building on it, adding pianistic techniques that make the music sparkle on this instrument. I get the intro down to a tee, but I can't remember much more of the original music and find myself fumbling to figure out the chords and melodies.

I only work on it when I'm alone, feeling somewhat uncertain about this new direction of creativity. Playing romantic pieces in front of an audience is no great feat. I know what I have to do, the exact notes to play and the expression to bring out. But making transcriptions is a discipline I haven't dabbled in before. So I keep it to myself.

A few days later, when Aleksandr chains me to the piano in the morning, I find a new book of sheet music on the side table, which I haven't seen on the shelves. It's the "Polovtsian Dances"—the complete original score for orchestra—along with a block of blank sheet music and a pen.

I turn to gaze after Aleksandr, but he's already gone. *Has he heard me playing little tidbits and fumbling to find the right harmonies?*

I immediately go to work, scribbling down what I've already transcribed. Then I study the score to find the right harmonies, which I twist and turn on the piano until I find the right way to fit the music on the new instrument.

For several weeks, I work on this—only when I'm alone—until I finally have a new version written down, just the way I want it.

Chapter 17

"I'M TAKING YOU to a party tonight," Aleksandr announces one morning when I'm kneeling at his side in his office, eating breakfast. "A seamstress will come in a few hours, and you'll try on some dresses in here."

The prospect of going somewhere—anywhere—has me all but bouncing, and the idea of wearing something other than the silky robes has my stomach fluttering. "Really?"

He gives me a nod of confirmation, and I think I see a small smile flicker across his face as he watches my barely contained excitement.

But then I imagine being at a party—the people, the noise, and the expectations to behave in a certain way. Will he expect me to make small-talk? I haven't carried anything resembling a normal conversation with anyone but Boris for months. Does he want me to act like an independent person? Someone with a will and opinion after having stripped it from me?

"I can't," I say hoarsely, fear scratching at my throat.

"You can do whatever I want." It's not a sharp reproach. It's a reassurance. Part of me wants to take it as such, but another part is too terrified about this new prospect of being around people.

"I don't know how..." He's broken me. He truly has. I only

know how to function in this closed-off environment he's kept me trapped in for...? I don't even know how long it's been. He took me in May, when the trees were a pale green. Now they are turning red and yellow, announcing the coming of fall. So, months? Almost half a year? The thought has another heavy pile of dread dropping into my stomach. "How long have I been here?" I ask, suddenly needing the information badly.

"It doesn't matter." Shutting his laptop, he turns to me in his swivel chair. He picks up a lock of my wavy hair and twirls it between his fingers as his eyes go distant. Then he tucks it behind my ear and continues. "I'll be at your side the whole night. You just have to do as I say, and everything will be fine."

"I can't. All the people... I don't know how..." I should probably see this as my chance to escape, but all I can see is the fear of returning to the normal world. My voice becomes shrill as I burst into desperate words of begging. "Please don't make me do this. Just let me stay here. I'll do anything. Just don't make me go."

Aleksandr's voice lowers to a frightening tone. "Don't start acting out because you're scared. If you can't handle it, I'll be happy to take you to the dojo for a good whipping."

Falling silent, I bite down on my lips. I hate the whip. But it's also the most effective way to free me of worries and tension. The pain is terrible, but the peace I feel once Aleksandr has whipped all the strain out of me just might be worth it. So I nod. It's the slightest movement of my head, and I'm not even sure he notices. I'm not sure I want him to.

But of course he does. I can almost hear the satisfied smile spreading across his face as he praises me. "*Takaya horoshaya devushka.* Such progress you've made." His warm breath prickles my ear as he leans down. "Remember the rules. You may scream and fight all you want. But if you even swear once,"—he pauses for effect—"I'll whip you so hard I can't bring you tonight."

My pulse skyrockets, and my head churns in a maelstrom of horror, shock, and endless questions. What have I done? How could I ask for something like this? Am I *this* broken?

He takes two padlocks and a short chain from a drawer and attaches one end to my collar, the other to a steel ring recessed in the floor below his desk.

"Boris will come get you in fifteen minutes." With that, he leaves me alone with my terrified thoughts.

Fifteen minutes later, Boris comes to get me as promised.

But I can't go with him of my own accord. I can't accept that I've asked for this myself. Once he has unlocked the chain on my collar, I scramble away from him and around the large desk.

I've never gone against Boris like this, and I start to regret it as annoyance settles over his harsh features. But I can't help myself. I've chosen my path, and when he rounds the desk, I run across the room and into the hall.

I should turn left, toward the door that leads to the stairs, but it's not the memory of the biometric scanner that stops me—it's the thought of being outside these familiar halls on my own. So I veer right, through the next door, into Aleksandr's bedroom and the en suite bathroom. I slam the door shut, but to my horror, I realize there's no lock. I've grown so accustomed to not having true privacy that I never noticed.

The thump of steady footfalls echoes through the bedroom, spurring me into motion. I jump into the empty jacuzzi tub and curl up behind the tall side. But it doesn't matter that Boris can't see me. He knows I'm here, and within seconds after the door opens, I'm hauled from the tub and over his shoulder.

I'm not done, though. I pound my fists against his back and kick my legs against his arms. But Boris is even bigger than Aleksandr and easily rearranges me, curling me around his neck and trapping my limbs in his impossibly strong hands.

I whimper and try to cry out, but when he descends the stairs, I have to keep my focus on breathing since my stomach bounces against his hard neck, making me puff with each step.

In the dojo, Boris places me stomach-down on the floor and pins me in place with a heavy boot on my back.

"Wonderful. She's in a troublesome mood." Aleksandr's voice is full of evil glee. He's provoking me. And it works.

I start to struggle again, writhing without getting anywhere. I stare up at him with furious eyes as he approaches, one calm step at a time. He's changed into his white karate pants, which hang low on his hips, and his upper body is bare, showing off toned muscles built for strength and endurance.

He crouches beside me and wraps a cruel hand around my nape. "You asked for this yourself, remember?"

He hasn't even hit me yet, and I'm already furious, his words feeding my anger. I throw my hands back and grab onto his arm until I feel his skin break under my nails. I'm unable to control the growling noises of rage coming from my throat, and I already know this will be one of the times I scream my voice raw.

My angry hands are no challenge for Aleksandr. He simply tugs them off and gathers them at my neck, and with Boris's foot remaining on my back, I'm effectively immobilized from my waist up. "If you put marks on me, I'll put marks on you." In a sudden movement, Aleksandr releases my hands and fists my hair.

"Get up!" he growls so hard I flinch.

Boris removes his foot and asks in Russian, "Do you want help restraining her?"

"No, I'll enjoy doing this myself." With a tug on my hair, Aleksandr pulls me up, and I scramble to take some of the weight off my head. As soon as I'm upright, he yanks me into him with a steely arm around my waist.

I fight him with all my strength as I hear Boris leave the room. I kick and claw, strain and jerk. I even try to bite him.

Not even when he has me spread out in chains do I give up. The only thing I don't do is scream—I won't give him the satisfaction. At least, I hold it in until the first crack of the whip. From then on, my screams don't let up until the whip has done its harrowing job and lands with a thud on the floor.

"I hope you got it all out?" Aleksandr comes up behind me and presses a kiss to my neck, his entire demeanor shifting from ruthless sadist to gentle protector. "You can't take any more."

Affectionately yet firmly, he wraps a hand around the back of my neck—the place he's gripped so many times to subdue my struggles. The place that makes me feel like prey. Today, there's no need to fight it. I crave his devastating possession.

I melt into his touch, seeking the comfort he so easily offers, and he rewards me with a "Good girl" and a soft kiss on my cheek.

After he's unchained me, he carries me to the garden room where he sits on the couch. Instead of curling me into his lap, he arranges me with my legs straddling his thighs and my stomach to his. Carefully, he presses a hand to the juncture above my butt, and when he strokes a finger down my back, I realize why.

I hiss at the sudden flare of pain.

He's broken my skin. Like I broke his. Or because that's what it took to chase away my rage?

How could I not realize he whipped me so hard? Somewhere along the way, I must have become so desensitized to the pain I didn't feel the full force of it.

"You're bleeding," he says in a low whisper, almost reverently. "No backless gown tonight, I'm afraid."

He leans his head on top of mine and holds me tenderly as I shake in his arms, coming down from the brutality and violence he unleashed upon me. Once the tremors die down, I'm a lifeless pile of limbs hanging against him. My head is blissfully empty, my chest free from heavy emotion, allowing an easy flow of breath.

"Boris," Aleksandr calls, the boom of his voice startling me. "Shh, sh, shhh," he soothes and rocks me with smooth side-to-side motions.

"She needs to have her back cleaned," Aleksandr tells Boris when he comes in half a minute later. "Maybe a few bandages."

Heavy thumps of boots leave the room, and when Boris returns, I'm half asleep in Aleksandr's arms.

"I have to go now," Aleksandr tells me, and I groan in dissatisfaction as he places me stomach-down on the couch. "I'm sorry, but I've already postponed an important meeting so I could whip you, and we need to see the seamstress soon, or the dress won't be ready on time." He slides his fingers into my hair, drawing small circles on my scalp. "Boris will take care of your back and bring you up to rest before it's time."

Aleksandr presses a gentle kiss behind my ear, gives Boris a couple of orders in Russian, and then he's gone.

I'm already on my way to a happy dream world when Boris

crouches beside me and runs a wet cloth across my back.

"Tebe ladna?" he asks softly.

Why wouldn't I be okay? My dazed mind scrambles for a moment before remembering.

The blood, the whipping.

I do register the extremeness of the situation, but it passes through my brain like a random thought. Nothing will disrupt the peace dulling my senses and pulling me into this floaty sensation.

"Mhh," I respond. I think I'm more than okay, but I can't form the words.

"*U tebya krovotechenie,*" he says, his frown palpable in his voice.

The knowledge that I'm bleeding sends a strange rush coursing through my veins. I'm not just bleeding. I'm bleeding from the marks Aleksandr gave me—marks of his possession.

Chapter 18

ALEKSANDR OPENS THE passenger door of a yellow sports car and holds my long gown as I get in.

For months, I haven't worn anything but robes and the occasional jeans and blouse when going outside in chilly weather. Now I'm in this long, golden, glittery gown that hugs my shape perfectly. Before Aleksandr took me, I would have loved this dress, but today it makes me feel awkward as hell. The shoes are even worse. High heels weren't exactly my forte before, and my feet struggle to remember how to keep a proper gait in the thin heels.

I pull down the visor when Aleksandr rounds the car. The woman staring back through the small mirror is hardly recognizable. Thick black lines and heavy dark shades surround my gray eyes, and a thick layer of bronze foundation, which doesn't fit my cool skin tone, covers my face. I've never been one for excessive makeup, having always kept it natural, but the stylist didn't ask, just applied.

Touching a finger to my sticky cheek, I wince. I want to smear the oppressive veneer right off.

"Too much makeup, I know." Aleksandr startles me as he gets into the driver's seat. There's no rebuke. He's simply agreeing with my unspoken disdain. Yet my face falls. Against the rational part of my brain—which doesn't have much say these days—I want him to see me as beautiful and desirable.

He sets the car into reverse and backs out of the immense garage that holds at least fifteen other sports cars and several black SUVs.

"I'll get someone else to do it next time," he says.

Taking one final look, I shudder and flip the visor back up. At least I got to wear my hair loose. The stylist gave me a nice haircut, but Aleksandr came in just in time to stop her from styling it further. I'm grateful for having one thing that feels familiar, but I'm not stupid. I know it's not for my comfort. It's to cover up the line of black numbers behind my ear.

My fingers unconsciously move to the collar. As if the numbers aren't enough, I have to wear this piece of metal around my neck. And now in public. Automatically, my fingers dig under the golden band in a futile attempt to loosen it as the air in my lungs becomes scarce. It hasn't felt this oppressive since the first night.

"Don't." Aleksandr gives me a sidelong look. "You'll want the reminder of who you belong to, or you'll just get lost."

I'm not sure I understand. He says so many cryptic things like this, which I can't wrap my head around—like he knows me better than I do myself. I want to be irritated by his assumptions, but the conviction in his voice makes my hand fall back into my lap.

"Most people will think it's an opulent piece of jewelry," he adds as we cruise down the long driveway lined with tall, beautiful trees.

Ignoring his words, I stare out the window and notice the black SUV in the side mirror. I saw Boris get into one of those earlier. It makes sense to bring a bodyguard for someone as rich as Aleksandr, but why the separate cars?

"Why don't you let Boris drive if he's coming?" I ask.

"I like to drive." Aleksandr flashes me a smile, ignoring my sour mood. The engine revs as he veers through the gates and onto the road. "What's the point of having nice cars if you don't get to drive them?" Bearing down on the speeder, he makes the car accelerate with staggering speed. My heart gives an extra thud as the car glides down the empty road with the ease of a mellow fifty miles per hour despite going closer to seventy.

"Is that why you kidnapped me in an SUV, then changed to the Jaguar?"

Aleksandr is unaffected by my hostile but truthful choice of words. Or maybe he simply has no problem acknowledging the fact that he kidnapped me.

"Exactly. The large car would be more practical if you put up a fight, and I needed Boris just in case."

"You drugged me." I don't follow. Why would he need a bigger car if I was out cold when he put me inside it?

"I did. But it wouldn't have been safe to stab you with a syringe if you were thrashing like a wild beast."

"I tried to fight you," I protest, unable to accept the picture he paints of me all but going willingly.

Aleksandr levels me with serious eyes. "You were very pliant, Astrid."

"You held a knife to my back."

Aleksandr makes an infuriating shrug. "Some people would scream anyway. You practically melted in my grip when I promised to catch you if you fell on the stairs. I knew right then that I had made the right decision to take you."

My stomach sours. Have I somehow brought this on myself?

Would he have let me go if I had fought a little harder? If I had screamed, maybe someone would have come to my aid.

As if reading my mind, he says, "Don't overthink it. You're where you belong now."

Turning my eyes back to the landscape outside, I ignore his words and lean my cheek against the expensive leather.

"Long drive. Try to get some rest." Aleksandr presses a button on the stereo, and smooth jazz filters through the speakers. The gentle rumble of the engine glides into the background, leaving only the vibrations that feel as good as having his gentle arms rock me after a harsh whipping.

He starts humming, and my eyes go heavy as I listen to his deep voice mixing with the warm notes of a saxophone.

I hear the rustle of fabric, and a moment later, he drapes his suit jacket over me. "Sleep, *krasivaya devushka. Dershu tebya.*"

Those last words send me straight back to that moment when I was staring down the long line of steps and he squeezed my arm reassuringly. They were the exact same ones. *I've got you.* The memory is as clear as if it happened yesterday. It seems cruel that he would repeat those exact words right this moment, but I'm not sure he's even aware that's what he's doing. When his large hand glides over my thigh, the gesture is reassuring and warm—there's no mockery. And why would there be? Those words never lie. It doesn't matter if he whips me, humiliates me, or kidnaps me. He always has me, and I don't doubt for a second that he would have caught me if I had tripped on those stairs.

We're still driving when I wake again. Out of habit, I'm about to rub my eyes, but Aleksandr stops me with a hand on my arm. I'm not used to makeup anymore. So I settle for blinking. "How long have I slept?"

"Over an hour."

"How long until we're there?"

"About forty-five minutes," he tells me.

I turn my attention to the serene landscape of fields and woods outside the car as I allow my body time to shed the cloak of sleep.

When the sluggish feeling finally subsides, I cast a glance at Aleksandr. He seems more relaxed than usual as he leans back in the seat, one hand resting on the bottom of the steering wheel, the other arm propped on the door.

"What is it you like about driving?" I ask.

"It's quiet. No phone calls or meetings. No people sucking up or wanting to call in favors. It's one of the few places I can leave my work behind."

"Where else?" I ask, curious to know more about this dichotomy of a man who has no qualms about locking a woman in a cage, yet also seems genuinely caring and protective.

He turns his head, and he hones his eyes in on me with startling darkness as his nose makes this predatory twitch that has my shoulders jerking with a sudden shiver.

"When I'm whipping you."

My eyes widen with something that might be horror, might be lust, and I become all too aware of the burning sensation lingering on my back.

"Don't look so shocked. You feel the same way."

"I don't." I shake my head, unable to accept any similarity between Aleksandr and me.

He scoffs. "No? Then why did you ask me to whip you today?"

I want to say I didn't, but he would only mock me because we both know what my minuscule nod meant.

Despite my lack of response, he keeps going, refusing to let me bask in denial. "You think it's so horrific what I do to you—lock you up behind pretty bars and whip you until you scream. But the truth is that your biggest prison is your own mind. The whip sets you free. So does the cage."

The only response I can manage is a shake of my head.

Furrowing his eyebrows, he watches me skeptically. "Tell me one thing that could clear your head before I took you."

"Whenever I was on stage. Playing."

He makes a tsk-sound. "You played great that night I saw you. But not more. Good technique, sense of detail and expression. Everything you've been taught. But your heart wasn't in it. Not truly. I wouldn't have chosen you for the festival program even if I didn't want you for myself. You were too much in your head, overthinking everything, wanting to impress."

His words are a stab to the gut, and my throat constricts with a growing lump. "That's because you were there."

"I saw you three weeks later when you played at a private dinner party. No pressure, nothing at stake. Just an extra wad of money. It was the exact same."

I turn my gaze to the scenery outside and press my fist to my mouth as I force back tears.

Sometime later when the trees and fields turn into dense neighborhoods, Aleksandr breaks the silence. "Remember that I've got you, Astrid. I won't leave your side for a second, okay?"

I turn my head to face him and am startled to find his expression alight with fierce protectiveness. It would be easy to think he says this to squash any hopes of escape, but his words are meant to reassure. And they work.

We take the highway leading around St. Petersburg and exit into an expensive neighborhood where the houses are big and far apart. Aleksandr stops in front of a large iron gate where he says his name into an intercom, and the gate slides open before us.

The grounds aren't nearly as big as Aleksandr's and neither is the house despite easily earning the title mansion. It ardently tries to seem even bigger and more impressive than it is with its many ornaments, statues, and columns. It looks vulgar, and I get the impression of someone with a small dick trying to compensate with his riches. What little green exists outside the shiny stone ground is under strict control—the grass pristine and flat, the bushes cut into round shapes. It might as well be plastic. There's none of the natural beauty of Aleksandr's wild, yet well-kept gardens.

"Who lives here?" I ask when Aleksandr helps me out of the car.

"A rich businessman." He wraps a protective arm around my waist and throws his keys to the valet.

"I don't like this place," I mutter half under my breath as we walk toward the imposing house. It's like it aims to intimidate with its tall, illuminated façade and excessive ornaments, and I unconsciously lean closer to Aleksandr.

He tightens his grip around me and leans down to whisper, "Neither do I."

"Then why are we here?" When Aleksandr doesn't answer, I go for another question. "Aren't you afraid I'm going to tell someone that you kidnapped me?"

Aleksandr stops, and I follow his eyes down to the place where my hand is clutching his suit jacket. My eyes slowly move back up to find his brows raised in a mocking expression. "Who would believe you?"

I loosen my grip and try to pull away, but Aleksandr refuses to let me go, and when we walk up the stairs to the large entrance, I'm more than grateful for the proximity.

My heart beats rapidly in my chest and anxiety twines around my lungs as we enter a huge lobby. Gilded moldings, painted marble, and lavish ornamentation assault my eyes. It's even more tasteless than the outside. But what's worse is not our surroundings. It's the people. A small group is gathered a bit farther into the large hall, and a din of noise drifts through the house from adjacent rooms.

I startle when a plump man breaks from the group and approaches us. "Aleksandr," he greets. "Finally, you decided to show up." He holds out his hand.

Taking his time, Aleksandr moves me to his left side and wraps his other arm around me before taking the proffered hand. "Viktor," he greets in a tight voice, and it's clear he doesn't like this man. He doesn't even try to hide it.

Turning his attention to me, Viktor drawls, "What do we have here? Is this your little pianist?" He extends his chubby hand to me, but Aleksandr intercepts with a hand on Viktor's arm, and I must say I'm relieved I don't have to touch this man.

Viktor flinches, but he clearly makes an effort to hide the humiliation. I get the feeling he's sucking up to Aleksandr when he ignores the dismissal and says, "Let me introduce you to my other guests."

Aleksandr steps straight past him, ignoring the offer as he takes me with him to the small group of people in fancy gowns and expensive suits. He shakes hands with the men but doesn't even spare the women a glance.

No one gets to shake my hand. Aleksandr stops the first two men like with Viktor, and the others get the hint. He doesn't even introduce me, and I tense up at his side, feeling out of place and unwelcome. Like he senses it, he starts caressing my waist as if to soothe me. It doesn't make much sense. The possessive grip and his soothing hand make me feel important and precious, but excluding me from the conversation insinuates unworthiness.

But as I watch him slip into conversation with the men, something dawns on me. He doesn't like any of these people, and I get why. They all seem overly saccharine and accommodating like the first man, and I remember what Aleksandr said in the car about everyone sucking up to him. A strange notion pops into my head. Could it be that it's not me who's unimportant, but these people who aren't good enough to socialize with me?

I hardly dare to believe it, but when a woman addresses Aleksandr, the notion solidifies.

"Where's Katya?" the woman asks. She's about my age and wearing the same vulgar amount of makeup. "She was more fun." Her eyes trail over me with unbridled disdain. "More... talkative."

Aleksandr levels her with an ice-cold glare, for the first time meeting her eyes. "She talked too much. Like you."

The woman goes positively rigid, her lips thinning into a firm line, and she doesn't utter another word. The man at her side does nothing to defend her, and I feel a small sliver of pity for her. She's quiet during the rest of the conversation, like me. But unlike me, she's uncomfortable and alone, whereas I'm comfortably tucked against Aleksandr's side with his protective arm around my waist.

Soon after, Aleksandr moves us farther into the house. He greets a few people in the crowded sitting room but doesn't stop to chat with anyone else even though several people try to engage him in conversation.

I can't stop thinking about what that woman said about

Katya. Who is she? His ex? Current lover? Just because he doesn't keep other women in his house doesn't mean he doesn't have a lover on the side that he sees in the city. I don't know why it hasn't crossed my mind before.

I remember Aleksandr saying he hadn't had a good fuck in a year. At the time, I thought he meant he had abstained from sex for a year, but as I think back to his exact words, I realize it might as well mean he hasn't had *good* sex in a year. Maybe that's why he never fucks me. He sates his needs elsewhere.

A painful stab of envy jabs into my chest, and I press my lips together to hold back the unwelcome emotion.

A waiter approaches and holds a silver tray full of champagne flutes up to me. I give him a small shake of my head. I don't dare to accept anything without Aleksandr's permission.

Aleksandr picks up a glass, and I'm surprised when he offers it to me.

Peering up at him with uncertainty, I meet a warm gaze so unlike the cold, almost cruel look he gave the woman in the hall. "Would you like one?" he asks when I hesitate.

With a nod, I tentatively accept the champagne and hold the glass awkwardly, like I'm not supposed to have it. "Uhm, thank you."

Aleksandr waves the waiter off without taking a glass for himself. "You're doing great, Astrid," he says, stroking his knuckles over my cheek.

"Who's Katya?" I blurt, the question too urgent to contain.

I wait for coldness to seep into his eyes and freeze out the warmth. But it doesn't come.

"Is that why you're so tense?" His hand curls around my fingers holding the flute, and his eyes darken. I think he's about to take the champagne away as a punishment, but I quickly realize it has nothing to do with my question. "Don't break the stem. I don't want your hands cut and bleeding."

Oh. Realizing I'm clutching my hands, I relax my fingers and stare longingly at the glass as he slips it from my hand and places it on a nearby table.

"You may ask questions." He tilts my chin up to bring my eyes back to his. "As long as you do it respectfully and I haven't ordered you to stay quiet. If I don't want to answer, I won't."

My mind works in overdrive as I try to process his unexpected gentleness.

"Have I ever punished you for asking a question?"

I take a moment to consider and go through all those times I've asked him something. Mostly, he's given me an honest answer. Sometimes an order to stay quiet. But never has he punished me for asking a question.

I give a slight shake of my head and let the calm blue of his eyes pull me in.

"Katya was a girl I used to see. Arm-candy." He shrugs. "The occasional fuck."

The idea of Aleksandr fucking someone who isn't me—past or present—has my stomach churning. I avert my eyes, but Aleksandr brings them back with a hard squeeze on my jaw.

"*Was*," he emphasizes, and a smile creeps into his features. "My dogs also get jealous if I pet other animals. I find it rather cute."

Red seeps into my cheeks, but I can't help the next question. "So you're not seeing anyone else?"

He releases my face. "I already told you, I haven't had sex in over a year."

"Why?"

"I don't care for women." His mouth curls in a sneer. "I'd

rather be without sex than bring them into my bed."

My eyes fall to the ground as my chest constricts. God, it shouldn't hurt this much. I should know that I'm nothing to him. But when his hand comes up to cup my cheek, the soft caress of his thumb seems to renounce the thought.

"I'm a woman," I say so softly I don't think he hears.

"Astrid, look at me."

I tentatively lift my gaze to his.

"You're mine," he counters with fierce determination. There's no further explanation, no reassurance. At least not verbally. Those eyes seem to reflect everything he's not saying. Being his somehow nullifies the fact that I'm a woman—renders it inconsequential—and because I'm his, he cares about me. Like he cares about his dogs. "Do you understand?"

I nod. I don't fully understand—Aleksandr is a riddle I don't know if I'll ever solve—but I'm slowly starting to get a sense of how this man works.

"What else do we need to get out of the way?"

Is he inviting me to ask more questions? Or is it some kind of trap? No, Aleksandr doesn't do traps. So I pull in a deep breath and accept the invitation. "Have you ever done this to someone else?"

"What? Taken them to a party?"

"Kidnapped them. Locked them in a cage." My words are barely a whisper as they leave the safety of my lips.

Snaking his fingers around my jaw, he hardens his grip, and his eyes go dangerous with primal lust. "No one's ever begged me so blatantly to be owned."

"What— I—" I can't find the right words. I can't find any words as I try to wrap my head around his statement.

He leans in close, his breath hot against my lips. "People

want a lot of things from me. Money, power, a better life. Marriage and kids. People have begged me for it all. But never have I seen such a blatant need for someone to be stripped bare and have everything taken away."

"I didn't—" I choke on the words.

"Oh yes, you did. The burden of freedom weighed so heavily on your shoulders that I went straight home and ordered the cage—even before I got a chance to examine my hunch further."

He releases my chin and picks up the champagne flute, which he hands to me. "Luckily, it proved to be right, so those beautiful bars didn't go to waste."

I stare at the bubbly liquid confined to the elegant glass in his hand, and it's not until he says, "Drink," that I take it and put it to my lips.

"Easy there," he warns, putting a hand on my wrist.

I take the glass from my lips and settle for a small sip instead of chugging the contents.

"Better." Aleksandr tucks me into his side again and leads me to another room.

He makes another round of greetings in a sitting area before he brings me onto a couch with him, where he starts chatting with a couple of the men. Since it's in rapid Russian, I only catch half of it. But I don't listen anyway. It seems to be business and politics, neither of which I've ever found interesting.

I've never been good at small-talk and idle chatting, and being silent among people would always make me tense and self-conscious. But there's something oddly freeing about being here with Aleksandr, letting him do all the talking and not being expected to do any of my own.

Even if I did feel like chatting, I wouldn't know who to strike up a conversation with. There seems to be a distinct separation between the sexes, and the women all seem snobby. Some even throw me a few disdainful glares. I think it's because I'm with Aleksandr—his hand is trailing affectionately up and down my thigh and not theirs.

Despite everyone looking rich and important, I get the impression that Aleksandr is above most. There are only a few men here who he addresses with genuine respect. None of the women get as much as a glance from him even though several cast long glances in his direction. It's only when one of them keeps glaring at me that he acknowledges her presence—although to her husband.

"Get your woman and her hateful eyes under control," Aleksandr says with cool authority.

The woman gets a hushed but stern admonishment from the man at her side. I can tell she tries to hold on to her dignity, but her disposition turns tense and meek. I should probably feel bad for her, but I simply can't muster it.

"Are you okay?" Aleksandr urges my attention to him with a squeeze on my thigh. His eyes have gone from lethal to calm and concerned in the blink of an eye, and I can't help feeling a little pride at being under this powerful man's protection—being the one woman he sees.

I give him a slow smile. "Yes."

He wraps an arm around me and pulls me closer. "Good. Let me know if anyone bothers you."

At my small nod, he turns back to the two men, who politely stopped talking. But even as he resumes the conversation, his attention remains on me in gentle strokes and reassuring squeezes.

I'm not sure how long we've been here when Viktor comes up to us—an hour maybe, if even that much. He leans down to

Aleksandr and says discreetly, "*My gatovy k nei.*"

I stiffen at Aleksandr's side. "What?" *Did he just say they're ready for me?* I try to straighten, but Aleksandr keeps his arm firmly locked around my shoulders. I beg as panic rises in me. "Please don't," I whimper and push at him, convinced some public humiliation is at hand.

Aleksandr grabs my chin and levels me with a sharp stare. "The piano, Astrid. You're playing the piano."

His words push the panic back, but another fear takes its place when my eyes drift through the room to the grand piano and all the people scattered around it.

"It's newly tuned, just for you, miss," Viktor says, clearly trying to reassure me. "It's a Steinway of the best quality, shipped in from America. I think you'll find it very much to your liking."

My eyes flicker back and forth between Viktor, Aleksandr, and the piano. What the hell is going on? Is this why we're here? So I can play in front of all these people? I can't do that. I haven't played for anyone except Aleksandr for half a year.

"I can't." I unconsciously grab at Aleksandr's slacks. *When did I get so comfortable around him?*

"Yes, you can," he says with conviction—that same confidence that so often seeps into my bones and makes me believe him. "You played for me this morning, and you will do it again now."

My eyes dart off to the many people in the room. "But—"

Locking my chin in a harsh grip, he forces my attention back to him. "None of these people matter. The only person you're playing for is me. *Yasno?*"

My hands start to tremble, but he gathers them both in his, and the strength in his grip chases away the worst anxiety. So I nod.

He brings me to him and hugs me tight. "You'll do this for me," he whispers. His fingers glide up under my hair to stroke the edge of my collar, and a surge of purpose washes through me.

But the confidence is brief. When he releases me and guides me to stand on my feet, a new wave of anxiety hits me. "What shall I play?" I ask in a low voice, only for him to hear.

His answer is without hesitance. "Borodin's 'Polovtsian Dances.'"

My breath lodges. I haven't even played that piece for him. I've barely even polished off the final details. "It's not ready."

"Sure it is. I heard you play it last night."

I fidget my hands in front of me and blink my unfocussed eyes. I can't do this. I just can't.

Aleksandr scoots farther out on the couch and takes both my hands in his. "It's the most beautiful thing I've heard you play. I want to hear it now."

He must have been listening in the doorway. The door is always open, and I get so absorbed in the music he could easily have stood behind me without me noticing. I can't refuse him when he says it like this. And I do want to play the piece for him. I've wanted to for a while but couldn't find the courage. But now, as I gaze into his certain eyes, I soak up his confidence and let it become my own.

I straighten my spine. "Okay. I'll play for you."

"Good girl." Releasing my hands, he gives me a go-ahead nod, and I make my way through the crowded room and take a seat at the piano. My hands are already itching to touch the keys as I take in the beautiful instrument before me.

Closing my eyes and inhaling deeply, I hear the notes I'm about to play. I've always done this, prepared the music mentally before sharing it with an audience. But this time, I also hear something else. It's Aleksandr's resolute voice, telling me to play for *him*. The remaining uncertainty dissipates, leaving me calmer than I've ever been before putting my hands to the keys in front of a crowd.

I lift my right hand to trace the solid steel around my neck. The feeling grounds me further, and my left hand is calm and steady as I put it to the keys and set off the uneven rhythm that is the pulsing heartbeat of the first part. My right hand joins in with the first notes of the melody before I add the flurry of notes that wraps the melody in lacy structures.

The music carries me on, making my fingers dance on the keys of their own accord, adding trills and ornamentations I hadn't planned. Everything comes naturally, without thought or contemplation, and I feel more alive than I ever have as I leave myself behind and merge with the music.

When I come to the bombastic part with the heavy chords and deep notes, goose bumps erupt all over my skin, and my breaths come in long gushes of air from deep in my lungs. Leaning in over the piano, I soak up the weight of it all, and when I move into the bright, snappy part, I straighten and let my fingers roll back and forth as the majestic life pervades my entire being.

Then I'm back to the first theme, and the lightness makes me soar even as my hands fly frantically over the keyboard to make all the notes and add on new layers I haven't practiced. I roll into an improvised cadenza, mixing bits and pieces of Borodin's melodies into my own structures and intricate webs. Then I finish with a resolute trill and a staggering descent and end it all on a thunderous note that makes me jump on the bench.

My heart pounds like a drum that wants the music to go on and on. It's the only sound. The room is quiet around me.

Disconcertingly so. I cast a nervous glance up, and the now overcrowded room breaks into a din of applause that assaults my fragile mind. I feel raw and exposed, like I've broken myself open and poured my soul out for everyone to see.

My music has never felt as personal as it does today, and suddenly, Aleksandr's words from the ride here ring devastatingly true. My soul wasn't in the music the first night he heard me play. It never was when I played for an audience. Not until tonight.

My hands start shaking as I realize how much I've given these people. I search the noisy crowd for Aleksandr, needing the stability of his eyes. But I can't find him. Everyone is watching me. Everyone but him.

The shaking spreads to the rest of my body, and I hug myself as I frantically flit my eyes across the room. No Aleksandr. Only strangers.

He promised he would be by my side the whole time. But now he's gone.

Black spots flicker before my eyes, and the room and all the people close in on me.

Someone grabs my arm, and I jump. Fear constricts my lungs, and I press my free hand to my chest as I gasp for air.

"I'm here. *Dershu tebya*," a familiar voice assures close to my ear.

Then I'm on my feet. A strong arm wraps around my waist and presses me into the side of a warm body. The grip remains on my arm. It's the same unrelenting hand that took me from the train station. The same hand that held me down when I was marked like an animal. But also the same hand that has held me so many times when I broke down—caressed me and put me back together.

I can't make sense of it. So I don't try. As I've done many times before, I give in to this powerful man and let his strength hold me up.

Fast-paced steps spur my feet to move at the same tempo. Then a gush of fresh air hits me as the overly bright lights disappear. The same hands shove me into a car and fasten my seat belt. The scent of leather and citrus lingers in the air, wrapping me in safety as the car begins to move.

It takes a long time before the haze settles and I finally turn my gaze to the man beside me—the beautiful, cruel, protective man who has become my entire world. A flood of emotion hits me without warning, and the shaking intensifies, rattling my entire body. I clutch my arms as the world spins around me and my stomach churns with nausea.

The car comes to a stop at the side of the road, and Aleksandr unclips my seat belt to pull me down to lie with my head in his lap. I clench the fabric of his dress pants as everything bubbles to the surface, spilling out from my eyes in streams of tears.

He presses one hand to my head while sliding the other over my back. Soothing strokes ease the flood of emotion, making the grief, longing, and overwhelming gratefulness easier to bear.

"It's a shame you're not going to play the Mariinsky. People would pay good money to see you." Blatantly and shamelessly honest, Aleksandr always gives me the truth.

But I don't care about the Mariinsky. I don't care about playing for a thousand people who are paying to see me. I only care that *this* man sees me. That *he* wants my music.

He carefully lifts me by the shoulders and takes my head between his hands. "You're mine. You're finally feeling it, aren't you?"

I nod between his warm hands, and the confession spurs

more tears from my eyes. They keep dripping into the cups of his hands as I stare at him, stark naked, bared to the bottom of my soul—a depth I've never encountered before. Now, it's his too. Just like everything else.

His eyes fall to my lips, and he slowly leans in. Hovering only a breath from me, he angles his head in anticipation of a gentle kiss. My skin hums, tickling and shivering beneath his warm breath, beneath the minuscule pulsing of muscles in his hands.

He closes the distance and presses his lips to my wet cheek. It's disappointing and heart-fluttering at the same time. And it's only the beginning. Languidly, he moves his lips to mine. A gentle brush sends shivers shuddering down my arms. Then he slants his head and unites our lips in a long, firm kiss.

My salty tears linger on his mouth, intensifying the intimate connection between us. I moan as his tongue ventures forth, parting my lips to gain entrance. I eagerly open, and my shoulders slump in surrender as I lean my head up in the frame of his hands.

Our tongues begin a languid dance of gentle strokes and swirls. It's sweet and seductive. Explorative and curious. Like tasting a new flavor of ice cream. But as with everything else this man does, tenderness can't exist without brutality. He slips a hand up and fists my hair close to the scalp as he crushes our lips together.

The ground falls away from beneath my feet as hunger and violent possession clash with desire and tender lust. I can't find my footing in the stormy haze, but Aleksandr keeps me steady even as he throws my world into chaos.

His free hand moves to my shoulder, digging his fingers in with bruising strength. Then it shoots up to my neck, flexing around my windpipe, and back to my cheek to feel the wetness that still coasts down my face. It's like he can't get enough. He growls through the intensity, and I helplessly succumb to the storm, soaking it all up—the pain, the pleasure, the overwhelming emotions still wrenching at my chest.

His hand moves to my breasts, massaging viciously as he holds me in place by my hair. Tendrils of fire flare in my core, and suddenly, I'm moaning and bucking uncontrollably. I want his touch like I've wanted nothing in my life before. I want this man more than anything else.

Breaking the kiss, he moves his hands farther down, shoving and pulling at fabric to gain access to my sex. But the dress is too long, and with a frustrated grunt, he releases my hair and grabs the fabric over my chest with both hands.

Riiip.

The sound of tearing fabric makes my eyes shoot down to stare at the ruined dress in shock. The golden fabric hangs in two pieces around my breasts, and another rip exposes my belly, another one my mound.

I whimper at the sight. The dress was stunning, and now it's ruined.

Aleksandr doesn't let me linger on the horror for long. Without preamble, he yanks my panties aside and thrusts two long fingers inside me.

"Oh God," I moan, my eyes widening as they shoot up to the fierce blue gaze in front of me.

Aleksandr's nostrils flare, and his expression burns with power and lust.

Driven by reckless, urgent need, I reach for his cock. It's hard and long behind his slacks—painfully so it seems. I fumble to open the button to free it, but Aleksandr grabs my wrist, and his fingers go still inside me.

"Are you ready to beg for it?" he asks with a simmering threat hanging at the edge of his words.

I give an almost imperceptible shake of my head. I want to. God, I do. But I still can't accept the defeat it would bring.

"Then keep your goddamn hands to yourself." He yanks my hand off, and I think this is it—he's going to shove me away and turn back to the wheel.

But Aleksandr is not done with me. Not by a long shot. Grabbing my hair again, he yanks my head back into the seat and picks up the thrusts inside me. This time, they are punishing, each thrust sending a deep stab of pain through my belly. I cry harder and strain against his hands, even as I'm moaning with desperate need.

"You're mine," he sneers against my ear. "Your music is mine. Your cunt is mine. Your orgasms are mine. And now I want you to be a good little slut and come all over my fingers."

My long wail fills the car, and my insides clamp around the merciless thrusts as I buck over the seat. I strain my head against the grip on my hair as the orgasm rips through me. The sharp pain—the relentless control—intensifies the acute pulsing in my veins. I keep squirming and spasming as wave upon wave of painful pleasure tears through my body.

"Good little slut." Aleksandr withdraws his fingers and smears the wetness across my tear-stained face. "Tell me who you belong to."

"You," I gasp as I slump in the seat. "I belong to you, Master."

Aleksandr turns my face to him, and a half-cruel, half-tender smile spreads across his lips. "You look like a goddamn mess."

I can't tell if he's mocking me or if it's a warped compliment, and when he claims me in a heated kiss that robs me of my breath, I don’t care.

Chapter 19

ALEKSANDR STARTS TO bring me to private parties regularly, and it's clear it's not so much about socializing as showing me off—putting my talent on display. Maybe it's even about granting me the opportunity to share my music with others.

After the first party, it slowly gets easier to play in public again. I don't talk to anyone at the parties, so the crowd is just a bunch of strangers. The only person who matters is Aleksandr. I find him with my eyes whenever I sit at the piano, and when I see his intent gaze trained on me and get a small nod, all the faces around him blur, and I play for him—and him alone.

It's not the same as when I'm playing for him back at his estate. The buzzing in the air and all the watching eyes somehow make it more important that he's the one receiving the music.

Ten minutes of recital quickly become twenty, and at some parties, I even get to play a full program of forty-five minutes. At those gatherings, I think I'm the main attraction, the reason for people showing up.

"Will she come play a concert at my place next weekend?" a man asks Aleksandr one night. "I have a great Steinway, and I'll make sure to gather a good crowd."

"I'll think about it," Aleksandr replies. It seems he's the one doing the inquiring man a favor rather than the other way around. I've become a desired feature that lends a party a certain degree of significance. And I'm making Aleksandr rich in the currency of favors, which seems to be more important than money in this world.

People even start asking for me at one point. "When are we going to hear her play?" they ask Aleksandr.

And some women address me directly. "What are you playing tonight?"

Aleksandr seems annoyed by this and often writes them off in some more or less impolite fashion. "You'll see," he'll say, or more blatantly, "Don't talk to her."

The men, though, seem to get the message more clearly, directing their questions at Aleksandr. He's respectful enough, but the large majority of people seem to fall into the category of wanting something from him, trying to suck up. Only a rare few incite respect in him. He's more engaged in the conversations with these men, and his beautiful smile draws small lines at the corners of his lips while the cold blue of his eyes becomes less hostile.

He generally seems less hostile these days. Not only at the parties does he loosen up more frequently, but also at home. So much so he grants me more freedom.

I get more time out of the cage room—in the immense garden, at the piano, and even in a big library downstairs. Though it's still with a guard to keep an eye on me or a chain around my foot.

I don't think it's because Aleksandr doesn't trust me or fears that I'll run off. It's about taking my freedom—blatantly and demonstratively. Flaunting my captivity in my face and making me feel it at my very core. Aleksandr has branded it so deep into me I have a hard time handling any choices besides the one he gives me at the piano.

There, my creativity blossoms like it has never done before. I produce splendid piano transcriptions of orchestra works and play old piano music with a new kind of vigor. But if Boris tries to be nice and ask me what I want for lunch or give me a stack of books to choose from, I get overwhelmed and end up saying I'm not hungry or that I'm fed up with books. Luckily, he brings me food anyway and leaves a book for me. Soon, he stops asking altogether.

The same inability to act independently goes for my new freedom of roaming the cage room on my own during the day. Instead of locking me inside the cage, Boris will lock me inside the room. The first time this happens, I sit on the couch and stare into thin air for what seems like an hour. The next day, I pace the space until my legs are tired, then try to read, and go back to pacing when my mind refuses to make sense of the words.

Part of me likes the freedom, but mostly I feel like a trapped animal pacing its cage. The urge to scratch the walls, kick the door, or jump out the window jitters inside me, and I can't rest for more than mere moments.

I might have found some kind of peace with my situation and accepted the futility of fighting, but I still can't accept how broken my mind is. I can't accept that I start wanting—no, needing—the horrible things Aleksandr does to me.

The self-deprecating thoughts are louder outside the bars, and when they screech like nails on a chalkboard, the only way to quell them is to crawl into the cage and pull the lid shut. There, in the safety of the confined space, they fade, leaving me blissfully calm. My mind won't even confront me with the fact that I voluntarily crawled into the cage. I save those disturbing thoughts for the next time someone lets me out.

The first time Aleksandr finds me half asleep in the cage, he emits a pleased rumble. I stir and gaze up with drowsy eyes to see him crouching beside me.

"So beautiful," he croons, reaching through the bars to caress me. "I knew you would come to appreciate the cage." He gets up, and when I hear the metallic click of a lock, a *thank you* hovers at the tip of my tongue.

From that day on, Aleksandr only allows me short periods of time alone outside the cage.

As Aleksandr becomes more lenient in some ways, he becomes more brutal in others. It's like he needs one to balance the other. Even though I rarely go against him and I readily seek out his comfort when emotions wreak havoc on me, he keeps whipping me every so often.

But apparently, the whippings aren't enough.

One day when Anton brings me to the dojo, Aleksandr's eyes gleam with a certain kind of cruel brutality I haven't seen for a long time. Instead of his usual karate pants befitting the room, he wears charcoal slacks, a blue shirt, and a midnight blue tie that hangs loose around his neck.

He hauls me into the room by my neck and shoves me stomach-down to the floor. Then he presses his foot to my back with a weight that makes breathing difficult. He's even wearing shoes, and the hard sole digs into my skin, making me whimper.

He flips my robe up and smacks my ass a few times before slipping his fingers through my folds. "Already starting to get wet," he mocks, then says to Anton, "You want a go at her?"

"What? No," I squeak and shove at his leg.

"Shut up." Aleksandr yanks my head back by the hair, into a position that forces me to go still and focus on breathing through my strained neck. Ignoring my labored wheezing, he turns back to Anton. "C'mon, I know you like a tight cunt, and this one, I tell you, is as tight as they come."

Anton looks down at my panicked face. "Are you sure?"

"Why else would I ask?" Aleksandr deadpans like it's a stupid question.

Aleksandr releases my hair, and I spend a moment regaining a steady flow of breath. But the sound of the tearing foil of a condom throws me back into a panting panic, and I strain backward, shoving my hands into the floor to push up. Once again, Aleksandr kills my struggles, this time by moving his foot to the back of my neck. The square heel digs painfully into the sensitive spot, and I don't dare to move. Instead, I whimper through clenched teeth as Anton sinks to his knees between my legs.

Aleksandr forces my attention away from the devastating sound of a belt and a zipper. "Why is this happening?"

"Because you want it to," I choke.

"Does anything else matter? Does your pitiful opinion make a difference?"

"No." I clench and un-clench my hands and scratch at the mats, desperate for something to hold on to.

"Grab my leg and hold on as I whore out your tight little cunt." His words are cruel, but amidst the coldness, I hear a sliver of care. And when I grab onto his leg and dig my fingers into his shin, a strange sense of gratitude mixes with the horrific humiliation.

Calloused hands spread my legs further apart and foreign fingers prod between my folds to reveal my devastating wetness.

"Is she wet?" Aleksandr growls.

Anton confirms. "*Ochen.*"

Aleksandr removes his foot from my neck and bends to push two fingers straight inside me. "You want this, huh? You're such a dirty little slut that you don't care whose cock goes inside that wet hole of yours?"

"Nooo," I whimper even as my pussy clenches around the intrusion.

He turns his fingers around in my wetness and pumps a few times. Then the fingers are at my face, and he grabs my neck as he holds two glistening digits to my mouth. "No?" he challenges. "Taste for yourself."

I open my mouth, just a smidgen, and Aleksandr shoves his fingers past my lips, onto my tongue.

"Your head might struggle to accept that you're mine, but your body has no trouble knowing who it belongs to." Aleksandr rubs his slick fingers over my tongue, and I whimper at the musky taste of myself. Humiliation courses through my veins, but instead of tearing at my soul, it drives me into that fluffy, submissive state where only his will matters.

"You're mine," Aleksandr sneers. "Everything you have is mine, and if I want to whore you out, you'll obediently spread your legs and thank me afterward. *Yasno?*"

I nod, and my legs spread further as his words sink into my very brainstem, where they settle like a fundamental truth. *I'm his, and only his will matters.*

Anton slowly presses his thick erection inside me. It's been so long since I've had anything but my own or Aleksandr's fingers in there that the stretch is painful. I groan and whimper, but my legs remain parted, making no effort to dispel the degradation.

"Good little whore," Aleksandr praises. "I knew you'd love having your pussy filled."

God, I wish it was Aleksandr's cock. But as my inner walls adjust to the stretch and Aleksandr keeps up the taunting appraisals, it doesn't matter who's inside me. Because this comes from Aleksandr. He's the one making Anton do it. He's the one telling him to go faster. The one holding me down.

Soon, my desperate whimpers turn into desperate moans as Anton picks up speed. Tension gathers deep in my belly, and my nerves hum with anticipation.

"Who do you belong to, little whore?" Aleksandr demands.

"You," I moan. "You, Master."

He leans down, his breath hot against my ear. "Come for your master, little slut."

His words throw me over. I scream through a violent orgasm, arch my back and curl my toes as pleasure shoots through my body. I can't remember ever coming like this. The orgasm keeps rolling on and on as Anton finds his release in me, and even after he pulls out, I'm twitching on the ground from the aftershock.

"Now, thank me for whoring you out," Aleksandr commands.

"Thank you, Master. Thank you so much." Against all my rational awareness, having someone fuck me on his order is as big a gift as the piano, and my gratitude is painful as I keep thanking him.

Just like he said I would.

Chapter 20

A FEW DAYS LATER, Aleksandr comes into my room in the middle of the day.

"Have you touched my cunt today?" His eyes are dangerously dark as he opens the cage.

My cheeks go positively red as I close my book and stare up at him. He has asked this question several times a day after he came in and found me with rosy cheeks and wet fingers a few hours after Anton had fucked me. Normally, I'd only masturbate at night when the lights have gone off, but the episode in the dojo stirred this intense desire that I can't quell.

That night, when he discovered that I'd touched myself, I expected him to be mad even though he's never forbidden me to do so. But when he grabbed my wrist and smelled the evidence on my fingers, a smirk spread across his face. "You dirty, dirty girl. Already craving more cock, huh?"

He shoved my fingers into my mouth and made me lick them clean, then ran them through the wetness between my legs before forcing me to lap up my juices again. He repeated over and over until I was begging him with desperate need.

"What do you want, dirty little girl?" Grabbing my chin, he leaned into my face. "My cock? Is that it?"

I nodded, a minuscule movement.

"Then ask me for it." He adjusted the massive length straining against his pants, and when I remained quiet, his voice became deadly stern. "Ask me to fuck you, Astrid."

I tried. I really did. I ached to say the words, but I just couldn't.

Aleksandr was furious when I shook my head, and tears streamed down my cheeks as I whimpered a pathetic, "I can't."

He burst out of the room and returned with leather cuffs to restrain me the same way he had when the lanky man nearly raped me—wrists in cuffs, chained to the bars behind my head.

I begged and cried, but Aleksandr was cold determination personified.

Instead of leaving me like he did the last time, he stayed in the room the rest of the evening.

My distraught condition clearly got to him. After a restless while of watching me from the couch, he started pacing, dragging his hands through his hair and sighing heavily. Then he tried to soothe me with gentle caresses. But he never relented and let me come.

When night fell, he took me to his bed and rocked me in his arms until exhaustion claimed me into a fitful sleep.

His first words when he left the bed the next morning were a growled, "Don't touch yourself."

I haven't touched myself since then, knowing he'd be able to tell if I was lying. My body is constantly taut with the need to come, but Aleksandr is determined to let me suffer for not begging him to fuck me. It's been three days now, and I'm about to go insane.

"Have you touched yourself?" Aleksandr repeats when I only shake my head.

"No," I say, staring up at him with indignant eyes.

Aleksandr opens the cage and grabs my chin, holding my head up to search for signs of deceit. But he doesn't find any.

"Give me your hands." He tastes all ten fingers, one at a time, then drags me out of the cage.

I stagger behind him to keep up with his long strides as he drags me through the room. When we reach the desk, he suddenly jerks me around and rips my robe off with one fabric-tearing jerk.

"Bend over the desk."

Too stunned to question, I bend at the waist and press my stomach to the cool surface.

"Spread your legs."

When I'm too slow to move, he kicks my feet apart, and I grab onto the wooden edge for purchase.

Anxious fear crawls over my naked skin. I have no idea what's coming. I just know it won't be good.

The grazing of fingertips along my spine sends an icy shudder through me. The touch is gentle, but violence crackles in the air around Aleksandr.

And in a flash of movement, it explodes.

Smack! The sound of his large hand crashing down on my ass echoes through the room.

I squirm on the table, but he effortlessly pins me in place with a single hand on my back as he rains a torrent of loud smacks down on my butt. The force screeches through my body. I whimper and cry out, but Aleksandr keeps going, only pausing to check if I'm wet.

At first, I think he's crazy. How will I ever get wet from this assault? But as he keeps going, the pain turns into tingling heat, my pained cries become moans, and my pussy becomes wet—

humiliatingly so.

Aleksandr is cold efficiency when he feels the slickness coating my inner lips. No taunting remark or rubbing it in my face. He's achieved his goal and proceeds to yank me to my feet, down the hallway, and into his office.

My breath stutters in my lungs when I see the half-naked woman standing beside his desk. She's tall and thin with long brown curls that spill over large tits. Everything about her gives off hooker vibes. Her trashy blue eyeshadow, Botox-pumped pink lips, vulgar lingerie, and platform heels. But knowing Aleksandr and what Boris told me about his dad's women, she can't be a hooker. He'd never fuck a prostitute. Right?

The thought does little to reassure me. She's clearly here to please Aleksandr. No amount of reasoning will change that. This is my punishment for not begging him to fuck me, and no matter who this woman is, it's going to hurt like hell.

I shake my head hopelessly. "Please don't."

"Don't what?" Aleksandr asks without emotion.

"Please don't make me watch." I can't do it. I just can't. Watching him fuck another woman will tear me apart. I'm not sure I'll ever recover from such a betrayal.

It's not a betrayal, a cruel voice reminds me. How can it be when I have no claim to him—when I have no claim to anything in this world? How can it be when he's never fucked me?

I start shaking all over, and I fall to my knees before Aleksandr. "Please don't."

"Oh, *krasivaya devushka,*" he says tenderly as he crouches in front of me and takes my chin between his fingers. A broad smirk spreads across his face. "She's not for me."

I don't understand. I stare blankly at him through blurry eyes as I try to gauge his intentions.

Turning me to face the slutty woman, he says close to my ear, "The whore is for you."

My eyes widen as I see the woman strap on a dildo harness. But I'm too relieved to protest when Aleksandr takes me to his desk and ties me down, bent over with my ass in the air.

It's only when he leaves me to go sit in a recliner a few feet away that my brain catches up. This woman—no, prostitute—is going to fuck me with a strap-on.

No, no, no, no. My brain reels from the realization, and I buck against the straps. It's no use. Aleksandr has spread my limbs so wide I can only move a few inches off the surface. Once again, I'm helpless to prevent his cruel humiliation.

"*Nachinay.*" Aleksandr orders the woman to begin, his voice cold as slithering ice.

"Please don't do this," I implore with all the urgency I can muster. "I won't ever touch myself without permission again."

"This is not a punishment, my sweet slut." With measured movements, he rises from the chair and stalks up to me. Fisting my hair, he leans down and sneers into my face, "My horny little slut craves her pussy to be filled, and so she shall get it."

He straightens behind the desk and waves a hand to the whore. *Come closer.* The prostitute steps between my legs, and shame courses white-hot through me. It should be her down here. Not me.

Aleksandr picks up a black tube, which I can only guess is lube, and leans over me. The slick sound of the dildo being prepared spurs me into a cascade of whimpering and begging. I feel utterly pathetic, but I can't help it.

A long finger flickers through my nether lips—Aleksandr's finger, to my relief. But it's not his fingers I'm going to take, and when he adjusts the slick dildo at my opening, I go frantic. I yank at my arms and legs and whip my head from side to side, but the dildo advances just the same, slowly but inexorably pushing its way inside me.

It's not a small dildo to suit my unused pussy. Aleksandr has made sure to get a wide, thick one to make me feel every little nuance of this new degradation.

I cry out as the toy stretches my walls. It's so devastating it kills my fight. My yanking becomes small jerks as tears slip free and patter onto the wooden surface.

A large hand closes around the nape of my neck, and Aleksandr leans down, close to my ear. "What does a little slut say when her master grants her a huge cock?"

"Please don't, pleeease." I clench my teeth as the prostitute positions the dildo against my opening and I feel her hips nestling in the space between my legs.

Aleksandr tightens his grip and lowers his voice to a frightening rumble. "What does she say?"

"Thank you, Master. Thank you."

His thumb strokes along my hairline, soothing and approving. "That's it. Good little girl."

Something flips inside me at those words—that touch. I suddenly don't feel so dirty anymore. Not in a fundamental way. I relax under his touch and relax my muscles around the violation seated inside me.

"Keep your eyes on me while I let the whore fuck you." Aleksandr's words are gentle, but when he retreats to the chair, his eyes are cold and commanding.

"Fuck her. Hard," he orders the prostitute without releasing my gaze.

The woman rears back, taking the dildo with her.

"It's very befitting that I have a filthy whore fucking my little slut, don't you think?" Aleksandr mocks.

His words should snuff out the desire he awoke with the spanking, but somehow, they drive it higher.

Thin, frail hands wrap around my hips, and before I can answer, the woman slams the dildo inside, all the way to the hilt.

My eyes widen, my mouth falling agape as I choke on a gasp. Pulsing fire thrums within my core, fiery and hot. I can't decide if it hurts more or spikes the thrumming need inside me.

Aleksandr smirks, wide and mocking, yet with a note of appraisal hidden in the depths of his eyes. "I knew you'd like this, you filthy little slut. Maybe I should have her fuck your mouth afterward—let you taste how wet you are."

I whimper, and the sound becomes a shrill wail as the woman repeats the hard thrust.

My hands clench and unclench around the edge of the desk. Pounding noises fill my ears, and the room goes blurry as throbbing pain bursts through my core.

"Look at me," Aleksandr demands.

I blink my eyes rapidly to focus on the mighty man who holds the strings to this degrading scenario—and to my very soul. As I stare into his blue, blue eyes full of unwavering power, I can't deny the feelings he stirs inside me. I'm not sure if it's love or even affection. It's something rooted at the base of my primitive instincts. Desire, lust, and most of all, the need to obey.

God, I want to exist under his command, earn his praise, and take his punishments. It doesn't matter which. I want whatever he gives me, and right now, it's a prostitute with a strap-on.

I relax in the bonds, and when the woman slams into me again, the pain isn't as acute. Another thrust and my nerve endings start to hum.

"That's it," Aleksandr croons. "Can you be a good little slut and come for your master?"

"Yeees," I groan as the dildo shoves inside me again.

"Faster," Aleksandr growls, addressing the woman behind me without releasing me from his sharp gaze.

The woman picks up pace, panting as she fucks me with merciless speed, her hips slapping against my flesh with each hard thrust.

All I hear is Aleksandr's voice. "You're such a dirty girl, masturbating in your cage," he mocks. "So filthy, moaning no matter what cock goes into you."

He goes on like this. It's vile and derisive, but it only solidifies my place beneath him—the place where I belong—and heat builds with every cruel word.

"Thank you, Master," I moan, craving every little piece of his devastating control.

The woman becomes wilder in her movements, and her fingers dig into my hips with punishing force. I don't think she gets to dole out degradation often herself, and she seems to relish in the vile energy. Somehow, it only drives me closer to the peak because I know Aleksandr is the one who controls her thrusts. She's nothing but a means to exert his will.

I'm teetering on the edge of an explosive orgasm when everything suddenly crashes.

"Dirty, fucking slut," the woman spits. Her words are Russian, but I understand every snarled vowel perfectly well. Too well. They are full of venom and hate, and it's all directed at me.

Shame and humiliation flare inside me, snubbing out my breath and strangling my chest as she keeps ramming her hatred into me with each thrust of her hips.

Her words cut my connection to Aleksandr and erase every *good girl* he's ever spoken to me. Suddenly, it's not him holding the power over me. It's this whore who gets to use me as a vessel for her rage.

I'm nothing. I'm truly nothing.

I see the moment Aleksandr detects the change in me. Alarm flashes across his face, and his features turn hard as stone. He bursts up, and the chair scrapes across the floor behind him as he charges for the whore.

His raging voice thunders through the room as he rips her off me.

"*Yebannaya slyukha*," he roars. There's a dull thump of a fist, then the thud of her body crashing to the floor along with her shrill scream. "*Pashla von*!"

The door opens, someone enters, and Aleksandr barks more commands and curses. There's a struggle behind me, short but livid. And then the whore's screams fade as the door shuts.

The clicks of Aleksandr's shoes echo through the sudden silence as he rushes back to me. "Astrid," he says with startling concern as he moves soothing hands all over my body. "*Dershu tebya*. I've got you now. She'll never touch you again."

But it's too late. I've already shut down and closed in on myself. Neither his words nor his hands will break through the withered shell of emptiness.

I don't fight him when he unfastens the straps and takes me in his arms. I just sit there and stare into thin air, stiff and unmoving, as he strokes my hair and whispers soothing words of comfort.

Aleksandr tells me how beautiful and precious I am, unlike the "filthy trash of a woman"—like he calls her—that he never should have allowed to touch me.

He says all the things I've longed to hear, but none of it registers. Nothing registers. I'm reduced to a blank slate.

The world is tinted in gray colors and lifeless shades. When Aleksandr takes me to his bedroom and tries to feed me, everything tastes bland, and I only get a few bites down. And when he tries to talk to me—ask me how I am—I just stare at the wall.

This continues for several days. I barely eat or speak. I shut everything out and exist in a narrow world of painless emptiness.

Aleksandr is constantly at my side, kissing and caressing me as he tells me over and over again that I'm his and he's taking care of me. He ardently tries to capture my attention, but my eyes won't focus on anything.

With each failed attempt to reach me, he becomes more frustrated and restless. He paces the room, drags his hands through his hair, and even shakes me occasionally.

"Please look at me, Astrid," he all but begs on the fourth day.

The desperation lacing his words is foreign, and it tugs at some unwanted emotion deep in my gut. My eyes flicker up to his, and the regret I find there is more than I can take. It takes me out of the numbness for a moment, but all I find is painful confusion. I don't want to face these emotions, so I shut them back off and invite the emptiness back in.

A frustrated growl rumbles through the room, and Aleksandr yanks me up by the arm and hauls me off. "If you won't look at me, I'll goddamn make you."

He takes me to the dojo, where he ties me up and whips me. The pain nearly breaks me, but somehow, I manage to keep everything bottled up. I don't scream, I barely even groan. I just stand there as chaos builds within me. It builds and builds until the pressure threatens to break me into a million pieces. But I refuse to give it to him.

"Goddammit, Astrid. Will you stop being so stubborn?"

My only response is to clench my jaw tighter.

"*Blyad*!" he growls and throws the whip to the ground.

Aleksandr just swore. And not just a *goddamn*. The Russian equivalent of *fuck*. That one little word speaks volumes, but I don't allow myself to dwell on the magnitude of it.

"Take her down," Aleksandr roars, and Boris comes in and starts working on the cuffs while Aleksandr watches me with an intense mix of rage, frustration, and something akin to powerlessness. He looks like he's either about to tear the place apart or throw everything out the window and give up.

I've never seen him like this. It should scare me, but I can't bring myself to care.

"Take her to her room," Aleksandr orders, and Boris puts a hand on my back to guide me out. The gesture is sweet and supportive, but I jerk away from his touch. Boris is an extension of Aleksandr's will like everything else here.

Staying close behind me, Boris lets me walk on my own, and I consider running—hiding somewhere in this enormous house to spite Aleksandr. He'd find me sooner or later and the consequences would be dire, but it would be worth the anger on his face—the sliver of control I would regain.

But as we walk through the house, my energy evaporates.

Boris locks me up in the cage, and I slip back into nothingness, staring through the bars. Wrapping my arms around myself, I try to soothe the shivers. It's not the room temperature that chills me; it's the coldness within.

When Aleksandr comes in a while later, I'm in the same position, staring into the blank world in front of me. I feel hollow. Everything could crumble into ashes and I wouldn't care. So I keep staring, hoping I will somehow disappear into the black void.

Is this what it feels like to be broken? Has he finally done it? Does it matter at all?

Bitterness churns my stomach, and I throw my hand up to wipe away a tear that threatens to open a floodgate.

Aleksandr is a large shadow looming at the edges of my vision, and I feel his grave eyes prickle on my skin.

"Will you please just let me go?" The words slip from my mouth without thought. I sound like someone who has given up all hope. And maybe I have, but hearing those words sparks something inside me. So I lift my head and repeat with more clarity. "Will you please let me go?"

Aleksandr's mouth twitches as he gauges me. I think he actually considers it, and hope blossoms in my empty chest. But there is also something else. A heavy feeling of something I don't want to acknowledge.

Dread.

I get no answer. Aleksandr studies me a minute longer. Then leaves.

Boris brings me breakfast and a pile of clothes early in the morning. Usually, I get to sleep until the sunlight reaches my cage in the corner, but today dawn has barely broken.

"Eat and put on the clothes when you're done," he says when I go to the bathroom to start my normal routine.

When I come back out, I'm surprised to find him gone. A bit disappointed. I could use the company to distract me from my self-deprecating thoughts.

I take the chair at the desk and take a few bites of the rich breakfast. As I sit here with nothing else to think about, the bitterness from yesterday resurfaces and turns my stomach into angry knots.

When the door opens, I'm staring at the food, my hands clenching with the urge to throw it across the room. But I can't. I'm frozen in place by bitter anger.

"Get dressed." Aleksandr's voice lights fire to the pyre building within me.

I shake my head and clench my jaw, refusing to meet his eyes.

He leans in against my ear and lowers his voice to a dangerous command. "Get up. Get dressed. Now."

The pyre dwindles to embers, and the urge to cry rises in its stead. I force it down with all my might, and all that is left is an empty pit of pain.

Aleksandr uncurls my hands from the desk and pulls out the chair with me in it. "Don't make me repeat myself."

I put on the clothes without another protest. It's casual attire. Jeans, blouse, coat, and flat shoes.

I feel like a zombie when Aleksandr leads me through the house and outside, where the red jaguar is waiting for us.

"Get in," he orders.

It's only when I see Boris load a suitcase into the trunk that my brain begins to function again. Is Aleksandr giving me what I asked for last night? Is he letting me go? Panic and dread wrap a fist around my lungs as I imagine all it would entail. The world. The people. The never-ending mill of expectations, goals, and struggling to get by.

I watch Aleksandr as he goes to say something to Boris.

I would lose him.

The idea should make me happy, but it does anything but. A lump grows in my throat, and my voice is hoarse with fear when

Aleksandr grips my arm and hauls me to the passenger's side.

"Where are we going?" I ask.

"Just do as you're told." He shoves me into the car and straps me in. His motions are quick and efficient, and I notice the tension in his jaw as he rounds the hood and gets into the driver's seat.

The engine revs as he speeds down the long, tree-lined driveway too fast. He turns on the stereo as we veer onto the road, and soft jazz seeps into the car. His fingers tap at the wheel, but it's not in time to the music. It's fast and stressed, his entire body teeming with restless energy.

"Are you—" My voice cracks. I can't say the words out loud. *Are you letting me go?*

"We're going to Southern Siberia. To stay with a friend of mine."

My exhale is loud. I shouldn't be relieved that he's keeping me. I should hate him for it, and I do try. "Why are you taking me? Can't you just let me stay with Boris like you usually do?"

"That would defeat the purpose," he snaps, his jaw clenching as he stares at the road and takes a bend at a hazardous speed.

"Will you please slow down? I don't want to die out here."

"Are you sure about that?" He shoots me an ice-cold glare.

"What?" I say, my voice shrill.

"Then you'd be free of me. Isn't that what you want? Or even better, I'll die in the crash and you'll get to run off, huh?"

Has he lost his mind?

I shake my head as I keep staring at him, shocked at his question. His tone. *He actually sounds hurt.*

Does this mean he cares about me? Like more than a prized possession?

I turn my eyes to the side window. Trees and fields swoosh

by with warm colors of red and orange, and I spend the next hour staring at them as I quiver through the unwavering tide of emotions rolling through me.

Chapter 21

WE DRIVE FOR AN hour before we arrive at a private airport and board Aleksandr's jet. Then we fly for four and a half hours, most of which I spend in the luxurious bedroom, away from Aleksandr. Another long, tense drive in a blue Maserati brings us to our destination.

The last half hour passes amidst the dark thicket of trees, bumping along a gravelly dirt road.

The trees finally give way to light as we enter a clearing. Or rather, a wide, open field with thick walls of trees on all sides. In the middle of it all rises a long, two-story house with a brown tile roof and wooden beams, well-kept with dark siding. Red window frames add a splash of life to the simple structure along with intricate carvings in the woodwork around the porch.

I can't help leaning forward in my seat as I take it all in. It's very different from Aleksandr's mansion, both smaller and simpler, yet majestic in its own right—a wooden mansion.

The gravelly road continues all the way up to the porch where Aleksandr parks beside two large SUVs and gets out.

I'm still gawking when he comes around the car with his suitcase in hand and opens the door for me.

Gravel crunches under my feet as I step out, and a gentle

breeze brings me the faint scent of pine needles. A serene calmness seems to permeate the open space between the trees, and my muscles loosen as it envelops me and invites me in.

With a hand on my back, Aleksandr guides me toward the house, and I'm too mesmerized by the wild beauty to pull away from him.

Just as we reach the porch, a large dog comes running out of the house, barking at the top of its lungs. I dart behind Aleksandr, instinctively seeking his protection.

As always, he provides it—from everyone but himself. Pressing a reassuring hand to my hip, he leans a knee on the steps and reaches his other hand out for the dog. The angry creature has halted in a fierce stand-off, ears standing at attention, head tall as it bares its teeth.

"C'mon Pasha, you know me." Aleksandr moves a little closer.

The dog growls as it approaches. Tentatively, it sniffs his hand, and then it's all petting and joyous reunion.

"Give me your hand," Aleksandr says.

I shake my head and take a small step back.

Aleksandr beckons me with an upturned palm. "Don't be afraid. *Dershu tebya.*"

I draw in a deep breath and place my hand in his. A tendril of longing rushes up my arm at the feeling of his warm hand around mine. The mere thought of rejecting him hurts, yet I've done it for days.

I remain behind the cover of his body as he guides my hand up to the dog. The black snout twitches as the dog sniffs my fingers. It shows no further sign of hostility, so when Aleksandr nudges my hand to the side of its neck, I let my fingers graze the soft fur.

"What breed is it?" It looks a bit like a husky, though mostly black with defined white markings—more elegant with its alert posture. And its eyes are brown instead of the startling blue of a husky.

"Karelian Bear Dog." Aleksandr gives the dog a good scratch behind the ear. "Great for hunting."

Bracing a hand on his shoulder, I bend sideways to get closer. I'm still not ready to give up my cover, but the soft fur entices me to sink my fingers in and stroke the fluffy creature.

"Sasha." A deep voice greets Aleksandr warmly, using his Russian nickname.

I pull back behind Aleksandr when I see a tall, lean man with observant eyes—too observant—step onto the porch. He appears to be around forty or so, and he's wearing a black turtleneck and slacks, which fit him to a tee. His hair is cut in an inch-long, controlled style, his strong jaw clean-shaven.

I eye him warily as he approaches us with firm steps.

He's the opposite of Aleksandr's blond hair, blue eyes, and light shirts. But the danger hanging thick in the air around him is the same—maybe even more acute.

Taking a step back, I watch the two men hug and exchange pleasantries. It's such a rare thing to see Aleksandr engage in a warm greeting like this. His posture is relaxed, his demeanor calm, his charming smile wide and full. It's clear he respects this man, maybe even considers him a friend.

Aleksandr's calm disposition dulls my anxious nerves, and I almost find the courage to step beside him and face the man.

But the courage snaps when dark eyes find mine over Aleksandr's shoulder. A new wave of anxiety scratches at my nerves when the man steps around Aleksandr—my shield.

"I won't bite," he says in accented English as if sensing my urge to retreat. “Neither will Pasha.” He gestures to the dog, which is happily wagging its tail, pink tongue hanging from its mouth. “I’m Vasily. Sasha’s friend since we were kids.”

Oh. Is this the man Aleksandr grew up with?

Vasily proffers a strong-looking hand, and I’m surprised when Aleksandr doesn’t stop him.

Casting an uncertain glance at Aleksandr, I seek both his permission and reassurance.

At his go-ahead nod, I take the stranger’s hand—or rather, hold up mine for him to take. A large, firm palm closes around my slender hand, and I gulp as I watch the unnerving connection.

“And who are you?” the man asks.

Again, I seek Aleksandr’s approval and get it.

“Astrid.”

“Astrid,” the man repeats, tasting the word. “It means passionate. Or divine beauty. Both very fitting, don’t you think?”

I’m too anxious to respond. I feel like a fish among sharks here between the two towering men, and the hand around mine feels like it’s about to swallow me whole.

“I’ve heard a lot about your passion, but I’m afraid I don’t have a piano, so I’ll have to settle for enjoying the latter.” Vasily shifts his gaze to Aleksandr. “If Sasha doesn’t mind.”

“Enjoy all you want. But try not to scare her, will you?” Sliding a protective arm around my waist, Aleksandr discreetly signals for Vasily to let me go. “She’s had a rough week.”

“I’m sorry.” Vasily releases my hand. “You’re quite safe here. Anyone under Sasha’s protection is under mine as well.”

Aleksandr leans in to press a kiss to my head, and I don’t miss the curious way Vasily watches him—like the display of affection is a novelty.

“Let me show you the guest room.” Vasily leads us into the

house and down a long corridor.

All surfaces, from floor to ceiling, are naked wood. Even the doors, which are adorned with square carvings. A few rosewood drawers and a striped carpet lend a splash of color to the hallway. It's warm and welcoming. Spacious yet unpretentious.

It's the opposite of the opulent palaces Aleksandr usually brings me to—rich people flaunting their wealth with absurd amounts of gilded moldings, walls of patterns, and monstrous chandeliers. Aleksandr has all these things too, but in moderate amounts. I don't feel like my eyes are about to pop from their sockets in his home. But it's obvious that he's rich, nonetheless. Here, the riches are more discreet, and it's only upon a second look that I notice just how delicate the carvings in the wood are and how finely woven the carpets.

The raw simplicity continues in the guest bedroom, where only a painting and a white rug get to disturb the beautiful knots in the naked wood. Three windows let in plenty of daylight, and white furniture with beautiful carvings and rounded corners add to the peaceful atmosphere.

I stand awkwardly in the middle of the room while Aleksandr throws his suitcase on the bed and starts unpacking. Vasily lingers in the door, watching me with curious fascination, like I'm a newly discovered rarity.

I try to avert my focus, but his sharp observation prickles in my awareness, making my feet shuffle and my hands jitter.

When he finally releases me from his inspection, my chest rises with a relieved breath.

"I can get Ivan to do that." Vasily gestures to the suitcase.

"Don't bother." Aleksandr carries a stack of clothes to the closet, and now it's my turn to be curious. Aleksandr doing something as menial as unpacking... That's a first.

He comes up beside me and puts a hand on my shoulder. "Get some rest. It was a long trip."

I scan the room, trying not to meet Vasily's eyes on the way.

"In the bed?" I ask. It's been so long since I've slept in a normal bed without a shackle on my ankle that I don't want to presume anything.

"The bed." Aleksandr doesn't seem the least surprised by my strange question.

"Am I sleep—" my eyes dart up to Vasily, and I stop myself.

"What?" The demand in Aleksandr's voice is not so subtle.

I direct my gaze to the wooden floor. "Am I sleeping there too?"

"In the bed, with me," he confirms.

I'm not sure I'm comfortable with this. After what happened with the whore, it's hard to be around Aleksandr. I'm in a constant struggle with myself, determined to shut him out even as I'm burning with the need to give in to him. The intimacy of sleeping together will only make it worse.

Vasily cuts in, clearly sensing my hesitance. "I have a spare guest room you may use."

My eyes light up with hope even as I realize I'm leaning toward Aleksandr.

Aleksandr wraps a possessive hand around my arm and shoots the offer down with the efficiency of a well-aimed bullet. "*Nyet. Ana so menoi spit.*"

Hands clasped behind his back, Vasily gives a polite nod. "I'll leave you to get settled, then." He closes the door on his way out, leaving me worried and relieved at the same time. With Vasily gone, there's one less danger, but with him gone, the danger of Aleksandr doubles.

Aleksandr goes to move the suitcase from the bed. "Come

here." His voice is soft, and I find the same softness in his almost regretful features.

My mind whirs as I take a step forward, hesitate, then close the distance. I would have expected him to be angry, or at least irritable. I shouldn't have said anything about the bed in front of Vasily. But his mood seems to have taken a general turn for the better since we arrived.

His fingertips stroke my cheek and catch a lock of hair on the way to tuck it behind my ear. "I'm sorry."

Somehow, those two innocent words make my chest tighten.

"For what?" I gulp as a hesitant hope grows within me. I badly want him to be sorry for letting the whore use me, but I know I'll never get an apology for that. In Aleksandr's mind, it's his right to let anyone fuck me. It's a miracle I get an apology at all. But it's not enough.

"I should have made sure she didn't speak to you." His lips curl into a sneer and soften again. "But we're here now. I think a couple of days here might do you good." He presses his palm to my cheek, and I have to stop myself from leaning into it.

He sighs at my resistance and lifts the covers on the bed, gesturing for me to get in.

If I can't get away from him, this is the next best thing. So I curl up under the covers and let him tuck me in.

I keep my back to him as he rummages in the room behind me, moving around and unpacking. Thoughts of the past week circle in my mind. The whore, my anger, the distance between Aleksandr and me. The loneliness.

Before I know it, my chest is shuddering under the weight of it all. Emotions press to get out in the shape of tears, but I don't want to cry in front of him.

Turning my focus to the trees beyond the windows, I

momentarily manage to dispel the ugly memories. But when Aleksandr climbs into bed and gathers me against his chest, they all come crashing back.

I try to pull away, but he locks me to him without effort.

"Don't," I say, turning the hurt into anger, like I've done so many times.

"Shh, *dershu tebya*," Aleksandr soothes, like I didn't just snap at him.

It takes everything I have not to cave in and sink into his warm embrace. "Just leave me alone," I try again, but he won't listen. He just tightens his arms around me, giving me the comfort I badly need but can't allow myself to take.

I don't remember falling asleep. I barely even remember relaxing in Aleksandr's arms. But I must have, despite my effort to reject him, because I don't remember him leaving either.

The bed is empty beside me now, the room murky, and I find that I miss him. Terribly.

The first thing I do is examine my body to search for chains or ropes. There's nothing. Only my collar. But it's not attached to anything.

This can't be.

Maybe it's because the door is locked. I slink over the floor and put my ear to the carved wood. There's an indistinct murmur of voices, but they are several rooms away. So I carefully push the handle down. The door slides free from the frame, and I peek into the long, empty hallway.

Carefully, I shut it again. Just because I can, doesn't mean I'm about to venture into the house. Bumping into Vasily is not something I'd like to risk. So I retreat back into the safety of the room.

After a quick visit to the en suite bathroom, I slip back into bed and let the darkness engulf me. It's peaceful. But it doesn't last for long.

When the door opens half an hour later, light streams into the room, forcing me to face the world. I'm relieved when the door shuts again, blocking out the light, less relieved by the sound of Aleksandr's footfalls. I've grown so accustomed to them I can identify their source in a heartbeat.

A familiar note of citrus wafts past my nose as the bed dips behind me.

"Are you asleep?" Aleksandr asks as he crawls under the covers and aligns his body with mine.

My chest tightens. It hurts to ache for someone you hate.

I force my breath to stay calm, hoping he'll believe I'm asleep, but when his knuckles brush my cheek, I can't help my answer. "No."

He keeps up the caresses as his warm breath moves against my temple. "Dinner is ready."

I'm not sure what to do with the information. No one ever tells me when it's dinnertime, lunchtime, or breakfast time. They just bring the food to my room and order me to eat.

"Come join us in the kitchen." Aleksandr sits up and turns on the bedside lamp. A soft glow lights up the area around the bed, gentle and unobtrusive.

I roll onto my back and face him. All traces of anger and frustration from our trip are gone. His features hold nothing but sympathy. It gets me every time. Tears prickle in my eyes, and I quickly turn to wipe them away.

"Come." He offers me a hand as he stands.

I take it and let him lead me down the hallway and into a large space with a seating area to the right and a kitchen and dining area to the left.

I flinch when I see a new man at the table—a large and bulky one. He looks menacing in the cross-armed position that makes his huge arms bulge beneath his black T-shirt. My eyes flicker to the other man in the room, and the sight is no better. Hands clasped behind his back and squared shoulders, Vasily remains standing as he waits for us to sit. Authority rolls off him in thick waves that make it hard to breathe.

All three men are poised and controlled, whereas I'm a mess. My eyes are swollen and puffy, my hair disheveled, and I'm unable to even fake a smile. I feel like one of the drooping flowers in Aleksandr's garden when it rains.

"This is Ivan." Vasily gestures to the new man. "He does a little bit of everything around here. If you need anything, he's the one to ask."

I glance at the bulky man in question, whose eyes flicker with life. He's massive like a bodybuilder, though without the excessive bumps and protruding veins. His strength is not meant to intimidate but to utilize, I think. Though, that idea does nothing to lessen the terrifying effect he incites. Neither does the thick bone structure of his face nor his shaven head, which gives off biker vibes.

I'm surprised when he smiles at me and his blue eyes turn warm, almost gentle.

It entices a small smile to my lips as I sink onto the chair that Aleksandr pulls out for me.

"She's afraid of me and not Ivan?" Vasily huffs as he takes his seat across from me, clearly having noticed my tension waning at the sight of Ivan's smile.

"Boris." Aleksandr's brief explanation insinuates I'm used to bulky men not being dangerous.

"There you go." Vasily shrugs, clearly satisfied with the explanation, then gestures to the table. "Go ahead and help yourselves. Ivan has been cooking all day, and I can guarantee it's delicious."

I'd been so busy watching out for the dangerous men that I hadn't noticed all the food on the table. My appetite barely stirs at the sight even though it does look delicious. There's steak, fried vegetables, pierogies, sauce, potatoes, beet salad, and home-baked bread. Everything the hungry heart desires.

"Have you killed the animal yourself?" Aleksandr asks as he takes the tray of steaks Vasily hands him.

"With some help from Pasha." Vasily pets the dog at his side. Tongue hanging from its mouth, it eagerly follows the food with its eyes. "It's a young deer."

A nudge on my arm has me turning to see Ivan hold up the platter of mini pierogies. Forking one of the small bread packages, he lifts his brows in silent question.

"Sure." I brush my hair behind my ear as I glance down at my plate. Despite his rough appearance, there's something very charming about Ivan's lively eyes. "Thank you."

He holds up several other plates the same way, scooping food onto my plate when I answer his unspoken question with a nod or a *yes*. I don't think I'll be able to get half of it down, but something in his gaze compels me to accept.

When he's finally done, I watch the mountain of food in front of me, feeling a bit overwhelmed.

Ivan gives me a go-ahead nod as he leans back in his chair with a satisfied smile. I pick up my fork and notice he hasn't taken any food for himself. Actually, he doesn't even have a plate.

"Aren't you eating?" I ask.

Ivan gives a shake of his head and pats his belly like he's already full.

Does Vasily have some *servants not eating with the guests* rule?

No. It doesn't make sense. Then why let Ivan sit at the table with us?

"Eat." Aleksandr's order is a gentle urge against my ear. Not the harsh command he so often issues when leaning against the desk in the cage room, watching me with hard eyes.

My appetite slowly emerges as I start tasting the food. Vasily didn't exaggerate. The meat melts on my tongue, and the vegetables are perfectly al dente.

Ivan points to my food, nodding at it with lifted eyebrows.

Not quite following, I furrow my brows, and he rubs his belly in clarification and nods at my food again.

"Oh. It's good." I give him a slow smile.

Ivan returns the smile. It's a pleasant one that softens his hard features and lights up his blue eyes. Unlike the bright blue of Aleksandr's gaze that resembles a clear sky, Ivan's eyes are a deep shade like a vast ocean.

I see why Aleksandr would compare him to Boris. My jailor also has a gentle disposition despite having the build of a brute. He's a bit of a teddy bear, and Ivan seems to be the same. It gives me the courage to spur on the interaction.

"Are you the one doing all the cooking around here?"

Ivan moves his head from shoulder to shoulder and makes a *semi*-movement with his hand.

"Vasily cooks too?"

Ivan shrugs and turns down his lips.

"Sometimes?" I ask and get a nod of confirmation. I still

haven't heard Ivan say anything, and I'm starting to wonder why. He doesn't seem shy or uncommunicative. He just doesn't speak.

"Is he as good a cook as you?"

He gives me a big smile that has my own lips tipping up.

"We were taught by the same woman," Vasily offers. "My grandmother."

My eyes dart to the intimidating man. I thought he and Aleksandr were preoccupied with their own conversation, but now they're both watching me. I shrink in the chair and hope they'll realize I'm not interesting and return to their own talk.

No such luck.

"Do you like to cook, Astrid?" Vasily asks.

What am I supposed to say? I don't even have the option to cook. And I'm not even sure I'm supposed to talk.

Aleksandr slips his hand onto my thigh and squeezes gently.

I suppose it's a go-ahead, so I glance at Vasily, down at the table, and up again. "Anna... my friend... she used to cook." Fuck, I don't think I should talk about this. How do I explain not living with her anymore? "She..." I shake my head and go for a simple answer. "No, I don't cook much."

Vasily's brow furrows, and he casts a suspicious glance at Aleksandr.

My hands start fidgeting, in and out of each other as I stare at the table. I fucked up. Aleksandr must be furious.

But there's no sign of fury. His hand moves back and forth on my thigh like he's trying to soothe me, and when I gather the courage to meet his gaze, it's calm.

Aleksandr turns to Vasily and explains on my behalf. "Her friend Anna did most of the cooking when they lived together. Since I got her, she hasn't been in the kitchen. I've got people for that."

My eyes flicker back and forth between Vasily, the table, and Aleksandr.

Aleksandr is cool and collected, but Vasily seems to have caught onto something, and his jaw hardens as he spears a piece of meat with his fork. "So, how did the two of you meet?" Vasily brings the meat into his mouth and points his fork between us.

Aleksandr answers without batting an eye. "I saw her at a concert at the conservatory, playing the piano. And well, Astrid practically begged me to take her." He gives me his charming smile, but the look in his eye is dark. Possessive.

My heart thumps so loud I think everyone must hear.

"So, you study at the conservatory?" Vasily directs the question at me, but Aleksandr answers.

"Not anymore."

Both Vasily and Aleksandr study me, and it's too much. Too dangerous. I want to slink under the table and hide. Bolt from the room. But I remain frozen in place, unable to move even when they turn back to a more casual topic and the tension dissipates.

Aleksandr's hand keeps rubbing my thigh, but it's Ivan's hand nudging my shoulder that drags me out of the paralysis. He nods to my plate, and when I don't react, he pulls it to him and cuts up the rest of the steak and pierogi, then pushes it back in front of me and nods to it as if saying *eat.*

I take a small forkful of the beet salad and a piece of pierogi and put my fork back down. My stomach is in knots.

I startle when Ivan curls his hand around my wrist. His hand is huge. It could easily encompass two of my wrists—maybe four. I shudder and let out a breath when he releases me to grab his own wrist the same way. It's big enough to fill his grip. Fuck, the man is huge. But what's his point? I'm weak; he's strong?

Lifting my gaze back up to him, I'm relieved to find humor in his eyes as he flexes his muscular arm, then points at me.

"That's not a fair comparison," I say.

He nudges me and makes a motion with his hands as if snapping something in two.

"Gosh, I'm not so frail my bones will break. Have you never seen a skinny person?" I eye him sideways and pick up my fork. "I swim and eat. I'm not that small."

Something dark flashes across his face at my question, but he quickly schools his features back into the easygoing smile as he grips my wrist for a moment again.

A tingling sensation erupts under his touch. I do feel breakable when his fist swallows up my slim wrist. But not in a bad way.

Suddenly feeling shy, I glance up at him beneath my lashes.

Ivan winks at me, and my cheeks heat with titillating embarrassment.

Is he flirting with me?

I take a piece of pierogi in my mouth and flicker my eyes to Aleksandr. To my relief, he's still engrossed in conversation. There's no telling how he would react to another man flirting with me. Or me flirting with another man.

Did I do that?

I fork another piece of pierogi and sneak a peek up at Ivan. He's leaning back in his chair with his arms crossed over his wide chest and eyes glimmering with mischievous satisfaction.

Boris is burly like a large troll; Ivan is impressive like a beautiful warrior.

Chapter 22

I'M STRUGGLING WITH myself when I get into bed with Aleksandr that night. He doesn't chain me up or tie me down. He just wraps his arms around me and tells me to go to sleep. I want to snuggle up against his warm chest—give in to the alluring sense of safety. But it's a hoax. There's nothing safe about this man. There's only humiliation and degradation. At least, that's what I try to believe.

But it's hard to convince myself. I remember the way he shot up from his seat and grabbed the whore with raging fury, then took me in his arms with startling gentleness. When someone else tries to do the humiliation and harm, all hell rains down, but when he's the instigator, it's supposed to be the natural order of things. And somehow, it has come to be.

Deep down, he's not the one I've been hating and shutting out lately. It's myself—for craving the things he does to me.

I feel sick. Brainwashed. Like I'm losing myself. It both terrifies and enrages me.

Nudging Aleksandr's arm, I shift on the bed. His arm moves without resistance. His breathing is level, warm air tickling my nape as his chest rises and falls in a calm rhythm against my back. I nudge his arm a bit more until it falls off me. He doesn't even stir.

Am I free to get out of bed?

I scoot away from him and sit up, listening for sounds in the house. It's quiet like Aleksandr's place. No traffic humming, planes buzzing, or drunken people yelling. It's peaceful, yet I don't feel the peace. I feel edgy and restless. Scared.

Scared of my own feelings, scared for my future, and scared that Aleksandr will grow cold and uncaring as with every other woman he meets. He's made me so dependent on him I can't exist on my own.

I get up and carefully grab Aleksandr's shirt, sliding it on as I pad over the wooden floor. It's the first time in months I get out of bed in the middle of the night, and the novelty sends a rush of equal exhilaration and trepidation through me.

I take care to open the door slowly, watching Aleksandr with nervous heart palpitations as I go. Still no movement. So I slink into the hallway and slide the door shut.

My heart beats like a drum as I look from side to side. There's a pale light at one end of the hall. Moonlight. The other end is pure darkness.

With my hand on the wall, I make my way toward the dim glow. The light increases as I go, and when I reach the hall, I see the bright, full moon that bathes the entrance in a pale light. I go to the door and grip the edges of the window as I admire the bright orb and the deep blue canvas of sky peppered with tiny dots of light.

I stare, mesmerized, for several minutes before my eyes drift down. The two SUVs and the blue Maserati remain parked in front of the house, waiting for someone to take them somewhere.

Maybe me? I haven't driven a car for years, but I surely remember how. If I can just find a set of keys, I can drive out of here and never return.

The idea sets a harrowing mix of emotions twisting in my belly.

This could finally be my chance to get away. Aleksandr barely stirred when I got up, so it would be easy enough to go search for his keys. With the car's GPS, I could find a city—find help. I just need to be brave.

My fingers go limp on the edge of the window, and my stomach sinks. *I just need to be brave.* I'm not sure I have it in me. I'm not sure I want to be brave even if I could.

A deep voice breaks me from my thoughts. "There's no place to go."

"What?" I spin around with a jerk to find Vasily in the doorway, hands clasped behind his back, eerily still.

My heart pulses painfully in my chest. How did I not hear him?

"The forest is a dangerous place at night, and unless you have a key fob…" The pale moon lends a chilly glow to his narrowing eyes as he steps in front of me and grabs my hands, turning my palms up. Finding them empty, he moves his inspecting eyes to my face.

"I—I just wanted some fresh air." I pull at my wrists, relieved when he lets them slip from his strong hands.

"Sure you did." Vasily's eyes glide down to Aleksandr's shirt, and I gulp as he reaches up to adjust the collar. His fingers work their way around my neck, close to the golden steel band. "In nothing but a shirt," he adds, watching me with calm intent as he holds the lapels. "It's better to stay quiet than to lie, Astrid."

My breathing barely moves as I stare up at him. His eyes are cool and observant. There's no threat, but I feel the danger lingering in the air around him. Vasily's intentions don't matter.

This man is a threat in and of himself.

My lungs expand to draw in a loud gulp of air when he releases the collar and turns. "Come," he says as he starts down the hall.

I watch him as he moves like a shadow in the dark, silent like a tiger, camouflaged in black clothes.

He veers into the kitchen, disappearing from my sight, and it snaps me out of my stupefied haze. Spurring my feet into motion, I pad after him. Chills spread down my arms as I move through the darkness, and the soft light above the kitchen island is a welcome relief as I enter the large room.

"Sit." Vasily gestures to the barstools, and I scoot onto one, watching as he fills the tea kettle and retrieves two mugs. "Green or black?" he asks, opening a cupboard.

"Sorry?"

"Green or black tea?"

"Oh. Green." I cast my gaze to the folded hands in my lap and add a polite, "Please."

Vasily gives me a sideways once-over before proceeding to fill two tea bags with dry green leaves.

The boiling water fills the silence as we wait. My eyes flicker over the dimly lit room, and I shudder when I see the black slab of window. Anyone could be out there. Yet I'd probably be safer there than here with this terrifying stranger.

Vasily fills both mugs and places them between us on the island. Pressing both palms to the surface, he levels me with a direct stare. "So, how *did* you and Sasha meet? Your words."

My eyes fall away to focus on anything but him as I push my hair behind my left ear. "Long story." I drag my hair back as I remember the tattoo.

The man is uncannily observant, I realize when I see him

watch my hand cupping my ear. I drag it away slowly like it would make my slip any less obvious, and he follows it down to the marble surface like a hunter following his prey.

He *is* a hunter. I remember him telling Aleksandr about the deer he'd shot himself. Is that why he managed to sneak up on me?

"I've got all night." Vasily returns his gaze to mine.

I clear my throat. "We met at the conservatory. Like Aleksandr said."

"That wasn't long at all." He cocks his head, eyes honing in like he can pry the rest of the story from me with the sheer force of his gaze.

"I guess not." I break eye-contact again, more than uncomfortable with his line of questioning.

"So what happened? From what I've heard, you have plenty of talent. Yet here you are. No prospect of playing any grand concert hall. On his arm instead." Pressing a finger to my chin, he turns my head back to him. "Or shall I say, under his foot?"

Horror pulls at my features. I try to turn away, but he curls his fingers around my jaw, forcing me in place as he searches my face.

"It's curious, really." His voice takes on a soft, almost marveling tone. "I've never seen him so... affectionate with a woman. And I've never seen a woman react to him the way you do. They usually grovel like slimy beasts around him, all wanting a slice of his wealth and power. But you don't want either. You unconsciously lean into him like you want *him*. Then you seem to remember yourself and pull away."

My mind scrambles to find an excuse to explain away his words. But all I can seem to do is stare at him. He's hit the dreadful nail spot-on.

Vasily's tone lowers as he reaches the conclusion on his own. "Ah, he meant it quite literally when he said he took you?"

His fingers become gentle around my chin, and I nod in his hand as tears pebble down my cheeks. Admitting this to another person is a heavy load off my chest.

"Do you want to be with him?" Vasily strokes his thumb along my jaw as he leans over the counter, studying my eyes with a strange intimacy.

I lift my shoulders and shake my head. "I don't know."

His brown eyes are warm with sympathy as he keeps stroking my jaw, and I can't make myself pull away. I know he's Aleksandr's friend and isn't going to help me, but his concern seems so genuine, and I can't resist it. It's the first time someone has shown any kind of understanding of my predicament, and I let the vulnerability shine in my wet eyes as I get lost in the depth of his brown ones.

He leans in and presses a soft kiss to my forehead. "Drink your tea, Astrid." Then he straightens and takes a sip from his mug, watching me over the rim.

I curl my hands around the other mug and stare into the green tea like it holds all the answers I'm searching for. Just as I'm about to bring it to my lips, the sound of firm footfalls halts me in my motions. *Aleksandr.*

Vasily lifts his gaze above my head. "Couldn't sleep?"

A warm hand slides onto my back, and Aleksandr's voice is both comforting and chilling to my ears. "Someone had wandered off in the middle of the night, so I had to come find her."

I don't detect any admonishment in his voice, but I don't dare to believe it's not there somewhere.

"I'm sorry," I say, my head lowered as I turn it to Aleksandr. I feel Vasily watching us, but I can't help it. I'm doing exactly what he said, turning to him even as I want to get away.

Aleksandr slides an arm around me and presses a long kiss to my hair. It's almost like he's relieved to have me in his arms again.

"Tea?" Vasily asks, and I feel Aleksandr's nod against my head.

The water spray beats in the silence as Vasily fills the kettle.

"Don't worry," Aleksandr whispers against my head. "If I don't want you to leave the bed, I'll make sure you can't."

I reach up and press my hands to his naked chest. His muscles ripple beneath my palms, his diaphragm moving in and out with his level breathing.

"Couldn't sleep?" Aleksandr returns Vasily's question from a minute ago as he wraps both arms around me.

"Didn't try to." Vasily fills another tea strainer and dumps it into a mug. "It's no use."

"And you?" Aleksandr moves a hand up and down my arm, and I shake my head against his chest.

"New place, new bed. A house full of strange men," Vasily says. "Can't blame her."

Aleksandr's chuckle is a delicious rumble beneath my hands. "Vasily won't touch a hair on your head. In fact, if anyone so much as gives you a strange look, he'll haul out one of his rifles. He's a bit of a softie like that."

"A softie with a high-powered rifle." Vasily laughs and hands Aleksandr a mug of steaming hot tea.

"You can take the man out of the military, but you can't take the military out of the man," Aleksandr says, bringing the mug to his mouth.

I lean my head against his chest and look at Vasily. "You were in the military?"

"Ten years. Five in Spetsnaz. Made captain." The pride is palpable in Vasily's tone.

"So, what do you do now?"

"He's retired." Aleksandr huffs, earning an eye-roll from Vasily.

"I do security consulting." Vasily takes a sip of his tea. "Large firms. Governments."

"The Bratva," Aleksandr adds.

Vasily shoots him a glare. "Whoever can afford me."

I glance up at Aleksandr. He's so at ease around Vasily. Their interaction seems almost brotherly. I've never seen him like this around anyone else. It would make sense if Vasily in fact is the guy Aleksandr grew up with.

Pointing a careful finger at Vasily, I ask Aleksandr, "Is this the guy you grew up with? The one with six dogs?"

"That's me," Vasily confirms with a laugh. "My father had a couple of dogs he used for hunting, and when he saw how much I loved training them, he got more. He figured I could transfer the skill to manipulating people once I took over his business."

"Wasted effort," Aleksandr chimes in.

"How so?" I ask.

"Well, Vasily didn't want the business. He took off to join the military. Didn't return home until the old man died. Took the inheritance and moved out here to live out his days in the wild."

"Don't act so disappointed," Vasily shoots. "You got the business—a quite lucrative one if I may add."

Aleksandr smirks and holds up his mug in a salute. "I did."

Vasily huffs and shakes his head before continuing the banter in Russian. "I had barely enrolled before he started grooming you instead."

"He knew you were a lost cause," Aleksandr retorts.

The two men continue like this, and I watch with fascination until I'm too sleepy to keep up with the now rapid Russian. I lean against Aleksandr's chest and revel in the feeling of his warm embrace, and when he carries me to bed a little while later, I'm already half asleep.

Chapter 23

I WAKE UP A LITTLE after eleven. I know because there's a clock beside the bed. A mellow light filters through thin curtains, announcing another gloomy late fall day. No sun at this time of year.

Usually, Aleksandr doesn't allow me to sleep this late, but he doesn't allow me to stay up late either, so I guess things are just different here.

My skin crawls with a restlessness I haven't felt in a long time as I turn under the covers. Maybe I should get out of bed? Aleksandr said he'd make sure I couldn't go anywhere if he didn't want me to, so since there's no chain around my ankle, I guess I'm allowed.

I find Aleksandr's dress shirt in the same place I took it last night and put it on. Then I go to peek behind the curtains.

Gray clouds cover the sky in a thick blanket, leaving no sign of the sun, and the grass and bushes are matted into a pale yellow. Everything is dimmed by fall, except for the thick wall of pine trees that stand tall and proud in the distance, green and resilient.

A knock makes me draw back from the window. Ivan appears at the door, clad in a gray T-shirt and jeans, his gruff features contrasting the softness in his eyes.

With a wave of his hand, he beckons me to come.

I pull the shirt closer and scour the floor for my pants. I should probably be used to going half-naked by now, but the new surroundings and Aleksandr's changed behavior have messed with my sense of routine.

Ivan clears his throat and points to the armchair where black jeans and a rosy blouse peek out from under Aleksandr's suit jacket.

"Thanks." I gather my clothes and point to the bathroom. "May I?"

Ivan's nod spurs me on, and I hurry to the bathroom and make quick work of emptying my bladder, brushing my teeth, and slipping into the clothes. Jeans feel uncomfortably snug with their stiff material compared to the loose robes I'm used to, but I'll take any kind of normalcy Aleksandr grants me. The blouse, though, is silky soft, molding to my torso like a second skin.

The curtains are open when I come back out, and Ivan is making the bed. Smoothing the bedspread out, he finishes and moves to the door with a *come-along* jerk of his head.

The scent of pancakes fills the air as we approach the kitchen, prickling at my senses with wistful recognition. I've eaten plenty of pancakes at Aleksandr's place, but I haven't experienced the scent so pervasively since... Anna.

My chest tightens at the thought of her. I miss our weekends together. She would cook pancakes in the kitchen while I sat on the couch watching Russian cartoons. Every now and then, she would rush to the TV, saying *oh, this is a good one* with a beaming smile, and we would both laugh at the punchline she had anticipated.

Ivan pulls out a chair for me by the table, and I must look as droopy as I feel when I sink down on it.

With a finger under my chin, he nudges my head up and does this weird thing where he pulls at the corners of my mouth as if saying *cheer up.* He seems warm and gentle despite his rough exterior, and it almost makes me want to smile. I manage a small one, and it's enough to earn me a nod of approval.

Ivan places a huge portion of pancakes with syrup and fresh fruit in front of me and shoves a fork into my hand. He's still towering at my side when I take the first bite. I glance up to see him shake his head and make a spoon motion, like he's eating fast.

This man really is adamant about getting food into me.

I fork a bigger piece, hold it up, and take it into my mouth. *Happy?*

Ivan shakes his head and grabs my utensils, stapling several pieces on the fork before he hands it back to me.

I huff and go for exasperation as I watch him with lowered eyebrows. But I can't quite conceal my humor when I shove the huge forkful into my mouth.

Ivan pats me on the head. G*ood girl.* He's beaming with playful satisfaction as he takes the seat across from me.

The room is silent as I eat, but it's the type of comfortable silence that frees the mind and allows a calm flow of breath.

Ivan leans back in his chair and watches me eat. With his face relaxed and his smile dormant, he appears dangerous—bald head, enormous build, and rough bone structure. I probably should be wary of him after what I've been through, but he has the opposite effect. He has this laid-back calmness that rubs off on me and makes me feel like I can trust him.

Though, it's hard to allow myself to do so fully. My inner compass seems to be faulty when it comes to men. No red flags popped up when I saw Aleksandr on the train, so I might well be missing the blaring alarm bells on this man too.

Fuck it. I'm tired of overthinking everything. There's not much I can do anyway.

I gobble up another mouthful of pancake and cut into the next one, stapling the pieces on my fork like Ivan did.

"Where's Aleksandr?" I ask halfway through the meal.

Ivan gestures to the windows, then makes a rifle motion with his hands.

"Hunting?" I frown as I shove the tower of pancakes into my mouth, savoring the sweet syrup coating them.

Ivan gives me two thumbs up and a warm grin, and I lower my head as I try to suppress the grand smile that wants to take over my face. When I have it under control, I swallow my food and look back up. "Vasily and Pasha too?"

A firm nod is his answer.

The information grounds me somewhat. Knowing the two most dangerous men have left the house makes it easier to relax.

When my plate is empty, Ivan retrieves the platter of pancakes by the stove.

I hold up my hands. "No, no, no, I've had more than plenty."

He gives an eager nod as he spears three pancakes and tries to dump them on my plate.

Shoving at his arm, I chuckle. "Forget it."

He pushes back with just enough strength to match mine, and hearty quips of laughter erupt from my belly as we struggle back and forth. I can't remember the last time I laughed like this, and I feel light and bubbly when Ivan finally gives up with a grunt.

After clearing the table, he motions for me to come join him in the sitting area.

Two upholstered sofas form an L-shape in the cozy nook, and a big flatscreen vies for attention with a large bay window overlooking the field in front of the house.

We each take a sofa, and Ivan turns on Netflix and hands me the remote.

I scroll down the home screen and see several familiar movies and series, but they all seem foreign. It's been ages since I watched TV, and I barely remember what I like.

Notting Hill. I used to love that movie, but I don't know if I do anymore. *Queen's Gambit.* Reminds me of Anna and TV nights. *Drive.* I used to find Ryan Gosling hot, but I can't remember why.

Everything reminds me of my old life, and nothing resonates with the person I've become. I feel like a foreigner in my own head, and I grow increasingly dejected as I skip through the immense amounts of content. I can't make a decision. I don't remember how. So I keep on scrolling.

Large hands fold around mine, and I realize I'm clutching the remote when Ivan pries my fingers off. The device slips from my hands, and it's a terrible symbol of all the other things that have slipped out of my hands over the recent months. It's like losing another part of myself.

"Please." I don't know what I'm asking for. Not the remote. The choices it offered were only a burden.

Ivan moves to my couch and carefully pulls me into him. At first, I tense up at the foreign contact. But he just holds me, pressing his large palms against my back as he molds his arms against my sides with surprising gentleness. So I tentatively lean my head against his shoulder.

Responding to my increasing openness, Ivan cups the back of my head and wraps an arm around my back.

God, it feels good. He's strong and warm. One big hug of comfort. So I give in to him, little by little, molding into his embrace.

There's no threat in his size. Rather, it's like a shield, providing all the security I can't find within myself. I'm not capable of feeling safe on my own anymore. I need the bars of the cage, a cuff around my ankle, or Aleksandr's arms. Or now, Ivan's arms.

My muscles melt beneath his touch and my energy slowly drains. I realize I don't have any left. I've been running on fumes, only holding myself up because I had to. Now someone else does it for me, and my eyelids grow heavy as my mind dulls.

I don't know how I end up in Ivan's lap. At some point, I realize I'm curled up there, shaking and whimpering as he rocks me with slow movements of his chest. Side to side, side to side. It's so calming I could sleep here. Maybe I already have. I'm not sure. It's like I've zoned out for a while.

Slowly, I straighten and push my hand into my hair, peering at him from behind its cover. I can't remember the last time I was intimate with a man without some component of force. It feels strange.

Ivan's eyes are full of gentle emotion, knowing, and understanding. Like with Vasily, I sense a genuine concern, like he sees the depth of my pain and wants to take it away.

I want him to. I really do. But I'm afraid of how Aleksandr will react if he finds me in the lap of another man, staring into his eyes. So I slip onto the couch, and Ivan seems as unwilling as I to lose the connection.

Hugging my knees, I stay at his side, close enough to feel the heat emitting from his body without touching him.

Ivan scrolls through Netflix and finds a nature documentary

about big cats. I've never been into nature shows, but as I sit here beside Ivan, watching the beautiful creatures and mesmerizing landscapes, I find it surprisingly soothing.

Casting a glance at Ivan, I wonder if he chose the show for his own enjoyment or because of its calming effect. I have a feeling it might be the latter.

Chapter 24

THE SOUND OF happy barking and claws scraping against floorboards stirs me from sleep. A wet nose tickles my fingers, and I open my eyes to see Pasha give my hand a big lick. Smiling at the creature, I reach out to stroke its fluffy fur.

Someone is stroking my hair too. A large warm hand. It's calm. *I'm* calm—almost weightless—the burden of worry gone from my chest.

The TV hums at a low volume, now with wolves instead of lions hunting in the wild.

Footfalls approach, firm and steady, pulling at something familiar inside me. A pair of legs covered in green outdoor pants appear before me, and I gaze up into a set of beautiful blue eyes. *Aleksandr.*

He crouches in front of me, and that's when I realize I'm curled up with my head in Ivan's lap.

Anxiety infiltrates my system like an unshakable virus, and I lift my head to move away.

"I'm sorry." I blink my heavy eyes in confusion. Everything's a blur, and my head scrambles to put the pieces together. Aleksandr and Vasily were out hunting. Ivan served me breakfast. Then somehow, I ended up in his arms.

"Shh, sh, shh." Aleksandr presses my head back onto Ivan's thigh and rests his hand on my cheek.

"I shouldn't..." I try to wriggle away from Ivan, but his heavy hand on my waist and Aleksandr's on my cheek prevent my retreat. "I'm sorry."

"It's okay," Aleksandr soothes. "I asked Ivan to take care of you."

My eyes flicker over the room and Aleksandr's features.

"Stay here while I go change. Don't worry." Despite his calm tone, the last two words are more of an order than a reassurance.

I try to obey while Aleksandr is gone, but the tension is back in my bones, rendering me unable to find comfort in Ivan's touch.

At Aleksandr's return, Ivan helps me to sit. With a brush of his knuckles over my cheek, he leaves me to go to the kitchen, and I don't miss Aleksandr's nod of appreciation as they pass each other. I blink my sleepy eyes like I'm seeing a mirage. It's such a rare thing to see any display of respect from Aleksandr, let alone such an appreciative one.

He takes Ivan's place on the couch and wraps an arm around me, pressing a kiss to my head. He's calm and relaxed, but I remain stiff and can't open up to the offered comfort.

"Do you like watching TV?" he asks.

I peer up at him as I try to gauge if this is a trick. But Aleksandr has never tricked me. He doesn't need to hide behind the pretense of being nice. He does whatever he wants. Straightforward and unapologetic.

"I guess."

He leans back to study me for a moment. "Maybe I should get a TV in the sitting room?"

"You still don't watch TV?" Vasily asks as he sinks onto the other couch.

"Why would I?"

"To do something besides work. Maybe it's time you learn what all the fuss is about." Vasily picks up the remote and turns to me as he launches Netflix on the screen. "What do you say, Astrid? Any preferences?"

An urgent grunt sounds from the kitchen, and Ivan gives a stern shake of his head when Vasily turns around.

I lower my head when Vasily's inspecting eyes turn to me. "Alright then," he says with a frown on his brow. He scrolls on for a minute, then says, "Let's go for something light."

Rhythmic music comes on as Vasily starts an action comedy and turns the volume back up. It's light with an undercurrent of suspense, meant to pull you in, but I'm stuck in my head, feeling disheartened. Here I am, with three strong men who have everything under control, and I'm this weak creature who breaks from the simple task of picking a movie. I can't do anything anymore, and I have no idea who I am.

Maybe the whore was right, after all. I'm nothing but a lowly cunt to be used.

A pained whimper escapes me, and suddenly I'm shuddering.

I try to pull away when Aleksandr takes me into his lap. Refusing his comfort despite needing it has become an ingrained reflex. A painful one. But I don't have much fight in me and don't want to make a scene in front of Vasily and Ivan, so I give up and let him hold me.

Icy shudders keep pulsing through me, and soon I'm clutching Aleksandr's shirt, desperate to feel him even as he's already holding me.

"It's okay. *Dershu tebya*," he whispers, only for my ears to hear. "Stop fighting and give in."

"I don't fight," I say, but I know he's right. I close myself off because I'm so angry with him. Or maybe it's myself I'm angry with—for not truly hating him.

I'm sick of fighting. Aleksandr, myself, my parents. Fighting to achieve dreams that would never fulfill me, fighting to fit in. It's always been a never-ending battle to get through the mud.

"I'm sorry," I murmur into his neck. I'm not sure why or if it's him or me I'm apologizing to.

"It's okay. Just accept it. Accept where you belong."

"I'm sorry." Tears start falling, and my shudders become shaking as I weep silently into his neck. So much for not causing a scene.

"*Takaya horoshaya devushka*," he soothes, stroking my hair affectionately.

We sit here for a long time, no one saying anything. It's just the TV, Ivan's bustling in the kitchen, and my sniffles. When my crying finally dies down, I realize it's a calm stillness. Despite my brokenness hanging thick in the air, no one seems bothered by it.

When Aleksandr nudges my hip, I straighten and turn to find Vasily standing beside us, offering me a steaming mug.

"My grandmother used to say a cup of tea could heal anything. Even a broken heart."

I gingerly accept the warm mug as I stare up at Vasily. He's lethal danger incarnate with his vigilant eyes and tall posture. I can easily imagine him with a rifle in combat, cool gaze trained on his target, aiming to kill.

Yet he poses no danger to me. His dark eyes glimmer with something warm, almost protective. In fact, all three men in this room seem oddly protective of me.

I have my whole world misconstrued, thinking danger lurks everywhere and every man means me harm. Some may do, but not the ones who count. Not Vasily, not Ivan, nor Boris or Anton.

Not even Aleksandr. Despite all the degradation and subjugation, he doesn't mean me harm. He just wants me to be his.

And God, I want it too. I just can't seem to see through all the norms and learned rationale polluting my mind. The notion that freedom equals endless choices. The notion that men and women should be the same. The notion of being weak and worthless if not independent.

I've never truly fit into any of those molds, but I didn't want to acknowledge just how ill-fitted I was for the normal world. But Aleksandr is helping me free my mind.

"Thank you." I reach out to take the mug, and a new trickle of moisture erupts from my eyes. But this time, it's not broken hopelessness. It's sincere gratitude.

Chapter 25

"WHY DOESN'T IVAN speak?" I ask when we lie in bed at night. My voice is hoarse from another crying fit. I've been feeling better during the day, but when Aleksandr brought me to bed, a flood of emotion came out of nowhere. Now I'm nestled in his arms, the expanse of his hard chest heating my back and his fingers drawing circles on my stomach.

"He had his tongue cut out." Aleksandr keeps up the circles, calm and slow, the complete opposite of the sudden thumps of my heart.

"How?" I croak. "Why?"

"The Bratva. His father sold him to pay off a debt. I guess he spoke out of turn."

"How did he get away?" Too horrified to stay in the intimate position, I turn around. The moonlight shimmering through the thin curtains reveals the outline of Aleksandr's face, but even there, I find no sign of disgust or outrage.

"Vasily has this reckless savior complex. He happened upon a boy without a tongue and just couldn't leave it be." Aleksandr scoffs. "He gathered a bunch of army friends, invaded the place, and took Ivan."

"Just like that? How did he get away with it? Is that why he lives out here? To hide from the mafia?" My heart beats faster with each blurted question.

"Nah, Vasily is just a recluse." Aleksandr props his head on an elbow and twirls a lock of my hair around a finger. "He burned the whole place to the ground. In and out in half an hour. No one outside knew there was trouble before he was long gone. If he had left a single one of those rodents alive, he would have been a goner. But Vasily is a war machine. Effective as they come. He's taken several jobs with the Bratva since. No one ever suspected a thing."

"And Ivan? Isn't he afraid someone will recognize him?"

"Ivan was a lowly servant. If anyone outside that house even remembered him, they thought he died in the fire. Because why would anyone be stupid enough to go after the Bratva for a boy without a tongue?"

I swallow hard as I consider what would have happened to Ivan if Vasily hadn't been *stupid enough* to get him out.

"The world is a dangerous place." Aleksandr runs his fingers along the curve of my face like he's trying to smooth away the worry. "But you're under my protection. You're safe."

"Am I?" I ask, my voice thick with fear. But it's not fear of what Aleksandr might do to me. It's fear he'll do something stupid too and get caught or killed—taken away from me.

He must sense my line of thought. "You have nothing to worry about. I'm not reckless like Vasily."

I bury my face against him and press my hands to his chest, needing his strength to say the next words. "You kidnapped me."

Aleksandr's laugh rumbles beneath my hands. "And what's reckless about that?"

"It's illegal," I whisper, my hot breath ricocheting against his chest.

He leans back and lifts a challenging brow. "And who would care?"

"My family. The police."

"Sure, your family made a fuss. That girl Anna was quite adamant, contacting the police several times. But nothing a wad of cash couldn't solve."

God, it hurts to hear that I'm worth no more than a sum of money. I try to pull away, but Aleksandr grabs my shoulder.

"This is not your picture-perfect Scandinavia. The police are good for what they're paid to do. A little money, and they'll sweep anything under the rug. Unless someone pays them to sweep it back out." He levels me with a hard stare that not even the darkness can pacify. "Does your family have that kind of money? Or your friend?"

I stare into the darkness behind him, my face taut with the effort of quelling the hurt.

When I don't respond, he digs his fingers into my skin, demanding an answer. "Huh?"

My eyes dart back to his, and my voice trembles with hopelessness. "I don't know." *I have no one.* No one important enough to make me count. And as always, Aleksandr doesn't hesitate to rub the cold truth in my face.

"Taking someone from the bratva is suicidal, but taking a girl who belongs nowhere..." He shrugs. "Like stealing an apple."

I turn around. This time, he doesn't stop me, so I break the physical connection and curl up on myself, cold and alone without his warm body.

A gentle hand slides onto my stomach, and I ache to feel more of him as his breath billows against my ear. "You're not just a stray roaming the streets without a collar anymore." His hand moves up and presses me back into him as it makes its way up between my breasts—farther up to curl his fingers around my collar. *His* collar. "If anyone tries to take you from me, there'll be hell to pay."

I shudder and suppress a sob, but a new one rises in its wake and erupts with a raw, mournful sound. I can't control it. Before I know it, I'm shaking and weeping, pressed against Aleksandr's chest and wrapped in his arms.

"*Dershu tebya*," he soothes. "You belong to me. There's nothing to be afraid of."

Except you, my brain screams, but all the realizations of the day muffle the sound. Aleksandr might have hurt me, used and abused me, and offered me up to a whore, but I don't care. When it's *his* humiliation, *his* pain, I want it. I crave it. It's nourishment for my soul. And when someone else tries to put me down, there's *hell to pay*.

He protects me from everyone but himself. And that's all I need. It's fucked-up and wrong. My rational brain knows this, but it doesn't get to control me anymore.

I want to be his with everything it entails. I want to feel his possession at the core of my soul. His hand on my throat isn't enough. My entire being shakes with the need for more.

"Please," I beg. "Please fuc—" I can't release the rest of the words. They're always stuck in the rubble of right and wrong.

"What?" Aleksandr grabs my chin. "What do you need?"

I glance back and forth between his eyes. They're fierce and piercing, and I find the strength in there to go against everything that's held me back for months.

"Please fuck me."

In one swift motion, Aleksandr shoves me to my back and rolls on top of me, trapping me beneath his weight as he cages my head in between his arms. "Why?" He presses his erection against my mound, spurring another stream of tears as the need to feel him flares inside me.

"I—I belong to you," I say, staring into his eyes. "I need to feel it."

His lips pull up into a smile. It's the same charming, heart-melting one that had my heart thumping when I saw him on the train. For the first time since that fateful day, I don't see a man who has kidnapped me and taken all I had.

I see my master.

"Spread your legs," he orders.

I obey immediately.

Already naked, Aleksandr doesn't waste time. He shoves his hard length against my opening, and the feeling is heaven. I moan through the tears and arch my back, wanting more. Wanting all of him.

Aleksandr grunts as he presses the tip inside. I can only imagine how painful the pleasure must be after a year of abstinence. Yet I don't think it's much different from what I'm experiencing. I've been waiting for this man for half a year. No, not just waiting. Craving, yearning, and aching. I haven't been able to admit it, but it's been there all along, the burning desire.

He pushes a little farther in, and I cry out from the sheer overload of... everything. Sensations and emotions rip through my body and mind. It's excruciating, maddening, and electrifying. It tears me apart and fulfills me in the deepest sense of the word.

"Please," I moan, arching my back high off the mattress.

His eyes spear me in place as he pushes in, one slow, agonizing push that fills me to the brim. All my focus gathers around the pulsing intrusion, wanting more, wanting less. But he just stays there, locking us together in this intense connection.

"Please," I repeat. My tears come a little faster as I strain against his body and grapple at his shoulders, the sheets, and his chest. "Master, please."

Gently—ever so gently—Aleksandr wraps his hand around my neck. The violence is subtle yet potent as he tightens, slowly but surely restricting my air.

Fear builds inside me, culminating in a wave of panic that has me struggling against the pressure. But Aleksandr squashes my fight with a single command.

"Don't," he growls, and the panic draws back, leaving me in a state of pure submission. I go still beneath him as I stare into the willful depths of his eyes. I can't move, I can't think. If he wants to snuff out my breath, I'll let him. That's the kind of power he holds over me.

A small twitch in his brow is my only warning. With a burst of movement, he pulls out and slams back into me. A choked scream stutters in my constricted throat as fiery energy bursts through my body. Aleksandr repeats the motion, spearing me with his enormous shaft.

His hand slackens, just enough to free my screams, and a keening mix of desperation and lust fills the darkness. I crash toward my orgasm, faster than I can handle. My entire body is strung with the need to come, my toes curling and my legs spasming.

"Not yet," he grits and stills inside me.

I whimper and moan, hating him and needing him at the same time.

"Such a good little slut." Grabbing my jaw, he flips my head to the side and kisses the sensitive spot behind my left ear. *His tattoo.* "Show me what a dirty little slut you are and come for your master."

"Yesss." My moaned response morphs into a scream as

Aleksandr sets my orgasm rolling with a forceful thrust. One more, and another. He keeps going, and I don't know how he's not coming. The wait must be agonizing, just like my orgasm that keeps rolling. It ripples off for a moment, but then Aleksandr presses his thumb to my clit, and I'm coming again. My entire body convulses and jerks with the onslaught of sensation.

His cock swells inside me, and my eyes roll back into my head as the sensations keep going and going, bursting through my nerves and throbbing in my veins. I'm fragmenting into a million pieces, helpless yet free under this dangerous man.

Finally, Aleksandr lets go. His hand tightens on my neck again as his motions become jerky and his face contorts with pleasure. A feral growl erupts from deep in his chest, and his eyes go wild and dangerous like he's prepared to kill.

"Little whore," he sneers cruelly, punctuating each word with a hard thrust. "*My* little who—" The word breaks into a groan as he comes down from his orgasm, and then we stare at each other for a breathless moment, both shuddering from the lingering pleasure.

Slowly, he loosens his grip on my throat. I breathe hard, reeling from the pleasure and his words—from him finally letting go of his control.

Fear slowly creeps up my spine as I wait for... somcthing. Will he shove me away now that he's gotten what he wanted? Shut me out with more cruel words because the emotional connection is too much? Act like nothing happened?

His reaction is nothing like what I feared. I keep expecting the worst from him—deceit, lies, distance. But despite all the humiliation, this man is capable of love. It's not the normal kind I might once have dreamed of, but somehow, it's just what I need.

His eyes come alight with warm emotion as he strokes a

hand across my damp hairline. "My good girl." It's like he's correcting his earlier statement. "I've been waiting for this since the first night I locked you in my cage."

My heart flutters, and gratitude swells inside me.

"Thank you," I say with as much clarity as my hoarse voice can muster. I'm not yet ready to tell him it's the cage I'm thanking him for, but I'll get there. Just like I got here, begging my captor to take me.

Aleksandr lowers himself back to the mattress and curls my body into his. "Sleep, *krasivaya devushka.*"

My eyes fall shut, and I drift away, feeling more at peace than I ever have anywhere else.

Chapter 26

ALEKSANDR AND VASILY are out hunting again the next morning. I spend the day with Ivan, helping him in the kitchen and watching nature shows while I lie with my head in his lap. It's surprisingly easy to be intimate with this man. It's clear he's known violence. I can see it in the darkness that occasionally flickers across his face. But deep down, he's a gentle soul.

In the afternoon, Aleksandr and Vasily return with a deer, which Ivan cuts up while I watch in equal disgust and fascination. Then he makes a hearty stew that makes my mouth water even before I taste it.

Along the way, I wonder how he can season the food without a tongue, but as he goes, I notice how he dips his head close to the stew and his nose twitches to pick up the scent. Even when he adds salt, he does this, like his sense of smell is so refined he can assess saltiness like this.

Dinner passes in a relaxed mood. I even feel good enough to carry a conversation with Vasily, asking about his job and telling him about my piano transcriptions upon his inquiry. Aleksandr seems pleased by this. He generally seems calmer and more relaxed than I'm used to, chatting with Vasily and laughing every so often. I can't help but admire him and cast lingering glances up at him. I notice how Vasily takes us in. His eyes roam back and forth between us like we're a riddle he's trying to solve. But instead of his earlier suspicion, I now only find fascination in his observant eyes.

Once our plates are empty and I'm helping Ivan clear the table, Aleksandr's disposition changes.

He watches me with this dark, unreadable expression as I walk back and forth between the table and the kitchen, his features set in stone and eyes hungry.

Maybe he wants to fuck me again? One taste, and his so-called control waned. My belly does a little flip at the thought, and I catch myself biting my lower lip as I walk back to him.

He gets up and tucks me into his side, and I think he's going to excuse us to take me back to the guest room and have his way with me. But what he does makes my jaw drop.

Looking from Ivan to Vasily, he asks casually, "Would either of you like to use Astrid?"

I go positively rigid, and my eyes shoot to the ground to avoid any and all contact with any of the men.

Vasily's response surprises me almost as much as Aleksandr's question. "I'm sure Ivan would like to borrow her. That is, if Astrid is okay with it."

Suddenly, all eyes are on me. I can feel the heavy weight even as I keep my gaze trained on the wooden surface of the table.

Aleksandr leans in and touches his warm palm to my cheek to turn my face to him. There's no cruelty or arrogance in his expression. *He doesn't do this to hurt me*, I remind myself. Yet I can't resign myself to the idea of another person taking me after the devastating episode with the whore.

"Please," I say in a weak voice. "Not again."

"*Bolshe ne budet,*" Aleksandr confirms, eyes grave with honesty. "This is nothing like what happened last week." He strokes his thumb along my jaw. "Ivan is rough, but he's not cruel."

Unlike you? A small part of me still resents him for letting the whore touch me. But as I stare into his sincere eyes, full of power, the resentment fades and gives way to a submissive urge.

"You liked it when I let Anton fuck you, right?"

I won't admit it, so I don't reply. And I'm not sure I'm supposed to. Aleksandr doesn't need my confirmation. He knows how wet I got when he forced my legs apart for his bearded guard.

Aleksandr gives Vasily an affirmative nod. Maybe he also knows I don't hate the idea of Ivan fucking me.

But why doesn't he do it himself? He did it last night, so why not now? Doesn't he want me again?

"Why don't you take me yourself?"

His mouth twitches cruelly as he curls his hand around my throat. "If I fuck you again this soon, I'll lose control. I won't have that. But you need this." He tucks a lock of hair behind my ear. "You've earned it."

Heat flares in my system along with a twinge of disappointment. But only a twinge. Because this is Aleksandr. I remember how he told me he doesn't let his dick control him. So it makes sense that he would feel like his lust got the upper hand if he gave in to it two nights in a row. He needs control like others need air. It's maddening, but also just what I need. I have no control, so he has to have enough for both of us, or I'll fall adrift.

My eyes flicker to Ivan when Aleksandr releases my throat.

He stands at the other end of the table with his arms crossed over his broad chest. I swallow hard at the sight. His gaze crackles with something cold and detached, all signs of the tender man I've come to know gone. I feel like a deer staring into the barrel of a gun, and I'm no longer so unflappable about him using me.

I'm breathing hard when Aleksandr catches my face between his hands. The room starts to bustle beside us—chairs scraping across the floor, drawers opening—but I'm trapped in the safety of Aleksandr's gaze. *For now.*

"I'm here all along," he promises. "Vasily too. We're both watching out for you."

What about Ivan? I want to ask, but the words won't leave my mouth, so I just nod in his grip.

He slides his hands down to my waist and slowly gathers the hem of my blouse in his large fists. My heart speeds and trepidation curdles in my stomach as he pulls upward, yet my arms willingly lift into the air for him to take it off. Next goes my pants at an equally leisurely tempo. It's both nerve-racking and soothing. The delay gives my nerves time to build, but the gentle strokes of his fingers subdue the unease.

Finally, my underwear comes off, and I have to fight the urge to cover my private parts as Aleksandr guides me to the end of the table. Vasily has taken a seat on a chair at a discreet distance. A spectator. The prickle of his perceptive eyes along my skin is unnerving.

Ivan hovers close by, a towering giant in my peripheral vision. He might not be as tall as Aleksandr, but he's twice as wide, and I can feel the brutality rolling off him without even looking.

I'm not sure it's not another case of my mind misconstruing male intentions. Ivan has been so gentle and caring for the last couple of days that it doesn't add up.

Aleksandr can be as gentle as he's cruel, I remind myself. So why wouldn't a brute like Ivan be capable of both?

An icy shudder ripples down my spine as I notice the ropes connected to the four table legs. I spin around to face Aleksandr before he can press me down on the surface.

"I can't," I say, hugging my chest. "I can't do this."

Aleksandr cups my chin and bends his knees to gain direct eye contact. "Sure you can."

I shake my head, but the movement is full of uncertainty. That's what Aleksandr's confidence does to me. It shoves away everything I believe to make room for his decree. "I can?"

"Of course. You're mine, Astrid, and I want you to do this, so you'll do it."

His unwavering certainty surges into me and steadies my erratic heartbeat. I don't need my own confidence when I have his. My throat moves with a gulp, and I give him a slow nod.

"*Takaya horoshaya devushka.*" He rewards me with a stroke on the cheek before he turns me around and urges me to bend over the table. He almost doesn't need to press to get me in place. A mere touch of his palm at my upper back is enough to make me bend of my own free will and rest my torso on the wooden surfacc.

"Will you do the ropes?" he asks Vasily, keeping his hand on my back as a stabilizing comfort.

Vasily approaches and hovers above my naked body. He doesn't speak a word as he slides his knuckles down the length of my arm. Calmness fills the air around him, clashing with the dormant threat that is an unwavering constant in this man. I clench my fists even as goose bumps erupt along my skin.

We're both watching out for you, Aleksandr said. I know it's true. I feel it like a promise in both their hands. They may be capable of devastating harm, but they won't direct that power at me.

My hands slowly unclench, relaxing on the surface in silent submission.

Vasily picks up one of my wrists and twines rope around it. He moves slowly but deftly. He's clearly done this before. The tightness is just right, holding me in place without cutting off my circulation, and the four circles of rope are perfectly aligned around my wrist when he tightens the knot. I watch in fascination as he proceeds to my next wrist. But when he moves behind me and I lose the distraction of watching him work, realization dawns anew. I'm trapped. In a few minutes, Ivan is going to fuck me, and there's absolutely nothing I can do about it.

I tug at the ropes a few times, testing their strength. *Unwavering.* Then I push against Aleksandr's relaxed hand at my back, and it immediately goes firm, holding me in place as efficiently as the ropes. Helplessness washes through me, titillating and terrifying.

The sensation explodes in my veins when I try to hide my feet behind Aleksandr. A firm hand snatches my ankle, making me yelp. The grip isn't like a leather cuff that will give in small fragments. Vasily's hand is like an iron manacle, firm and controlled, staying exactly where it snapped into place.

I was right about this man. *Pure danger.*

It should terrify me out of my mind, yet my blood rushes a little faster and gathers between my legs, heating my core.

Once I'm bound into strict compliance, my range of movement reduced to mere inches, Aleksandr and Vasily leave my side.

The room remains eerily quiet as they both take a seat at the edges of my vision.

I wait. A minute, maybe two. And then I feel it, the energy shifting behind me. It's like a brewing storm, quiet yet dark on the horizon.

Ivan moves behind me, approaching the table to stand between my legs. It's like a wolf sneaking up on me. Silent and deadly. I can't feel him, but I can feel the threat, raising the hairs on my nape and chilling my blood.

The sound of a belt breaks through the quiet, followed by a low grunt. It's raw and hungry, exuding all the violence I hoped to be an illusion. I hear him sheathe his cock, and his growls grow frustrated with impatience, sounding nothing like the gentle man I've come to trust during the past two days.

Large hands slam onto my waist, drawing an abrupt yelp from my throat. Fear coils my muscles as the head of a thick cock presses against my entrance. It's foreign and unwelcome. I screw my eyes shut to block it out, but there's no ignoring the intrusive sensation. Shudders erupt through my body, and a wave of dizziness blurs my mind.

"Look at me," a deep voice demands.

I force my eyes open with a whimper. Craning my head, I meet my master's eyes. They're as steady as they're demanding, promising both pain and protection.

The first comes when Ivan shoves inside me. One earth-rattling thrust has my eyes rolling back.

"Nooo," I wail, clawing at the edges of the table.

"*Ty uveren chto eta khoroshaya ideja?*" Vasily's concerned voice flickers somewhere in the background—something about this not being a good idea.

Aleksandr's sharp command follows. "Astrid," he snaps, and my eyes immediately dart to him, so instinctively it dulls the pain and fear. His eyes lock onto me with willful determination. "Do this. For me."

Another hard thrust has me shaking, and I clench my jaw to keep my teeth from rattling as I nod my agreement. "Mm-hmm," I whimper, keeping my eyes on Aleksandr's.

But when Ivan picks up pace, I lose the connection. The painful thrusts come at a staggering speed as he fucks me with punishing violence. I never knew it was possible to fuck so hard so fast. If I did, I'd hope I'd never get to experience it.

I yank at the ropes and wail into the room, clawing at the table and whipping my head back and forth.

In a blur of motion, Vasily darts up and shoves Ivan back. His cock falls out, and there's an enraged grunt, more animal than human. It's like Ivan has become a completely different person. Like he's possessed.

Aleksandr is right at Vasily's heel. "*Podazhdi*," he barks, making Vasily pause. Grabbing my hair, he sinks to my level. "Look at me," he demands, yanking at my hair.

I cry out through the pain, but the sound dies in my mouth when I focus on the man in front of me. The force of his gaze knocks the panic straight out of me.

"The pain is mine," he growls.

God, the pain. My scalp screams, my pelvis pounds, and my skin smarts from the bite of Ivan's hands, which are still lodged around my hips. It's all I can think about, and it takes me a moment to realize what Aleksandr is saying.

He's the one who controls the pain. He's the one who gives it to me—directly or by proxy.

"Take it for me," he demands, and it's like the whole world flips at those words. The pain dulls. Or rather, morphs into something else. A throbbing heat, a melting desire. An extension of Aleksandr's will. And God, I crave it badly.

Aleksandr briefly lifts his eyes to Vasily, demanding he releases Ivan.

The moment Vasily steps back, Ivan slams back into me. The pain is still there, but it drowns in the pulsing need, or maybe it merges with it, and it drives me toward an explosive orgasm.

"That's a good little whore. *Malenkaya shlyushka*," Aleksandr croons, and I moan at the warped compliment, relishing in the depravity. "Come for your master."

The effect is instant. My legs spasm in the ropes, and my body strains in Ivan's grip as I combust in a vicious orgasm. It's pain and pleasure, crashing against one another in violent harmony.

Suddenly, Ivan is coming too, with an almost pained sound. The room becomes a cacophony of echoing screams, loud moans, and roaring growls.

The moment I feel his orgasm wane, he pulls out and releases my hips. My orgasm has barely rolled through me, and I shudder with the last ripples, groaning with dissatisfaction. I'm not ready to lose the connection. But Ivan is determined to break it. I stare after him in stunned surprise as he leaves the room with pounding steps and shuddery shakes of his head and slams the door bchind him.

"Did I do something wrong?" I manage through labored breaths as I lift my head to watch the two men. My eyes flicker to Vasily and halt in a new flash of surprise. He's staring at me, eyes wide and amazed, his hand rubbing the back of his head like he doesn't know how to react.

"You did everything just right," Aleksandr whispers close to my ear.

Vasily agrees with a firm nod. "Ivan hasn't come inside a

woman for years. I always have to stop him before he gets that far."

"Stop him?" My voice slurs as the effect of the whole ordeal knocks into me with delayed effect. My head drops to the table, and my eyes blur.

Vasily chuckles warmly. "A little masochist." His next words drown in the drowsy hum covering my ears.

It's like someone has drugged me. A blissful, peaceful drug.

I blink against the blurry vision of the two men bustling to untie the ropes. Someone lifts me up to sit on the table and drapes a steadying arm around me as my head droops against a shoulder. I inhale a deep whiff of citrus.

"Master," I murmur into Aleksandr's neck as fluffy darkness claims me.

The sound of a door and the patter of paws wake me. I'm curled up in Aleksandr's lap on a couch, wrapped in a blanket.

Slowly, I lift my head to see Ivan come in with Pasha on his heels. He's wearing nothing but jeans and a towel slung around his neck, his sculpted torso on full display. I can't help lingering on the sight. Where Aleksandr has the elegant strength of a swimmer, Ivan has the rugged strength of a lumberjack—a body built for hard work. He's not beautiful in the traditional sense, but God, his resilient stature and the warmth in his eyes make for a potent combination that makes it hard not to marvel.

Except, his eyes aren't warm right now. They are livid. And all his rage is directed straight at Vasily.

"Relax, Ivan." Vasily lounges on the other couch, by no means perturbed by the angry mountain of a man coming straight for him with accusation written all over his face. "I told you it was okay."

Clenching his jaw, Ivan points an angry finger at Vasily. There's no doubt he'd sputter curses if he could.

"There was no need for me to stop you. Aleksandr had it under control. She's okay."

My blurry mind scrambles to follow. Why should Vasily have stopped him? Couldn't Ivan do it himself? And why didn't he stop when I screamed at the top of my lungs? I know he doesn't want to hurt me.

Ivan shakes his head, fury seeping from his pores.

"Come see for yourself," Aleksandr offers.

Ivan's steps thud angrily across the floor until he reaches the couch. Something shifts in him as he watches me, and his movements become careful as he lowers himself to the couch and reaches out to touch my cheek. I blink my sleepy eyes against his now soft gaze. All traces of rage are gone as he carefully studies me. There's only regret and concern. An unspoken *I'm sorry.*

I reach for his hand, gripped by an urge to soothe away his worry. He seems hesitant to take it at first, but when I squeeze his big paw, he closes his hand around mine in a warm, soothing grip.

I straighten on Aleksandr's lap as I get lost in Ivan's warm gaze.

"Thank you," I say softly.

A deep frown curls Ivan's brows. I'm not unaware of how strange my words are. Thanking someone for shrouding your world in pain and panic is not normal. But my world isn't normal. I'm not normal. I don't know if this dark urge that makes me orgasm under brutal force has always resided somewhere deep inside me or if it's a product of Aleksandr's conditioning.

What does it matter anyway? The urge is there regardless, real and potent.

When dealt by the right hand, pain and cruelty make me come alive in a way I never have before. Just like Aleksandr almost prophetically said. I do feel free under the fiery lick of his whip, I do need a master, and I do crave the raw possession of his cock. He sees things in me I don't see—don't dare to see—myself. So maybe he's right about the first night too. Maybe I did beg him to strip me bare and take away the burden of freedom.

I gulp and shove the idea back into the dark recesses of my mind. I might not deny the idea, but I'm still not able to cope with it.

"Do you want to hold her?" Aleksandr asks.

Ivan nods eagerly.

Aleksandr lifts me and passes me to Ivan. I tense at the feeling of Ivan's large, calloused hands as he settles me into his lap. My fear isn't conscious. It's an instinctive reaction as my body remembers what those hands did half an hour ago—the brutal force unheeding my screams.

None of the brutality lingers now, though. Ivan is as gentle and careful as I came to know him. Maybe even more so. The regret is palpable in the tentative way he holds me, like I'm a fragile thing he's afraid to break.

I don't want him to hold back out of guilt, so I sink into him and curl my arms up against his chest in a silent gesture of trust. I have no idea what came over Ivan when he fucked me or why he couldn't stop himself, but deep down, I know I'm safe here in his arms now that the storm has passed.

Slowly, Ivan relaxes. The tension in his shoulders drains, and his arms go firm around me as he presses me closer.

If I thought Aleksandr was strong, I'm not sure what to call

Ivan. Deadly? His chest is wider and thicker, the muscle hard and unbreakable beneath my hands; his thick arms are massive branches wrapping around me. It should feel dangerous, but he carefully tempers his strength—just enough to cocoon me into a tight grip, but not enough to restrict my airflow.

The fingertips that trail featherlight strokes down my arm are so gentle it's difficult to believe this is the same man who brutalized me at the dining table.

Aleksandr catches my attention with a hand on my thigh. "I need to go make a call. I'll be right back." He gives me a reassuring squeeze. "You are safe here."

I follow him with my eyes as he stalks through the room, his phone already at his ear.

"Does he ever take a break from business?" Vasily asks as he strokes the fluffy creature that snuggles up beside him on the couch.

When he's whipping me. I don't say the words out loud. They're private. Plus, I'm still too sluggish to carry a conversation.

Vasily goes to the kitchen to retrieve a bottle of wine and a couple of glasses. When he returns, he grabs a bottle opener from a nearby drawer and uncorks the bottle.

"I would offer you some, but I don't think Aleksandr would be happy if I served you alcohol without his permission." The cork makes a small pop as Vasily pulls it from the bottle.

He pours two glasses and hands one to Ivan, but sets it on the coffee table when Ivan doesn't let go of me to take it.

Vasily sits back down beside Pasha, propping his ankle up on his knee as he sips the wine and pets the dog. He looks almost normal like this, laid-back and relaxed. Though, the eerie observation lingers in his eyes as he studies Ivan and me.

"Are you okay?" he asks me after a few minutes of silence.

I snuggle closer into Ivan's embrace and nod. How can I not be?

How can I be? is probably the more appropriate question and the intent behind Vasily's inquiry. But why try to explain the inexplicable?

Ivan presses me tighter in response and presses his large hand to my cheek like I'm a child in need of comfort. I listen to the steady flow of air as his chest moves up and down, lulling me deeper into the comfort of his arms.

Silence stretches through the room, calm and effortless. Vasily turns his eyes to the window and the murky dusk outside as he sips his wine. The lack of his intent focus makes it easier to relax—easier to open up.

"Why do you need Vasily to stop you?" I murmur as I press my palm against Ivan's sculpted chest.

I feel Vasily's gaze return to us before I see it. There's a question in his eyes, and Ivan responds with a nod.

"He can't stop himself," Vasily explains. "He was forced to do some pretty bad things to women when he was just a kid." He takes a sip of his wine and gazes into the distance, and I think he's going to stop the explanation there—abrupt like Aleksandr. But then his gaze trails back to me, grave and somber. "It's how he knows sex. Once he opens the door, he can't shut it himself. So he doesn't have sex without my supervision."

"But you're so gentle." I trail my thumb over a scar on Ivan's chest.

"It's conditioned," Vasily explains. "Deeply rooted in his subconscious. Like the instinct of a hungry wolf to pounce on a deer. When he's not hungry,"—he shrugs—"no danger. But when the urge is roused, so is the need for violence."

"I'm so sorry." I press the side of my head into the crook below Ivan's head.

A low murmuring sound escapes him as he rocks me, like I'm the one in need of comfort and not him.

"He doesn't even sleep with the door unlocked when we have women in the house," Vasily adds.

My heart aches. The horror this man must have seen is unfathomable. Despite it all, he's retained his gentleness, and I can't help but marvel as his hand strokes my cheek and he nuzzles my hair. There's so much love and tenderness in this man. So much strength even though someone once tried to break him.

"Do you often have women here?" I ask, curious about these two men who both seem to incite the rare occurrence of Aleksandr's respect.

"Rarely. But we both like it when we do." Vasily points his glass at us, and his eyes warm. "I don't bring my women out here. Not unless I fully trust them, and I rarely meet anyone I want to be with long enough to find out if she's trustworthy. And since Ivan prefers to stay here, he rarely meets anyone. That's why I suggested he'd be the one to take Aleksandr's offer."

Turning my head to glance up at Ivan, I give him a shy smile, which he reciprocates with a warm one that makes his deep blue eyes light up. I can't believe I might be the only woman this kind and gentle man has been with for a while.

I lean my forehead against his chest and feel the steady thuds of his heartbeat. It's strong and firm. Unwavering.

Ivan nudges the hair off my left shoulder and slides his hand onto my nape. When Aleksandr grips me like this, it's possessive and primal, but with Ivan, it's a gesture of affection. The intimacy fills the air around us and wraps us in a silent peace that stops the world from turning.

Seconds pass. Minutes pass. I lose track of time as my surroundings slip into an inconsequential blur.

A hand behind my ear makes me jump. It's not Ivan's. His are still on my nape and waist.

It's Vasily, I realize. Despite the quiet, he managed to move up behind me unnoticed, and now he's touching my neck, stroking my hair away, and resting his fingers just below my ear.

The gesture is surprising, but not shocking. I still recall the tender way he kissed my forehead the night we drank tea together, and his touch fits perfectly into the bubble of intimacy. So I stay there.

Until he flips my ear back.

The tattoo. That's what he's doing. He's studying the numbers that mark me as property.

I shoot my hands up to cover them, and immediately, the energy shifts.

"*Dezhi yeyo,*" Vasily grits, ordering Ivan to hold me.

Betrayal stabs through me when Ivan grabs my arms and traps them between us. I try to wriggle free, but there's nothing I can do. Ivan has me locked in place with the efficiency of steel molded to my skin.

"Has he done this to you?" Vasily asks, horror lacing his words.

I whimper as he drags a finger over the numbers, and when he presses my head to the side so Ivan can see too, I want to cry. Not because Aleksandr marked me. It's the horrified grunt coming from Ivan's throat that has despair building in my chest. That grunt confirms all the beliefs I've stubbornly held onto for so long but was finally starting to be free from. *This is wrong, sick, and depraved, all wrapped up in one devastating package, and I shouldn't want any of it.*

Vasily doesn't say more. He doesn't need to. Horror and anger roll off him in waves—off both men. It's devastating. I want to get away. Hide my shame and hide from their pity.

But I have no resilience left, and when Vasily curves his hand around the back of my head, the emotions burst free.

I've craved sympathy for my predicament for so long, and now when it's here, I don't want it. But I can't help taking it. Like a parched cat offered poisoned water, I lap it up.

I weep silently into Ivan's chest. I weep for everything I've lost, every depraved thing I've gained, for their disapproval, and for my own that I can't seem to shake. I weep because I want him—the man who's torn my world apart and forced me to see all the things I didn't want to see.

I want him. I want him so badly. Maybe I've been conditioned like Ivan, or maybe I've finally come to see what was there all along. It doesn't matter. I just need him.

Firm steps sound Aleksandr's return, and a gush of relief washes over me.

"What's the matter?" Aleksandr urges as he rushes to my side.

Vasily steps back, and Aleksandr splays his hand on my back. Warm and strong. Familiar.

"Just some aftereffects," Vasily says. "Do you want some tea? I don't suppose you've started drinking alcohol since the last time I saw you?"

"No. I need to get Astrid to bed." Aleksandr takes me from Ivan's arms and carries me from the room.

Curling my arms around his neck, I bury my face against him and inhale his comforting scent.

"I'm scared," I confess, letting the vulnerability flow freely.

"What are you scared of, *krasivaya devushka*?" Aleksandr places me on the bed in the guest room and sits on the edge beside me.

I grab onto his waist and bury my face in his lap.

I'm afraid of the things he's doing to me. The way he affects me. Myself. For not hating those numbers behind my ear. For not hating the collar around my neck. I'm scared I'll lose myself so completely I won't be able to find my way back. But most of all, I'm scared of what will happen if I grow so dependent that I'm nothing but an empty shell if I lose him.

"Please don't leave me," I whimper into his legs as my tears wet the black fabric.

"I'm not leaving you. Not ever." The fierceness in his voice manifests in a grip on my nape. And right at this moment, the strain whooshes out of me, and peace settles in my bones.

I may like the tenderness of Ivan's touch, but I *need* the possessiveness of Aleksandr's grip.

Chapter 27

SAYING GOODBYE THE next day is a strange affair. Vasily keeps watching me like he did the first day. Seeing the numbers behind my ear has clearly changed something for him.

When we came, he thought I was an unwilling victim, but then he saw how I clung to Aleksandr and the affection I received, and now he knows the truth.

At least he thinks he does. The truth can no longer be boiled down to Aleksandr kidnapping me and marking me as an animal. It's far more complex. So much so I struggle to comprehend it myself even though it's becoming clearer every day.

But Vasily doesn't know that, and I'm not ready to acknowledge it out loud.

"Don't be a stranger," Vasily says as he shakes Aleksandr's hand, and I notice how his voice has become lower than usual, his gaze a bit sharper.

Aleksandr takes the proffered hand in a firm shake, and the goodbye becomes more of a standoff as the two men stare each other down, one more intimidating than the other. "Don't become a recluse."

I have no idea if Vasily has confronted Aleksandr or if Aleksandr has figured out what happened after he left last night, but it's clear something is going on between the two men. They aren't on the same easygoing, friendly terms as when they greeted each other three days ago.

Ivan pulls me in for a tight bear hug after Aleksandr has shaken his hand and moved on to put our luggage in the trunk. Leaning his cheek against the top of my head, Ivan once again wraps us in a quiet bubble of intimacy.

I wonder what he would say if he could speak.

I hesitate with my own words, afraid they're too intimate or he won't understand the true meaning.

"Thank you," I finally whisper.

He squeezes me tighter with one arm and gently cups the back of my head with the other. I think he understands what I'm thanking him for—mending my brokenness and giving me a safe place to heal, opening his beautiful heart for me, and not least, using me.

When Ivan moves me back by the shoulders to meet my gaze, tears are trickling from my eyes. Bowing my head away from Aleksandr and Vasily, I dry one cheek, and Ivan swoops in to take the other, giving me a wink when I peer back up at him. *No one noticed.*

I can't help but laugh, though strained. I really like this man, and I'm sad to say goodbye.

Next, I step up to Vasily, seeking Aleksandr's approval before taking his hand.

Vasily closes both hands around mine and gazes deep into my eyes. "It was lovely to make your acquaintance, Astrid. Maintain that fierce strength of yours." He lifts my hand like a true gentleman and presses a kiss to the back. Then he opens the passenger's door on the blue Maserati and watches me as I get in.

"Take care of her, Sasha." Vasily props an arm on top of the car as he leans down, and I don't miss the slight reproach in his tone.

"I always take care of what's mine, Vasily," Aleksandr shoots with a not-so-subtle hint of irritation. He turns on the engine, sets the car into drive, then turns back to Vasily, this time with sincerity. "Thank you for taking care of her."

"My pleasure." Vasily shuts the door, and then we're off.

The drive to the airport is quiet, but the tension from our last trip is gone. Aleksandr keeps taking my hand whenever he doesn't need both to steer, and he gives me these affectionate glances I haven't seen on him before.

I know he cares about me on some level, but these looks seem to hold more than the normal *you're mine, and you do what I want* affection. There's something almost like longing—maybe even apprehension.

When we're on the airplane, seat belts buckled, engine whirring as we prepare for take-off, Aleksandr leans in and takes my chin in his hand. "I'll never leave you. *Ty imeish moyo slovo,*" he says. No threat, no warning. It's a promise. Sincere and deep-felt.

But there's also a sort of worry in his eyes. Like he senses something coming. I don't know what. I believe him when he promises he'll never let me go, yet there seems to be some trepidation that this will all be over soon.

Is he afraid I'll leave him?

How can he be? Even if I wanted to, I couldn't.

But would I if I had the chance?

The thought sends chills running down my skin, and I

shudder.

“Are you cold?” Aleksandr asks and wraps me up in his jacket even though I tell him I’m fine, and when I shudder again sometime later, he pulls me into him and rubs his hands up and down my arms.

The motion soothes the most immediate unease, but the ominous sensation lingers like a brewing storm around the edges of my mind.

Chapter 28

THINGS CHANGE AFTER we get back from visiting Vasily. Not in a blatant, obvious way, but on a discreet level. Aleksandr still brings me to the dojo for a good whipping every now and then and lets Anton fuck me. He still locks me in the cage and insists I'm his property.

But there's something inherently different about his touch. A different urgency to his tenderness, like he tries to hold on to me, afraid I'll suddenly slip away.

He'll often sit beside the cage and stroke my hair long after he's shut off the lights, and sometimes, I'll wake from him carrying me to his bed in the middle of the night. There, he'll often make me come on his fingers, or on a rare occasion, have me suck his cock.

But he won't fuck me again even though I've become quite blatant in my begging.

"Please take me," I say, my voice full of need and frustration when I feel his hard length against my ass.

"No," he always replies, firm and unwavering.

"Why not?" I ask one morning after he's made me orgasm multiple times.

"I'm not sure..." he answers cryptically.

"About what?"

"You."

I shake my head and stare back and forth between his very blue eyes. "What do you mean? I'm yours. I've accepted it."

Aleksandr's features harden as he gets up and rounds the bed. Grabbing the leather cuff, which has become a permanent attachment to his bed, he shoves the covers aside and grabs my foot.

"I'm not sure you have." He tightens the strap around my ankle and snaps the padlock in place and leaves.

I stare stunned after him. I have. *Haven't I?* I willingly follow him to the dojo, beg him to fuck me, call him Master, and wear his collar with pride.

I'm his.

Despite Aleksandr's mistrust in my submission, he slackens the reins. He lets me walk the grounds without Boris at my heels—though I know there's always one of his men keeping an eye on me, only now from a distance—and he lets me wander off to get hors d'oeuvres or use the bathroom on my own whenever we're at a party, and one night, he even takes me to the opera.

I'm absolutely flabbergasted when we stand in front of the Mariinsky theatre—the opera, not the concert stage, which is in a separate building. I never had the money to come here much, but Anna and I managed to save enough to see two shows a year, and it was always a highlight in our meager lives.

Now, I'm staring up at the impressive building with saucer-sized eyes, feeling like a child who got the biggest present under the tree.

“I hope you like the opera.” Aleksandr squeezes my hand and studies me.

I stare back and forth between the towering building and the towering man. *Of course I like the opera.* I can’t believe he’s taking me!

“I didn’t think you’d be ready for the concert hall yet,” he adds.

My eyes lock on his, large and vulnerable, as a wave of emotion rolls through me.

There’s no mockery in his words to remind me he has the power to take away my dream. It’s a genuine, considerate gesture, not wanting to cause me further hurt by confronting me with my loss.

Aching longing crashes with fierce gratitude. The dream of the Mariinsky concert stage hasn’t faded from my mind even though I know it can never be more than that. A dream. Yet I feel utterly grateful for this man even though he’s the one who’s crushed my chances of getting there—touched he would do this for me.

“If you don’t like the opera, we can catch a movie instead.”

My lips part. “I…” But the words won’t come out—they won’t describe how I feel. So I fall into his arms, hugging his waist and inhaling his characteristic scent.

Not caring that people are milling around us, Aleksandr brings me into a tight embrace. There’s no aggressive possession or fierce power. He just holds me tenderly. It’s almost like we’re a normal couple out on a date—a man and a woman who love each other.

“I love it,” I finally say, squeezing my arms around his waist. I love it so, so much. And maybe I even love him.

Do I love Aleksandr?

I lean back and stare up, up, up, until my eyes collide with the stark blue of his.

The words hover right at the tip of my tongue. I want to say them—badly—but something holds me back. A shroud of memories. The fact that he kidnapped me. Took me from my dreams. Will it always be there? Hovering like a dark cloud, never fully revealing the open sky?

Aleksandr is right again. I have not fully given in. I've accepted my situation and come to terms with the fact that I crave his warped brand of affection, but I haven't accepted the finality of it. I haven't accepted that I can't get out—that he took me against my will.

It shouldn't matter. Aleksandr has done so many things against my will. I've even accepted the mark behind my ear. So why can't I forget the small detail of how I came to be his?

My eyes roam up to the beautiful building. And there's my answer. I'm stubbornly holding on to the dream of grand stages and concert posters with my name. I'm no longer sure if I truly want it, but I'm afraid to let go of the dream because it's the last remaining part of my old life. I'm afraid to let it go, because if I do, I have nothing else. Then I'm only his, and that thought scares me more than anything. There'll be nothing to fall back on, no other place to fit in. If I lose him, I lose it all. So I stubbornly hold on. I can't help it. I'm just so fucking scared.

Tears gather in my eyes as I stare back at Aleksandr. "I'm sorry," I say. *I'm sorry I can't let go, sorry I'm so stubborn, sorry I can't fully give in.*

Aleksandr answers by taking my head between his hands and pressing a long kiss to my lips. It's strangely vulnerable, full of emotions I rarely get to see in him. It's frightening and heady at the same time. Tears spill from my eyes and onto his powerful hands. Aleksandr has got me no matter what happens. He always catches me. So I let go. For now.

Pressing my hands against his chest, I lean into him, and there's that possession. Aleksandr snakes his hand around my nape and deepens the kiss, imbuing the movements of his tongue with all the might of his possession.

The world around us slips away, and I'm free in the steady grasp of his command. Free to let go of my dreams, the hurt, the longing. The fear. But when he releases me, it all filters back in, infecting my mind and squeezing my heart.

Aleksandr grabs my chin and leans in. "One day, Astrid. One day, you'll figure out that all this doesn't matter." He gestures to the world around us. "All that matters is that you belong to me. And that's enough."

Aleksandr straightens and trails a finger over my collar. His lips flatten as his hard façade falls back in place, and he takes my hand to lead us into the building.

The show is every bit as spectacular, moving, and beautiful as I thought it would be. But it's also overwhelming, all the people, emotions, and the whole newness of the situation. So when we leave the private box three hours later, I'm tired and want nothing more than to get into Aleksandr's car and let the rumble of the engine lull me to sleep.

Aleksandr brings me into his side as we make our way through the crowded lobby, and I lean into him and cast a sleepy smile up at him.

"I'm happy you liked it," he says with a smile of his own.

"I really did."

"Pletnev," a man calls from behind us.

Annoyance hardens Aleksandr's features as he halts and looks back.

A slightly plump middle-aged man in an expensive suit approaches us. "Do you have a minute?"

"We're going home," Aleksandr replies, about to pull me along.

"It's about the Nevskii account."

Aleksandr stops again, his eyes hard and unwelcoming as the man steps up to us. Before facing him, Aleksandr leans down to me and brushes my cheek, his eyes softening for a moment. "Go use the bathroom. I'll be done when you get back."

I nod and reluctantly slip out from under his arm to make my way through the crowd. I used the bathroom in the last break, so I just adjust my hair and check my makeup before I go back out.

My chest lifts with a heavy sigh when I enter the lobby again. There are even more people here now. How am I supposed to find Aleksandr?

I start making my way through the crowd when I hear the soft lilt of a feminine voice. "Astrid?"

I halt, and my heart stops when I hear the voice again, this time a little louder.

"Astrid?"

No, it can't be. I turn around and stare straight into a set of familiar almond-shaped eyes.

"Anna." My pulse speeds up and my head spins. It's like seeing a ghost. I thought I'd never see her again.

"Astrid?" she repeats in a whisper, shock and confusion widening her beautiful eyes. She shakes her head like the vision before her is as surreal as the one before me. "Where have you been?" She shakes her head again, and concern softens her features. "Are you okay?"

She's about to reach for me, but then her eyes scan downward and take in the diamond necklace below my golden collar, the expensive gown, and designer shoes. Her expression falls and hurt strains her beautiful features.

"Have you any idea how worried I've been?" she asks, staring at me like she doesn't know me.

"I've..." My throat constricts, killing the words. There weren't any, anyway. Because how do I explain this? I've been gone for half a year, and now, suddenly, I show up at the opera house, dressed like a princess.

Her eyes shimmer with unshed tears, and my heart clenches at the sight of the always stoic girl about to break down in the middle of a crowded lobby.

"I—I'm sorry," is all I can say. I know it's not my fault, but it's the only emotion I can feel right now. Regret. Deep, painful regret.

I reach for her, wanting to take her hand, soothe away the pain I've caused her, but someone grabs my arm. I flicker my eyes up to meet Aleksandr's hard expression.

When I glance back at Anna, her entire demeanor has changed. Her confusion has morphed into horror, her hurt into anger. It takes her a moment to get her façade back in place, and she exudes a willful energy that would scare most men. Seeing the man beside me tells her everything she needs to know—that I'm not here of my own free will; that I haven't left her by choice.

"Let her go," she demands.

But no one but Aleksandr makes demands in his world. He doesn't even acknowledge her, just drags me away.

"Wait." I try to pull back. "Just let me talk to her. Just for a minute."

"We're leaving," he says without a hint of emotion.

"No, please." I turn my head and see Anna rush after us through the crowd, but suddenly Boris is there, intercepting her. He's always there, hovering close by to do just that. Stop unwanted people from approaching us.

"Why couldn't you just let me talk to her," I say when Aleksandr shoves me into the passenger's seat of his yellow Alfa Romeo. "Just let me tell her I'm okay."

Aleksandr gets into the driver's seat and sets the car into drive. "You don't belong out there anymore."

"I won't say anything." And I mean it. I could never do anything to incriminate Aleksandr.

He leans in, just as he was about to drive off, and grabs my chin. "You're mine, Astrid," he says with all the force of his possessive dominance. "You belong with me. No one else."

His words hold a startling finality that leaves me breathless—shoves away any doubt or uncertainty that crept in when I saw Anna.

I can't even tell him he's right as the full force of his words pounds through my system.

No matter how much I fear or try to fight what's happening to me, I can no longer deny that I'm his. He alone controls my fate, my body, and to some extent, even my mind. All he has to do is say those words and the impact of seeing Anna is already fading.

Chapter 29

THE ROOM IS buzzing around me, the chattering of mingling people mixing with the smooth sound of a string quartet. But no one grants the musicians much attention. I'm the real attraction here. People keep glancing my way expectantly, whispering to each other, probably wondering what I'll play tonight.

A thrill of purpose rolls through me. It may not be the Mariinsky concert stage, but I get to share my music here at these private parties. I hunger to step up to the grand piano and pour my heart out as much as the people here hunger to see it.

The man throwing the party, Roman I think is his name, comes up and gives me a saccharine smile that sends shivers running down my spine. I think he's about to tell me it's time when he addresses me, but instead, he says in English, "Do you mind if I borrow Aleksandr?"

He clearly hasn't gotten the note that I'm not to be spoken to. And I don't answer.

"What?" Aleksandr shoots Roman an annoyed look.

"Relax, Sasha," Roman drawls in Russian. He probably doesn't know I speak the language. "I just want to discuss our investment deal. No one's going to take your precious pianist away." At that, he looks back at me, and there's something in his smirk that makes my skin crawl. *I don't like this.*

"Don't go," I say in half a whisper and grab Aleksandr's hand.

He gives me a squeeze to let me know he's heard me without taking his eyes off Roman. "We closed the deal long ago. There's nothing more to discuss."

"I might be interested in doing another one—even bigger—with you." Roman scratches at his beard and casts another unnerving glance my way.

"Well, I'm not." Aleksandr turns his attention back to the man he was talking to before Roman interrupted.

But Roman won't let it go. "I can get you a controlling share in the mother company."

This gets Aleksandr's attention.

"Let's discuss it in my office. I'm sure your woman would like a break to use the facilities anyway. I'll get one of my guards to escort her and she won't even know you're gone." With a snap of two fingers, Roman summons one of his men.

"Boris," Aleksandr calls, and Boris appears at our side, blocking the approaching man with his humongous build. "Take Astrid to the bathroom."

I still have a nervous feeling rattling in my stomach, but I'm relieved Aleksandr asks Boris to take me instead of sending me off with a stranger. There's something fishy about this whole situation, and I don't want to be left alone.

I take my time in the bathroom, not wanting to come out before Aleksandr has returned.

I'm washing my hands when there's a metallic sound coming from the door, like someone tries to pick the lock.

Retreating a step back into the room, I watch with horror as the lock turns and the door handle moves. Suddenly, my pulse pounds in my neck, and I frantically scan the place for some way to defend myself or escape. But it's too late. The door opens, and a tall man clad in all black steps inside.

My breath catches when my eyes fall into the dangerous trap of Vasily's gaze, and then relief floods my system. But the unease doesn't quite go away.

Vasily exudes the same calm poise that made me trust him when we spent a few days at his house in Siberia. He's still in complete control of every particle surrounding him, but today there's also a potency in the air around him, an urgency like he's here with a purpose.

Clasping his hands behind his back, he stops in front of the door and directs the acute sharpness of his gaze at me. For a moment, he just stares at me, taking in my every nervous twitch and flicker of apprehension. I feel like I'm staring into the barrel of a sniper's rifle, and I take a step back like retreating into a corner would do me any good.

"Do you want to get out of here?" he asks.

It takes me a moment to process his words. The genuineness is at odds with his purposeful stance.

"What do you mean?" My heart speeds up in my chest, chasing after his words as I realize what he's saying before he clarifies.

"Do you want to get away from Aleksandr? To be free?"

Get away from Aleksandr? No. Never. *Be free?* God, yes. It's all I've ever wanted. I wanted to be free from the constrictions of society, do my own thing, and chase my own dreams. Aleksandr took me away from it, trapped me and robbed me of the only freedom I ever knew.

But didn't he grant me another type of freedom? Didn't he

free me from my own mind, the worrying, the pondering, the yearning that nothing could ever quell?

Vasily breaks off my spinning thoughts. “I can get you out of here. Tonight. But you need to make a quick decision. We only have minutes.”

This steadies the turmoil in my head for a moment because I know he can’t. I won’t have to make this impossible choice. “Boris is in the hall, looking out for me.”

Uncertainty spills into my mind the moment I say the words. *Then how did Vasily get in?* Boris would have stopped him, right? Or did he let Vasily pry the lock because he knows him? No, it doesn’t make sense. Boris would have knocked or had him wait for me to come out.

Vasily shakes his head calmly and surely, confirming what I’m thinking.

“He wouldn’t leave me,” I croak, doubt sprouting a feeling of betrayal. *He wouldn’t.*

“Only if he thought Aleksandr was in danger.”

My heart pounds so hard I feel faint. “Is he?” *Please, God, let him be safe.*

Reaching for the wall, I try to steady my suddenly wavering legs, and Vasily steps closer and grabs my arms to do it for me. “He’s okay, Astrid. It’s only a diversion.”

Realization filters in. The diversion began with Roman. My stomach twists. I knew something was off. “Please, I need to go back to him.” I need *his* hands to be the ones steadying me.

“Astrid.” Vasily shoves back my rising panic with his demanding tone. “This is the only chance you’ll get. Aleksandr isn’t going to let you go. He’s too proud. But I can get you out.”

“I just want to go back to him,” I say, badly needing to see for myself that he’s okay.

"Are you sure?" Vasily seems somewhat perplexed. "You can be free. All you have to do is say yes."

"Why would you do this? Is this some kind of test?" Aleksandr is his best friend. They've known each other since childhood. It doesn't make any sense. Vasily wouldn't betray him like this.

Vasily lifts a hand and brushes my hair behind my left shoulder. Knowing what he's doing, I step back, but Vasily's grip prevents anything but a slight shuffle of my feet. I gasp when he presses the shell of my ear forward to reveal the black line of numbers that mark me as property.

The angry look in his eyes hits me as hard as it did the first time. Shame burns white-hot in my stomach, and suddenly, I can't find my way through the flood of emotions that wells up inside me.

It's wrong, yet it's so very right. It's humiliating, yet it frees my mind. I want it, yet I don't want it.

But most of all, I'm so terribly scared. Fear still pounds in my chest from the thought of something happening to Aleksandr. I've grown so dependent on him that I'm not sure how to cope if I lose him.

"Treating a woman like a slave is unforgivable," Vasily says.

A slave. Kidnapping. Keeping me against my will.

The words flicker through my mind, and I'm surprised to find I truly don't care. Not when I think about the golden bars and the safety of Aleksandr's arms. But he's not here right now. He's somewhere else. Out there among those dangerous people. I don't think anything has actually happened to him, but the idea that something might scares me so much I can hardly breathe.

I clutch my chest as my mind runs rampant, imagining something happening to him a year from now when I'm completely dependent on him. I'll be like one of his dogs he found in the streets of St. Petersburg. Helpless and lost. And who will take me in then? No one. Because no one wants a broken woman, and I won't be able to cope on my own.

I can't let myself become so dependent on one single person with no backup or safety net. I just can't.

So I nod and look up at Vasily. "Get me out of here."

The next five minutes pass in a flurry of hasty movements, pulsing heartbeats, and bated breaths.

Vasily helps me out of the window and onto the pristine lawn outside. It's so easy. No one sees or hears a thing. We simply jump out of the window. The entire act seems mocking to me. *Why didn't I do this myself?*

Next, I'm in Vasily's arms, bouncing against his hard chest as he hurries across the lawn, moving through the shadows on stealthy feet.

A black SUV waits for us by the road, and just as Vasily sets me into the back of the car, I see someone come running down the long driveway. Tall, broad, and fast, Aleksandr moves like a deadly predator. The lamp posts light up his face, revealing his terrifying expression—the urge to kill. But there's also something else hidden behind the hard façade. I'm not sure anyone else would see it, but I know him well enough to spot the hurt hidden deep in his beautiful eyes.

A sharp ache spears my chest, and I move to jump out of the car and run to him, but the door slams shut, and then the car is moving, taking me away from him.

Resolve hardens Aleksandr's features, and I think he's going to speed up, but then he stops.

He stops.

I press my hand to the window as a searing pain bursts through my insides. Is he letting me go? Without a fight?

My throat constricts, and I grip my collar as I heave for air, needing the symbol of his possession to steady me.

He's letting me leave. Just like that.

Vasily, who's beside me in the back seat, misjudges my panic. He quickly reaches for me and inspects the collar. A grunt of frustration escapes him when he sees the locking mechanism.

He pulls me face-down into his lap, takes a bobby pin from my hair, and goes to work on the lock. A few moments of metallic scratching and the lock gives with a click.

I've sometimes thought back to that fateful night when Aleksandr took me from the train station. The ominous prick in my shoulder. Aleksandr has done many things to take my freedom since, but the defeat was never quite as stark as the moment the sedative kicked in.

Now, the same stab of defeat hits me as the collar loosens around my neck. It's like being robbed of my very essence.

A hollow cry escapes my lips and fills the car with a horrible sound of pain and despair.

I want to grab at the collar as Vasily removes it, scream for him to put it back. But I'm the one who made the decision. I'm the one who left Aleksandr. And if I'm not with him, I can't wear it.

The realization stabs into my chest, and I release another agonized cry. Vasily takes me into his arms, and I desperately claw at his chest as I wail into his shoulder. He holds me with the same tender care Aleksandr always did. But it makes no difference. I feel broken apart, torn into shreds, and nothing will repair me this time.

Chapter 30

I KICK AT THE snow on the ground as I wait for my mom outside the grocery store like I do every time I let her convince me to join her. She thinks being around other people will do me good, and I keep hoping she'll be right. I've tried to go in with her a few times, but it always ends with me darting out of the store, clutching my chest as panic threatens to pull me under. Still, she keeps trying, and I keep letting her convince me. We're back in the same poisonous routine we've been stuck in since the first day she set me off at school—her pressuring me and me trying to accommodate her.

I remember clutching the hem of her blouse when she opened the door to the crowded classroom and a thick din of noise assaulted me. She had to pry my fingers off the silky fabric and all but push me to make me go in.

Thus began many years of retreating to the bathroom at every chance I got, covering my ears and shutting my eyes when I felt like I was drowning, and learning how to cope in a world I wasn't meant for.

Every morning, I begged my mom not to leave me, and every time she did anyway, it chipped away at our relationship. She never listened when I told her I felt like I was drowning; she just kept telling me I'd get used to it. But I never did, and at some point, I stopped trying to explain it to her and shut in on myself instead.

Somehow, I learned to cope, but all those mechanisms are long gone as I stare at the sliding doors and consider if I should give it one more go. I need to get used to this world, after all.

A shrill, whining noise breaks me from my anxious thoughts. I step around the corner to find a small, golden dog with huge eyes and long fluffy ears yapping for its owner. It's just a puppy. A puppy that seems as lost as I.

I carefully approach it and sink to my knees with my side to it at a few feet's distance, slowly reaching out my hand to let it sniff me. Like Aleksandr taught me.

My chest squeezes at the thought of him, and I quickly shove away the memory as a black, wet snout brushes my hand.

The puppy rises on all four legs to get closer, nose working eagerly as it moves up my hand, tail wagging with curiosity. I move a bit closer too and brush my fingers over the fluffy fur on its neck. The dog leans into my hand, and soon it's pressing itself against my leg and lifting its head as it eagerly accepts my petting.

I realize I'm smiling widely—my first smile in six weeks—when an outraged voice breaks the moment.

"Haven't you learned anything?" my mom snaps, grabbing my arm and pulling me away from the innocent puppy.

I stagger to follow the sudden force, but the moment she releases me, I fall onto my butt, and a sharp pain shoots up my spine and into my head.

"I don't have time to drive you to the emergency room today," my mother snaps, already having turned her back to me, on her way home.

Tears well in my eyes, and I quickly swipe them away and swallow the lump in my throat before getting up and following her. But it's not the pain or her sharp rebuke that has me on the verge of tears. It's the memory of strong arms catching me, never letting me fall.

I lift my hand to rub the spot behind my left ear. I can't see the black line of numbers and letters, but knowing it's there calms me. It makes me feel like I haven't truly lost him—like I still belong to him. It's about the only thing that will soothe the constant tension in my chest these days.

"Are you coming?" my mother calls without turning. She's probably struggling to hold back tears of her own. She's been doing that a lot since I came back, perpetually obsessed with keeping up her proper appearance.

Even when the police asked me if I'd been raped, her face was cold and stoic.

I told them no, of course. And that's about the only question I answered. For two long weeks, both my parents and the police tried ardently to pry answers from me, but I simply didn't know what to say. So I stayed quiet.

My parents threatened to kick me out or have me locked up at a psychiatric facility. None of it worked. They didn't know I had enough money to make it on my own—thanks to Vasily—and they didn't know the idea of being locked up soothed the nervous rattle in my mind.

Finally, everyone gave up. It was all empty threats. Cold as my parents may be, they don't want society to see them kick out their traumatized daughter, and I'm not crazy enough for any facility to want me. And since I wasn't pressing charges and the police had no perpetrator or any leads to go on, there was nothing they could do. It probably also helped that Christmas was coming around and that no one wanted their precious holiday ruined by my tragedy.

I follow my mom home at a distance, not wanting to talk to her. She'll only try to pressure me to apply for a job as a music teacher at the local school—the same one that drove us apart in the first place—or to start dating.

Once we get home, I head straight for my room, shut the door, close the blinds that my mom keeps opening, and flop onto the bed.

Then I lie there as I've done for the better part of a month and stare into the murky gray that swallows up my childhood room. The stark white of the globe-formed IKEA ceiling lamp stands out in the darkness, as does the nondescript white drawer, which every middle-class home has at least one of here in Norway.

Everything's the same here. Obnoxious. Stifling. It should feel like home—nostalgic and comfortable—but I can't remember that it ever did.

I miss the tall ceilings and open rooms of Aleksandr's mansion. The vast gardens which I could roam in peace without bumping into curious eyes at every turn. The clean air, the lake, and the white moonlight spilling in through wide windows.

But most of all, I miss the safety of the bars—or strong arms that would close around me. The certainty of a firm command. The peace of belonging. All the things I lost because of one stupid decision.

I often think back to the night Vasily took me away. I remember telling him no. I wanted to stay. Yet somehow, he convinced me. He brought back all the poisonous shame and uncertainty Aleksandr had almost released me from. All the fear.

I thought Aleksandr had brainwashed me, but being here

now and looking back, I realize he did the one thing I could never manage myself. *He set me free.*

Vasily thought he did the same, and even though I find myself hating him at times, the hate never sticks.

He did what no one else would do for me—not Boris, not any of the men who helped mark me like an animal, and surely not any of the stuck-up, entitled people at the parties Aleksandr brought me to. Vasily risked his oldest and deepest friendship to get me out, and I'm grateful for that despite the insipid life it has brought me back to.

He had prepared everything. A private plane to take me home, a thick wad of Norwegian cash to keep me going for a while, and a car to take me anywhere I wanted once I landed. Even a hotel room in case I didn't want to go home straight away. I chose the hotel and stayed there for two weeks until I finally worked up the nerve to go face the world, my parents, and the police.

I still remember the fierce look in Vasily's eyes when we said goodbye in front of the stairs to the aircraft. "You're so very strong, Astrid," he said.

"I'm not," I replied, feeling anything but strong with my eyes all puffy from crying and my body quivering from shock and grief.

He took my hand in both of his, and I badly wanted to ask him to take me with him as I gazed into his assertive eyes. "Only a few people can withstand Aleksandr. It takes immense strength to be around someone like him. I don't know the finer details of what he put you through, but I know whatever it was, it took a hell of a woman to survive without breaking. Remember that."

I think about those words whenever I feel weak and broken. But as the weeks have dragged on, the words grow more distant—

a faraway echo that doesn't ring true.

Turning in bed, I burrow deeper under the covers and try to recall the citrusy scent of safety and calm instead. I know the scent well. It hovers right there at the edges of my nostrils. So close.

I inhale deeply through my nose, desperately wanting it to permeate my senses, but instead, I take in the dead smell of potatoes and sweet detergent. I clench my fists harder around the sheets. It's wrong. All wrong. The scent is familiar, but not to me. Some distant, long-gone version of myself recognizes it, but it holds no meaning anymore. All I feel is dread as I inhale again without catching the citrusy notes.

Needing to get rid of the flat scent and distract myself, I throw the comforter aside and grab the phone on the nightstand. It's a strange thing to hold a device like this again, using the internet and being able to contact people—having people contact me.

I don't care for it. I deleted my Facebook account a few days after I got the phone, and I have several unopened texts sitting in my inbox. Too many people contact me with the pretense of wanting to know if I'm okay. Really, they just want the newest gossip and attain the information about what happened to me.

I blink against the sharp light as I click the Google icon and type in *Aleksandr Pletnev.* I need to see his face, see the sharp blue of his gaze, which becomes blurrier to my mind's eye by the day. My finger hovers over the search button, twitching with the need to press it. But I end up pressing the power button instead. I always do. It's like those many months of hoping he would show up at a recital, thinking that knowing what he looked like would jinx my chances. I know it's stupid, but what I'm hoping for this time is too important to take the risk.

One good thing I do get out of the phone is calling Anna. It takes me six long weeks to gather the courage. The hurt expression on her face when I saw her at the opera still haunts me. She thought I had up and left without a goodbye or explanation. I could never abandon her like that, yet I feel like I somehow did. Because I didn't fight. Not truly. I could have tried to gain Boris's help or sneak off when Aleksandr took me to parties. Something. Anything. Gain the sympathy of one of the many women he spoke condescendingly to.

I never tried. I just stood by his side, quiet and pliant, like some mindless idiot—an expensive acquisition he could show off to his rich friends.

Part of me hates myself for having been so meek. But the frightening thing is, I didn't hate it when I was there, safely tucked into his side, any looks of pity and contempt dispelled by his authoritative presence. It's only now that I'm back in the real world, where women are supposed to hold their own and no person is property, that I feel bad. Even so, some warped part of me misses it.

But as I sit with the phone clutched in my shaking hand, Anna's number dialed on the screen, I only feel regret and shame.

She picks up on the third ring. "Hello." Her gentle voice is tentative. Almost scared. She won't recognize the number I'm calling from, but she can see the country code. She probably thinks someone is calling her to tell her I'm dead.

"Anna." My voice is thin and brittle, shaking from the effort it takes not to cry at the sound of her voice.

Silence stretches on the line, and my heart beats so hard I can barely breathe.

"Astrid?" she finally says, her voice breaking. She is also fighting off tears. It's rare to experience such a vulnerable side of this girl who always meets the world with a shield of strength and composure, and it hurts to hear how I'm the one to have cracked that strength.

"I'm so sorry." I repeat the words several times as my free hand works to catch all the tears streaming down my cheeks.

"No, Astrid. I'm the one who's sorry. I'm sorry for ever doubting you." Her voice goes from resolute to brittle. "I should have never thought... I know you, Astrid. And I'm so sorry I didn't try harder to get you help. When I saw you with him, I went back to the police, but they wouldn't hear any of it, and—"

It's my turn to cut her off. "There's nothing you could have done." I'm the only one who could have done anything, and I didn't do shit.

After another stretch of silence, Anna tentatively asks, "What happened?"

I tell her how he took me from the station, but when I get to the part about the beautiful, detestable cage that I miss every day, I fall apart. I cry for ten minutes straight while Anna murmurs gentle words, telling me it's okay, that I'm out of there and never have to see him again. What she doesn't realize is that those words only wrench more tears from my eyes.

When I finally go quiet except for heavy breaths, she asks how I got out, and I spend half an hour telling her about Vasily, how he came to get me, and about the month I've spent here in my parents' home. Then I spend another ten minutes crying before I turn the conversation to her life.

She's been doing well after she graduated—as well you can after losing someone you hold dear.

She has not become the famous, world-touring pianist I hoped she would, but she's gotten a steady job playing at a fancy restaurant, which generates other gigs playing at parties of the customers, and it's enough for her to maintain her life in St. Petersburg.

When we end the call, it's with a promise to see each other soon. A promise I'm determined to keep.

Four days later, the doorbell rings early in the afternoon. A few minutes later, my mom is in my room.

"You've got company," she says, her eyes sharp with annoyance. If I had a distant relationship with my mother before, it's been all but frigid since I came back and refused to tell her what happened to me.

"I don't want to see anybody," I say and turn my back to her.

"Oh, hush, Astrid. Will you get out of bed for once and take some responsibility."

God, I hate that woman. But I'm in her house, and she's got a point. I can't keep lying around here. So I climb out of bed and walk through the house with my mother at my heels.

None of my former friends have been so brazen to show up at my house, and I'm more than fine about that. I don't want to be their topic of gossip more than I already am. Plus, they'll come up empty-handed if fresh gossip is what they're looking for. Or maybe not. My appearance alone might satisfy their need for something dramatic to talk about. The sight of me is not a pretty one. God knows I try to avoid the mirror as much as I can. Seeing myself is not much better than seeing a ghost. Black circles surround my lifeless eyes, my shoulders slump, and my cheeks are thin like everything else on my body.

I freeze when I reach the hallway. There, in the open doorway, is Anna. Beautiful as ever, wearing high-heeled boots that would make any Norwegian scowl at this time of year, and tears glistening in her almond-shaped eyes.

I run to her and fall straight into her arms, both of us sniffling like little girls. For the first time in weeks, I feel like I can breathe again.

"I've missed you so, so much," I say into her silky hair, and her arms tighten around me in silent response.

My mother's condescending voice destroys my newfound peace. "Who is your friend, Astrid?" I had blissfully forgotten about her, and I tense at the sound.

Anna gives my arm a reassuring squeeze, like she would always do when I talked to my mother on the phone.

"Thank you," I whisper and gulp to clear my voice of the strain. "Mom, this is Anna." I step away from my rock and best friend to let my mother greet her. "We studied together at the conservatory."

Anna shakes her hand and introduces herself, exhibiting just the right amount of politeness, but without a smile or a "Nice to meet you." When the exchange is over and my mother has turned her back, Anna's lips curl up in half a laugh.

I realize it's because I'm almost laughing myself. Anna hasn't met my mother before, but she's heard enough and seen me talking to her enough to get a good impression. I love how she doesn't show any fake enthusiasm.

We go up to my room, making the same polite introduction when we pass my father in the living room. We talk for several hours on end about everything and all, except for the last eight months of my life.

For the first time since I left Russia, I laugh, and for the first time since I watched Aleksandr disappear behind the car, I feel something resembling home. It's a good feeling, and I find myself craving more of it.

We join my parents in the dining room for dinner. My mom shows the same expected amount of politeness as Anna does, but her mouth remains flat, and anyone could tell they don't like each other. But I don't care. I finally have someone on my side.

My mother can't help but pass a snarky comment about Russians being impolite when Anna is preoccupied with a less tense, equally trite conversation with my dad. Yet she reluctantly offers Anna to stay the night. My mother is so obsessed with norms, proper behavior, and the judgments of society that she'll do something like this even though she clearly itches to send my Russian friend packing.

"Nonsense," my mother says when Anna says she'll find a hostel. "We have a spare mattress."

Anna starts out on the mattress on the floor, but when I'm shaking and trying to suppress my whimpers after a nightmare, she climbs into my single bed and holds me, and I have the best sleep since I left Russia.

Chapter 31

"COME BACK WITH me. To St. Petersburg." Anna's face lights up like a light bulb, hope shimmering in her amber eyes as we sit on my bed like two teenage girls after breakfast.

Hope sparks in me too—an eagerness that has every cell in my body working double speed, my stomach jumping from the rush. But my hope isn't the same as hers. My hope is not something I dare to admit to, and my face goes hard as I shove it down.

"I'm sorry," Anna says, misreading my reaction. "He might come for you again."

I shake my head. I don't know if he will, and if he does, it doesn't matter. Or maybe it does. My stomach makes that flip again.

"How do you know?"

I shrug, unable to give her an answer without revealing the sick urge churning inside me.

"Maybe he's found a new obsession," she suggests. "Otherwise, he would already have come for you, right?"

I gulp down the sorrow that wants to fester inside me at the idea. "Maybe."

"Or I can come live here. I'm sure Norway must have plenty

of fancy restaurants that need pianists. We could move to Oslo and—"

"No," I interject. "I want to go back."

"Are you sure?" Anna says hesitantly. "I mean, I know I suggested it, but he might come back for you."

"I'm not worried." I'm really not. If anything, I'm hopeful. But Anna doesn't need to know that.

Her eyes light up. It's tentative at first, but as she gushes, her entire face comes alive with hopeful excitement. "You can come live with me. I have my own apartment. It's small, but we'll make do. Like we did before. I even have a cat now. Stravinsky. He's black and furry. Hisses if you refuse to pet him." She bobs her head up and down, eyes wide and happy. "You'll love him."

The cat was always Anna's dream, but I know I'll love him. If for nothing else, because she loves him.

Anna squeezes my hand and continues. "You don't have to worry about rent or anything. I'll take care of you like you did me. I know how many times you stocked the kitchen, thinking I wouldn't find out." She gives me a sheepish smile, and I can't help but laugh.

"I thought you'd have my head if you found out."

Anna shrugs. "Well, I did consider it. But then I decided to pay you back in pancakes."

"I can't make pancakes for the life of me, so it's a good thing I have some money to last me a while." *Enough to go back and undo everything Vasily did for me.*

"I'll help you find a job. I know people, and my boss has great connections and likes me enough to help." She's all but bouncing on the bed as she speaks. "You'll be playing at your own restaurant within weeks, I'm sure."

My face falls and I avert my gaze. "I can't play." I gather my hands in my lap, wringing them in and out of each other. "Not anymore."

"What do you mean?"

"I can't play. I've tried many times since I came back, but I just can't."

Anna stares baffled at me for a while before her optimism returns. "It's just a blockage. Like writer's block." Her tone is full of hope, but there's no hope for my playing. Deep down, I know I'll never be able to touch a piano as long as I'm away from Aleksandr.

"It's not. I've tried." Whenever I sit on a piano bench, watching the black and white keys, all I can think about is Aleksandr and how he's not there to hear my music. My fingers refuse to touch the keys as if bound by some invisible spell that only allows me to play for the man who owns my heart and soul.

"What do you mean? Did he hurt you?" Her tone goes shrill and urgent as she grabs my hands. "Did he injure you?"

"No!" My eyes dart up to hers, and I rip my hands free. *He would never!* "It's not physical."

"Okay," Anna says, surprise etched into her features. She reaches for my hands, slowly this time, and I let her take them. "If you don't want to play, you don't have to." She trails off. "Just don't change your mind about coming back with me."

"I won't," I assure her, and with that, it's settled. I'm going back to St. Petersburg.

Chapter 32

THE NEXT DAY, we go to the city to get me a passport and some new, much-needed clothes. I've been wearing my old teenage clothes because the idea of going shopping and being among people without Aleksandr at my side is too daunting. Anna is not him, but she's the next best thing, and I find myself able to walk through the crowded city center with my hand in hers without lurching straight for a panic attack.

When we walk by an upscale hotel, Anna suddenly drags me through the swinging doors and up to the reception.

"Can we try your piano?" she asks the young man behind the front desk. "We are trained pianists from St. Petersburg, here to play a few concerts, and we saw your beautiful instrument from the window and couldn't resist."

I barely hear her voice as I stare at the instrument. It truly is beautiful. A shiny black grand piano with the lid open, keys bared. Black and white. I can almost sense how they would feel beneath my fingertips.

The receptionist flashes Anna a flirtatious smile. "Go ahead."

Anna drags me through the fancy lobby and nudges me onto the padded bench. "Play," she tells me the same way a mother would tell her child to eat her broccoli.

I close my eyes and try to recall the patterns of the music. Any music. But it's like staring into a black void. There's nothing. No notes, no music.

"Rachmaninoff," Anna says. "His G minor prelude."

It's the piece I played for Aleksandr in the concert hall at the conservatory. One of my favorites.

My memory flashes—sounds flickering. I widen my fingers, remembering the large grip. I start to play, and my fingers work automatically, the piece so deeply ingrained into my muscle memory I don't have to think. But it's mechanical and soulless. I can't feel it. I can't feel anything.

He's not here.

It's like a grave transgression to play for anyone who isn't him. Like cheating. Like violating my most fundamental morals.

I burst up from the bench. I can't do this. My music belongs to him. It's not mine to share with anybody else.

People start clapping—I hadn't realized a crowd had gathered—and I start running, through the carpeted lobby, through the revolving doors, and down the street, barely veering around the many people I'm about to crash into.

"Astrid," a voice calls out. "Astrid."

I swerve around a corner, down the next street, through throngs of people, not caring where I'm going. I'm out of breath, my frail limbs weak and tired from the sudden burst. The world is closing in, my lungs constricting. Too many people, too much noise. Too many painful feelings.

A few hundred feet more, and my feet lose momentum. I all but collapse against a brick wall.

Feet click urgently against the pavement, coming up behind me. Then delicate arms wrap around me, and I turn around and cry into Anna's shoulder. People pass us from both sides, but we just stand there, frozen in time.

I always thought losing the ability to play would be the worst thing that could happen to me. But it's not the loss of the piano that has my heart aching and my chest shaking with hollow sobs. It's a loss so profound everything else pales against it.

I left Aleksandr and gained my freedom. But what is freedom when I've lost my very reason for existing?

Chapter 33

A WEEK LATER, I have my passport, plane ticket, and a packed suitcase, and I am on my way to St. Petersburg.

The past five days since Anna left have been some of the most restless of my life. Being stuck in a bad place is one thing, but being stuck there and knowing I'll soon move on is aggravating, to say the least.

I waited until I had my suitcase in hand, about to head for the bus, before telling my parents. And I was right to. They went absolutely bananas, telling me I was crazy, reckless, and even sick. My mother even ran after me and grabbed my arm, telling me in no uncertain terms not to return if I left.

Mustering all the determination I could, I shoved the tears back and told her I wouldn't.

Anna's apartment is small but cozy, a small upgrade from the one we had before. Her cat is a hairy mess with the cuteness of a puppy and the pushiness of a goblin.

I spend a week getting settled, another looking into work opportunities. It's not easy. My only skill set is music, and I can't play. I can barely even speak about music without my chest constricting, so even if my inadequate Russian wasn't a complication, I couldn't even teach music theory.

I'm down to menial work, cleaning and working at dingy cafés. Hard work for bad pay. I dread it and keep postponing sending out job applications, living off the money Vasily gave me for another two weeks. So when Anna tells me her boss is willing to consider me as a waitress at the fancy restaurant, I'm more than happy to go meet him.

I put on my best new clothes and let Anna do my makeup and lend me a pair of high heels. I feel like Bambi on ice as I make my way down the slippery streets of St. Petersburg in mid-February. The streets are covered in ice, topped with a fresh layer of snow, and the temperature is a freezing twenty-five degrees that has my teeth chattering.

Somehow, I manage to smile and speak enough for the manager at the upscale restaurant to offer me a job, starting the next night.

The work is exhausting. It's not because of the chores, but all the people I have to tend to, the smiles I have to fake, and the small-talk I no longer know how to engage in. I'm awkward and out of place, and I feel the manager eye me like he's considering firing me. So I ramp up my effort, making my smiles extra bright, my voice extra cheery.

It helps a bit to have Anna around, cheering me on and making goofy faces from the piano, but I'm always depleted when I get home. On the upside, it means I sleep at night. And with Anna constantly slipping me a sandwich or urging me to eat a bit more when I'm about to leave half a plate of food, I slowly gain weight. It's not much, but it's an improvement.

One of the biggest challenges is to cover up the tattoo behind my ear. As a waitress, I have to keep my hair up, and crude amounts of foundation barely do the job.

"What is that?" Anna asks one night when we get home and

collapse on the couch.

"What?" I say, blinking my tired eyes.

"Behind your ear."

"Nothing." I slap a hand to my ear and hurry to the bathroom, but Anna is right behind me.

"Astrid, you know you can tell me."

I try to get rid of her, but she's adamant, and finally, I let her remove my hand.

The gasp that escapes her is disheartening. She watches me with horror through the mirror and says in a hoarse whisper, "Did he do this to you?"

I lower my gaze and remain silent. I don't want to explain how I made an appointment to have it removed three weeks after returning to Norway and ran out of there right when the dermatologist lifted the laser gun.

I can't bear to erase the last part of me that links me to him. Sadness still weighs heavily upon me whenever I lift my hand to my neck and find the collar gone.

Anna doesn't pry. She must see how much it hurts to think about it. So instead, she offers to cover it up every day before we leave for work, and somehow, it eases the pain, having her there with me even though she doesn't know the story.

"I knew he was dangerous," she says in a regretful voice one night when she's applying foundation to the tattoo. "I should have done more to warn you. I should—"

"Anna,"—I turn around and take her hand—"You couldn't have done a thing. He had set his sights on me. He has money. Connections. No one could have stopped him."

"I know. It's just..." She stares at the foundation tube and heaves a heavy sigh. "I knew what he was capable of." Her eyes come back up to meet mine, wide and horrified. "I had seen it,

Astrid. But I never thought he would do anything like that to you."

"What had you seen?" I give a slight shake of my head as I furrow my brow. "Will you tell me how you met him?" I still remember the fear in her eyes on the night when he showed up at our recital and she told me he was dangerous.

"Do you remember how I told you about Kirill? The rich guy I dated for a while."

"Yeah. The one who was involved in some dangerous business."

Her expression fills with a strange combination of longing and hurt like it does whenever she mentions him—which is a rare occurrence. She seems to have locked the memory up tight, refusing to confront the lingering feelings she clearly has for this man.

"I was with him that time when I met Aleksandr. We were going to this business meeting with this man that both Kirill and Aleksandr did business with. Sergei was his name. I initially didn't want to come, but Kirill convinced me because it would help him seal a deal. Apparently, Sergei wanted to meet me, and Kirill said it was just to have something pretty to look at. But that wasn't it. I think he just wanted to see the fear on my face when he showed us his basement."

"Kirill was about to decline when Sergei offered to show us his collection down there," she continues. "But Aleksandr made this cut-throat expression that made it clear that saying no would be a really fucking bad idea. So we went down into his basement, and—" Her eyes flicker back to mine as her thoughts seem to take her in another direction. "Astrid, I saw things. Things I can never unsee."

I take the foundation tube from her hand and interlace our

fingers. "What did you see?"

Her gaze goes distant as her thoughts seem to flicker to something else. "I often think back to that night—how I think Kirill looked as horrified as me the moment we stepped into the dank hallway underground. But the expression was gone so fast I couldn't be sure it was ever there. And I was so goddamn scared when we left. So scared I ran without even giving him the chance to explain himself."

A hurt unlike any I've ever seen on her before tightens her features. But Anna is good at schooling her reactions, and the pain fades when she straightens her spine. "It's for the best anyway. It's dangerous to be around people like that. You can't be rich in this country without doing shady business dealings and getting involved with such people."

"What was in the basement?" I ask again.

Anna shakes her head as her eyes take on a haunted look. "It's—It doesn't matter. It was horrible. And Aleksandr showed no sign of remorse. Rather, he was curious and kept asking questions like he wanted it for himself."

"Maybe he did it for show? To please this guy?" I suggest.

"No. That wasn't it. I could see it in his eyes. The fascination." She turns me back around to recommence covering up the ear mark. "That's why he did this."

"Did what? Take me?"

"Yes." Her voice tightens like she's on the brink of tears. "I'm sorry, Astrid. I can't talk about this anymore. I just can't."

With that, the conversation is over. Whatever was in that basement was bad. But it doesn't matter what it was. I know Aleksandr. I know he can be cruel and unforgiving, but I also know he'd never hurt me. Not truly. Everything he did was ultimately to set me free—from my own mind. He saw what I needed and opened my eyes to what I'd never been able to find on my own. And then I went ahead and threw it all away because of a moment of fear. Because that's ultimately what drove me away. Not the insecurities about being the person he'd made me realize I was. But the fear of being so utterly dependent. Fear of what would happen to me if I fell even deeper under his control and something happened to him.

But what I didn't realize when Vasily offered to get me out was that it was already too late. I don't think I'll ever truly feel like myself again. Not as long as I'm away from Aleksandr.

It's ironic, really. Anna's story was supposed to make me see how dangerous he is and help me move on. But it has the exact opposite effect, and I find myself slipping away from her as my thoughts keep drifting to the man whose control I crave with every aching beat of my heart.

Chapter 34

MY WORLD TILTS on its axis one night when I step out of the kitchen and see the man at the center table. It's a round table for six people, but he sits there alone like anything smaller wouldn't fit his larger-than-life authority.

With his back to me, I can only see the gray suit jacket hugging the expanse of his broad shoulders, his neatly styled blond hair, and his tall and straight posture. But it's more than enough to recognize him. I could close my eyes and still feel Aleksandr's commanding energy permeate the air.

My knees nearly buckle, and I halt in my tracks, unable to move. I hold my breath as I wait for him to turn. He must surely feel me too. Aleksandr senses everything around him, and he grew attuned to me like I grew attuned to him during the seven months I spent under his control.

But he never turns.

Five minutes pass. Still no sign that he has sensed me. I barely notice when the piano music stops and a new piece doesn't begin.

"Astrid," a soft, lyric voice says. "Are you okay?" Anna puts her hand on my shoulder. Her touch usually comforts me, but nothing will ease the blaring ache tearing at my heart right now.

"It's him," I mutter, keeping my gaze on the man I've ached for since I sat in that car and felt the collar loosen around my neck. My eyes sting after barely blinking for several minutes, but I'm trapped by his magnetic power, caught in the control he wields over me without even trying.

"Who?" Anna asks. Her gasp reveals the moment she sees him. She recognizes him too. "What the fuck is he doing here?" She grabs onto my shoulder. "We need to get you out of here."

She starts pulling, but I remain in place, my otherwise sluggish muscles now tightening to resist her—to stay close to him.

"Astrid, come on. What if he's here to take you?"

"He isn't." My voice sounds dead, devoid of life and hope. I just know it. He's not here to take me.

Our boss comes up to us and pries Anna's hand off me. "Get back to work. Have you any idea how unprofessional this is?"

"I'm sorry," Anna says, and I can feel her worried glance as she ambles away and returns to the piano.

"And Astrid," he continues. "You are not to serve the man at table seven." *The center table.* "If he needs anything, get one of your co-workers, and keep a wide berth around him. But clear his table when he leaves. Do you understand?"

I nod, and my heart clenches painfully as I keep staring at Aleksandr. Is he mocking me? He surely is the one to have issued this demand.

Maybe he's here to taunt me with his presence.

Or maybe he simply likes this restaurant, but wants nothing to do with me?

A whimper escapes me at the thought. But I quickly shove the pain back. Because if he truly didn't want to have anything to do with me, he'd simply have my boss fire me or require me to be off work when he comes in. That's the kind of power he has.

No, he's here to torture me. To punish me for leaving him.

"Get back to work. Now!"

My feet stutter into movement at my boss's low but furious command. I'd better pull myself together, or I won't have a job in a few hours. It's already hanging by a thread.

Aleksandr shows up every night for the next week, ordering three courses, drinking tea, and staying for hours.

Not once does he look at me. It's like the first time I saw him on the train. I was right there in front of him, but he never graced me with his attention. I may walk around in his line of sight, staring at him while I clear tables and take orders, but he never moves his gaze to me.

I struggle to keep my focus on the tasks at hand, and sometimes, I even struggle to move.

To make matters worse, it drives Anna and me apart. Since the first night he came here, she's been begging me not to go back to work, and each time I do, tension accumulates between us. Not only does she think I'm putting myself at risk, but also her job.

One evening, she takes me aside during her break to give it to me straight.

"Astrid, I really don't want to say this, but I feel like I have to." Her lips pull into a thin line as she averts her eyes, and then she turns her focus back to me with a serious gaze. "If you insist on being here, you have to do a better job of acting like you don't care, or we're both gonna lose our jobs. I—" She shakes her head, looking utterly lost. "I can't afford that."

"I'm sorry," I say. "I'll try harder."

As I walk back into the restaurant, I try to gulp back the growing lump in my throat. Despite Anna's words and my promise, all I can see is Aleksandr sitting at his usual table.

I hate him so much. I don't get why he'd torture me like this. A cruel way to get revenge?

I was getting better. Clawing my way out of the pitiful dark hole increment by small increment. But with him here, everything shatters. I can't even find my way back to the numbness of those first days back home in Norway. Now it's only soul-crushing pain, and Anna can barely make me smile.

I stop in the middle of it all, just staring at him.

"Astrid," Anna hisses in my ear. "Pull yourself together."

"Fuck you," I exclaim, and several customers plus my boss turn their heads. But not him. Aleksandr keeps his attention straight ahead, never ever noticing me.

I dart out to the back and lock myself in the bathroom. I feel like the whole world is against me—now Anna too—and I don't think I can take it much longer.

It takes me twenty minutes to shove back the hurt and anger so I won't break down in a sobbing or screaming mess when I go back out to the dining area.

I'm barely holding it together. My legs are shaking, and my tear ducts keep welling up. I try my best. I really do. I don't want to let Anna down. But despite my best efforts, I know this is my last night here. My boss keeps eying me sternly. I know he's waiting until closing time to fire me because he's afraid I'll cause a scene.

If I'm on my best behavior, maybe he'll let Anna stay, so I keep straining to keep myself upright through the rest of the night. But when Aleksandr rises to leave, I can no longer keep myself in check. I halt in the middle of it all, staring at his back as tears stream down my cheeks.

Is this the last time I'll see him?

My chest constricts so hard I can barely breathe.

He takes his time, putting on his jacket, closing the buttons, and leaving a tip. Then he saunters toward the exit without a single glance in my direction.

I want to collapse on the floor and combust into the shattered fragments I'm desperately trying to hold on to. I want to call out for him, gain his attention. Or just a sign that he knows I'm here. I want to run to him and stop him—beg him to take me back.

But all I can do is stand there, frozen in place, and watch him leave.

A waiter opens the door for him, and Aleksandr disappears into the chilly February night.

He's gone. Out of my reach. Gone for good.

My whole being trembles—pain, longing, and utter broken despair tearing through my system.

I turn my teary eyes back to his table. It's always me cleaning up after him. It's such cruel mockery. I don't get to be near him, but I get to pick up his dirty dishes.

Anna is once again at my side, whispering in my ear. "Get your shit together, Astrid, or we're both out of here tonight."

My legs start moving, and it's only then that I remember he left a tip. *Aleksandr never leaves a tip.* He knows I'm the one to clean up after him—he's probably the one to have ordered it—and I'm not worth a single penny.

Suddenly, my feet are moving hastily across the floor. My breath catches when I see the small folded piece of yellow paper on the white tablecloth. It's not a tip. It's a note. His plate is pushed to the side, leaving the note at the center where I can't miss it.

My hands tremble as I reach for it, and my vision blurs from tears and blinding emotion as I unfold it. I have to blink several times before I can read the lonely line scribbled in cursive across the paper.

Are you ready to be mine?

I stare dumbfounded at the words for a minute before the meaning registers.

Then I dart through the restaurant, knocking into a waiter, who drops his tray, pushing my way past entering customers and out the door. My eyes flicker frantically over the dark street, the snow, and the cars lined at the side of the road.

And there he is. He's leaning against his red jaguar, calm and casual.

Staring straight at me.

My legs stagger down the stairs and toward him. I only make it a few steps before I can't go any farther, too paralyzed to move at all. But Aleksandr is moving too. Straight for me.

I fall to my knees, into the cold slush on the pavement, unable to keep my weight up anymore, unable to stand upright in his powerful presence.

His black leather shoes stop right in front of me, and his demanding energy wraps around me like a safe blanket, welcoming me back home.

"Are you ready to give me everything?" he asks, and I shudder at the beautiful sound of his deep timbre.

I lift my gaze, up over his slacks, his jacket, all the way up his large frame to meet his stark, blue eyes.

"I'm ready," I say, and even though I'm shaking from emotions and the biting chill in the air, my voice is even. Because I've never been so sure about anything in my life.

He leans down and grabs my hair, and his entire countenance emits threat and anger, yet it's the best thing I've felt for months. "I won't just have a part of you this time. I want it all," he sneers into my face.

"I'm ready. All of it is yours. I'm yours." I barely even flinch as his grip smarts at the back of my skull. The pain makes me feel alive—makes me feel like I'm back where I belong. *With him.*

He tightens his grip, his nose twitching with that fierce possessiveness of his. "I want you to leave everything you have—everything you are—here at the curb. I don't want any of your doubt or self-loathing. If you want to be mine, you go in with everything you have. Accept that I'm the only thing in this world that matters. *Tolko ya.*"

"Only you," I confirm, and it feels like the truest thing I've ever said. When Vasily got me out, I thought I could salvage what little part was left of the old me. And maybe I could. But I didn't want to. All I've wanted since I sat in that car and watched Aleksandr disappear was to belong to him. With all my heart and soul.

Aleksandr straightens and bores the full force of his gaze into me. "Strip."

I don't hesitate. His word is my command. If he wants me to strip in the middle of the street in the frigid February night, I'll strip.

With my fingers already stiff and frozen, it takes forever to get the long row of buttons on my waitress shirt undone, and by the time I shrug out of the fabric, I'm shaking so hard my teeth chatter.

A sudden commotion at the restaurant entrance catches my attention, but I don't remove my eyes from the only man that matters. Not even when I hear Anna's desperate voice do I turn my head.

"Astrid," she cries, and in my peripheral vision I see her rush toward me, but someone stops her. A giant bulky man. Boris.

"I'm sorry," I say, tears springing to my eyes. But I still don't break away from the icy blue of Aleksandr's gaze. Because no matter how much I love her, how much I owe her, I can't stay for her.

I throw the shirt to the side and rise on staggering feet to remove my shoes and pants. Anna is yelling and crying frantically somewhere in the background, but I don't really hear it. I don't truly feel it. The only thing that matters is the sharp command from the mighty man who has taken over my world.

"Underwear too," Aleksandr demands, his eyes sharply fixed on me.

I gingerly reach back to open my bra and shed it to the side. Then I do the same with my panties.

I'm stark naked in the middle of the street, and the cold air bites into my skin, horrified eyes making my hairs stand on end. But none of it matters.

With a hand on my shoulder, Aleksandr presses me back down on my knees. It's the first time I feel his skin on mine, and tears run in streams from my eyes at the familiar feeling. It's not until he releases me that I notice the icy slush around my bare legs.

"I don't want your insecurities or any goddamned doubt." He kicks my legs apart, and my knees scrape painfully against the unforgiving concrete. But I don't let out as much as a whimper. "I want your pure submission and nothing else."

With a single rip, he tears the necklace from my throat and casts it aside. It's a necklace Anna gave me. A symbol of our friendship. A stab of grief tears through me, but it's brief. I know

I need to lose it to be his. *I need to lose everything, and Aleksandr intends to take it all away.*

My eyes widen as he retrieves a knife from his pocket. The cold steel glitters unforgivingly beneath the street lamp.

"Are you ready?" He holds the knife in front of me to let me feel the acuteness of the threat. He wants to know for sure, and I think I need to feel the depth of my submission too.

I have no idea what he plans to do with that knife, but it doesn't matter. I gulp back my fear and nod. "I'm ready, Mast—" I stop myself. I'm not sure I have earned the privilege to call him Master yet.

Aleksandr's lips tip up in a cruel smile. "*Ne zeichas.* You may say the word once you thank me for taking the next thing."

A stream of horrible scenarios bursts through my mind as Aleksandr steps behind me, but I keep my back straight, accepting his will, whatever it may be.

He grabs my ponytail and tugs hard enough to make my scalp sting, tilting my head back to make me stare straight up at him. Then he leans so close I can feel his hot breath on my face, and it's a welcome relief from the cold.

Someone screams as he runs the back of the blade down my cheek. But I barely notice. I don't care what he does with the knife. I'll let him take anything he wants. So I close my eyes and pull in a steadying breath, and when the knife runs down my neck, the sharp tip nicking my skin like it did my back that first day, my whole world hones in on him.

I don't hear anything but our shared deep breaths, don't feel anything but his hand in my hair and the tip of his knife—his warm breath against my skin as he leans dangerously close.

"You are mine," he sneers. "All mine." Suddenly, he straightens and shoves my head back into position. Something tears as he rips the knife upward, and a wail bursts through the night behind me. The grip on my hair eases, but it's not until Aleksandr stands in front of me with my ponytail clutched in his hand that I realize what he just did.

Horror washes over me, but when my eyes flicker back up to his, I can't do anything but stare. His gaze is willful, alight with the power of what he has just taken. *My hair. My long, wavy, blond hair.* The part of me that wants to scream at the loss falls silent as his command wraps around me, shutting out the world and all its norms.

He wants to take my hair to make me his, and I realize that's what he meant when he said I had to leave everything here at the curb. I can only be his if I shed all the norms and expectations of society; all insecurities, dreams, and wants; everything that made me *me.*

He slowly opens his hand, and the wind takes my beautiful hair, blowing away everything I once was. A sense of freedom washes over me. A new beginning. It's like I needed him to strip me bare in every sense of the word to finally accept where I belong and go into it wholeheartedly.

The words slip past my lips quite automatically. "Thank you, Master."

Aleksandr leans down and takes my chin, and this time, there's nothing cruel about his smile. "You're welcome."

He presses a chaste kiss to my forehead, then shrugs out of his suit jacket and wraps it around me before lifting me into his arms. I bury my face into his shoulder, shutting out the world and inhaling the comforting scent of him. *My master, my world.*

"Bring my car back," he orders someone in Russian and gets into the back of a black SUV with me in his lap.

Boris takes the driver's seat, and then we're off—away from

the crowd, my best friend, and everything I once was.

Aleksandr adjusts me to straddle his thighs and presses me close, rubbing my arms, back, and legs with his strong, warm hands. Hands I thought I'd never get to feel again.

I moan into the crook of his neck and inhale the fresh notes of citrus I came to know as his when he pressed a knife to my back and steered me out of the train station ten months ago. It seems like a lifetime ago. Everything has changed since then. Me, my dreams, and the very premise of my existence.

The road has been full of pain, guilt, and bone-deep hurt, but I don't regret a single moment of it. Because it has all led me here, into Aleksandr's arms.

I burrow a little closer and soak up his heat to let it soothe the icy chill lodged in my tissues. Slowly, the cold wanes, and as my shaking turns into shuddering, I ask the question that has been haunting me the most since the night Vasily took me away.

"Why didn't you stop me?"

"I knew you would come back," Aleksandr says, arrogant in his conviction as ever. And yet again, he's right.

Shoving his hand into my hair, he grabs a fistful. He might have cut off my ponytail, but there are still plenty of thick locks to grab onto. Angling my head to the side, he spears me with intense eyes. "You are mine, Astrid. Irrevocably. There's no doubting it. But you needed to figure it out on your own."

I flicker my eyes across his face, reacquainting myself with the hard features and stark blue eyes that my mind has been trying to conjure for weeks without achieving more than blurry images. Now he's here, right before me, his warm, possessive hands gripping me with a fierceness I thought I'd never get to feel again.

It's overwhelming, scary, and dangerous. But most of all, it's safe. I should feel no safety in the arms of the man who has kidnapped, hurt, and humiliated me and is going to keep doing so. But I do. Because despite all his brutality, this man also protects me with all the power and strength of an unconquered king. In his arms, I find the most devastating possession and the sweetest tenderness.

I belong here.

I belong to him.

Irrevocably and without a doubt.

Chapter 35

DESPITE ALEKSANDR HOLDING me and rubbing my cold skin all the way back to his estate, I'm still shivering when he carries me up the marble stairs. I'm not sure whether it's from cold or adrenaline. Either way, it feels heavenly when he lowers me into the hot water in the jacuzzi in his bathroom.

He strips out of his clothes and joins me in the water, where we stay until my body finally warms and I sink into a peaceful state of mind.

"You're so beautiful," he murmurs as he threads his fingers through the remnants of my hair. "Bare and vulnerable. All mine."

I nestle closer into him and relish the familiar feeling as I soak up his strength to balance the lack of my own.

But despite my lack of strength, everything feels new and hopeful as I sit here. I finally feel free, having shed all the shoulds and coulds and expectations of the world. But one fear lingers. The one that ultimately drove me to leave him.

"What if something happens to you?" I whisper into his neck.

"Nothing will happen to me," Aleksandr assures, wrapping his hand around my nape in an equally reassuring and possessive grip. "You're mine, and you're staying with me."

"But— What if—?" I pause to find the words. "You don't know that for sure." I let out a shuddery exhale against his skin. "I can't live out there." The mere thought of going back and existing beyond his control has me quivering again.

"Shh, sh, shh," he soothes, stroking my back with the other hand. "I'll figure something out."

"Are you sure?"

"*Ty imeish moyo slovo.*"

This is the only thing that matters to me anymore, knowing my world isn't so precarious it would crash into dust in the blink of an eye if the worst imaginable thing were to happen. I have no idea how he'll solve it, but I trust him.

"Thank you," I whisper, and as the last tension drains from my system, I drift off in the safety of his arms, finally back home where I belong.

I spend the first week in the cage, like when Aleksandr brought me here back in May. I only get out to pee or eat, but unlike then, I don't fight or protest.

Aleksandr brings me food himself two or three times a day. He doesn't utter many words, but his eyes say everything. They are so intent as he watches me eat that it feels like they penetrate my skin.

"Eat up," he says when my appetite runs out halfway through a meal. So I keep going. It takes a long time for me to get it all down, but Aleksandr remains where he is, his demanding nature looming over me.

His patience never seems to lessen. I get no *hurry* or irritated grunts. He just stands there, and I feel myself shrink under his watchful gaze, becoming so small I can't stand to sit upright.

I want to sink to the ground, kneel at his feet, and display my submission. And when I've finally finished the meal, I get to do just that. I sink to my knees in front of him, bowing my head in deep reverence. He always accepts me—with a smarting grip on my hair or a gentle hand on my head.

Either way, it has the same effect. My blood surges through my veins, loud and wild, yet everything is perfectly calm, my breaths slow and even, my head free and silent.

After letting me relish the feeling for a while, he locks me up in the cage again. The clatter of the bars and the click of the lock is like hearing a long-gone lover's voice again. The bars close in on me like a protective shield, and even though I get to keep a book under my pillow, I'll often just lie there and let the feeling of being back where I belong roll through me.

I'm grateful for the recuperating week in the cage. I knew I was depleted, emotionally and physically, but being here and finally releasing all the tension the world out there brought upon me, I realize just how much. I think this is what it must be like to take a vacation on a sunny beach after being stressed and overworked for months.

On the eighth day, Aleksandr brings me down to the pool. It's strange to leave my room after a whole week of seeing nothing else. It's like stepping into a new world, scary and dangerous. The few men we pass and the many rooms and large spaces, ornamentations, and chandeliers, are a sensory overload that has me clinging to Aleksandr's side. I have no idea how I made it three months in the real world after having spent seven months here.

Another week and I'm back at the piano. Yet another week, and he lets me sleep in his bed occasionally, fingerfucking me into multiple orgasms.

"I'm sorry," I say one night when I lie in his arms in the darkness.

"For what?"

"Leaving." It's the first time since the restaurant either of us touches upon the subject, and my heart is already thumping. "Can you forgive me?"

He's quiet for a minute before he says, "I'm going to punish you, but I'm waiting for you to regain your strength."

"Thank you," I whisper. But it's not for the waiting part. I need redemption for what I've done, and the only way to get it is to take my punishment. "Do you hate me?" Suddenly, my voice is thick with unshed tears, and I curl into myself, feeling like I don't deserve the comfort of his arms.

"No." He brushes his hand over my cheek and pulls me closer. "You needed time out in the world to realize that you don't belong there. Why else would I not come for you?"

I turn to face him, needing to see him when he answers my next question. "Would you come for me if I left again?"

His eyes turn cold as he shoots his hand up to my neck and grabs it in a steely grip. "If you ever try to leave again..." his voice is a menacing sneer, and his nostrils flare as his eyes move back and forth over my face with something akin to fury or desperation.

I've never seen him like this. It scares me, and I cower beneath his sharp stare, but I don't try to escape. Rather, I lift my chin to make room for his large hand as I stare up at him with wide, vulnerable eyes.

As he watches the unbridled submission unfold over my features, something happens to him. Realization strikes. His eyes soften, and he says with all the certainty of his powerful being,

“You won’t.”

Chapter 36

"I'M TAKING YOU to the dojo," Boris says one night when he enters my room.

I've waited for those words for nearly two weeks—since the night Aleksandr told me he would punish me—and I have imbued myself with calm acceptance. But now, as I see the worry etched into Boris's hard features, it's no longer possible. I bite down on my lips as I try to keep the anxiety at bay. If Boris is concerned, I definitely have cause to be.

He grabs me by the arm and leads me through the house. The hand is unnecessary; I would come of my own free will no matter how scared I was. But it stabilizes me, and I think it does the same for him.

When we reach the dojo, my hands tremble, and my knees are weak like they're about to give in.

"Shackle her," Aleksandr orders. He's standing in the middle of the room, arms crossed, whip coiled in his right hand. There's something menacing in his wide stance, and when I meet his eyes, I immediately have to look away again. There's no trace of mercy to be found. He's pure, primal dominance.

Boris takes me to the center of the room, and my every instinct beckons me to run when he places me between the chains that fall from the ceiling with leather cuffs dangling from the ends. But I can't. Another more important part of me knows this is where I'm supposed to be. So I let him slip off my kimono and strap cuffs to my four limbs. Once he's done, I'm spread into an X, naked and vulnerable, ready to take my punishment.

"Leave." Aleksandr's harsh tone makes me flinch, and anxious energy crawls up my spine as I hear the thuds of retreating steps and the click of the door, which tells me I'm now alone with the beast.

Aleksandr moves up behind me with slow, measured steps. "Why are you here?"

"To"—I squeeze my eyes shut and push the words out with a gush of air—"be punished."

Aleksandr steps around me and tips my chin up, and the look I meet in his eyes has me clutching the chains. "It's been long overdue."

He steps away and cracks the whip through the air, and a yelp escapes me as I pull frantically at the restraints.

His palm presses to my upper back, and I jump again. But he just keeps it there, warm and calm. "This is as much for your sake as it is for mine."

A few months ago, I would have called him crazy. But today, I know he's right. I need this to atone for leaving him—atone for failing not only him but also myself.

My breath stutters past my lips as I wait for the first strike.

It comes with a force that rips a desperate scream up my throat, shoving all strength from my body in one cruel lash. I collapse in the shackles. For a moment, I hover on the edge of panic, panting and whimpering. But somehow, I manage to gather myself and straighten my knees as I brace for the next strike.

The whip cracks through the air, and another lash sends searing pain into my flesh. I collapse with a wail, gripping the chains to support my weight.

I don't know how I manage to get back up. Aleksandr doesn't say a single word, doesn't make any motion for me to do so. I do it of my own accord, instinctively needing to please him and take what he wants to give.

So I keep straightening every time I collapse.

I take ten more lashes like this. Wailing, collapsing, and getting back up.

"Please," I whimper when blaring alarms and flashes of red shroud my world. "Please, please. I can't take any more."

"Why am I punishing you?"

"Because I ran off." My eyes prickle with unshed tears, but they won't fall even though my chest keeps heaving with the need to cry.

"And why does it matter? Why do I care?" His words are cruel, belying the suggestion that he does care.

"Because... I—I don't know," I stutter through tearless sobs.

He curls his hand around my nape and leans in. "Because you're mine." The startling gentleness in his voice finally makes my tears flow. "Mine to take care of, mine to protect, mine to punish." His fingers tighten on my neck. "And I can't do that when you're not here, can I?"

"I'm sorry." I sniffle and wipe my wet cheek on my shoulder. "I'm so, so sorry."

"*Ya znayu.*" He brushes his thumb along my skin. "I know. But I'll keep going until you bleed for me."

"No, no, no, no." The chains clatter as I flail against the restraints.

The whip falls to the ground, and Aleksandr's arm shoots

around my waist, slamming me back against his chest as he grabs my chin with the other hand. "Where does the pain come from?"

"You," I croak.

"And what do you do when I give you something?"

"Accept it. With gratitude."

"Good girl. I've trained you well." Aleksandr nuzzles my cheek, and I melt into his punishing grip as determination rapidly grows inside me.

After a few minutes of tender affection, he steps back again and picks up where he left off, whipping me with unmerciful force.

But my head is no longer in the same place. All alarms and flashes of panic are gone. In their stead is the urgency of his possession. Nothing exists beyond his ownership. Not the guilt, not the fear. The pain becomes an extension of his will, and even as I wail with each strike, I welcome it.

I feel more alive than I ever have—more cherished and even loved. Because if I didn't mean so much to Aleksandr, he wouldn't punish me like this. He wouldn't free me of my guilt and fill me with his command.

Gratitude swells inside me even as my back burns like he's set fire to it. It grows so big I can't hold it in.

"Thank you, Master." The words spill past my lips without thought. It might well be the sincerest words I've ever spoken.

"That's it," he croons, trailing his fingers over my ribs and waist as he moves close to me. "I knew you'd get there."

I expect him to give me a reprieve, maybe even take me down. But Aleksandr steps back and strikes me again. The whip tears into my flesh with a pain unlike any I've ever known.

I scream and wail and thrash. My mind, my back, my every nerve feel like they're about to burst. I can't take it, but Aleksandr forces me to as he swings the whip again.

"Accept it," he growls as the leather cracks through the air.

A hot trickle runs down my back. Blood, I realize. Dark spots form before my eyes, and I can't breathe. I heave and drag in breaths, but the air won't stick. I grapple at the chains as the room becomes a blur and my mind spins.

Strong arms embrace me from behind, and a voice whispers in my ear. "Easy now. *Dershu tebya.*"

I collapse in his embrace, and my arms dangle in the chains above. Then I weep. Like a child in need of comfort, I press my back against the strong body behind me as tears stream down my cheeks.

"I need you," I say between whimpers, feeling more vulnerable than ever.

"*Dershu tebya,*" he assures. "I'm never letting you go again. You're mine."

"I'm yours."

Keeping one arm around my waist, Aleksandr moves the other down between us. It's only when the thick head of his cock prods at my entrance that I realize what he's doing.

"Please, no," I beg, too wrought to even cry anymore. "I can't. Please. No more." There's no room left to take the intensity of his carnal possession.

Aleksandr doesn't listen. He presses inside me, and my slick walls betray me as they clamp down on him. I pant and weep, twitching in his arms as I beg him to stop. But as he slowly makes his way in, stretching me to the point of new pain, my body numbs to the strain, and moans mingle with my sobs and pleas.

When he settles deep inside me, my head empties. I'm helpless. There's not a single thing I can do to change his mind. The realization is like a drug, thrumming through my veins and igniting my desire. I moan and arch my hips, now desperate for more instead of less. But Aleksandr just holds me there, letting me feel my utter powerlessness to the bone.

That's when I realize something. He's taking me without me begging. *He's taking me against my will.*

The thought should scare me. Instead, it builds my desire to the point where I scream with desperation. This is the purest testament to his ownership.

He didn't want to fuck me until I submitted so much that I begged him. Now his will is branded so deep into me he doesn't need to hear the words to know that every little part of me belongs to him.

Aleksandr starts moving, dragging his cock in and out at an agonizingly slow pace. I cry and beg, but he keeps going, exerting his devastating control over both me and his own body.

It's only when I give up and hang silently in his arms that he finally picks up speed.

He thrusts into me with such force it seems he's trying to punish me all over again.

"Come for me," he demands, and I scream through an orgasm so intense it's painful.

Aleksandr growls into my ear as he finds his own release. It prolongs my orgasm and drains me of every last drop of energy. He keeps taking like he's taken everything else, and my world blackens as I go slack in his arms.

Chapter 37

"I THINK WE CAN keep the bandages off from today on," Aleksandr says one night when he peels the bandages off my back.

It's taken a whole week for the welts to close. Aleksandr drew blood in several places when he punished me, and the cleaning process hurt so badly I cried through the whole ordeal twice a day for several days.

"How do they look?" I've asked the same question with a strange combination of nervousness and fascination every time he has removed the bandages.

"Come see for yourself." Getting off the bed, Aleksandr offers me his hand. I gingerly take it and let him lead me across the room, where he cradles me in his arms with my back to the tall mirror—the same response to my question he's had whenever I've asked.

I lean into him and turn my head to take in the angry red stripes. The scabs may be gone, the welts having closed, but the vision is a clear testament to the violence my back has undergone.

My breath catches like it does every time. I still can't believe how I took such a whipping without breaking. The pain must have been unspeakable, yet I don't remember it that way. It was bad, yes, but it was also freeing and intoxicating.

Aleksandr trails a featherlight hand down the length of my back. "I can't wait to see the scars once the redness fades."

Aleksandr brought a doctor the day after the whipping to make sure the welts didn't get infected. I was quite horrified when the doctor informed us I would need a plastic surgeon to treat my back to avoid scarring.

I clearly remember the tenderness in Aleksandr's expression when he crouched in front of me. "Would you like me to get a plastic surgeon, or do you want to carry my marks on your back?"

I still can't believe he gave me that choice, and it's even harder to believe I chose the latter. The way he said it made it sound like such a beautiful thing, carrying the marks of his whip on my back as yet another testament to his ownership.

"Me neither." I arch into his touch as I imagine how the scars will look once the redness fades.

He presses his lips to the crook by my neck and whispers, "One day, I'll take you to a party in a backless dress to show off my marks."

The old me would have been horrified, but the new me sways my hips as a tendril of desire snakes its way down my spine.

Aleksandr trails his hand back up and wraps it around my neck and the golden steel of my new collar. "Everyone would know that you belong to me, body and soul."

"Yes," I say, and the word comes out as a moan.

Using his grip on my neck, he turns me to face him, and his eyes flicker back and forth between mine like he can hardly believe what he sees. "You really are mine, Astrid. Through and through." He tightens his grip around my windpipe, marveling at the way I let him cut off my air without a flinch. "I always knew you had it in you, but I hardly dared to hope you'd ever get here."

Aleksandr backs me up toward the bed. My vision blurs as my air becomes scarce, and my feet shuffle clumsily. But I don't fall. I never do when Aleksandr is by my side.

Lowering me onto my back on the mattress, he eases his hold on my neck just enough to keep me conscious. Then he plunges his tongue into my mouth and kisses me so deeply I lose track of time and place. The air in my lungs becomes irrelevant as I submit to his will.

"You're mine," he grits as he shoves his other hand between us to free his hard length. Without preparation, he pushes inside me and slides right in. I'm already wet, and it doesn't take many thrusts before I hover at the edge of an orgasm.

"Be a good little slut and come for me," he sneers into my mouth.

My gasps wheeze in my constricted throat as I come apart beneath him, shuddering and spasming from the intense pleasure.

He makes me come like this two more times before he finally lets me feel the ultimate pleasure of him spurting his release inside me.

"Thank you, Master," I say repeatedly as he lifts me farther up on the bed and cradles me in his arms. "Thank you so, so much."

"You're welcome, *krasivaya devushka*." He peppers sweet kisses all over my hair. "You've deserved it."

As I come down from the breathless high, something else pops into my mind. Something I've wanted to ask him for a while but haven't dared to. It feels like walking into a minefield. He has just started to trust the full extent of my submission, and I'm afraid he will think I haven't truly given in after all if I ask this.

But I need to do it, and this moment of intimacy might be the best time.

So I take a deep breath and let the words out. "Will you please check on Anna for me?" I've been worried about her. I can't imagine her boss keeping her on after she put in her word for me and I caused such an offensive scene outside the restaurant.

Aleksandr is quiet for a while, and I'm preparing to resign myself to the prospect of never knowing when he finally speaks. "I'll check on her."

Relief expands my chest with a deep breath, and hope blossoms inside me. If he'll do this for me, then maybe someday he'll let me see her. I hardly dare to hope, but despite Aleksandr's uncompromising control, he cares about me and ultimately wants what's best for me.

"Will you let her know that I'm okay?" I ask, feeling bold.

This time, there's no hesitation. "I will."

"Thank you." My heart fills with gratitude, and the words blurt out of me. Three small words I could once never imagine speaking to this man, but now say with all the fierceness of my heart. "I love you."

There's no trace of reaction on Aleksandr's hard face, but the deep vulnerability of his kiss says it all. He might not ever say the words back, but as he holds me close and kisses me like it's the last kiss he'll ever have, I know I won't ever need to hear it as long as I feel it.

Chapter 38

"SOMEONE IS COMING to see you tonight," Aleksandr says.

I'm sitting on the floor beside him in the dining room, forking delicious pasta into my mouth. He'll have me eat dinner in my room most nights, but occasionally he'll bring me down here and let me sit at his feet the same way I do when eating breakfast in his office.

Hope blossoms in my chest, and my face lights up. *Could it be?* I hardly dare to ask the question, but I've grown bolder around Aleksandr—more hopeful. "Is it Anna?"

His face becomes serious as he slowly shakes his head. He rises from his chair and crouches in front of me, stroking my newly cut jaw-length hair. "I haven't been able to find her," he says in a quiet voice.

I stop my hand from bringing another forkful of pasta into my mouth as my stomach twists. "What do you mean?"

Curving his hand around my cheek, he watches me with regretful eyes. "Boris went to her apartment two weeks ago. It had been upended. Someone else is searching for her too, it seems."

A clank resounds as I drop my fork to my plate. I stare at him, frozen by the fear that snakes its way up my spine.

Aleksandr takes my hands in his, lending me some much-needed stability. "I've got some of my contacts working on finding her, but it has to be discreet since we don't know who's involved and what they want with her. So it might take some time."

"What if she's in danger?"

"I don't think she is. Not imminent anyway. Her rent has been paid six months in advance, and there's no trace of her anywhere. I think someone might be hiding her. But I'll have my men keep looking to see what they can dig up."

He shoves my plate aside and brings me into a tight hug. "We'll find her," he says against the top of my head and presses a kiss to my hair. "Don't worry."

Taking a deep breath, I allow myself to trust his words. It doesn't erase my worry, but it dulls the throbbing fear. After a few more settling breaths, I remember what led the conversation to Anna, and I lean back to watch him with a confused expression.

"Who's coming to see me, then?"

"Vasily."

"Vasily?" I furrow my brow. Why would he come to see me? And why would he come here at all? Aleksandr must be furious with him for getting me out. That is, if he knows it was him. He surely must. He saw us drive away. Tentatively, I say, "You know what he did, right?"

Aleksandr's countenance hardens. "Of course."

"Why—" Baffled as I am, I struggle to find the right words. "Aren't you mad at him?"

Aleksandr's nose twitches with primal anger. "Vasily took the most precious thing I own, so yes, I did consider having him killed." His jaw flexes as he considers for a moment. "But taking out Vasily would be a very expensive operation since I neither deal in arms nor military forces. And I guess I owe him a free pass for all the things he's done for me."

I gulp back the urge to thank him for not going after Vasily. I couldn't stand it if something happened to him because he helped me. My veins thrum with nervous anticipation at the prospect of seeing him again. I like Vasily and am deeply grateful for what he did for me, but I'm afraid of how he feels about me since I went and undid everything he did for me.

"Why is he here?"

Aleksandr squeezes my hands. "To put your mind at ease."

His words have the exact opposite effect when he snaps his fingers, prompting Boris to enter with the chubby, rosy-cheeked man I recognize as Aleksandr's lawyer.

The lawyer doesn't spare me a glance as he sets a briefcase and a stack of papers on the table.

"What's going on?" I say, my voice suddenly high and thin.

Aleksandr grabs my chin and levels me with a stern look. "This is for you, Astrid," he says, just like he did when he marked me like an animal or whipped me until I screamed.

I wring my hands, wanting to say something but knowing it's no use. Whatever Aleksandr has planned is going to happen.

"Who do you belong to?" he demands.

"You," I reply without hesitance.

"That's right. You belong to me. So it doesn't matter what you think, now does it?"

I gulp back the fear building in my throat and shake my head. "No."

A smile tips his lips up, and he releases my chin to brush his knuckles over my face. "Now be a good girl and go with Boris back up to your room. I'll be up when Vasily arrives in an hour or so."

My heart pounds like a jackhammer as I wait in the cage. But it's not just from fear. A weird sort of anticipation courses through my veins, speeding up my pulse and tingling in my extremities.

Unlike the last time Aleksandr's lawyer was here with a stack of papers that involved me, I want—no crave—Aleksandr's warped brand of possession. I crave the bars around me, the mark behind my ear, and the scars on my back. And even not knowing what is coming, I want whatever he has in store for me.

My body is thrumming with nervous energy when the door opens. The air grows thick with powerful masculinity as Aleksandr and Vasily step inside. My tongue darts out to wet my lips as I watch the two men, each dangerous in their own right.

Vasily is clad in all black, and his entire stance exudes measured authority, his eyes simmering with a latent threat—the kind that lurks in corners and jumps out when you least expect it. He's refined and subtle in his power. Aleksandr, on the other hand, is unapologetic in all his dangerous authority. Threat crackles in his stark blue eyes, and his mere presence incites intimidation—like a vast glacier rising above the ocean.

I pull the comforter over my legs and wrap my arms around myself. The protection of the bars isn't enough as Vasily approaches the cage.

I glance at Aleksandr. He's made himself comfortable on the couch, ankle propped on his thigh and an arm over the back. He shows no signs of unease at his best friend seeing that he holds a girl in a cage. And why would he? To him, it's his right.

And it is. I belong to him. If he wants to lock me up, he may do so. I don't care that the world outside would deem him depraved. I don't care how they'd explain my behavior as a result of mindfuck. I stopped caring the moment I fell to my knees in the cold street, stripped bare, and let Aleksandr cut off my long hair.

But as Vasily approaches me with firm strides, I find that I do care what this man thinks.

I feel like I've let him down. He risked his friendship with Aleksandr, and now I'm back here, in the place he helped me escape.

Crouching in front of the cage, he watches me with those perceptive eyes. I flutter my gaze back and forth between the mattress and him as I wring the comforter in my hands.

"How are you, Astrid?" he asks, tone grave and somber.

"I'm okay."

"Tell him the truth, Astrid," Aleksandr shoots from the couch. It's a stern order with a mocking edge that would have anger boiling in most people, but I'm not like most people. My spine straightens even as my head falls into a lowered position, and my hands flatten on my thighs as a surge of calmness steadies me from within. Instinctive submission.

"I'm good." I keep my eyes lowered as I feel Aleksandr's demanding gaze on me and add, "I'm more than good."

I blink up to see Vasily cast Aleksandr an annoyed look. Whatever frustration or incredulity he holds, though, he keeps to himself.

His voice softens as he turns back to me, like he's speaking to a scared animal. "Are you sure?"

Lifting my gaze to his, I imbue my words with all the strength of my newfound confidence. "I'm sure."

Vasily seems to gauge me for a moment before he gives a

nod. “It’s good to see you.”

A smile tugs at the corners of my lips as my eyelids flutter shyly. Vasily really is a beautiful man, and despite his harsh and disciplined exterior, he’s also a warm and caring person.

“It’s good to see you too.” I cast a glance up at Aleksandr, hoping my reaction to Vasily won’t offend him.

It doesn’t. He gives me a nod of approval, and I turn back to Vasily.

“Your hair is shorter.” Vasily reaches through the bars and tucks a jaw-length lock of hair behind my ear. “It suits you.”

His hand remains behind my ear, the featherlight touch of his fingertips tickling my sensitive skin, and my cheeks flush as my heart beats a little faster. He reminds me of Aleksandr in so many ways despite the immediate differences.

A crease forms between his brows as his eyes flicker over my face, like he doesn’t believe what he’s seeing. “You look radiant, in fact.” Turning to Aleksandr, he says, “Can I see her outside the cage?”

Aleksandr gets up and saunters across the room to open the cage. The lid clanks as it comes up, and I gingerly rise on the mattress, taking Aleksandr’s proffered hand to let him help me out.

Even as I keep my gaze lowered, I feel Vasily’s perceptive eyes roam over me like he’s trying to solve a riddle. I can’t help clasping Aleksandr’s hand, seeking his protection. Vasily is all mighty power as he towers in front of me, hands clasped behind his back.

My breath quickens when I glance up to find him watching me in stoic silence. Nothing on him moves except for his eyes that slowly trail across my features, down my body, taking in every nervous twitch and bated breath.

"Do you like being in the cage, Astrid?" he finally asks.

I gaze down at the golden steel—the bars I once detested but now ache for whenever I'm away from them for too long. Lifting my eyes back up, I let out a sincere, "Yes." I'm not ashamed anymore. This is where I belong. It's who I am.

"Why?" There's no worry or horror in Vasily's expression this time. Only curiosity. So I answer truthfully.

"It clears my head. Makes me feel free in a way I never did out there." I nod toward the windows and the outside world like Aleksandr has done so many times. "It's peaceful."

Aleksandr's voice is a gentle lull close to my ear as he reaches around me to open the belt on the robe. "Let him see what else clears your mind."

His soft words are like a caress, but the moment the meaning registers, I grab onto his hand. "No. Not that." I may have no trouble admitting I like the cage, but I'm not ready for Vasily to see the scars on my back.

"Yes. That." Aleksandr pulls the tie open despite my clutching hand. "Keep your arms at your sides."

His firm demand has my arms falling down of their own accord. There's no way I can disobey him, no matter what.

The robe slides off me like water, and I squeeze my eyes shut as I become naked under Vasily's sharp stare.

Aleksandr's hands are once again gentle as he turns me around. They're comforting and warm, but they can't prevent the icy surge that freezes me in place at the sound of Vasily's startled gasp.

"Look at me," Aleksandr demands as he clasps my shoulders.

Pressing my lips together, I open my eyes and stare up into the willful depth of Aleksandr's gaze.

"You belong to me, and I like the scars. That's all that

matters."

I give him a small nod, and Aleksandr pulls me into him, wrapping an arm around my waist and curling a hand around my neck—protective and possessive. I press myself into him as Vasily's fingers come up to touch the scars. He starts exploring the marks, tracing and pressing lightly. At first, I feel the strain in his touch, the horror rolling off him, but slowly, it turns into something else. Curiosity? Maybe even fascination?

"How do you do this?" Vasily asks with a strange kind of wonderment. "Keeping her locked up and whipping her without... breaking her."

"I'm just giving her what she needs."

Vasily's breathing deepens as he keeps stroking up and down like he's in awe. With a sigh, he finally removes his hand and touches it to my shoulder instead. "Astrid, will you turn and face me?"

Aleksandr loosens his arms around me to let me turn.

I'm shocked to find Vasily's face tight with something that looks like regret. His eyes soften with sincerity as he brushes my hair aside and curves his hand around my cheek. The intimacy is startling, and I can't help but lean into it as he speaks.

"I owe you an apology, Astrid." His mouth flattens in a wry expression before he continues. "When I saw the tattoo behind your ear, I was blinded by something else I've seen. Women who weren't happy. Women who were misused and mistreated." Lifting his gaze, he addresses Aleksandr. "Have you told her how I found Ivan?"

I feel Aleksandr nod behind me as he presses me into him and gently caresses my stomach.

Vasily turns his attention back to me. "The women Ivan—a thirteen-year-old boy—was supposed to train had ear tattoos. So when I saw yours, it hit a little too close to home, and I forgot all the other things." He swipes his hand along my skin and tilts his head a bit as if to deepen the connection between us. "How you kept leaning into Aleksandr unconsciously. How this peaceful look would settle over your face when he took you in his arms." Vasily gives a slight shake of his head. "I'm sorry Astrid. I shouldn't have taken you away from that."

I'm speechless. Astounded. Unable to find the words.

Before I get the chance to gather my thoughts, Aleksandr speaks. "Let's finish what you came here for." He leans down to pick up my robe and holds it up for me to push my arms through the silk. Then he ties it at the front, and I'm more than a little relieved. I thought he was going to offer me up to Vasily, and even though I am attracted to him, I don't think I could handle the vulnerability of submitting to him like that after the strange, intimate moment we just shared.

"Come." Aleksandr clasps his warm hand around mine and leads me to the desk, where he pulls out the swivel chair for me. I sink onto it and lift my legs up to hug them in front of me as Aleksandr goes to open the door and let his lawyer in.

Now there are three men, all clad in suits and exuding power, and tiny me dressed in nothing but a robe, exposed and vulnerable.

My finger goes up to rub the mark behind my ear. That day was a traumatic experience for me, yet somehow, the memory has shifted. I no longer shudder at the thought or feel broken. Rather, it brings me a strange kind of peace knowing how far Aleksandr will go to cement his ownership over me.

Rather, it levels my breathing, knowing Aleksandr holds that kind of power over me. And when he comes to stand at my side with a warm hand on my back, I close my eyes and sink into the steady current of his control. I have no idea what's coming, but I know that as long as Aleksandr is in charge, I'll welcome whatever it is.

The men exchange a few words in Russian, and there's the sound of paper and the scratch of pens.

I keep my eyes closed until Aleksandr leans down and slides something in front of me on the desk. "I've had one drawn up for you in English."

My heart thrums in my chest as I grab onto Aleksandr's arm and peel my eyes open to find a document in front of me. With a hand going in circular motions on my back, Aleksandr offers me his steadying support as I read the header.

Last Will and Testament - Pet Clause.

I swallow and glance up at Aleksandr as my throat tightens with emotions. *Is this him doing what he promised? Making sure I'm safe if something were to befall him?*

His warm eyes confirm the notion. This is not to humiliate or put me in my place. This is to protect.

I return my focus to the document and read the same information about the pet as the last time. My name, gender, origin, etc.

Then I get to the part that says *Appointment of Caretaker,* and gratitude swells inside me at the sight of Vasily's name. This time, I look up at the commanding man towering before me. He's intimidating as ever with his tall, proud posture, eerie calmness, and observant eyes. But I've learned that dangerous men aren't necessarily the ones who pose a threat to me. I know their keen air of control can also mean safety and protection. And the idea of going into the care of this man if my world were to crumble is a huge weight off my chest. I won't have to return to a world I'll never find my footing in. I'll be under the command of another powerful man.

"Thank you," I say with all the gratitude of my beating heart.

"I'd be a proud man to have you." The hard lines of Vasily's features soften somewhat as he gives a small nod.

Biting my finger, I lower my eyes to scan the rest of the document. When I reach the end with the scrawled signatures, another thought has my eyes darting back up to Vasily.

"What if something happens to you?"

"The same as all my other belongings." He makes a slight twitch of his lips, and I think it's because he's not used to categorizing a person as property. "You go to Ivan."

Ivan. The beautiful, gentle giant with a dark side. That definitely wouldn't be a terrible place to end up. I push out a shuddery breath and nod.

Aleksandr presses a long kiss to my head. "No matter what happens, you'll be safe."

I start shaking. At first, it's a small quivering in my hands, then it moves up through my arms and torso until my whole body trembles.

Aleksandr picks me up and sits with me in his arms, pressing me close to him.

"Are you sure this is the right thing to do?" Vasily says, the doubt back in his voice.

"I'm sure," Aleksandr replies with all the certainty of his powerful, intelligent being. "This is not fear. It's relief."

Aleksandr is right. The relief is so strong I can't stop shaking.

Right from the start, when he watched me on that stage, he saw straight through me—into the hidden parts of my soul that I could never access myself. He saw the restless yearning for what it was. A need to belong.

Now I'm his with all it entails. Devastating brutality,

violence, and humiliation. But also care and safety. It's freeing in a way nothing ever was. No matter what happens, Aleksandr always catches me. And this is the ultimate way to make sure I'll always land safely.

"I'm yours, Master," I whisper, burrowing my head into his neck.

He tightens his grip fiercely. "Always."

Glossary

Ladno, prosto povtarayem i ty sdashsya: It's okay. We'll just go again until you give in.
Prishol: He's here
Spokoyno: Slow down
Dershu tebya: I've got you
Yasno?: Are we clear?
Takaya horoshaya devushka: Such a good girl
Ty russki znayesh?: Do you speak Russian?
Spasibo: Thank you
Krasivaya devushka: Beautiful girl
Kakaya khoroshaya sabatjka: Such a good dog
Sidet: Sit
Slyuka: Whore
Nakonets-to, vot plennaya slyuka Aleksandra: Finally, here we have Aleksandr's captive slut.
Prosti menya: I'm sorry
Ty imeish moyo slovo: You have my word
Vso horosho s nei: Is she okay
Poshol: Leave
Derzhi za nog: Hold her legs
Smatri na menya: Look at me
Dershi golovu: Hold her head
Horoshaya devushka: Good girl
Tebe ladna?: Are you okay?

U tebya krovotechenie: You're bleeding

My gatovy k nei: We're ready for her

Ochen: Very

Nachinay: Begin

Yebannaya slyukha, pashla von: You fucking whore, get out of here

Blyad: Fuck

Ana so menoi spit: She sleeps with me

Ty uveren chto eta khoroshaya ideja: Are you sure this is a good idea?

Bolshe ne budet: It won't happen again

Podazhdi: Wait

Malenkaya shlyushka: Little whore

Dezhi yeyo: Hold her

Tolko ya: Only me

Ne zeichas: Not yet

Ya znayu: I know

Dear reader

First of all, thank you so much for reading! If you'd be so kind as to leave a review (one or two lines is all it takes), it would make me very happy!

You're probably wondering about Anna. Is there more to her story?

Yes, there is.

I have a book planned for her, but I have no idea when I'll finish it. I'm working on so many books and have others I want to release before I dive into her story. I debated with myself about whether to hold back the last four chapters (after Aleksandr takes Astrid back) and wait to announce that Anna will get her own book, but Aleksandr and Astrid's story wouldn't be complete without those last chapters. I also considered leaving out the part where Astrid asks about Anna, but that also seemed wrong. So I decided to keep it. After all, I don't think the suspense is too great. I hope you won't get too anxious waiting for her story. <3

Sign up for my newsletter and be the first to get updates on my books and exclusive excerpts:

www.ellajacobs.com/newsletter

Ella

Acknowledgements

To my Dom, there are no words to express my gratitude for you. But I will try anyway. Thank you for constantly reading and rereading and helping me shape me into the author I've become. Thank you for fulfilling all my kinky fantasies and providing the best of inspiration. Thank you for putting up with me when I get lost in my stories and refuse to go to bed. Thank you for simply smiling and telling me how much you adore me when I'm stressed and cranky. And thank you for putting up with my endless infatuation with my fictional men. But you know they all hold a part of you.

You're my rock, my inspiration, my greatest supporter, and the man who stabilizes the chaos within me and fulfills my deepest, most depraved desires. None of my books could have been without you.

Thank you to Jakob for enriching my story with Russian phrases. This might be the only mark you've set on this book, but you've already set a deep mark on my mind, and this will undoubtedly come to show in my future writings.

I can't wait to see what other kinky games you have in store for me.

A huge thanks goes out to my amazing beta readers. Lauren,

Rachel, Klara, and Willow. Your feedback and support is always invaluable, and I'm so grateful for all the time you spend reading and providing honest and thorough feedback. You guys are the best!

To all the people in the BDSM community, who have supported me on my author journey. Writing what I write, I can't talk about my passion with most people, so thank you for providing me with a space where I can truly be myself.

Last but not least, I want to thank all my readers who support me in one way or another. For all your amazing reviews, for posting about my books and helping spread the word, or just reading and loving my work. You mean the world to me! I hope to bring you many more books that will have you crying, swooning, and rushing off to the bedroom for much-needed breaks ;)

About Ella Jacobs

Ella Jacobs writes BDSM and dark romance. She loves exploring the emotional sides to Dom/sub relationships and subjecting her heroines to overbearing men with gray morals.

Besides writing, Ella loves music. It inspires her to write, and when her characters are messing with her head, she sits down at the piano and plays Chopin and Liszt to regain her sanity.

Ella lives her own age gap romance with a stern, loving Dominant, who is always ready for some character analysis and rarely gets jealous when she falls in love with her fictive men.

You can read more about her own experiences with the BDSM lifestyle on her website.

www.ellajacobs.com

Printed in Great Britain
by Amazon

30564432R00227